# KINGFISHER

## PATRICIA A. McKILLIP

ACE BOOKS, NEW YORK

**ACE**

**An imprint of Penguin Random House LLC**
**375 Hudson Street, New York, New York 10014**

This book is an original publication of Penguin Random House LLC.

Library of Congress Cataloging-in-Publication Data

McKillip, Patricia A.
Kingfisher / Patricia A. McKillip.
pages ; cm
ISBN 978-0-425-27176-6 (hardcover)
I. Title.
PS3563.C38K56 2016
813'.54—dc23
2015007963

FIRST EDITION: February 2016

PRINTED IN THE UNITED STATES OF AMERICA

10  9  8  7  6  5  4  3  2  1

Cover photographs: woman © Nina Pak / Arcangel; wet stones © Scorpp/Shutterstock;
water © Zffoto/Shutterstock; decorative elements © il67/Shutterstock.
Cover design by Judith Lagerman.
Interior text design by Laura K. Corless.

Penguin
Random
House

For the excellent folk of the
South Slough National Estuarine Research Reserve.
With a tip of the hat to
Roger's Zoo and Bizarretorium for inspiration.
With very special thanks to Susan Allison.

# PART ONE

# CHIMERA

# 1

Pierce Oliver was pulling crab rings out of the water off the end of the dock at Desolation Point when he saw the knights.

They were throwing doors open, clambering out of a black touring car half as long as the dock, it looked, and inset with strange devices depicting animals so rarely seen most were presumed extinct. Three young men, sleek and muscular, adjusting their black leathers and quilted silks, heads turning this way and that as they surveyed the tiny harbor, caused Pierce to forget what he was doing. The line went slack in his hands. The tiered, circular frames of the net he had hauled up, dripping and writhing with crabs, slumped into one another. A fourth door opened; another head rose out of the driver's side, black-capped and masked with sunglasses. His voice queried something lost in a sudden squall of screeching gulls. The three shook their heads, turning from him toward the dock.

They were all, Pierce realized abruptly, staring back at him.

A crab hit his shoe, skittered over it. He glanced down hastily, pulled the rings taut again, knelt to shake crabs back into the net and bat the smaller escapees back into the sea. He felt the tremor of footsteps along the dock. Boots, black, supple, and glistening like nacre, came to a halt under his nose.

"Sorry to interrupt your work there, but could you tell us where in Severen's name we are?"

Pierce, the crab net rope in one hand, a lime-green plastic measure in the other, opened his mouth. Nothing came out. The shadow stretching out from the boots on the dock seemed to have grown wings. They expanded darkly across the wood, rising to catch the wind. The boots under Pierce's transfixed gaze refused to levitate, ignoring the wings.

Then the broad, shadowy wings were gone, and he could lift his head finally, look helplessly up at the speaker, who had hair like cropped lamb's wool and eyes like a balmy afternoon sky in some other part of the world. The eyes were beginning to look more bemused than tranquil at Pierce's silence.

"He doesn't know either," the dark-haired man with a green jewel in one ear the color of his eyes guessed with a laugh. The third, a golden-haired giant as solidly massive as a slab of oak, flared suddenly, flames licking out all around him. Pierce jumped, dropping the crab measure.

"Cape Mistbegotten," he gabbled hastily, not wanting to rile them into further displays of weirdness.

"Mistbegotten?"

"Des—Desolation Point."

"Des— Seriously?"

A gull landed on the dock beside him with a sudden, fierce cry. After the crabs, he thought, but it stayed very still then, raking the strangers with its yellow-eyed glare. He retrieved the crab measure, stood up shakily, and realized that he had forgotten to take his apron off. It hung limply around his neck, untied and grubby from the kitchen, the trellis of green beans on it like some stained mimicry of a heraldic device. Another crab was snarled in his shoe-lace, trying to untie his ancient, cracked trainer.

"Desolation Point," he repeated more clearly, though his mouth was still dry. The dark-haired man's shadow seemed to have grown a barbed tail; it lashed sinuously, soundlessly, as though to sweep the crabs off the dock. It stilled finally. Pierce closed his eyes tightly, opened them and his mouth again. "It's the only town on the cape. The sign got blown into the ocean during a winter storm. It's still a little early in the season for tourists; we haven't bothered to replace it yet."

They were gazing at him with varying degrees of incredulity. "People come here?" the fire-giant said dubiously. "On purpose?"

Pierce shook the crab off his shoe; it landed on its back, legs waving at him furiously. "Like I said, it's the only town on Cape Mistbegotten."

"Then why isn't it on the map?" the blond with the temperate eyes asked reasonably. "Our driver couldn't even find it on paper."

Pierce grunted, puzzled. Something in the gull's grim eye, its oddly motionless stance, enlightened him. "Oh, that was probably my mother. Sometimes she hides things and forgets."

"Your mother." The burly giant's face flattened suddenly, all expression gone. "Hides. An entire cape." He had shifted suddenly very close to Pierce, forcing Pierce's head to angle upward. "Are you mocking us? Do you have any idea who we are?"

Pierce, caught helplessly in the hazel-eyed smolder, finally registered the odd crunch in the giant's wake. "Not a clue," he said breathlessly. "But you just squashed a perfectly good dinner crab."

The giant looked down at his boots, raised one slowly, grimacing at the legs dangling from the sole. The fair man with the wings dropped a hand on his shoulder, shook him lightly, fearlessly.

"Temper, Bayley," he murmured. His eyes, on Pierce's face, widened in sudden comprehension. "We must have wandered off the map into the realm of a sorceress."

"Or a lunatic," the giant muttered, shaking crab off his boot.

"No." The intense gaze fixed Pierce, held him motionless. "He is the sorceress's son. That's why you couldn't speak. Isn't it? You saw something in us. Tell me what you saw."

"I saw—" Pierce whispered, losing his voice again, "I saw your shadow. Your wings. And I saw your fire," he added to the giant, then to the dark knight, "I saw your barbed tail."

Suddenly, they were all smiling.

"No wonder you lost your tongue," the giant marveled. "We've been up north, hunting our ancestors." He held up his brawny arm; Pierce saw the fine embroidered medallion on the black sleeve: a white bear outlined in flames. "I am Sir Bayley Reeve. My ancestors took the Fire Bear. I'm not sure how," he added with wonder. "She's huge. She topped even me by a head."

"And mine took the wyvern," said the man with the sea-green eyes. "I am Roarke Wyvernbourne."

Pierce swallowed, speech swollen like a lump in his throat. Even Desolation Point, the outermost stretch of isolated land along the coast of Wyvernhold, got a newspaper now and then.

"And mine the great Winter King of the north," the pale-haired man said. "The Winter Merlin, who taught the ancient mage of the first Wyvernbourne king. Back when there were a dozen petty kingdoms and as many kings. That's what you saw in me: the falcon's wings. I am Sir Gareth May."

They waited, gazing at Pierce expectantly, until he found his wits again. "Oh. Pierce Oliver." He started to hold out his hand, felt the crab net rope still in it.

"Oliver," the Wyvernbourne prince murmured. "Wasn't there something . . ." He shook his head, shrugging. "Well."

"Did you— Ah— Did you actually— I mean, with weapons? I thought they were already pretty much extinct?"

The knights were silent for a breath; Pierce saw the memories, complex and mysterious, in their faces.

"We came as close as we could," Gareth May said slowly. "They leave a track. They leave a rumor. I climbed into the high forests, found the ancient nesting places of the Winter Merlins. I heard their voices in the wind. Maybe I saw one. Maybe it was a cloud. Maybe it was both."

"I searched in fire," Bayley said. "At night. Fire licking wood as the Fire Bear licks her newborn to turn them into flesh and blood; she swallows their fire, their immortality. Maybe I did that."

"I found the caves where the wyverns raised their young," the Wyvernbourne prince said. "I saw their high nests, hollows of stone where they laid their eggs, said to make a noise like thunder when they cracked."

"What we hunted, what we took, is what you saw," Gareth said simply. "That you saw it so quickly, so easily— that's the wonder. We were searching for what we found. You weren't looking for anything at all."

Again they were silent, consulting one another with their eyes. Pierce watched, fascinated by their closeness, their fellowship. The motionless gull, which he had forgotten, gave such a sudden, piercing cry that he nearly leaped off the dock. It sounded, he thought as he caught his breath, like a curse.

He glanced down, saw more crabs wobbling to the edge of the rings, toppling onto the dock. He bent to pluck a couple of likely-looking dinners up, toss them back into the net.

"Look for us," he heard, "if you come to Severluna. You might find a place for yourself in King Arden's court."

He straightened again, blinking at the thought. They were smiling at him again, welcoming him to their world, making him, for a moment that melted his heart, one of them. The moment passed; he was himself again, in all his awkwardness, his isolation, his inexperience: a young, tangle-haired man wearing a filthy apron at the end of a dock at the edge of the world, chasing after crabs instead of wyverns.

"I've always lived here," he explained. "It's home."

Bayley glanced bewilderedly at the tiny town lining the

main street, doors facing the setting sun. The others refrained from looking. "Oh. Well," the giant said gruffly, and added, "Sorry about your dinner. Luckily there are more in your net."

"They're for my mother."

"Oh."

"She owns the best restaurant on the cape. I was working in the kitchen earlier; that's why I'm wearing this ridiculous apron. Most of these are too small to keep."

"What about that one?" the prince asked of the one Pierce had just thrown back into the net.

"Let's see . . ." He pulled it out again, turned it over. "Nope. It's female."

They gazed at it. Bayley broke the silence.

"Hell can you tell?"

Pierce tapped the band on the underside of the shell. "It's wider on the females." He let it fall into the water; the young men watched the splash.

"I could eat," Bayley murmured wistfully.

"Her restaurant's open. It's called Haricot. There's crab on the lunch menu. Follow the street the direction you were going; it's just past the Wander Inn." He watched them query one another again. "A motel," he explained. "If you keep going the same direction out of town, the road will loop around the cape and take you back to the highway."

"Thank you." They stirred then, stepped toward the waiting car, thoughts shifting away from Pierce, back to their journey. "We appreciate the help."

"We'll tell them at Haricot that you sent us," the dark prince said with his father's charming smile.

You won't have to, Pierce thought as the dock swayed

under their receding steps, and the gull finally flew off. She knows.

The knights were long gone by the time he pulled up the rings in the late afternoon and carried them and a bucket full of squirming crabs to the Haricot kitchen.

His tall mother, nibbling a strawberry, glanced at him past the ear of Cape Mistbegotten's only sheriff. Her eyes, a rich blue-green, narrowed, questioning. Pierce took off the apron and scrubbed his hands at the sink, hearing her voice through the falling water.

"Well, I can look, Arn. But it's been a while since I've done anything like that. I've been retired for years; cooking is my magic now."

Ha, Pierce thought, and felt her gaze between his shoulder blades.

"Thanks, Heloise," the sheriff said. "It's the third time those interpretive signs and telescopes on the point have been vandalized, and I still haven't got a clue. If you could just— Well, keep an eye on them now and then, when you have a moment."

"I'll try to remember."

There was a short silence. Pierce, drying his hands, heard what Arn Brisket was not saying, what he'd not been saying since the third time Heloise had told him no. Not for the first time, Pierce wondered why. Arn was decent, honest, with maybe more shoreline on his head since the first time she had said it, but his chestnut mustache was still bold and thick as a squirrel's tail. And it would be a timely solution. Pierce froze then, at that unexpected thought, staring at the towel in his hands with its little edging of green beans.

"Pierce."

He looked up dazedly. Arn had gone; his mother, trying to retie her apron without tangling her long red braid in the strings, nodded in the direction of her office. Pierce went to her, took the ties out of her fingers. They seemed oddly chilly. He swallowed something hard in his throat.

"I'll just get the crab pot on to boil first."

She nodded again, briefly, left him without looking at him, her backbone straight and rigid as a flagpole.

Staff chattered again, voices muted, as he filled the huge pot with water. Arn, they talked about softly, and his stubborn, persistent longing, since his wife's death a decade ago, for the sorceress turned cook and gardener. Pierce heaved the pot onto the stove. His thoughts drifted to the strangers who had gotten so completely lost they had managed to find Desolation Point, the westernmost thrust of land on the entire Wyvernhold coast. So did everyone else's thoughts, then. The knights might have come and gone from Haricot, but they had left behind them vivid impressions. Pierce responded absently to the questions and comments as he lingered beside the crab bucket. The strange idea in his head took on clarity, dimension. He nudged an escaping crab back into the bucket and felt his mother's eyes again. But she wasn't visible; she was in her office, checking the evening menu or balancing accounts while she waited for him.

Or maybe sitting motionlessly, watching him out of a borrowed pair of eyes.

He left the crabs to the staff, went out the back door through her rambling, burgeoning kitchen garden, and drove home.

Home was on the outermost cliff on the cape, where it jutted into the wild sea amid the shards and wreckage of time and the raw, irresistible forces of nature. Shreds of morning mist still hung from the high branches of the ancient trees around the pile of stone and wood that had been Pierce's father's house. And his father's before him, and his father's father's, back to some distant past long before the watchtower that had guarded the headlands had been torn down to add a wing to the family hall.

"This house is yours," his mother had told him years earlier, when he was too young to understand what she wasn't telling him. "Your father gave it to me before he left us. Now I'm giving it to you, so that you'll have something from him. So that you'll always have a home here with me and the trees and the sea."

Even then he had felt the twist of bitterness that this place was all he knew of a father: no voice, no expressions, no touch, only these huge, silent rooms full of heavy, ornate furniture and paintings of the dead who had lived in them. There was no picture of his father. As Pierce grew, so did his questions. But his own mother seemed to know little more than he did about his father. He was gone, she only told him. He had left the house to her, and now it was Pierce's to keep forever. At any request for even the simplest of answers, she flung up a mist of silence, or sorrow, or absentmindedness, and disappeared into it. Pierce had no idea if his father was alive or dead. Nothing, anywhere in the vast house, including his mother, indicated that he even had a name. Pierce asked the housekeepers and gardeners, many of whom had grown up in Desolation Point, what they knew; he flung questions at random through the rest of the town. Everyone, wearing the same slightly uneasy expression, gave him the same answer.

"Ask your mother."

He veered his small, weathered Metro away from the rutted, overgrown drive to the house, parked instead on a paved overlook at the cliff's edge. Crenellated stonework marked the edge of safety. Beyond it, waves heaved and hammered at gigantic slabs of stone that had been, at some lost point in time, determined to burrow beneath the edge of the earth. The cliff bore signs of that ancient struggle. Layered and veined with changing eons, it had been twisted upward by the power of the collision. Jagged, broken edges of land reared out of the water like the prows of a ghostly fleet of ships. Time had laid a thin layer of dirt and decaying things on the top of the cliff. The house, the trees, stood on that fragile ground while the battle, frozen but not forgotten, bided its time beneath.

Pierce got out of the car and wandered to his favorite corner of the wall, where tides in their raging broke high above the land, where the cliff swallows nested, gulls rode the wind below him, sea lions and whales slid through the waves as easily as he moved through air. That afternoon sea was calm, idling between tides. Waves gathered around the rocks, broke indolently against them, creating brief, lovely waterfalls of foamy white that flowed over the dark, wet stone and drained back into the sea.

His thoughts were anything but calm. Old questions surfaced urgently, obsessively, along with new. Who was his father? What was he like? What had he done? Had he ever left Cape Mistbegotten to follow the long road south to Severluna? Had he known such as those formidably trained, confident, trusted young knights?

Had he been one?

Was he alive or dead? If dead, how had he died?

If not, where was he?

There were no answers, Pierce realized finally, in this place where he had been born. Wind, sea, the ancient house, even his mother all told him nothing. Sitting on the wall, staring at the fog bank rolling across the horizon told him nothing either. He stood, backed a step or two away from the land's edge, perplexed by an impulse growing in him, as mindless and undefined as the forces under his feet. It was not until he finally turned, got back into the car and started it, that he understood what he would do.

He went as far, then, as the end of the drive. He turned the engine off again and was gazing at the closed door of the garage when his mother stepped into view through the driver's side window. She bent to look at him as he jumped. Her eyes were wide, her red-gold hair loose and roiling in the wind. It dawned on him, as they both fumbled to open the door, that she had been waiting for him. She had known what he was thinking before he did.

"Pierce?" she said, as he got out. Her husky voice, oddly tremulous, the pallor in the lovely face, the green rainbow of letters spelling Haricot arching over the embroidered bean vine on the apron she had neglected to take off, amazed him. He had never seen her afraid before. He was going to do this thing, he realized, astonished anew. He was actually going to leave home.

"It's okay," he told her. "Mom. Really."

"It was those knights," she said bitterly. She was trembling, her hands tucked under her arms as though she were cold. "Their fault."

"They just got lost." He put an arm over her shoulder, turned her toward the house. "Let's go inside. Don't worry. It's just something I have to do."

"No. I need you to stay here, help me at Haricot. You can't leave. You need to know so much more than you do. So much that I haven't taught you yet."

He pushed the heavy front door open. The great hall, a shadowy, drafty remnant of a bygone age, held as many cobwebs as there were oddments to hang them on. The full body armor of some long-dead knight stood on one side of the huge fireplace so rarely lit that the pile of logs and driftwood in it probably housed any number of creatures. The knight's helm, a beaky thing with slits for vision, seemed to stare speculatively at Pierce.

He asked impulsively, "Was my father a knight?"

Heloise sank into one of the worn couches scattered around the room. She eyed the cold hearth expressionlessly; Pierce thought that, as ever, she would maneuver around an answer. Her face crumpled abruptly. She tossed a streak of fire at the dry wood with one hand, and with the other, brought the hem of the apron to her eyes. The pile flamed amid explosions of resin, cracklings, and keening that, to Pierce's ears, might not have entirely been the voices of wood.

"Yes," she snapped. "Yes. And he still is."

Pierce's breath stopped. Everything stopped; his thoughts, his blood, even the fierce, hungry ravages of the fire froze in a moment of absolute silence. He sat down abruptly on the couch beside his mother. He took a breath, another, staring at her, then heard the fire again, and his own breathing, as ragged as though he had been running.

"He's alive?" He felt the blood push into his face, the sting of what might have been brine behind his eyes; he seemed, weirdly enough, on the verge of crying for the man who had not died. "What—where?"

Her full lips pinched; her own face had flushed brightly, furiously. If he had touched her cheek, she might have burned him. Her lips parted finally, gave him the word, a hard, dry nugget of sound.

"Severluna." He didn't move, just let his eyes draw at her, asking, asking, until she finally spoke again. "He has been, since before he was your age, a knight in King Arden's court. We met there—"

"You—"

She held up a hand; he waited. More words fell: flint; fossils; hard, cold diamonds. "We met and married there." His throat closed; he swallowed what felt like fire. "I had a child. A son."

His mouth opened; no words came. He felt the wave break again behind his eyes, the ache of salt and blood.

"The year your father took my small son to King Arden's court to be trained and educated was the year I knew, beyond all doubt, that he had never loved me. He loved the queen. Only her. Always her. Before, during, and even now.

"So I ran." Her own eyes glittered. Pierce watched one tear fall, saw her catch it in her palm, her fingers close over it, so rare it was, so powerful. "I took you with me. I didn't—

I didn't know that then. I came here, to the place we chose, during the first year of our marriage, to be alone together. I thought we were alone. I had not realized then that he had brought her with us; even then he carried her everywhere in his heart." His lips parted to ask; she opened her empty hand to stop him. "No one lived here; it was his inheritance. He came looking for me. Once. To ask me back to Severluna. I told him no. Never again.

"By then I knew about you. I didn't tell him. I kept you here, after you were born, so far from king and court that you would know nothing of your father's life. Down there, no one gives a thought to the distant, isolated margins of the world. I wanted to raise you so far from Severluna that anything you heard or read about it would seem as unreal as a fairy tale."

Pierce, motionless, staring at her, felt the world change shape under his feet. No longer bounded by the sea, by the little, ancient town, the dark, endless forest, the narrow road that circled the cape, it expanded to immeasurable lengths, grew complex, noisy, mysterious, shocking.

He opened his mouth, realized with wonder, as no hand came up, that she was waiting now for him to ask.

"Who is he?"

Her eyes grew luminous under tears she would not let fall; in that moment, he thought she would answer. Then she stood up so fast she pulled the next breath he drew into her wake. "Enough!" she told him fiercely, pacing in front of the roaring fire, rumpling the hearthrug. Her hand, searching for something to worry—beads, the restaurant key on a chain—found the apron front. She glanced down at it with surprise, then untied it impatiently and tossed it on the floor. Pierce, watching her, had a sudden, wrenching glimpse of the young woman she had been in Severluna, married to an illusion and fleeing in pain and fury to this difficult place, where memories rooted themselves more implacably than anything she could coax out of the miserly soil.

"Who?" he pleaded again, his voice grating; she only shook her head.

"Find your own answers," she said harshly. "I've been trying since I came here to forget all this." Then she halted, midwhirl in her pacing, to stare at him. "No. Don't. Don't leave me, Pierce. There's nothing you need in Severluna. Your father does not even know you exist, and even if you find him or your brother, what can they do for you? You're not trained to the ways of the court. I have no family there to take you in. You'll be alone in a city full of strangers—what will you do with yourself?"

He gazed at her, wondering that she could show him such things—a father, a brother, a world not governed by wind and tide and how many crabs came up in the net, but by wealth, power, knowledge, and the sources of the strange magic she knew—and expect him not to want what she herself had wanted.

He stirred, beginning to think. "What I do here," he answered slowly. "I work for you. I'll find another restaurant."

"But how will you find your way? You can barely read a map."

He shrugged. "People do. Find their ways. Even people as ignorant as I am of anything beyond Cape Mistbegotten.

I'll put one mile behind me, then another, until I get where I'm going."

"And what," she asked helplessly, "will I do without you? Without the sound of your voice in this rambling old house? Without the sweet face I've known all of your life? Here everyone knows your name. You have a place here, everything you need. How will you know even how to look for a bed in Severluna?"

"Mom." He leaned forward, caught one of the long, graceful hands working anxiously around the other. He tugged at her gently until she dropped beside him again on the couch. "What I don't know by now, it's time I learned. Stop worrying. The road runs both ways. If I get into trouble over my head, I can find my way back. Anyway. When in my life have you not known where I am?"

She was silent at that; she sat tensely looking into the fire, fingers kneading the sofa cushions. "Yes," she said finally. Her grip loosened slowly; she met his eyes again, her own no longer angry, grieving, but calmer and beginning to calculate. "Yes. Come and work with me for one more evening. Please," she begged, as he stirred in protest. "I'll be understaffed without you. And I need you under this roof one last time, while I get used to the idea that you are leaving me. At Haricot tonight, I can teach you a little sorcery, some arcane methods that will be useful to know in a strange kitchen. All right?"

He nodded absently, hearing only every other word of kitchens, sorcery, cooking, as he conjured up the knights again in memory. They might remember him, he thought:

the young man who had seen the legendary shadows of their ancestors.

"In the morning, if you still want to leave, we can make proper plans. Yes?"

"Yes," he said absently, and realized then that he was already gone, on his way, the roof over his head, his bed, now only his first temporary stop, and her advice among the possessions he might take or leave behind when he continued his journey.

# 2

Merle was chanting again. Carrie heard his voice coming out of the old rowboat hauled to dry dock under a hemlock. Keys in hand, she paused beside the pickup door, listening. She couldn't make out a word of it. The old crow perched on the wind-bowed crown of the hemlock burst into sudden, raucous song. Carrie wondered if Merle and bird understood each other. It seemed as likely as anything else about her impossible father.

She tossed the keys onto the driver's seat, walked into the long grasses under the shadow of the forest. She and Merle lived at the southern edge of Proffit Slough, high and back far enough so that the daily ebb and flow of tidewater pushing into sweet water didn't find its way into their house even in the most violent weather. Several other houses, old, patched, painted long ago in muted colors, stood peacefully among the silent pines. They were relics of a past when farmers had drained the land and built the only road that ran between the fields and up to the highway. Farmers and crops and cows were long gone; the land had been repossessed by streams and tidal channels, the labyrinthine sea nursery regulated by tides and seasons and the ancient rhythms of the moon. Only farmhouses remained, inhabited by the artistic, the eccentric, the reclusive.

And Merle, who, Carrie's mother said for years before she left them, was just plain demented.

The chanting from the boat was getting eerie, high and reedy, like some ritual litany that should have been accompanied by gourd rattles and drums. Carrie looked down into the boat. Merle stopped his chanting abruptly and stared at her with such astonishment and wonder that she felt like something he had been trying, with no real hope, to summon. Well, here I am, she told him silently. As suddenly, he recognized her. He smiled. He was lying on his back beneath the broken seat planks, his head cushioned on a monstrous dandelion blooming through a hole in the boat bottom.

"Are you drunk?" Carrie asked.

He considered the question. "Not this morning."

"Do you want some help up?"

"No, thanks. I'm good."

"Coffee?"

"There's a thought," he answered, but showed no other signs of interest.

"Well, what exactly are you doing?"

"Waiting."

"For what?" she demanded bewilderedly. "A bus?"

"For an answer."

He'd been out all night, she guessed, as often happened on tranquil spring nights. He watched the reflection of the moon in the slough streams, or swapped tales with some transient beside a fire in the backwoods. Fish stories, hunting stories, war stories: Carrie had overheard some of those earnest, drunken conversations, when neither listened to the other, and whatever events they spoke of seemed to have happened in different countries, maybe even in different millennia.

"I have to go to work, Dad. You sure you don't want a hand up?"

Merle murmured something inaudible. Then he said more clearly, "I'm working."

Carrie glanced at the sky, saw a flock of geese in a ragged V flying the wrong direction for spring. "You'd be more comfortable out of here."

"I can see better down here."

"How about that cup of coffee?"

"You'd shudder, your blood would roar, your hair would stiffen tendril by tendril like quills upon the fretful porpentine if you could see, if you could see."

Carrie gave up. "Okay. I guess that would be no."

Her father's eyes lost their vacant passion; he smiled at her again.

"No, thanks."

"Don't forget that Mom's in town for the night. She wants to meet you for lunch. Call her?"

"I won't forget," he promised.

"You have a good day, Dad." She hesitated. "You won't forget, but will you do it?"

"Whatever you say, Sweet."

"I have got to get out of Chimera Bay," she said fiercely to the saint dangling on the rearview mirror of the pickup. Her father had found the medallion on his rambles, hung it in the truck because it protected travelers. How her father, who shied like a vampire at the shadow of a church spire in his path, knew one saint from another, Carrie hadn't a clue.

She and the truck rattled across the old farmers' road, then up the steep, rocky, rutted grade that joined a paved road at the top of the hill. In the mirror, before she turned, she could see the north end of the slough, the distant estuary waters broadening between the low, coastal hills to meet the tide. The paved road wound for a few miles along the crest of the hills before it dipped down to follow the sea, where it flowed around the headlands and into Chimera Bay.

The Kingfisher Inn stood at the edge of the broad bay, looking out over the deep shipping channel and the calm waters beyond it that ebbed twice a day into shallows and mudflats. From the highest curve, Carrie could see all of the inn at once, the huge central building with the two round turrets at its back corners, and the wide, graceful, four-storied wings that once overlooked lawn, rose gardens, and the docks where guests who sailed in on their yachts would tie up for the night.

It had all been a wonder: so the old photos, letters, and yellowed reviews, framed and hanging behind glass along the walls, told her. And what had happened to it all? Something had happened. She was uncertain what; everything had changed before she was born. For all the vagueness in everyone's eyes when she asked, the good fortune might have vanished a century before. Not even her father could come up with a coherent explanation, and he had been there, she knew, beside the much younger Hal Fisher in a tuxedo under the blazing chandelier, his golden hair clipped, his mustache wild and thick, bracketing his confident smile, lord of all he surveyed, including Merle at his elbow, wearing a dress suit, of all things, and looking, in the old sepia photo, oddly watchful, as though from very far away he saw the something coming.

The glimpse of the earlier inn vanished in a turn as the road wound down into town. Now the inn was peeling paint, shuttered windows, walls hidden under scaffolding, its proud turrets piebald where slats had blown off. Carrie parked in front, where lawns stretching the entire length of the inn had vanished under tar and gravel. She recognized the half dozen cars already there, the usual bar dwellers.

She found her way under the plyboard tunnels beneath the scaffolding to the front door of the restaurant and let herself in. No one was there yet but Ella; Carrie came early to help her prep. Walking through the kitchen doors, she blinked at the morning light streaming in from the back wall of windows overlooking the bay. Around her in the kitchen, things burped, bubbled, steamed. She smelled oil, rosemary, yeast. For a moment she thought she was alone among the cupboards and counters, the wheeled chopping blocks, the stoves, refrigerators, dishwashers, everything that still could, in the mix of antique and modern, making noises at once like an orchestra tuning up.

Then she saw the tiny woman with her head in one of the refrigerators, rummaging through the shelves. She straightened abruptly and turned, her arms full of eggs, two kinds of cheese, mustard, pickle relish. She smiled at Carrie. Her hair was a mass of white curls, her face pale and seamed like a piece of old diner crockery, the only color in it her periwinkle eyes. The corner of the egg box slid. Salad dressings and sauces, Carrie guessed, and went to help her.

"Thanks, Hon."

"Do you want me to make them?"

"No. I want you to start on the crab bisque. But take the note up first."

She was, everyone swore, Hal and Tye's mother. Carrie didn't believe it. Nobody could be that old and move the way Ella did, everywhere at once, it seemed, even during the most chaotic of All-You-Can-Eat Nites. And she was elfin; how could she have come out with those tall, big-boned sons, themselves at least half the age of the inn? Whoever and however old she was, she knew everything about everything, though she could be half a heaping tablespoon short of explaining, even, for instance, the why of the note Carrie picked up off the countertop to take upstairs.

She went the quickest way, through the back door of the kitchen, down a battered wooden walkway to the only staircase, of the four built to give guests access from every floor to the grounds, that didn't threaten to pitch her back down through a rotting tread. Lilith Fisher lived in one of the turret suites that once overlooked the lovely gardens and the yachts at the docks. Now it overlooked a weedy lawn and a couple of fishing boats. She was said to be writing a book about the history, the celebrities, the gossip surrounding the inn during its glory. Carrie had never seen her actually working at the big desk cluttered with books, papers, and old photos in the turret. Hal, it seemed to her, was the one doing the writing: every morning a note, elegantly hand-penned in real ink on heavy, deckle-edged paper tucked into a matching envelope with his wife's name on it, asking her to join him that evening for dinner.

Lilith opened the door when Carrie knocked, then flowed away, scarf ends, sleeves, trouser hems fluttering as she said into her cell phone, "No. No! Really? He really did that?" She reached the far wall and flowed back, seeing Carrie this time, tossing her a preoccupied smile. "I can't believe it. After all you did to protect him."

Like Hal, Lilith was long-boned, tall, still willowy despite her ivory-white hair. She wore it coiled on top of her head, an untidy cinnamon bun held in place by a couple of colored pencils. Her eyes, behind half-moon glasses, were big, sunken, luminous, the creamy green the sea sometimes turned during a nasty storm.

Carrie held out the note. Lilith took it on an ebb turn and surged again. "No. Yes. I will." Carrie backed a step toward the door; Lilith whirled abruptly, midroom, swirled back to her. "Of course, Heloise. The mourning doves. They can watch for him from my turret."

She dropped the phone in a pocket and finally stood still. "Thank you, Carrie." She opened the envelope; her eyes flicked over the note, then at Carrie again, some memory surfacing in them as frigid as an iceberg in a northern sea. "Please tell Ella that I will take my dinner alone tonight."

And that was that for the lovely, old-fashioned note.

"Okay," Carrie said, confused as always, wanting to ask why? What did he? Couldn't they at least talk about it over dinner even though that might mean a few broken plates? Lilith's eyes flashed at her again, this time without the chill, reading her expression, Carrie guessed, or maybe, in some nebulous way, her thoughts.

Lilith pushed her glasses up toward the cinnamon bun, worked a pencil back into place. She turned, gazed down at the bay through the turret's curved windows, where Hal and his brother Tye, tiny figures in a small, rocking boat, sank lines into the shipping channel to see what they could lure up from the deep.

"We have no more plates to throw," Carrie heard her murmur. "We broke them all long ago."

"What?" Carrie's voice came out in a whisper.

Lilith dropped her glasses back down onto her nose and peered more closely at the boat. "Ask Ella to send Hal's jeans up with my dinner. I'll mend that back pocket. How's your father this morning?"

Carrie, staring incredulously at the tiny nail-paring-sized blur that was Hal's jeans, answered absently, "He was lying on his back in a broken rowboat talking to a crow about fearsome porpentines."

"Really? He said porpentines?"

"He did. Dead sober."

"And the pickup? Did you get the brakes fixed?"

Carrie nodded, sighing. "I had to use some of my creel money, though."

A smile flickered through Lilith's delicately lined face. "Works for me," she said. "The less you squirrel away in that old creel, the longer you'll stay with us."

But I need to leave, Carrie cried silently, her whole body tense with desperation, and Lilith nodded.

"I know."

Carrie went back down an inner stairway that took her through the great dining room behind the reception hall. It was an empty, silent, beautiful place in which the backwash of the past, layers of memory, had accumulated. Huge windows overlooked the water, each framed with stained-glass panels depicting wild waves, cormorants and albatrosses, the frolicking whales and mermaids of the deep. The old glass was bubbled and wavery; passing boats and birds grew distorted in it. Sometimes, Carrie glimpsed odd things in the shipping channel through those windows: small ships with rounded hulls and too many sails, or leaner vessels with ribbed sails raked at an angle that might have crossed over from exotic seas where fish flew and whales had horns like unicorns just to visit Chimera Bay. The round mahogany and rosewood tables still filled the room, circled by their chairs. Waiting, maybe, for the doors to open at last, the guests in their glittering evening clothes to enter and feast. But the silver sconces and candelabra had grown black with age; the fireplace, its mantel carved from a single slab of myrtle wood, had been cold for decades.

In the kitchen, she gave Ella Lilith's message and got to work on the bisque.

Bek and Marjorie came in at eleven to serve. Purple-haired Jayne brought in a couple of lunch orders from the bar while they were putting on their aprons. After that, things got hectic. Ella worked the grill, flipping burgers, tuna melts, fillets of salmon and halibut; Carrie kept an eye on the two pots of soup—crab bisque and chicken-veg—while she lowered into bubbling oil anything that could possibly be deep-fried. At odd moments, between orders, she experimented. She fried croquettes of chopped salmon, sour cream, onions rolled into a web of uncooked hash browns. She added one or two to a plate, flagged them with toothpicks, beside the usual skewer of orange slice and pickled crab apple. They were pretty much successful; only the toothpicks came back. Her deep-fried minced eggplant, green olive, and feta croquettes mostly came back with a set of tooth marks at one end. The implacable Marjorie, who had worked in restaurants for a quarter of a century, eased her plump body and her tray like a dancer through the kitchen, nibbling Carrie's experiments as she passed. Angular Bek, who wore nothing but black and was waiting on tables while he made up his mind what to do with his life, always looked on the verge of dropping his tray as he tossed a croquette in his mouth. Somehow, his sharp elbows avoided the soup pots and doorposts; he threatened but never achieved a head-on collision with the hanging copper pans.

Jayne called in another bar order, then saw Carrie's little pile of experiments and crossed the kitchen to grab one. Carrie watched her eyes, lined and shadowed with black and purple, widen, then close. For a moment, her young, cynical face grew ethereal.

"Eggplant," she breathed. "Everyone is so afraid of it. I adore it. I color my hair eggplant. I wear eggplant. I inhale eggplant. Make more."

Marjorie and Bek began to argue about something. Carrie heard snatches of it whenever they passed each other.

"It was," Bek said.

"Couldn't have been," Marjorie answered adamantly. "No way. Not here."

"Was."

Marjorie called for the dessert tray. Carrie added another of her experiments to the slices of pound cake, pots of dark chocolate mousse, strawberry tarts. Marjorie looked dubious. "Nobody here eats pears for dessert."

"Not even poached with vanilla and black peppercorns, and drizzled with warm salted caramel and grated lemon peel?"

"Try some ice cream on it."

Carrie grinned. "I'll eat it if it comes back."

The dessert tray returned without it.

"It was her," Bek insisted to Marjorie as he came in under a precarious load of dirty plates. "She ate Carrie's pear."

"No way," Marjorie said tersely. "Must have been a tourist."

"I worked for him for five days, once. I know it's her."

"Only five days?" Carrie echoed, replenishing the dessert tray. "Five days where?" Then she asked, "Who?"

"Got another pear?" Bek asked.

"No," Ella said quickly from the grill. "I want the other half of that."

"She ate the croquettes, too. Even the eggplant ones."

"Who are you talking about?" Carrie asked again, pulling the soup pots to back burners to wait for supper.

"Sage Stillwater."

In the sudden, odd silence, Ella slapped her spatula down on a burger and pushed it flat until it hissed. For the first time, Carrie saw her angry.

"What on earth would Stillwater's wife be doing here?" Marjorie demanded of Bek.

"Spying," Ella answered succinctly. They stared at her; she added darkly, "There's something here Stillwater wants. Maybe a cook, maybe a server. Maybe just a taste of something he hasn't thought up himself. In a week, you'll find Carrie's croquettes on his menu."

"I really doubt it was her," Marjorie said soothingly, though she sounded unconvinced. Carrie had never met Stillwater, but she knew enough about him to doubt that the owner of the classiest restaurant in Chimera Bay would ask his wife to eat in a place that offered fried-chicken nibbles for lunch.

Ella, still upset, brooded at the burger, flipped it to reveal the blackened underside, and upended it into the trash.

"I've known Stillwater on the prowl before," she said, reaching for fresh meat. "I've seen what he can do when he wants something."

Carrie felt her arms prickle into goose bumps, despite the heat in the kitchen. "What did he do that time? And why," she added puzzledly, "didn't he come himself?"

Ella started to answer, then closed her mouth and shook her head at some unspeakable, unholy tangle of memory. "It's complicated," she said grimly, and left it there, in the place where every other inexplicable event at the inn ended up.

Carrie stayed late to help Ella clean the kitchen after supper; they lingered in the weird, soothing rhythms of the dishwashers, eating crab bisque and Ella's olive and black pepper biscuits at the kitchen counter. It was late when Carrie drove home, but as she climbed out of the truck, she heard Merle still chanting. She couldn't see him. The only light in the slough came from the moon, and from the little flashlight on her keychain. She paused beside the truck, wondering if she should check on him. His voice sounded hale, if a little hoarse, and he seemed to be moving away from her, deeper into the wood. She went indoors, crawled into bed instead.

Her father's voice, or the memory of it, drifted in and out of her dreams until she wove it into a rich night-language that almost made sense, that almost made her see what it was conjuring.

Then the moon set, and the wild chanting stopped.

# 3

Somewhere south of Cape Mistbegotten, a sign in one of the little towns along the coast highway caused the traveling Pierce Oliver to veer impulsively off the road.

ALL YOU CAN EAT FRIDAY NITE FISH FRY the sign said. His sudden, overwhelming hunger drove the car to a halt beneath it.

He got out. It took a moment to find the door, hidden within a makeshift tunnel beneath scaffolding that went up and up, higher than he would have expected from such ramshackle beginnings. Part of a turret, a cone of white, jutted incongruously from behind a plywood wall covering the face of the building. There were no windows in sight. The sign was scrawled in chalk on a large board hooked to the scaffolding. It clattered and swung in the gusty wind blowing in from the west, or from the south, or from anywhere, according to the tipsy weather vane on top of the turret, which squealed crankily as it spun.

Odors wafted through the door as Pierce pulled it open. He smelled citrus, garlic, onions, and felt his empty stomach flop like a fish out of water. The vast cavern beyond the door was shadowy; he stood blinking, aware of a bar at his right, stretching off into the dimness, ghostly glasses floating upside down above it, a body or two on the stools, the dull gleam of amber and silver and gold from the bottles lined behind it. Other things were scattered among them: weird paintings, masks, street signs, totems that had drifted into the place through the years and clung. A mobile of porcelain Fools' heads hanging from the gloom above the bar swung slowly, glint-eyed and grinning, as though his entrance and the wind that pushed in behind him had disturbed them.

"Hello?" he called. He couldn't remember when he had last eaten. That morning? The evening before? Time blurred in his head like the light and shadow blurred in this twilight place where, in the depths of the cavern, near the ceiling, a star blazed suddenly with light.

"Up here," a voice said briskly from above. "What can I do you for?"

"I saw your All-You-Can-Eat sign?"

"Ah. Dinner will be along anytime now as soon as my brother gets the crab traps in. Crab cakes tonight—your lucky night. You can wait in the restaurant through that door, or in here."

Pierce's eyes were growing accustomed to the gloom, threaded here and there by golden, dusty tendrils of light of no perceptible origin. The size of the place shifted by greater lengths and depths. He blinked again. A ladder stood in a muddle of tables, chairs, stools, worn couches, odd, mismatched pieces of furniture. Above the ladder, an immense crystal chandelier depended: a lovely ice flower with a hundred petals. That, he realized, explained the star. The speaker stood near the top of the ladder with a cloth in his hand, polishing the prisms.

A voice from one of the barstools near Pierce rumbled, "Join me?"

Pierce felt eyes, glanced around to meet them. "Thanks."

The man had long, shaggy, dark hair, a wolf's pale eyes, beads in one ear and braided into his forelocks. For a second Pierce, light-headed with travel, saw the full face of the wolf, taking him in through its long, lean muzzle as well while it regarded him without discernible human expression. Then the man was back, beginning to smile, gesturing with one broad, capable hand at the barstool next to him.

Pierce sat. The stranger pushed a bowl of assorted pretzels, chips, and nuts over to him. "Tye'll be down in a moment to take your order. Passing through?"

Pierce, his mouth full, nodded and swallowed. "From the north coast. Cape Mistbegotten."

The man sipped beer, musing. "Isn't that where the sorceress lives?"

Pierce's fingers drummed on the mahogany; he wished suddenly, urgently, for a beer. "She retired. She's running a restaurant now." He felt the wolf's eyes, alert, waiting. He added reluctantly, "She's my mother."

"No shit."

He shook his head. "Nope. She spends her time trying to grow weird heirloom vegetables for the only decent restaurant on the cape."

He heard rhythmic descending steps. "Which would make you Heloise Oliver's son Pierce," the bartender said, reaching the floor. "I'll be a cockeyed halibut. Have one on the house."

"How—" Pierce began, then stopped, not wanting to know. She was his past, what he had left, like the perpetual mists and the big, silent house up the twisty coastal road. How could she have found her way into this bar with him?

"What'll you have?"

He consulted the chalkboard dangling, by no visible means, above the draft handles. "I'll try a Goat's Breath Dark."

"Excellent choice. You look like her. That red hair. Those eyes."

Pierce nodded briefly, wondering how they knew her. He didn't ask. He didn't need to know; he was on his way south, and he would keep going until the voice of the ocean changed from a roar to the siren song of Severluna. The bartender, a tall, burly man with lank hair the color of duck fluff and a pair of square, dark-rimmed glasses on his nose, set a beer in front of Pierce. He drank deeply, came up for air, and found the mild eyes behind the glasses studying him.

"I'm Tye Fisher," he said. "My brother Hal owns this place. He and your mother are related in a roundabout fashion; they know each other in the way that big families do. You need a place to stay, we can open one of the rooms for you." Pierce felt his expression change, lock into place. Tye added quickly, "Stay the night, I mean. The old hotel hasn't been officially open for decades."

"Hotel." He swiveled on the stool, trying to find it. Remnants surfaced in the shadows: a huge stone fireplace at the far end of the room, what might be stairs inset to one side of it, the kind that fanned out over the floor, then did a slow curve upward and out of sight.

"We're trying to get at least part of it back in business. We've been trying for years. Soon as you get one leak fixed, another starts, then the wind picks up, slats go flying into the bay, and the windows cloud up. You know how it goes." He nodded toward the chandelier. "This used to be the old reception hall. Through those doors there along the inner wall was the sitting room, even bigger than this one. The restaurant's in there now. Kingfisher Grill."

Pierce glanced behind him, then turned back to his beer, not wanting to know, wanting to make himself clear from the start. "I'm just passing through," he said. "On my way south. I want to find a job cooking in Severluna."

"You any good?"

Pierce smiled. "I don't know. My mother taught me a few things. I'm hoping to learn on the job in a restaurant on the beach. Someplace like my mother's, simple, fresh, and local, only down where it's warm, and nobody has to wear socks."

Tye grunted. He pulled a square of wood and a knife from under the bar, then, as if he had a little orchard down there as well, an orange and a couple of limes. He began to slice them. "We could use a cook. Ella—that's our mother—she's been running the kitchen since the Grill opened, and she needs to slow down a little. If you meet anyone down there who wants a job up here. Or if you don't find the right beach."

Pierce took another swallow. "I'll keep that in mind." He put his glass down, met Tye's easy expression, whatever was in his eyes hidden behind a blur of light over his lenses. "I could use a room, thanks. Just for the night. I have my stuff in the car. It steered itself into your parking lot when I saw the sign."

"Fine." Tye scraped wedges of orange and lime into their condiment dishes, then plucked a lemon from the mysterious garden under the bar. "Fine, then. We'll see what we can do for you."

The front door opened, banged shut. The wolf man beside Pierce breathed a sudden exclamation into his glass, then huddled around it, head bowed, shoulders hunched. Brisk footsteps across the floorboards came to an abrupt halt.

"Hi, Dad."

"Amazing," the man murmured, "how much weight those two innocent words can carry."

There was a swift, indrawn breath, held for a moment in which nobody, not even the placid bartender, moved. Then came a gusty, exasperated sigh, and the footsteps marched on, to Pierce's ears sharp with pointed recrimination. He risked a glance, saw a slight, straight-backed young woman, her dark hair in an impeccable French braid, disappear through the swinging doors between rooms.

The bartender cocked his glasses at the wolf man, who said glumly, "I was supposed to take her mother to lunch. She was in town visiting friends. It was all too much for me. Name's Teague, by the way," he added to Pierce. "Merle Teague. That dark wind that just blew through is my beloved offspring Carrie."

Pierce frowned. "I know your name. I don't know why."

"Do I owe you money?"

Pierce shook his head puzzledly. The front door rattled and smacked open, in the same moment that the double doors flew open, and Carrie Teague reappeared, under Pierce's fascinated gaze, a bit like a bird popping out of a cuckoo clock.

"Ella says Hal's at the dock," she announced tersely, and waited in strained, forbearing abeyance, for a response.

The two men who had just entered nodded to Tye and tacked away from the bar. One was young, the other not so, both comely, with gold beards and hair neatly trimmed, lean, lanky bodies that wore their jeans and work shirts with casual elegance. Father and son, Pierce guessed, and felt a sharp, unexpected pang of envy.

"We'll help him," the older said, and they followed Carrie back through the swinging doors. Pierce found himself watching their empty flapping, waiting for what would happen next. He turned quickly, picked up his glass again.

"Shouldn't be long now," Tye told him, whittling thin curls of lemon peel off the pith. "Ella and Carrie will have those crabs boiled up in no time. Ella makes the sweetest crab cakes you ever ate, and Carrie does a mixed pepper aioli that's just this side of heaven and that side of everlasting fire."

Pierce felt his stomach roil again and whine. "Can't wait," he breathed, and Tye grinned. He put his knife down, made a few indiscernible passes under the bar, and came up with a bowl of hot, salted popcorn.

More people came in while Pierce ate it. Some disappeared into the restaurant; others lingered at the bar or carried their drinks to the couches and chairs. Tye poured another beer for Pierce without asking; Pierce drank it without caring. The road was untwisting behind him, the gray sky becoming less desolate. Some kind of young minister or priest with a backward collar came in; he and Merle started an amiable argument about what sounded like cannibalism. Smells melted between the swinging doors, floated through the room, disrupting conversations, making people forget what they were saying to stare mutely, expectantly at the doors.

They opened finally. Pierce, hoping for supper at last, turned eagerly. It was Carrie again, dodging swiftly through the crowd toward the bar.

Merle seemed to sense her; this time he looked toward her, waiting. The priest watched silently as well. She said nothing to Merle, just handed him an old-fashioned brass key that looked big enough to open a cemetery gate. Perhaps feeling Pierce's curious gaze on her, she gave him a brief, wide-eyed stare back, revealing pale eyes like her father's. A fairy tale impression of her stern, graceful face—skin as white, lips as red as—clung to memory as she whisked herself away.

Merle rose, too, nodding to Pierce. "Just another minute or two. You're that close."

He followed his daughter; the man with the backward collar followed him. Pierce turned to try for Tye's beleaguered attention and found the cold, foaming beer already in front of him.

After what seemed the slow march of time toward forever, both swinging doors opened wide and stayed open, held by the gold-haired father and son, standing like sentinels flanking the man who entered.

People rose, murmuring, greeting him, raising their mugs and wineglasses in salute. He was very tall, broad-boned, lean, and muscular, a warrior in frayed jeans and a faded flannel shirt. His white-gold hair hung thick and wild to his shoulders; an ivory mustache like a pair of ram's horns curled down the sides of his mouth. He held a gnarled staff in one hand, a carved, polished hiker's stick he used as a cane. He needed it, Pierce saw. Though he smiled broadly as he entered, the lines on his face tightened slightly at every other step as pain bled through him and into the shifting, halting staff.

The young man whose collar announced he was holy followed, carrying a gaff the length of a spear. The metal pirate's hook at the end of it glistened oddly with a sheen of red, as though it had tangled with something closer to human than fish. Merle came after him, holding a huge oval platter with the biggest salmon on it Pierce had ever seen. The platter, an ornate, old-fashioned piece with bumps and ruffles and flutings all over it, looked as though it were made of pure gold. The knife laid across the edge of the platter beside the fish riveted his attention. The blade was crafted of hand-hammered metal with a sandwich of polished ash fitted along the length of the metal handle. Long, broad, and sweetly curved to its point, the blade would rock with a satisfying heft in the hand, finely mincing anything it was fed with its thin, wicked edge: elephant garlic, delicate chives, hazelnuts, words.

I want that, he thought, and found Merle's eyes on him across the room as though he had heard.

Carrie, oven mitts on both hands, followed her father, carrying a cauldron etched all over with an endless, dream-like tangle of circles and knots. The cauldron filled the room with the smell of seafood seasoned in brine and aged sherry and mysterious spices from some land so exotic it hadn't yet appeared on a map. Even she was smiling a little, her ivory skin flushed in the steam.

Under the chandelier, which was still all cold stars and

no visible light, Hal stopped. Everyone stopped. No one spoke. Candles burning on the bar tables, small lamps along the walls shed a misty, golden glow over Hal's white-gold head, the oak in his hand, the bleeding gaff, the salmon and the blade, the silver cauldron. Pierce watched, wondering. Then time flickered; past and present seamed together in the moment; what was old became new, and new became more ancient than he could imagine.

I know this, he thought, then: But what is it?

"Welcome," Hal said, "to the Kingfisher Bar and Grill. We have an inexhaustible feast of crab cakes, shrimp, scallops, halibut, salmon, oysters, clams, all you can eat and any way you like them. Come into the restaurant or stay here and eat as you please. Just let us know what we can do for you."

The odd procession broke apart; the gathering in the room and in the restaurant itself, visible now beyond the open doors, dissolved into jovial chaos. The restaurant tables, Formica-topped rounds with a single plastic flower in a bud vase on each, began to fill. A gray-haired woman, a skinny young man in black, a gum-chewing girl with purple hair, moved among them, taking orders. Pierce looked around for the gaff, the platter, the knife, Hal with his staff. They all seemed to have vanished.

What was that? he wondered. What was that about?

"Something you need?" Tye asked, unexpectedly in front of him despite the crowd around the bar. He lingered as Pierce gazed at him mutely, wondering at his attention amid the clamor. "Anything?"

Pierce shook his head abruptly. He was on his way south. No mysteriously crippled fisher, no amount of goodwill and fellowship, no hints of lost glory would strand him there with the Formica tables and the chandelier that didn't work anymore. "I'm fine," he said. "Thanks." He raised the beer with an appreciative smile, and Tye moved away.

The girl with the purple hair came soon after to take his order. He sat there at the bar and ate the seafood stew, trying to identify its tantalizing backwashes of seasoning, then the crab cakes with their outrageous sweet-fiery sauce, and, when he could positively eat no more, a few bites of deep-fried salmon, which seemed a disgraceful end for such a noble fish until he tasted it.

"God," he said reverently, and Tye, rattling a martini shaker, smiled.

"Nope. Carrie."

He found himself with yet another beer in his hand and smiling mistily at the memory of the meal. The room around him was quieting. Most of the diners had left; there were rumbles and clangs of cleanup from the invisible kitchen. The homely tables within the next room had been tidied, set for the next day. Through the swinging doors, propped open now, Pierce could see the ghost of the hotel in the high, shadowed ceiling too far above the modest restaurant area, and the hint, behind three makeshift walls around the tables, of the long, wide, empty husk of the older room enclosing them.

Someone loomed into his dreamy stupor. He started, found the disquieting Carrie in front of him, holding sheets and a towel now instead of a cauldron.

"My dad told Ella you're staying the night," she said briskly. "She asked me to take you upstairs." She raised her chin slightly, catching Tye's eye. "Number three okay?"

"Far as I know, nothing leaks in there."

"How much do I owe—?"

Tye shook his head. "Don't worry about it. We'll settle up in the morning."

"Thanks." He drained his glass and stood up. Nothing fell over; the floor didn't rise to meet him. He laughed a little. "I lost track of how long I've been sitting here."

"You're not the first," Tye answered. "Sweet dreams."

Carrie led him to the far side of the room, where the old reception desk with slots behind it for mail and keys emerged bulkily out of the shadows. She had begun to climb the stairs when he remembered his manners.

"Here. Let me carry that stuff."

"I've got it, thanks."

He trailed after her around the elegant curve, trying not to gaze at the taut figure on the step above, sure she would read his mind and dump the linens on his head. He thought of food instead.

"That salmon was unbelievable. How— What did you do to it?"

"The salmon?" She sounded incredulous.

"Yeah. I would never in a million years have let it anywhere near a deep fryer. My mother would have fired me. But you—"

"You're asking me about the salmon?"

"Well. Yes."

She flashed him one of her wide-eyed glances, a bewildering mix of amazement and exasperation. She made a noise indicating something major wrong with his head, and opened the door at the top of the stairs.

"Ella, Hal, and Tye all sleep on this floor; you won't be alone up here." She dropped her armload on a tapestry-covered chair and flicked on a lamp. "Bathroom's in there. Don't worry. It's not a chamber pot, and there is hot water."

"What did I say?" he asked softly, genuinely wanting to know. To his surprise her expression became complex, bittersweet, and strangely sad. Should I ask you to stay? he wondered. She turned away quickly, whipped a sheet open across the bed.

"Nothing. You said nothing." She shifted around the bed, tugging the corners tight without looking at him. "There are so many things nobody will answer when I ask. I thought you might—they might answer you. If you had asked."

"Asked what?"

Her lips pinched again; she only said, "Go down and get your things while I finish this."

When he came back, she was gone.

He woke sometime in the dark of the night, chasing down a fading dream in which something he wanted very badly kept eluding him, no matter how fast he moved, how desperate his desire. He was covered with sweat, as though he truly had been running. It took him a few groggy moments to remember where he was. When he finally did, he fell back into sleep as into some soundless, bottomless nothing.

He woke with a start in a pool of light from the unshaded window. He saw blue water, a paler blue sky, the sun burning away the last of a morning fog. He groped for his watch. The lovely room caught his attention first: the rich, dark wainscoting, the pale rose walls, the high ceiling and fine moldings of an earlier era. Light, airy, full of morning, it drew him upright to walk down the shaft of sunshine, peer at the bay and wonder, as he saw the fishers already out, how long the world had gone on without him as he slept.

He showered, dressed, and packed quickly. He heard no sounds in any of the rooms around him. Everyone was up, he guessed, and he hoped the restaurant might still be serving breakfast. When he went downstairs, he found the bar empty. He dropped his bag on a velveteen couch and went to push at the swinging doors. They refused to budge. He found the sliding bolts holding them fast, pulled them out of the floor and looked into the restaurant.

He heard nothing from the kitchen: not a voice, not a clatter of pot or plate, not a sizzle.

He turned after a moment, slid the bolts back into place, and listened. Not a floorboard creaked; not a door opened or closed. Maybe they were outside on the water, or running errands, shopping. The bar had been cleaned, everything tidied, put away, shut up. He wandered aimlessly a moment, waiting for Tye to appear, present him with a bill.

A gleam in the shadows near the reception desk caught his eye, drew him over to look at it more closely, for something to do while he waited. A tall, wide glass cabinet stood between the desk and the massive fieldstone fireplace. Its curved door was made of intricate diamonds of beveled glass framed with thin brass rods; its latch and hinges were a bygone age's fantasy of brass, curved, etched, scrolled. Inside the cabinet he saw the gaff, the gold platter, the cauldron.

He gazed at them. Again they teased at him, eluded him when he tried to make sense of them. He turned finally, beginning to feel the oppressive weight of the silence, the emptiness around him. He wondered if he had partied with ghosts.

He saw the knife then, lying on the desk, along with the brass key. He stopped, holding his breath. The knife hadn't made it into the cabinet with the other oddities. He picked it up, weighed it in his hold, turned it in what light he could catch from the high windows to study the hammered silver, the blade and haft shaped of a single piece of metal. It fit his hold like a friend's handclasp, its fine edge, under his thumb, keen, dangerous, and ready for anything.

He felt his throat dry. He wanted it. He would take it. He set it down on the desk noiselessly, as though someone might hear the faint slide of metal and come to its rescue. He had never stolen anything in his life. He would not steal this, he told himself swiftly. He would pay for it. He pulled out his wallet, rummaged recklessly through his cash, wondering how much his room, all the beers he had drunk, the amazing supper he had eaten, and the knife would cost him. How much it had all been worth.

He pulled out a credit card finally, tossed it on the desk. They would find it there beside the cabinet key, and know who had taken the knife. Let it cost whatever they wanted.

He crossed the room swiftly, hid the knife in his bag under a shirt. Then he left as quickly, closing the bar door quietly behind him. There was no one in the parking lot, nothing but the little Metro, like the last boat left at the dock.

As he pulled out, he thought he heard a shout. He sped up and out onto the highway. The place was empty, after all, no one left to call him back. Everyone who knew his name was gone.

# 4

Carrie, wakened early the next morning by a cacophony of crows saluting the sun, listened, before she opened her eyes, to the quality of silence within the walls. The old farmhouse, with its plain pastel paint, its ancient linoleum, and flaking sills, had its own familiar language of creaks and rattles. It seemed strangely still that morning, as though it, too, listened. No random snores, no running water, no comments from floorboards or door hinges. No Merle, she thought, and opened her eyes.

She was used to that. Her father was a random occurrence, like most of the weather around Chimera Bay. A squall, some sunshine, hail, a rainbow, one followed another in a perpetual guessing game. Merle might be asleep in his bed when she woke; he might be just coming through the door to fall into bed. He might be on a log, or up a tree, or sitting in the truck having a beer for breakfast with one of the nameless forest-dwellers who carried everything they owned in a leaf-and-lawn bag. More surprising, he might be getting out of the truck with a bag of groceries. Sometimes, he was simply nowhere at all, where he'd been since the Friday Nite before.

Carrie showered and dressed for work, then wandered outside, chewing on a piece of toast. There was no Merle on the horizon. The noisy choir of crows had disappeared as well, leaving the landscape to a single moon-white egret, standing motionless in six inches of silvery flow. Beside the stream, and staring as raptly at some flowering skunk cabbage, was Zed Cluny in his pajamas.

He raised his head and saw her as she started toward him. He had moved into Proffit Slough the previous year, renting a tiny cabin that stood on a knoll above the stream. Carrie had found him chatting amiably with Merle one morning; the fact that Merle was sitting on Zed's cabin roof at the time didn't seem to bother either one of them. Carrie went over to claim her father and got a pleasing eyeful of Zed. He and Carrie had worn a trail through the grasses between them, much like the rest of the wildlife in the slough.

He watched her from the other side of the narrow stream that was a vein in the vast tracery of water constantly pushed and pulled, rising and lowering in the tidal flow. He had a sweet face that hadn't yet hardened into itself, straight white-gold hair that he trimmed into a lank bowl on his head, dark caramel eyes that had grown patient, far-sighted with his meanderings through the world.

"I just saw a baby salmon go by," he told her. "I think. Smelt?"

"Smolt. You working this morning?"

"In a couple of hours. Thought I'd get my camera, try for a shot. What are you doing up so early?"

He had so many odd jobs, Carrie couldn't keep track of his schedule: afternoon at the Food Co-op, driving an elderly woman around on her errands a couple of times a week, morning lifeguard duty at the city pool, night shifts at the ancient Pharaoh Theater. Years of swimming had given him a broad pair of shoulders and muscular legs which, at the moment, were hidden by flannel penguins waddling all over them.

"The crows woke me up," she answered. "Then I couldn't go back to sleep; the house was too quiet. My father finally stopped chanting, and now he's vanished."

He chuckled. "Yeah. I heard some of that, last night when I got home after the midnight show. What was he—"

"Haven't a clue. He never tells me anything. Or he does, but he never makes sense. He's probably asleep under a tree."

"Maybe he's got a girlfriend."

"My dad?" she said, surprised at the notion. "I suppose maybe. But it's hard to imagine who."

"That's because he's your dad."

Somehow, at the thought, they were both moving toward the weathered plank Zed had laid across the stream. He reached it first, balancing easily on his bare feet. Carrie was there at the bridge's end to gather armfuls of frayed flannel, muscle, warm skin, to inhale the familiar scents of dreams and soap and sweat on the penguin pajamas.

"Come inside?" his lips said against her hair.

"I told Ella I'd come in early to help her hull strawberries and bake shortcakes." Reluctantly, she peeled herself away from him. "I should go," she told his eyes, which were heavy, full of her now instead of salmon and skunk cabbage.

"Tonight?" he said. "Wait. What's today?"

"Saturday. I'll be home late."

"So will I—nine to two again at the theater. Wait for me here when you get off work? If tomorrow's Sunday, I won't have anything until noon, when I drive Mrs. Pettigrew to church and walk the Hound of the Baskervilles until she gets out. What about breakfast at the beach? Coffee and hard-boiled eggs, and I smoked some tuna—"

"Yes," she said, laughing. "Yes. I want it now." Her feet backed another step, moving against the tide, it felt. "See you tonight."

She realized much later, as the dinner crowd shifted from the grill to the bar, that it would be one of those nights. Knight nights, she called them: the slow, informal gathering through the evening of the men closest to Hal Fisher. Ian Steward, Jarvis Day, Curt and Gabe Sloan, Josh Ward, Father Kirk from St. Benedict, and Reverend Gusset from Trinity Lutheran, Hal's brother Tye, and Merle made up the steadfast, reliable core of the group. Others, less familiar, wandered in from the mountain towns, or from the wilds along the rivers and lakes, the farthest reaches of the sloughs. Carrie couldn't name all of the knights, but she recognized them by the fierce, mute loyalty and respect she saw in their eyes as one by one they went to greet Hal first, and only then, turned to the bar and the stalwart Tye behind it. They even occupied the single round table at the place, overflowing around it, chairs pulled up two or three deep, always Hal with Merle at one side of him, and the vacant chair on his other where no one ever sat.

Of course, Carrie had asked Ella about that. Ella's lips had thinned until they vanished; she couldn't have pushed a word past them if she had wanted to. She just shook her head and disappeared so far into a pot after a scorched spot that Carrie thought she would fall into it.

She had asked Gabe Sloan, Curt's tall, golden-haired son, who with his father held the restaurant doors open for the Fish Fry procession. But he didn't know the why of the empty chair beside Hal Fisher either.

"My dad says it's all connected," he had told her. "Hal Fisher getting hurt, the hotel failing, Lilith Fisher going to live in the tower suite, the quarrel between them, even the Friday Nite Fry—it's all part of the same story. But the ones who know the story won't talk about it, and those who don't won't ask for fear of causing pain."

Merle knew, Carrie guessed. But he only said, when she asked him, "It's like an evil spell cast over the place. When the right person comes through the door and asks, the spell will be broken. That's what I know."

It wasn't all he knew, she thought grumpily. But it was all he would say.

The knights of the forests, the mudflats, and the waters were still sitting around the table when she finally finished late that evening, cleaning the kitchen and setting up for Sunday brunch. The men leaned back precariously into one another on their chair legs; they balanced scuffed boots on knees, and held their drinks as they talked, winding down now, a rumble of male voices tweaking the thread of some endless story, eliciting a deep roll of laughter that tapered slowly into silence as the men reminisced, privately, dreamily, until it seemed

they must have come to the end of the evening, then someone
else spoke, plucked a thread, and the thunder reverberated
through the circle again. A middle-aged couple sat in the
shadowy edges of the room talking quietly; another nonknight
sat at the bar, staring into his drink and ignoring the group.
But no Merle. His chair was oddly empty that night.

Carrie sank wearily onto a raddled velveteen couch left
over from the gilded age and parked now against the wall
near the restaurant doors. Tye gave her a smile and poured
her the cold, dark, molasses-edged beer she liked. In the
sprawling circle of men, she saw Gabe's sleek, trimmed head
turn. He got up a moment later, took the beer from Tye,
and brought it to Carrie.

"Here you are," he said, handing it to her, and sat, while
his eyes went back to the company he had left. "How'd it
go tonight?"

"Thanks," she said, yawning. "I had to do some serving;
Marjorie missed lunch. I made thirty-six dollars in tips.
That's going into the creel."

He grunted, shifting as though a broken spring under
the ancient velveteen had bit him. He didn't like the idea
of the creel full of Carrie's escape money any more than
Carrie liked the idea of accidentally falling in love with him
and spending the rest of her life in Chimera Bay. So they
kept their distance from one another, though Carrie sensed
sometimes that he was simply waiting for her to come to
her senses and realize where she belonged.

She added, to take his mind off the creel, "Ella rolled
cheese biscuits for dinner. So I took the dough scraps,
wrapped them around chopped green apple and boiled

shrimp with some grated ginger and a spritz of lemon juice, and baked them."

"Weird."

"They all got eaten. Did my dad come in tonight?"

"I'm not sure. I got here late. You can ask; they're almost done."

"How can you tell? What do you talk about?"

He shrugged. "What comes up," he said finally, "out of the deep."

She looked at him silently; his eyes, back on the group now, were intent and burning with the mystery that Hal Fisher carried around with him. "Fish stories," she said, and his eyes came back to her, earnest, unsmiling.

"Sort of. Not exactly, but in a way."

She swallowed more beer, added restively, tired of hints, riddles without answers, "If you see my father, will you tell him I'm looking for him? I'm going home. It's been a long day."

"Sure," Gabe said, his attention on her now that she was going to leave him. He rose as she did, watched her silently as she took the glass to the bar. She waved to him, and he nodded, still not moving; she felt his gaze until she closed the screen door behind her and stepped into the parking lot.

A shadow shifted beside the pickup as she crossed to the driver's side. She stopped, more startled than frightened; nothing much ever happened in Chimera Bay. The shadow stepped forward, let the light from the streetlamp fall on its face.

She didn't recognize him, but he knew her.

"Carrie. I'm Todd Stillwater."

He was, she thought incredulously, the most beautiful

man she had ever seen. If a Greek statue of an athlete had landed in the Kingfisher parking lot, alive, dressed in jeans and a sweatshirt, he would have looked just like this, complete with the wonderful straight nose, the mobile, curling lips, the wide-set, guileless eyes. Even his voice was perfect, deeper and more tempered than she would have expected from his youthful, open expression.

She was staring, she realized, frozen and mute. She opened her mouth; a bat squeaked out, by the sound of it.

He smiled a little, reassuringly, though the charming little frown, like the most careful chip of the sculptor's chisel between his brows, remained.

"I startled you. I'm sorry. I usually don't skulk around scaring people in parking lots. I just drove over on the off chance you'd still be here. I closed earlier this evening."

He paused, waiting. She cleared her throat. "Yes," she managed. "I'm Carrie Teague."

"My wife Sage dropped into this place a couple of times recently. She likes the way you cook. Your ideas. We wondered if you'd like to come and work for me." She opened her mouth again; nothing came out this time. He added, "I run my own kitchen; Sage helps me. She also bartends, sets tables, serves, cleans up after—"

"Oh," Carrie breathed, enlightened. "You want me to set tables."

"No. Sage doesn't mind doing all that. But it's too much for her to have kitchen duties as well. So I've been looking for someone else to cook with me. I'm asking you. If you can bear to leave this place. I can pay you very, very well." He smiled again. "I think you'd be worth it."

She felt something break loose in her chest or her brain, float slowly aloft like a hot-air balloon ascending from earth into warm, endless blue. "I don't—" She pulled in a breath dizzily. "I don't know what to say. Except thank you. I could never afford to eat in your restaurant. But I've heard your cooking is—well, unlike anything else around here. Magical. I think that's the word I heard when I started paying attention. My experiments—my little bites—they're just for fun. Mostly I fry fish. Make clam chowder. French fries for lunch and garlic mashed for dinner."

"Yes," he agreed, waiting patiently, she realized, while she dithered, tried to talk him out of what he wanted. Why, she wondered, didn't she just say okay, then shut up and dream how fat that creel would get and how fast?

Then she saw Ella's face, tight with anger at the thought of Stillwater, her spatula pressing down on a spitting round of burger until it seared.

As though he read her mind, he said swiftly, "Think about it. I can be patient. You know where to find me."

He gave her another sweet smile, opened a big, graceful hand in farewell.

A door opened, slapped shut behind her; she jumped.

"Carrie!" her father called sharply. She turned, her own hand still raised. Merle stepped out from behind the scaffolding, scanned the parking lot, looking as though he were scenting it, tense and watchful, like some four-legged beast with its hackles raised.

"What?" she wondered bewilderedly. Now what? Nobody ever explained anything, so how exactly was she to know? She glanced behind her; Stillwater had already gone. "Where have you been?" she asked Merle, but he didn't explain that either.

"Who was that?" he demanded.

"You sound exactly like someone's father," she said irritably.

"Well, I am."

"Well, now is not the time. And never mind who that was. It's my business."

"I know," he said grimly.

"You know what? Who that was, or that it's my business?" She threw up both hands, scattering questions everywhere into the night. "You want me to make decisions without giving me anything! I might as well go work for him—it's got to be less mysterious than this falling-down place. Rituals with letters, rituals with cauldrons, a bloody gaff, a missing knife, everyone in a time warp, looking back at the past, wishing for the good old days, hinting of portents, speaking in riddles, knowing things but never saying, never explaining—and you're mad at me for just thinking of going to work for Stillwater. How did you even know he was out here?"

He was silent, looking at her, and still, so still that for a moment he seemed to fade into the night, become one of those half-invisible things, both seen and unseen, so familiar that no one ever bothers to look, to recognize, until it's too late.

Then he did vanish. A wolf sat in the place where he had stood, its muzzle lifted and open in a long wild cry. Carrie, stunned motionless, heard in its fierce energy, its plaintiveness, the only answer that Merle could find to give her before the wolf ran off into the dark.

She was still trembling, her hands still icy, when she

stopped the truck beside Zed's cabin. She couldn't move except to wipe away the stray tears that told her she wasn't entirely a solid lump of ice. A solitary thought surfaced now and then from what seemed the completely functionless tangle of her brain. Why am I surprised? was one of them. Another came eventually, when she saw Zed's car lights turn onto the slough road: How long ago were there wolves around Chimera Bay?

After another silence, she heard her door open, felt Zed's hands tug at her.

"Hey. It's me. Carrie. What's wrong? Why didn't you wait inside? You're so cold . . ."

He took her inside, wrapped her in a blanket, and gave her something hot in a cup to thaw her fingers. She couldn't seem to stop shaking. Finally, he took her shoes off and pulled her into bed under the covers, where he could wrap himself around her.

"What happened? Carrie? Do you want me to call 911? Is it your dad? Did something happen to him?"

She drew a long breath, finally feeling bits of her—a lung, a nostril, an earlobe—begin to come back to life.

"No," she whispered. "And yes. Either I'm going crazy, or my father turned into a wolf in front of me."

She felt his chest rise as he sucked breath. "No. Merle's a werewolf?"

That had not occurred to her; she thought about it.

"No. I don't think so. It wasn't like that. It was more like— We were arguing in the Kingfisher parking lot—and he needed—he needed a different way to get me to understand what he was saying. Or not saying."

"Wow." He pulled up, leaning on an elbow, gazing down at her. "That is so cool."

She felt her face melt, remember how to smile. "So. No 911."

"Where'd he learn to do that? What is he?"

"I don't know." Both eyes heated at once; the candles he had lit blurred and swam. "Another unanswered question." The tears broke; she wiped at them, smiling again. "I hope he doesn't run around Chimera Bay like that and get himself shot. I should have known. I should have known by now not to be surprised at anything he would do. He talks to crows. He talks to the moon. Sometimes he makes me wonder exactly how long he's lived in this world. He says things— things that seem to go so far back that I don't understand how he can know them."

"It's so amazingly bizarre. Like the life cycle of a salmon."

"What?"

"That old, that strange. Or like sharks that never seem to sleep. Orcas. The leviathans of the deep that take your hook and don't let go until you're the one struggling on the end of the line, and they've changed the way you look at the world."

A shiver ran over her, gossamer and cold as a ghostly finger.

"I wonder," she whispered, "what leviathan is making my father afraid."

# 5

On a stretch of coast road between towns, where traffic was light and the wind from the sea soughed through thick stands of hemlock and spruce, the Metro blew a tire. The small car shivered under Pierce's grip and tried to crawl up a tree trunk. Pierce turned the wheel wildly, got it stopped before they met, but not before something groaned under the car and he heard a crack like a bone breaking. He sat a moment, breathing raggedly. Nothing passed him on the road, which, he realized belatedly, was fortunate since the rear bumper was angled out into the lane. He moved finally, opened his door, and got out to survey the damage.

The right front tire was in a ditch and pretty much flattened. The right back tire seemed to have run over a milepost, which had not gone down without a fight; the metal had taken a bite out of the tire as it warped. The broken bone had been a sapling caught under the car as it slewed off the road. The slender trunk had splintered above the root; the rest of it was wedged under the car.

Pierce swallowed dryly. He stood for a moment, listening, and heard only wind, no traffic. He reached inside the car, loosed the handbrake, then got behind the car and pushed. It rocked a moment wearily, then moved abruptly, mowing down whatever it had left standing, and rolling the front tire deeper into the ditch. At least the rear end was out of the road. He stood another moment, looking helplessly at the car, then pulled out his cell phone to call a tow truck. The phone rang in his hand, and he started. He should, he realized, have expected the call.

"Hi."

"Pierce! Are you all right?"

"Yeah," he sighed. "I'm fine. You must know that already."

"Where are you?" Heloise asked. "I don't recognize anything."

He glanced around, looking for her borrowed eyes. A jay squawked at him suddenly, harshly, as if he had trashed the neighborhood on purpose.

Mom? he thought, then saw the hawk circling high above the trees, silent, dark-winged against the blue.

"I'm fine," he said again. "I just had a blowout. I'll call a tow truck to take me to the nearest town, stay there until the car is fixed."

She was silent a breath, circling with the hawk. "Wait. I think I know—"

"Mom—"

"That little town. Biddie Cove. I stayed a night there a long time ago, when I ran away from Severluna. It has the highest sea stack on the Wyvernhold coast, and a wonderful old diner that served the best chowder—"

"Mom. I have to call a tow truck."

"No," she said quickly. "No, you don't. I'll call Lilith Fisher. She can get Tye to send someone to help you."

He caught his breath, startled and suddenly panicking. "No—I've come all this way—I don't want to go backward. Anyway, who is Lilith Fisher?"

"She's Hal Fisher's wife."

"How—how did you—"

"We've known each other for years. Of course I told her that you were driving down this way. She called me yesterday when you pulled into the old Kingfisher Inn. She said that Tye offered you a room."

"You never told me we had family in Chimera Bay."

"Of course I didn't. Why would I want to give you any reason to find your way there?"

He gripped the phone, his fingers chilled. "Well, I'm not there now, and there's no reason why I should go all the way back. I'll get a tow to whatever garage is around here."

"But they'd be happy to help you, and put you up as long as you need."

"I know." He swallowed, his eyes riveted on the pack in the car as though he could see the ritual blade and his guilt jumbled in there along with his shirts and underwear. "It's just that I need to solve my own problems. You need to let me. How will I make it in Severluna if I run to you for help

anytime something goes wrong? Mom?" He listened to the
sea wind, the silence in his ear like a breath held. "Mom. Let
the hawk get on with its life."

Finally, he heard her sigh. "I know you're right. It's just
hard for me not to want—"

"I know."

"Will you call me later and let me know where you are?"

"I will. I promise."

Chimera Bay, the tow-truck driver told him an hour later.
They had the best parts and service department within
a hundred miles any direction. And if it couldn't be fixed, the
town had more car dealerships. Pierce climbed glumly into the
truck, watched his past reel backward along the road until it
came to a halt again at the place he had just left.

He spent a couple more hours waiting to hear the verdict,
then walked up the highway to the nearest motel. He was
closer to the busy south end of town than to the Kingfisher
Inn; with luck he could skulk around unnoticed until the
car was fixed. He saw several bars, a fish market, a wine
market, a supermarket, a bookstore, a shoe store, one each
of every kind of fast-food restaurant. He wandered among
the streets as evening fell, looking into windows, reading
menus, hoping nobody he had met the previous night would
chance along and remember him. He glimpsed, inside the
lobby of an old theater, the huge, golden body, the kohl-
rimmed eyes of an ancient ruler upon his throne, welcoming moviegoers with a placid, perpetual smile. On a side
street, he came across an elegant little restaurant tucked

into what had been a bank building. The round tables wore black cloths; red cut-crystal vases on them held a single small white calla lily. Stillwater's, the restaurant door said in simple lettering. No menu was posted.

"Excuse me," someone said behind him as he looked curiously through the door's tinted window.

He turned. A woman stood on the sidewalk, smiling at him. He knew her. He did not. He lingered on the top of the steps in front of the door, trying to place her in his past, those eyes, that smile. He recognized her face finally from one of the few ungloomy things in the house on Cape Mistbegotten: a lovely painting from some romantic era of a medieval maiden welcoming her knight home from his travels. She had that same generous mouth, the same abundantly flowing champagne hair, those same widely spaced, heavy-lidded gray-green eyes that seemed to carry light from a sun already gone for the day.

"Oh," he said, feeling his transfixed bones galvanized into motion. "Sorry. I'm in your way. Sorry."

She laughed a little, a lovely sound that he imagined a rill would make, or a warbler. "That's okay." She opened the door, then paused, looking down at him now. "Do you want to come in? We start serving a little later than most, but the bar is open."

I just wrecked my car, he told her silently. I left my credit card smoldering in last night's bar. I'll probably have to ask my mother to sell the painting of you so I can pay my motel bill. No way should I follow you into this place.

"Sure," he said dazedly, and followed her in.

"I'm Sage Stillwater," she said, as she seated him on one of the four leather-cushioned stools at the tiny bar.

"Pierce Oliver," he said, taking the piece of paper she

handed him without seeing it, still caught in the wonder of watching a painting move, change expression, talk. He made an effort. "Do you own the place?"

"My husband does. I do some cooking. I also serve food, clear the tables, mop the floors, and tend bar. If you'd like a drink."

He shook his head, changed his mind, changed it again. "I don't know," he said finally as she smiled. "Will you have one with me?"

She considered that, her head bent slightly, long, rippling hair falling like a veil behind her lovely profile. "Let me just see what Todd needs."

She moved among the tables toward curtains hanging over what might have been the bank-vault doorway, doorless now, but still heavily framed with steel set into the gray and white marble walls. He watched her mindlessly, her long limbs in black skirt and gray silk shirt moving quietly, gracefully. She disappeared. He straightened, feeling as though he had been for a few timeless moments utterly bewitched. He noticed the paper in his hand, laid it on the bar. No one came in while he waited. He felt oddly alone though he thought he heard the rise and fall of voices from far away, maybe from the street. Or maybe it was only the incoherent sound of distant traffic. The café curtains, black like the tablecloths and shadowing the lower half of the broad windows, gave him a view of the bay at the end of the street, the water gull-gray with the coming twilight and absolutely still.

He heard footsteps. But they were outside, he realized, on the sidewalk. He looked around, wanting a drink now. His eyes fell on the paper lying on the marble bar. It wasn't so much a menu, he saw as he scanned it, as a manifesto. Something that seemed utterly pretentious, absurd, amid the prosaic diners, car lots, chain motels of Chimera Bay.

Eat, it pretty much commanded, what I give you. I'll tell you what it will cost you when I decide the meal is over.

His cell phone rang.

He jumped wildly. "Mom," he breathed, hunched over the phone as though he were in church. "I can't talk now."

"What in the world were you thinking?"

"What?"

"When you stole that knife?"

Her voice sounded strange, amazed and completely bewildered. But he was the stranger, he realized, unrecognizable, unpredictable. "I wasn't," he said tightly. "Thinking. I just wanted. I'll let you know why when I know."

"But, Pierce, you don't— You've never done— This is so unlike you. Where are you? You promised to let me know. I can't find you anywhere, and I've been so worried, especially after Lilith told me. She said that things of such ancient power find their own paths; they take what they need. That is hardly comforting. Sweetheart, be careful."

"Mom—"

"Better yet, just come home. Return the knife and come home."

He opened his mouth to answer, found no argument, no answer, nothing at all that either one of them would understand, except that he could undo nothing.

He gave up, turned the phone off, and dropped it into his pocket. Sage pushed aside the dark, heavy curtains, came toward him carrying something. Again he was drawn into the timeless vortex that seemed to flow around her, a spell she cast without awareness, with every movement, every shift of expression. As she drew closer, he sensed the disturbance behind the calm, saw the faint flush of red in her eyelids. He swallowed, stunned at himself, at what he felt and saw, at her for making him see.

"I'm sorry." Her voice seemed unchanged, but her smile was less luminous, more controlled. "Todd says he won't cook tonight. We are now closed."

"Oh."

"It happens, sometimes."

"Was it—" He stopped, cleared his throat. "Something I did? Or didn't? Do?"

"Oh, no." She shook her head but without letting him see her eyes. "No. Maybe he just knows that no one else will come in tonight. Sometimes he knows things like that. Sometimes they matter, sometimes not. He made this for you."

She put a small, covered plate down on the bar, and let him see her eyes now, direct, unsmiling.

"A consolation?" he asked, gazing back at her. "Or to make me regret what he won't give me?"

"Maybe," she answered simply, "so that you will come back."

His hand hovered over the black cloth covering the little plate. Then he dropped his hand, stood up, still holding her eyes. "Then I'll come back," he said, and turned away from her. As he closed the door behind him, he looked back at her, saw her staring down at the plate, still covered on the bar.

He wandered the streets a while, aimlessly, while the sky over Chimera Bay grew black. Traffic thinned, shops closed, a couple of restaurants turned out their lights before he finally bought some take-out sushi and a six-pack to carry back to the motel. When he was nearly there, something furry and four-legged darted in front of him and hissed furiously, every hair on its body standing on end.

He blinked down at it, then rubbed his eyes tiredly. "I'm sorry. Just let me get in out of the dark."

The cat wailed at him, stalked away, hair still erect. After a few feet, it shook itself, then sat down in the middle of the sidewalk and looked around a moment. It gave up trying to figure out what it was doing there, and began to lick a paw.

I know just how you feel, Pierce told it as he passed.

He ate sushi and drank beer on his bed in the quiet motel, staring mindlessly at the news. Sometime in the middle of the night, he remembered his mother and the phone he had never turned back on. He pulled the pillow over his head and went back to sleep, dreamed of cooking strange and wonderful dishes, none of which seemed to be made of anything he would have recognized as food.

The Metro was fixed by noon the next day, but Pierce couldn't persuade himself to get into it and go. That day passed. Another. A third. He watched TV; he wandered out for food when he had to, trying to look inconspicuous and dodging growling dogs, spitting cats, a crow that fluttered into his face and yelled at him. He picked up his drained phone at one point, hunted around for the charger, then stood looking blankly at it, unable to find the energy or the interest in connecting one to the other. At noon and again at twilight, he wove a labyrinthine path through the streets that led him surreptitiously closer and closer to the heart of the matter: Stillwater's.

No matter what time he reached it, no matter how elaborately he stalked it, winding his way through side streets and alleyways, trying deliberately not to think about it until he finally permitted himself to pass it, the restaurant was always closed. He would wait, skulking across the street. It would stay closed. Finally, he would walk down to the waterfront to gaze at the quiet bay, where a neatly painted tugboat or a sailboat or a barge full of logs might be following the shipping channel out to sea. If he was lucky, and wasn't accosted by his mother's familiar of the day, he would turn finally and walk the complex labyrinth again.

The restaurant would be closed.

Incredulous, he wondered if the restaurant was closed only to him. Other people entered when his back was turned, ate and drank, were spoken to and served by the long-limbed, rippling-haired beauty with her eyes full of secrets, her air of one moving imperturbably through her tasks while listening for a distant voice. Somehow the chef had seen Pierce's heart among her possessions; somehow, through the power of his arts, he denied only Pierce entry to his enchantments.

Or maybe, Pierce thought in saner moments, they were just taking a vacation.

He could wait.

He wandered into a scruffy bar along the waterfront one twilight, a place where faces grew blurred on entry since nobody came there to be seen. He would sit and have one beer, he decided, then take the shortest route to the restaurant, just like any other diner expecting to be fed, expecting Stillwater's to behave like any other restaurant. Maybe if he changed his attitude, stopped slinking through the streets, sending an aura of guilt and confusion ahead of him, the sadistic chef wouldn't recognize him. He would just step in, sit down as easily as he had taken a stool in this shabby cave where nobody expected him and nobody cared. He—

"It's not you he wants," the man beside him said. "That's why he won't let you in."

Pierce froze. The voice seemed something out of a vague, half-forgotten past, which, he realized as his head turned stiffly, reluctantly to face it, had been only a scant few days ago.

"Merle."

The man's eyes held only a faint, friendly smile. "Thought you left town."

"I had car trouble."

Merle nodded, took a sip from his bottle. The stolen knife hung between them, an unspoken word haunting the air. I wanted it, Pierce explained as silently, so I took it. Now I want a man's wife. So.

"Is it fixed?"

"Yes."

"Then you might as well get back on the road. Nothing for you here. Oh." He reached into a pocket, pulled out a credit card. "You left this behind. You're family; Tye wouldn't charge you for anything. You might need this, south. I hear cities can be expensive."

"How did you know?" Pierce asked helplessly. "Why I'm still here? How could you know something like that?"

Merle shrugged, beads in his hair speaking softly together. "I know Stillwater." His eyes slid away from Pierce's face, gazed over his shoulder at the night gathering across the water. "What he wants has nothing to do with you."

"But Sage—I can't just walk away from her—"

"He doesn't think you will. That's why he bothers tormenting you. It's just a game."

Pierce swallowed. "Is it a game to her?" he asked painfully.

"Oh, no." He gave Pierce's shoulder a reassuring pat. "No. But you can't do anything for her. He knows that. He just likes having you around, wanting what he has. Think about this: Maybe you'll learn something in Severluna that will help you here. But you need to go." He grimaced slightly, touched his temples, rattling beads again. "And call your mother. She's been on my mind."

"Who are you?" Pierce whispered, trying to see into the pale eyes, fathom the mists there. "Who are you?"

Merle lifted his beer. "I go back," he said simply. "Find your way to Severluna. See what you can do with that knife."

# 6

Carrie was ruthlessly and shamelessly ransacking her father's possessions.

She had seen very little of Merle since he had turned into a wolf. She pursued his human voice through the trees in the bright dawn, in the twilight mists; he lured her but refused to let her find him. She glimpsed him a couple of times through the swinging doors between the bar and the grill, leaning against the mahogany and looking at her, his eyes unreadable. When she hastily dumped the tray of silverware and napkin holders she carried, and went out to find him, he would be gone. Vanished. Disappeared. Wherever he slept, it wasn't at home.

He was a mystery. She would solve him, she swore, if every other mystery clinging like the old year's dead wet leaves to the Kingfisher Inn eluded her. This mystery was her father. He had loved her mother once. They had made her, Carrie, with his dark hair, his eyes, and her mother's urge to run.

"Well, I'm not," she whispered tersely to the boxes she pulled out of closets, dragging their frayed lacework of cobwebs adorned with desiccated sow bugs into light. "I'm not running yet."

She opened drawers, photo albums, tool chests, shoeboxes full of letters, rusty tackle boxes, suitcases that had been in the dark since her mother left. Her mother, who had fled as far south as she could go without leaving Wyvernhold, was back home from her brief visit north, and no help whatsoever when Carrie called her.

"Why did I leave your father?" she repeated incredulously. "If you're asking that question after all these years, then you already know the answer. Why are you still up there? Move down here, where it's warm and beautiful. We'll have fun together."

Zed, whom she'd hardly seen in a couple of days, appeared one morning as a step across the threshold of the farmhouse, making her straighten, turn eagerly toward the sound. After another step or two, she recognized him and drooped a little over the box of photos she had pulled out from under Merle's bed.

Zed himself appeared finally, walking carefully, tentatively through the old parlor, around piles of clothes, scattered papers, yawning chests and cases, their contents strewn across the floorboards like tidal debris after a tempest.

She blinked at it, startled at the scale of her devastation.

"He won't let me talk to him," she explained tightly. "He won't let me ask. So I'm looking for clues."

"Find anything?" he inquired with caution.

"No."

He thought a moment. "Maybe I could ask? He talks to me now and then. I think he likes me. I'll buy the wolf a beer and tell him you're—ah—worried?"

She sighed. "Tell him I miss him, and I don't understand a word he's not saying." She stared at the hillock of photos she had pulled out of the box, saw herself, gap-toothed and curly-haired, laughing up at her father. "I'm missing something," she said slowly, frowning at the past.

"What?"

"Something. I'm not seeing it. Something's under my nose . . ." She looked up at Zed again, saw his patient, mystified expression. She got to her feet finally. "Do you want some coffee? I think I made some. Maybe I didn't."

He smiled, shook his head. "I can help you with this later. If you can tell me what you're looking for. I'm working at the co-op this morning. You?"

"Prep and lunch."

"I'll come to the Kingfisher after work; maybe I'll run into Merle."

"Good luck with that," she said grimly.

She took a question along with Hal Fisher's daily note to the one other person she knew who could read minds, and whose behavior was also generally incomprehensible.

"My father turned into a wolf a couple of nights ago and howled at me," she told Lilith as she handed over the note. "Did you know he could do that?"

Lilith stood stock-still in front of her writing desk, staring at Carrie through the half lenses balanced on the end of her nose.

"Why did he do that?" she asked slowly. "What did you say to him? You're not leaving us, are you?"

Carrie swallowed what felt like a spoonful of dust. "You did know," she whispered.

Lilith looked at the envelope in her hand, fanned her face with it. "Well. Not that exactly. I've never seen him do that. But—"

"But you're not surprised." Her voice shook. "What exactly is he?"

"Ask him."

Carrie flung up her hands. "How? He won't let me. Nobody answers questions around here! Nobody!"

Lilith tried; Carrie saw the impulse in her eyes. But when she opened her mouth, nothing came out. She closed her mouth, and a floodtide of pain, sorrow, hopelessness broke across her face, deepening the fine lines on it and leaving a sheen of unshed tears in her eyes.

Carrie put the back of her hand against her mouth, her own eyes filling. "I'm sorry," she breathed, without knowing for what. "I'm sorry."

"Carrie." Lilith paused, swallowed. "Whatever you said—whatever you did—to make Merle shape the wolf, listen to him. Listen to that howling. He's trying—"

"I know. I know. But I don't know why." She blinked back tears, added, her voice a harsh husk of itself, "I don't understand wolf."

"You understand fear. You understand beware."

"But of what?" she asked helplessly, and was unsurprised when Lilith did not answer.

She saw Zed alone at the bar when she went through the swinging doors. She caught a glimpse of Merle later, when she was about to leave, alone again in the late-afternoon crowd, his pale eyes intent, unblinking, on her face. She blinked, surprised, and he was gone again, like shadow melting into shadow.

He was talking to her, she realized then; he had her attention; he was telling her something.

What?

He didn't have much, she thought, for a man who had lived in the same house at least since Carrie was born. Where were the elegant suits he had worn in the old photographs of the Kingfisher Inn during its shining years? Where were the silk ties, the expensive shoes? Locked away somewhere in the past, she guessed, in the ghost of the old inn. What he bothered to keep in drawers was frayed, worn. There was no word to express the state of his socks. She did find a few things her mother had given him in the years when she still liked him: beads for his hair, a gold earring, a piece of butter-colored amber on a leather tie.

All signs of his previous life he had left elsewhere; only the Merle that Carrie thought she knew lived in that house with her.

But I don't really know you at all, she told him, and kept looking.

She found the photo in a cardboard box of papers shoved into a corner of his bedroom closet. It was buried under old check stubs and statements from the years when he actually kept a bank account, tax forms from when he actually had jobs, outdated receipts that should have been tossed long ago. A handful of photos lay at the bottom: herself as a toddler on Merle's shoulders, her parents in their wedding finery, her mother, very young, with long, wild hair and feathers hanging from her earlobes; she was standing beside one of the winding tidal streams, lifting her skirt above her muddy boots as she watched the water.

The final photo startled her: Hal Fisher and Merle in all their glory, both in tuxes beneath the enormous chandelier with every light in it ablaze, and the reception room around them filled with women in heels and dark lipstick, men in suits and ties with jeweled pins. Hal and Merle were both smiling. It might have been opening night at the Kingfisher Inn as they welcomed the first guests. Behind them, a chef stood at the open doors of the huge dining hall, all its tables bright with cutlery, glassware, candles, and vases full of roses from the old gardens. The chef wore an old-fashioned cream-puff hat, black stovepipe pants; he, too, was smiling. Carrie, studying his smile, felt her skin constrict. She peered more closely at him. The warm, wide-set eyes, the Greek athlete's profile looked oddly, disturbingly familiar.

Todd Stillwater's father, it had to be. He must have done something so unspeakably wicked that every mention of that name, his history at the Kingfisher Inn, was forbidden even unto the unborn generations. She crouched over the photo for a long time, gazing at the three of them: Hal, Merle, the chef. Finally, the idea floating around in her head became coherent.

No way could she ask Hal. Her father refused to talk.

Maybe Stillwater would.

She took the photo with her when she drove to his restaurant on her day off. She went in midafternoon, in the calmer hours between lunch and dinner. No wolf chased the pickup through the streets, nor did Merle fling himself between her and Stillwater's name on the door. Why? she wondered. Where was he, if he felt so strongly about protecting her from some horribly lurking menace? She slammed the truck door a little crossly, climbed the worn marble steps, and opened the door to find Todd Stillwater sitting at the tiny bar, surrounded by paperwork.

"We open at seven for dinner," he said absently, without turning around. Carrie, surprised to find such cool elegance in the genial patchwork of downtown Chimera Bay, looked curiously at the black linens, the red cut-crystal vases, the thick marble walls of the early bank that stood sentinel against sound from the busy highway.

"Pretty," she said, and he turned.

"Carrie," he said, smiling, and stood up. "I wasn't sure you'd come."

"Is this a good time?"

"Perfect."

In the light of day rather than streetlamps, so was he, she thought dazedly. His black tie was loosened around his unbuttoned collar, his sleeves rolled halfway up forearms lightly furred with gold against a darker gold that, her fingers anticipated, would be warm and textured to the touch. She swallowed, wondering why she had never noticed forearms before, or the amazing bones of the wrist.

"I just came to talk," she said uncertainly.

"Good idea. I'm just going over accounts, nothing that can't wait." He rose, pulled out a couple of chairs at one of the tables beside the windows. "Sit down. Or would you like to see the kitchen? Sage is out shopping; she should be back anytime now to help me plan the dinner menu. Much as it ever gets planned. I'm impulsive, like you with your bites. You'd be welcome to stay for that. In fact, it might—"

"I came to ask a question," she interrupted.

"What's that?" he asked promptly, and she sat down awkwardly, with a thump, laying the envelope on the cloth between them. He sat, too, looking at it expectantly. "One of your recipes?"

She shook her head and drew out the photo.

He sat silently a moment, gazing at it. His brows peaked; he bent closer to it suddenly. "Is that—is that Hal Fisher? In a tux? Wow. Where— Wait. Is that— That's the chandelier in the Kingfisher bar."

"It's the old hotel." She tapped Merle's smiling face. "That's my father."

"I'm damned."

Her finger shifted to the face under the cream-puff hat. "That looks," she said steadily, "like you."

He picked up the photo wordlessly, angling the old black and white to deflect the light from the window. "It does," he breathed. "It could be me." He dropped it onto the table, stared at her. "I had no idea."

"No idea what? Is that your father?"

"I have no idea," he said, his eyes, wide and startled, meeting hers, and she felt the sudden rush of blood from her neck to her hairline.

"Oh."

"No, it's okay—"

"I am so sorry."

"It's just that—"

"I only just found the photo hidden away in my father's closet. I'd never seen it before. And the chef—he looks so—"

"Yes, he does." He brooded over the photo silently while Carrie, her face still burning, watched him. Thoughts whirled in her head; she caught at them, trying to make sense of them. If Todd Stillwater didn't know his father—if that chef was his father—then whatever horrors he had inflicted on the Kingfisher Inn resonated in his name—in his son's name—but had nothing to do—

"But had nothing to do with you," she whispered. He glanced at her, his eyes, silvery gray as a blade, tarnished with thoughts, memories.

"My mother fled from my father as soon as she could after I was born. She took me south to Severluna. I always thought my name—Stillwater—was her maiden name. But maybe not." He touched the photo lightly, near the chef's face. "That might—that might explain— It must have been something he did—"

"Yes."

"The tensions I've felt around that place—"

"Yes."

"Do you know what he might have done? Anything at all?"

She sagged against the table, sighing deeply. "How could I? No one ever answers any of my questions. I was hoping that you knew what happened. Why everything fell apart at the Kingfisher Inn, why Hal and Lilith stopped speaking, why Ella blames somebody with your name for everything, but she draws in small and tight like a snail whenever I ask."

His eyes dropped; he studied the photo again, while she studied his eyelashes, the exact color of his hair, the pale matte brown of a walnut shell, against the warmer shade of his face. Where does he find that sun around here? she wondered. He was gazing back at her suddenly, and she felt the fire across her face again, but not even that could make her look away.

He seemed oblivious; he only said, "I'm glad you brought this; it explains a lot. I had no idea what I was asking the other night. I don't want to cause worse feelings by taking you away from the Kingfisher. Maybe we could work something out part-time? Let's think about that. No decisions yet. But while I've got you here, let me show you what I do. I have some bites left over from lunch you might be interested in. Can I bring you a taste?"

"Sure," she said dazedly.

"I don't use menus, but I have written down a few of my recipes. Let me bring those, too; they'll give you an idea . . ."

He vanished into the old bank vault. She waited thoughtlessly, amazed at the notion of snacking on the ideas of the best cook in the county. He returned with one arm lined with small plates, papers under the other arm. He let the papers splash on the table, and arranged the little plates like offerings around her. They held treasures, she saw with astonishment: geometric shapes of this and that layered on one another, unexpected colors catching the eye, orange topping cranberry topping an airy cloud of licorice, another of chocolate, none of it, she suspected, tasting anything like the fruit or meat or sweet that the colors might suggest. Stillwater pushed a plate toward her, a tower of diamonds and squares and circles of the thinnest, brightest colors topped with a coiled ruby garnish, like a designer hat.

For an instant, as she raised her eyes from the lovely little makings to smile in amazement at him, she saw a stranger's eyes gazing out of what suddenly seemed the mask of a beautiful face. Tree-bark dark, they were, flecked with gold and luminous with an ancient light that had long since faded from the world she thought she knew.

He lifted the plate.

"Eat."

PART TWO

# WYVERNBOURNE

# 7

In Severluna, the youngest son of King Arden IX tied on his apron deep beneath the intersection of Severen Street and Calluna Way, and edged behind the water bar of the ancient cave. The apron was striped blue and green, the colors of water and moss, of the river goddess Calluna, from whose warm, steamy, smelly fountainhead within the stones behind the prince, the infirm, the depressed, and the curious had come for millennia to drink.

Prince Daimon picked up the sacred water pitcher, toasted the comely ticket-taker who sat on a stool at the cave entrance. He began to fill the little blue and green paper cups lined along the bar. The water, at least, was free. The god Severen, whose river began in the great, jagged snowy peaks to the east and crossed the land to merge with the Calluna and the bay, was worshipped for the precious metals he carried in his waters. His shrines were everywhere, even there at the holy birthplace of the goddess. His gold, silver, and copper changed hands upstairs at the ticket window, the coffee bar, and the ice-cream bar whose specialty was blueberry-pistachio in honor of the goddess. Below, near the entrance to the sanctum, there was the small prayer pool in which pleas to the goddess were accompanied by gifts of coins and the occasional semiprecious stone. Despite the heat, the strong mineral odors, the depths to which visitors must descend seeking the goddess in her underworld beneath the streets, the domed and tiled antechamber seldom stayed quiet long.

Raised voices on the stairs, a gabbling echo of high-pitched bird cries, indicated a busload of young schoolchildren gamboling down the steps. Daimon brought up more cups from underneath the bar as the first of them exploded into view. A couple of tour guides from the upper regions divided them expertly, took one group through the jagged stone opening into the ruins of antiquity around the pool, while the others tasted the holy waters in the cups. The children made the usual gagging noises after a sip of warm liquid laced with lithium salts. Daimon showed them the spittoon-shaped vessel in which to pour the dregs or spit the unswallowed mouthful, while their gimlet-eyed chaperons watched.

"Skylar, either swallow or spit into the pot—don't you dare spit that at Sondra."

Finally, the second group snaked through the narrow opening; for a moment, there was peace under the dome.

Daimon took a mop to some spilled water on the mosaic floor, which had been painstakingly repaired a century earlier after the streets had been laid down above the river, and somebody got around to wondering where the goddess's cave had gone. One of the chaperons, who had lingered in the quiet, took a second look at the young man behind the water bar.

"Prince Daimon!" she blurted. "What are you doing down here?"

"Serving the goddess," he answered, and wrung the mop sponge into the spittoon. He recognized the woman: Lady Clarice Hulte, whose elderly husband, Sir Lidian Hulte, was one of the king's knights. Her daughter, a plump, prim little girl with pigtails, had dumped her water into the hair of an obnoxious boy scrabbling for coins in the prayer pool, an action which the goddess, who had issues with the greedy Severen, would surely have approved.

Lady Clarice, whose pale, protuberant eyes her daughter had inherited, transferred her stare to the mop handle. "You're a noble of the realm, not a housemaid."

"We choose the weapons that best serve the goddess," Daimon said mildly. "I was in my father's service last week, putting his weapons to use. This week I'm in the queen's. She asked me to work in the shrine, learn the rituals of the goddess."

"But she is not your—" Lady Clarice began, addicted as she was to arguing points of protocol. Then her mouth snapped shut; she flushed an interesting shade of plum. Behind her, the ticket-taker caught her lips between her teeth and stared raptly at the floor.

"Technically, no," Daimon agreed. "The queen is not my mother, so I was not dedicated at birth to the goddess. But I see no reason to displease either of two such powerful women. Do you?"

A faint squeak came out of the ticket-taker, a similar sound out of Lady Clarice. "I do beg your pardon—" she managed faintly.

Daimon shrugged a shoulder and began lining more cups along the bar. "What for? Nobody cares. Even if I weren't a bastard son of my father, I'd have to outlive four siblings and their offspring before I could possibly be king of anything. And when you consider—"

The ticket-taker straightened abruptly on her stool. "Oh, stop. Forgive him, Lady Clarice; his true mother took one look at him when he was born and dropped him on his head."

Lady Clarice, stunned and swaying to stare at the ticket-taker, recognized the youngest offspring of Queen Genevra and King Arden. She swallowed audibly. Princess Perdita gave her a friendly smile, then shifted her gaze to frown at her half brother.

"Shame, Daimon. Apologize to Lady Clarice for teasing her."

"I am sorry for teasing you, Lady Clarice," Daimon said amiably, turning a spigot to refill the sacred water pitcher. In the silence before the water began to flow, the distant voices of children deep within the cave echoed incomprehensibly off the stones.

"I'll just—" Lady Clarice said weakly, taking a step or two backward. "I'd better see to—"

She turned, plunged into the cave. Perdita looked reproachfully at her retreating shadow.

"She didn't give me her ticket."

Daimon and his half sibling had been born in vastly different circumstances, but so closely in time they might have been twins. The fair-haired, gray-eyed, muscular Daimon had entered the world in a busy public hospital on the outskirts of Severluna. Willowy Perdita, with the king's black hair and golden eyes, had been born minutes earlier in a pool of warm water within the palace, surrounded by midwives and attendants of the goddess Calluna. By some royal sleight of hand, Daimon, howling in his crib in the hospital nursery, had been spirited away within an hour to grow up with Perdita.

Daimon had never known his mother. The queen had given him only the most meager bone of truth at an early age: that his mother had died after giving birth to him. What Queen Genevra actually thought about the matter, she never said. Gossip said a great many conflicting things for a few years, as the court watched Daimon grow. Then it lost interest. When he found the reckless courage to ask the king, his father said briskly, "You are my son. The rest is my business." Daimon guessed from the place where his mother had chosen for him to be born that she was used to taking care of herself. She was nobody, or anybody at all, until she had caught the king's eye. That the king had not left him nameless and orphaned but had reached out to find him, told Daimon something. But he was never sure what.

Daimon finished filling cups, put the mop back in a cupboard, and emptied the dregs in the vessel down the drain in the floor where it was filtered, cleaned, and piped back into the river downstream. He was aware of Perdita's voice— something about an upcoming fete, someone she hoped would be there—as a light, pleasing counterpoint to his thoughts. When her voice suddenly invaded his distraction, he was startled.

"Daimon! Where are you? I've been talking at you—you might as well be on the moon for all you're listening. What are you thinking about?"

He shook his preoccupations away, smiled at her. "Sorry. You were saying?"

"No. Really. What were you thinking? I've never seen that expression on your face. Are you in love?"

He knew the one on hers well enough. He felt that glittering, potent gaze from the place where, in a different myth, his third eye might have been, down to the soles of his feet. Witch, he thought. Sorceress. He shifted, dropping his own eyes, and took a cloth to a nonexistent spill on the bar.

"How should I know? I've never been there before."

"Who is she?"

"You were saying about a fete? Hoping who might come?"

He still felt that intense, ruthless regard, heard her draw breath. Then the children came spilling out of the cave, running upstairs in anticipation of ice cream, despite the unreasonable demands to *Walk! Walk!* Some unfortunate visitor coming down against the tide stopped and pressed himself against the wall until the frothing school of bodies vanished into the upper realms. He descended finally, interrupting Perdita's single-minded pursuit of her half brother's private concerns.

"Gareth!"

She sprang off the stool and flung her arms around the visitor. Daimon's mouth crooked. He couldn't, himself, appreciate the subtle fascinations of Gareth May that turned the willful Perdita into a boneless butterfly. But he was grateful for the interruption. The young knight gave him a little, formal nod over Perdita's shoulder; Daimon saluted him genially with the bar cloth. In the little, quiet interim between visitors, while the lovers murmured, Daimon could hear the voice of the goddess, whispering as the waters quickened against the stones in the distant underground.

He stepped from behind the water bar and slipped into the cave.

Underwater lights limned the large, round pool of the headwaters that in earlier centuries had been caught in a basin of brick and colored tiles, ringed by stone steps where sufferers could lower themselves into the soothing embrace of the goddess. Pillars, plaques, broken statues haunted the shadows, wandering downstream as far as they dared. Seeking the upper world and light, the Calluna would ultimately find the swift, broad waters of the Severen as well. The river god would sweep the slower, shallower waters of the goddess into his bed, dissipating hers as god and goddess became one. Now the goddess's waters were trapped in enormous underground pipes beneath the city streets. They never saw the light before they joined the Severen in its chilly, muscular flow to the sea.

Daimon stood at the edge of the pool, where Calluna's first visitors had painted their gifts to her on the raw stones: animals, birds, flowers. The earliest image of the goddess's face floated among them, inspired by the moon, archaeologists thought, reflected through a hole in the upper ground onto the dark water below. She had enormous, staring eyes; a wreath of hair or light rippled around her face. She watched. Daimon, meeting her dark, urgent gaze, found as much pain as power in it. She understood the sufferers who sought her. She understood her fate.

Moved by the glimpse of ancient glory and sorrow, Daimon bent, dipped his fingers into the pool, watched the ripples form and slowly spread.

Perdita called his name, needing him back; he heard the clamor of other voices in the antechamber. As he turned, a pair of bewitching eyes opened across time, space, memory, and smiled, blurring the face of the goddess in his thoughts.

In the dark privacy of the cave, he smiled back. But, he remembered, he had a lunch to get through first with his father, whose unexpected summons earlier that day took precedence.

When his shift behind the goddess's water bar ended, he ascended to the upper realms, unlocked his electric bike from the parking rack, and made his way through the busy, labyrinthine streets of Severluna to the calmer, tree-lined avenues that ended at the vast grounds and high towers of the palace of the Wyvernhold kings on the cliff above the sea.

"The queen asked me to talk to you," King Arden said.

They sat in the king's private chambers, eating a seafood stew, a salad of strawberries, hazelnuts, and a dozen kinds of baby greens, and chewy, sour rolls flavored with rosemary. The servers had withdrawn; they were completely alone, which Daimon found disquieting. As the youngest of Arden's five children, and illegitimate to boot, he enjoyed a certain amount of lax attention, an absence of scrutiny from his father as long as he did what the king asked when he remembered that Daimon was around.

"About what?" Daimon asked bewilderedly, and caught the flash of the wyvern's attention. But the king hesitated. He trawled for a bite, then lost interest in it, and let go of his spoon. He sat back, gazing at Daimon, an odd, quizzical expression on his face. He was a handsome, energetic man who commanded respect, explained succinctly when he had to, and held his secrets as close as any gambler; Daimon was unused to seeing him uncertain about anything.

"She said it's time. High time, her exact words. That I talk to you about your mother."

Daimon, stunned, felt the blood flush into his face.

"Now? Why?"

"I have no idea. Genevra is an acolyte of the goddess. She pulls things out of the air sometimes. Ties up a loose thread before anyone else sees it. She herself never wanted to know anything more about your mother. And I never meant to not tell you. The time just never seemed—easy. But she said you have a right to know, and now is better than not." He was still again, frowning at the past. "I wish," he breathed finally, "that I understood it better myself." He raised his salad fork, aimed it toward Daimon's plate. "Eat. While I find the place to begin."

Daimon took a few tasteless bites, listening to his father's silence. "I always thought," he said slowly, trying to help, "that she must have been independent, maybe poor, considering where I was born, but someone who didn't expect—who wanted to take care of herself." He looked at the king, so lost in the past, it seemed he had all but forgotten his son. "She must have had a name. You could start there."

The king stirred, rearranged a few leaves in his salad. "Her name was Ana. That's all I knew of it. I met her at a party. I don't remember whose. I was much younger, then; life and details blur. Her face never did. It is as clear in my memory as yesterday." He paused, seeing her again, Daimon guessed, the face that had never changed with time because she had so little left of it. "She had come to Severluna at the invitation of your great-aunt Morrig. They were related in some far-flung way; they shared ancestors in a family whose name is in annals older than Wyvernhold. Are you in love?"

Daimon coughed on a hazelnut. "I don't think so," he said vaguely, and was held in the wyvern's intent, powerful gaze.

"You know that what you feel is not love? Or you don't know, yet, what love is?"

Daimon felt the burn again in his face and guessed that perhaps his life was not so comfortably ignored as he had thought. "I don't know enough," he said finally, "even to answer the question."

His father nodded. "That's a good place to begin learning. I didn't realize how much I didn't know until I met your mother. And you are right: She was very independent. She wouldn't let me give her anything. Morrig helped her find work; she took an apartment in the hinterlands of the city, which is why you were born out there." He broke a piece off a bread roll, crumbled it absently. "All we had was that one night together, after the party. Not even a night, just the few early-morning hours. She wouldn't see me again. I had no idea where she went after she left Morrig's house; my aunt wouldn't tell me. But they kept in touch with one another. It was Morrig who told me when and where you were born. And that your mother had died." He paused; his mouth tightened, more rueful than bitter. "It was Genevra who taught me a few more things about love, then. How far it can bend, and in how many ways, without shattering. I knew your mother so briefly. But to this day, I have never forgotten her. And I have never understood exactly what had hold of my heart that night." He picked up his fork again, missing Daimon's sudden, wide-eyed stare as the king's words echoed in his own heart. "You look like her. That's all I can tell you. I'm sorry. I don't know how much you've wondered about the matter, but if you need more, you might ask your great-aunt Morrig. These days, she seems to remember the distant past much better than she remembers last week. Another thing," his father said, moving on with a touch of relief, "I might as well bring up while you're here. There is a matter that Sylvester Skelton brought to Lord Ruxley's attention; he brought it to mine."

Daimon, struggling with his father's startling revelations, responded to the simplest of them. "They can't stand each other. Why would Sylvester take anything to Lord Ruxley before he brought it to you?"

"It is a matter for the Mystes Ruxley, not the lord. Some ancient artifact of the god Severen's—a cup, a pot—came to light in a manuscript Lord Skelton has been translating." The king paused a moment, studying his bread plate as if the crumbs on it might shift into language and illuminate a mystery. "I don't entirely understand the significance. Which isn't surprising, considering the maze of Sylvester's mind. The part I do understand is that he says the object is ancient, valuable, and powerful beyond belief."

Daimon pursed his lips to whistle, refrained. "What on earth is it?"

"Sylvester seems to think it important enough to call an

assembly of the knights of Wyvernhold. He and Mystes Ruxley will explain it." He paused, chewing over the matter with a bite. Daimon recognized the more familiar expression in his eyes, now: the gleam of the wyvern, roused. "I have no idea what this object is, but I think what Sylvester has in mind is along the lines of an old-fashioned quest. It sounds to me like the perfect diversion."

"You've lost me."

"You must have heard the rumblings of discontent from knights born in more isolated parts of Wyvernhold—in the eastern mountains, along the north coast—about regaining the sovereignty that was lost when the first King Arden Wyvernbourne's army pulled all the little, bickering kingdoms together under his rule and created Wyvernhold."

"Something of it. Surely nobody's serious."

"The notion seems to spread more often in peaceful times, when there's little else to complain about. That somehow the romance and glory of those realms would return along with their reclaimed boundaries and their names. It's a foolish, dangerous idea. Something as common as water rights could tangle the courts for years, not to mention the temptation for each small kingdom to build up its own standing army, just in case. If the magus and the mystes can sell this idea of an artifact that powerful and valuable free for the finding and the taking, it will scatter the knights across Wyvernhold and give them all something else to think about besides reclaiming long-lost kingdoms. I have no intention of becoming Arden the Last, who let Wyvernhold scatter into thousand-year-old fragments."

Daimon, trying to imagine such a marvel, found a flaw in his father's thinking. "What if it's real?"

He felt the weight of the wyvern's regard again, golden and unblinking. "Then one of my children had better find it for me."

D aimon joined Vivien Ravensley that evening for dinner in the Gold District. The district was one of the outermost in Severluna. Blessed a couple of centuries before by the god Severen with a stray nugget of gold, it had attracted swarms of prospectors. A sanctum had been built near the site of the finding. The gold ran out not long after the sanctum was completed; the disappointed prospectors moved on. Even the god himself moved on; at least the sanctum's Mystica did. The sanctum, unsanctified, wore many faces through the years. Now it was The Proper Way, a restaurant and brew-pub named after the street on which it stood.

They sat at one of the little outdoor tables overlooking the distant lights floating on the dusky blue Severen: nightfishers, barges, cruise and container ships following the river to the sea.

Vivien had caught Daimon's eye at a party one late night, an endless affair that drifted from place to place by the hour, its cast changing across every threshold. He kept seeing her at odd moments: once leaning against a colorful paper-covered wall, her hair a sleek helmet of burnished copper around her face, another time between two marble statues, her own face as matte white as theirs, her eyes a rich peacock blue flecked with gold that turned fiery when someone struck a match to light a candle next to her. Looking for her, he didn't find her; she seemed to become visible only when he thought she had gone. Then she would appear again across yet another threshold and give him something new to notice: her very long, thin fingers, her smile that made him think of otherworldly beings whose names were slowly vanishing from the language.

Finally, she turned that smile to him and beckoned.

They put in an order for steak and vegetables and watched their supper cook on one of the blazing grills on the restaurant deck. As they ate, Daimon told her about his lunch with the king.

"It sounds like a fairy tale," Vivien commented. "Your mother enchanted the king for a night and—"

"Came up with me. Yes. It seems extremely tactful of her to vanish like that. Asking for nothing from my father, no money, no help—and then considerately dying. If it hadn't been for my great-aunt Morrig, not even my father would have known I existed. I certainly would never have known. I could be out in the dark now, repaving highways or working on one of those container ships, instead of having a palace to return to after sitting here with you."

She looked at him over a forkful of blackened carrots. Passing car lights caught her eyes, kindling that strange golden fire in them. "You're not. Returning. Are you?"

He smiled, entranced by that fire. "How could I?"

He was very familiar with her tiny, untidy apartment overlooking the sleepless streets and the broad, busy river. But he had no idea where she worked. She only laughed when he asked, and hinted of something involving dogs, or small children, or the elderly. "Very boring," she told him. "I do it; I get paid; I don't want to think about it."

She scattered her past in riddles around the apartment. A photo of an ancient village hung on her wall; it seemed made entirely of stone, its cottages and streets and the lovely little bridge that arched over a meandering brook he could not find on any map. A hundred-year-old sketch of a hoary castle stood framed on the table beside her bed. It was ringed with water, one tower split and sagging, the drawbridge drawn up tight, like a mouth clamped over a secret. "Where I was born," she explained of those things. "Only it's not in that photo—that's just the antique part of Ravensley." When he asked about the name, she shrugged. "It's old. Common in south Wyvernhold." Again, he could not find it on a map. "Too small," she told him, laughing. "The tiniest village in the world."

She had come from there to Severluna, sometime in the previous year. Even that was vague. But her vagueness would be accompanied by that bewitching smile. He felt oddly comfortable with the lack of detail; it mirrored his own sense of something missing. Half of him seemed anchored to his Wyvernbourne heritage, but the other half lacked a solid place to stand. That part of himself drifted aimlessly, feeling the lack, wondering what it was he could not see.

He said, cutting into his steak, "I am glad my father finally told me about my mother. I wish he had told me what little he knew years ago. It would have put an end to my endless imaginings. And I wish there had been more to tell."

"A happier ending?" Vivien guessed. "She didn't die? But nothing in the world stays private these days. Her death made things tidy." He eyed her; she lifted a shoulder. "Nothing to tell, no one to know, nothing muddled or messy."

"Only between the queen and my father," he said dryly.

"But Queen Genevra has been—" She paused. "Well. If not perfect, at least perfectly discreet."

"Not entirely if such gossip travels even into tiny villages not on any map."

She reached out quickly, wrapped her long, pale fingers around his wrist. "I'm sorry, Daimon. I shouldn't have said that. The village of Ravensley might have been asleep the last hundred years for all it knows of court gossip. I picked up a thread of that rumor about the queen's lover here in Severluna. But everyone here is discreet as well. Everyone is kind about the queen. No one blames her. And the story has been around so long, it's beyond gossip now, anyway. It's more like folklore."

He studied her curiously, struck. "Folklore. Fairy tale. Is that the context in which you live?"

She sat back; shadow from a grill hood hid her eyes. "It's where I grew up," she said lightly. "Time passed so slowly there. Centuries overlapped. Like the cobblestone road through the village that bikers always take too fast, bouncing across it when the paved road suddenly vanishes. Here in Severluna, I might as well be on the moon; everything is still so strange."

"Centuries overlap here, too."

"But things change constantly; now is always becoming new." She laughed at herself, shifting out of the shadow. "I still leave country dust in my footprints when I walk. I learned to cook in a cauldron." She picked up a charred bit of parsnip with her fingers, absently or to prove her point, Daimon was unsure. He watched her mindlessly, her slender, graceful hand, the movements of her mouth, wanting to seize that hand, pull her away from the table, scatter plates, forks, chairs behind them as they ran for the door. She laughed at herself again, and at his expression, wiping her fingers on her napkin.

"Sorry," she said again. "Bumpkin."

"Alien."

"Is that all you talked about at lunch?"

"I don't remember." Then he did, dimly. "Oh. My father brought up some artifact that Sylvester Skelton unearthed in his studies. Something even older than your village, and with mysterious, unlikely powers. My father talked about sending the knights out looking for it, to take their minds off—whatever it was. Politics. Reclaiming their ancient kingdoms. He's calling an assembly. I'll have to behave like a knight for a few days. Can we go?" he asked restively at the thought and snared the attention of a passing server. "I might not be able to get away so easily, then."

Her eyes flared again, as nearby coals flamed; she looked like a wild thing, he thought, a deer, a fox. "Another fairy tale," she breathed. "What is this marvelous thing?"

"I don't know. A cup, a vessel, your cauldron for all anyone knows. Are you finished?"

She gave him her entrancing smile and stood up.

"I've barely begun."

# 8

Above ground on the final afternoon of their weeklong shift at Calluna's cave, Princess Perdita watched Daimon melt into the traffic on his electric bike. As though he felt her narrow-eyed gaze between his shoulder blades, he vanished quickly around the nearest corner. Meeting someone, she guessed, but no one he would talk about. She wondered why.

"Is something wrong?" Gareth asked.

She was standing in the middle of the crowded sidewalk, gripping him by his forearm with both hands, frowning intently at nothing. Total strangers were grinning at the couple, pulling out phones. Gareth wore that look he got when confronted with the powerful, exasperating bond between the half sibs. Perdita looked at him quickly and smiled, and his face eased.

"Maybe nothing. Maybe not." Wind blew her long black

hair across her face; she pushed it away, laughing. "I'm starving, and my hair smells like Calluna's cave. No respectable place will let me in. There's the car."

He grimaced as he folded his tall body, packed as it was with knightly virtues and muscles, into her tiny Greenwing. "Be easier to carry this under my arm," he grumbled.

"I know, I know, but father says it's good for the earth and sets an example. More likely he had Lord Skelton put a spell on the engine that makes it impossible to speed. What's the greasiest, smokiest, darkest pub you know?"

He thought a moment, then guided her there.

They sat in a corner of the antique pub, surrounded by oak and smoke-stained stone, along with a mix of tourists and students from an equally archaic local college. Everything on the menu was fried, including modern versions of rustic dishes with weird names. They ate Straw Dogs and Fishwife's Cobble, along with Wyvern Eggs, which turned out to be balls of deep-fried bread stuffed with golden, peppery cheese. Perdita watched people come and go, some fashionably dressed in black and metal, others who might have just gotten out of bed and tossed on some laundry in one of the aged flats down the streets. Gareth meandered absently through a tale about getting lost during his recent trip north and finding an invisible cape with an unusual name.

Perdita felt the name come alive in her head, possibly a portent, or a detail in some obscure scheme of things. "Mistbegotten?" She tucked it away for later scrutiny as Gareth nodded.

"We met a young man with a net full of crabs and a sorceress for a mother."

"Really. What's her name?"

"Heloise Oliver. She runs a restaurant there; she served us the most amazing crab chowder. Beautiful woman. Red-gold hair and eyes that glitter like bluebottle wings." He bit into a Wyvern Egg, rendered himself speechless with hot cheese. Perdita eyed him speculatively. "Her son takes after her," Gareth continued, when he could. "He seems to have something of her gifts, as well. I can't imagine what the pair of them are doing up there in that forgotten little corner of—"

Somebody skidded across the floor and landed in Perdita's lap.

Before she could move, Gareth mesmerized her, seeming to be sitting in his chair and standing in front of her in the same second, holding a strange, spiky fistful of metal she guessed was a weapon under the nose of the man on top of her.

He said, "Get. Up."

The entire pub had frozen, along with the stranger, who smelled of piss, sweat, and the spilled beer that was soaking into Perdita's skirt. She nudged him; he remembered how to move, gathering himself slowly, clumsily, while the peculiar weapon with its mysterious red light like a mad little eye glared an inch from his face. His long hair was a tangled mass of gold and silver; he tied his torn pants with rope, and there were no laces in his mismatched shoes. He lurched a little as he rose, causing the red light to roil suddenly amid a steam-kettle hiss of breath from the onlookers.

Perdita stood up, then, and edged around the man to see his aging, befuddled face. He had gone cross-eyed, staring at Gareth's weapon.

"Are you hungry?" she guessed. "Can we treat you to lunch?"

His thin lips opened and closed a couple of times before he finally spoke. "That would be kind, miss. Ah. Will I be alive to eat it?"

She glanced at Gareth. The weapon was gone as suddenly as it had appeared. Gareth stood with a quizzical look on his face, wondering, it seemed, why everyone was riveted in place and dead quiet in the middle of their drinks.

The bartender came to life, bringing a cloth to mop up the beer. The unfortunate who had sat on the princess cleared his throat.

"Sorry, miss. I'm a little unsteady at this particular juncture in time. Sorry, young sir. My fault absolutely. I believe the entire incident was occasioned by an olive."

"An olive."

"Under my heel. I slid on it."

"Go and sit down, Henry," the bartender sighed. "And thank your lucky stars. And thank you, Princess Perdita," she added with a charming smile at Perdita, then at Gareth as he passed her a paper bill with Severen's face on it. The god, his hair colored gold, his face masked in silver, looked not unlike the wild-haired, silver-stubbled man staring raptly at Perdita. "If you'll come with me, Princess, I'll unlock the private facilities, and you can wash off the beer."

Perdita drove Gareth to the palace. He had a meeting; she had a ritual to attend. She turned out of the city traffic through the hoary, lichen-stained arch at the south end of the palace grounds. The broad, graveled drive ran through parklands and gardens toward a view of the vast expanse of wind-whipped blue that was Severluna Bay. It began to curve at the white-stone walls of the palace rising as high as the cliff it stood upon. At the deepest point of the drive's horse-shoe turn, the wide steps of the palace flowed down from the doors to meet it.

It was, on ordinary days, the most efficient way to get home. But the princess had barely cleared the archway before she found herself at the end of a long, slow line of official vehicles, private cars, motorbikes, electric bikes, blue-and-gold city cabs, and the sleek, dark, fast sedans favored by knights on duty. She felt, in the Greenwing, like a sprat that had wandered into a school of sharks.

She asked Gareth incredulously, "What is this? Is this your meeting?"

"It might well be. The king called for an assembly of the knights of Wyvernhold, which means everybody still capable of hobbling into his presence."

She glanced into the rearview mirror to back out, but a car had already pulled in line behind her. She recognized the device on the pennant flying on the hood. "Lord Kraken," she marveled. "He's got to be at least a couple of centuries old. What is my father up to? Are we going to war with somebody? You'll tell me, won't you?"

He laughed. "I wouldn't know how to keep secrets from you."

She caught sight of Daimon, then, ahead of them in the line. Wherever he had come from, he hadn't yet had time to change into the formal black leathers and quilted jacket with the golden wyvern opening its wings across his shoulders, and depicted on the crest over his heart. He balanced on his bike with one boot on the ground, listening to the giant Sir Bayley Reeve, who stood athwart his own motor- cycle five times the size of Daimon's.

"Gareth," Perdita said, coming to an abrupt decision, "can you drive this?"

He looked pained, as though she had asked him to pedal a tricycle to the Assembly. "Must I?"

"I'm going to be so late . . ." She leaned over to kiss him before she opened the door. "Just leave it anywhere near the garages, with the keys in it. Thank you, Sweet."

She jogged down the drive and slid onto the bike behind Daimon, interrupting Bayley Reeve's move-by-move rendi- tion of a wrestling match he'd won.

"Sorry," Perdita told him. "I'm desperate. Daimon, can you cut through the garden to the back courtyard?"

She felt his silent grunt of amusement. "You reek of beer," he commented.

"Please?"

"Well. Possibly the guards will recognize us and we won't get shot. But I will be viewed askance for days from every conceivable direction."

"Just hurry, and maybe no one will notice."

He was already veering out of line. As they sped on the verge along the drive to the nearest paved path through the immense garden, Perdita took a firmer hold on him and aimed for his ear.

"Do I know her? This woman you're in love with?"

The bike careened abruptly, nearly sending them into a fishpond. Daimon righted them, curved around the water, then made his own path between the hedgerow and the herbaceous border, to the consternation of the gardeners deadheading the roses between them.

"Sorry!" Perdita called to them. "Daimon—"

"I'm not in love." The bike sped from grass to gravel as it met the drive again, this time edging between taxis that had already deposited their passengers at the king's front door, and were moving more quickly. Half a dozen palace guards spilled down the marble steps after the racing bike. Perdita turned quickly to call to them.

"Sorry! I'm late! So you are seeing someone."

"I didn't say that." He churned up gravel turning along the side of the west wing of the palace, then veered again, heading for an arch in a walled courtyard. Perdita, clinging tightly, wondered if he was trying to throw her off the bike.

"Do I know her?"

She felt him draw breath, let it go. "No."

"Why not?" He didn't answer. "We've always told each other who our latest passions are. Why is this one such a secret?"

At the arch, guards raised their weapons and shouted, then recognized the pair as they skidded through into the broad, quiet yard behind the palace. Daimon brought the bike to a halt at the stairway to the goddess's sanctum.

He said, as Perdita got off the bike, "Because I'm obsessed. Because I don't know, in a clearer light, exactly what I'd see."

She stood still, gazing at him with sudden, rabid curiosity. The expression in his eyes, above an implacable smile, warned her away.

"Thanks for the ride," she said, and ran for the stairs.

The stairway curled up the inner walls of a lovely white-marble tower inlaid with a winding filigree of blue and green marble. A briny wind off the bay whistled through the filigree. Perdita pushed open the upper door and stepped into another world, this one entirely Calluna's.

It was the antechamber to the sanctum, where water piped from Calluna's cave filled richly decorated pools for giving birth, for meditation, for healing. The antechamber had no windows, only blue and green walls down which Calluna's water slid endlessly, silently, reflecting fire from candles of every size and shape lined along the walls on river-smoothed stones brought up from the goddess's cave. A carved replica of Calluna's earliest face hung above the closed doors of the Inner Sanctum, watching her waters fall.

As Perdita hurried across the wide antechamber toward the line of private rooms where the mystes and the acolytes kept their robes and effects of office, a door opened softly and closed. Perdita slowed, blinking. The man turned swiftly down the inner stairway nearby without noticing her. But in that brief glimpse she recognized him, as well as whose chamber he had slipped out of.

Leith Duresse.

She had grown up aware of him, not really knowing why for years, only understanding finally that it was her mother's awareness of him she had sensed at a very early age. Other knights could come and go, their faces blurring into one another; she always saw Leith clearly: the tall man with the black hair and broad shoulders, eyes the turquoise of Calluna's walls in the sanctum. Always shadows in them, Perdita saw, always something she could not grasp. Then one day she did.

Maybe someone had said something. Maybe it was the way he had looked at the princess, from behind that tangle of passion, guilt, love, acknowledging his fault. Or maybe he had opened the door of her mother's chamber in that place where only women came, just at the moment when she was old enough, knew enough, to understand what she saw.

Her mother opened the door a moment later. Perdita saw her glance down the stairwell. Then she heard Perdita's step and turned her head quickly to meet her daughter's eyes.

Perdita saw only recognition and a faint touch of relief. The queen stepped back, opening the door wider. "You're so late. Hurry and dress."

"I know. I got tangled up in the line of knights." The little chamber, richly appointed with chairs, couch, wardrobe, mirrors, cupboards, was already draped with the queen's garments. Perdita began to throw clothes off as the queen closed the door and opened the wardrobe where Perdita's acolyte's skirt and tunic hung. Genevra, who rarely smiled, gave a sudden, helpless laugh.

"You smell like a brewery."

Her mother was a mermaid, the child Perdita had decided. What else could she be with that long sea-foam hair, those green eyes, that skin as luminous as pearl? Decades of marriage, two walloping sons and two daughters, an adopted son from her husband's lover, her own long, discreet affair, had added a line here, a shadow there, and deepened the intensity in her eyes. She knew that Perdita knew. Others in that women's sanctum knew as well. But no one spoke of it. Passion had no part in Calluna's world, which was an escape from the ruthless carelessness of the god Severen.

"There was an accident in a pub," Perdita said, pulling off her boots, "involving a homeless man, an olive, and Gareth's beer. Mother, what is my father intending, with all those knights on his doorstep? Are we threatening someone? Is someone threatening us? Are the old kingdoms going to rise up and rebel?"

Her mother, handing Perdita her sandals, hesitated a moment, then said simply, "I sent for Leith to ask him that. The sanctum has always been the last to find out what's going on among the knights. He said it involves something Lord Skelton discovered in his endless prowls through his books. An artifact of Severen's, Sylvester calls it."

"For that I had to ask Daimon to give me a ride through the rosebushes? What on earth is it?"

"Something to do with Severen in his early aspect as the dying and reviving god. It's quite old, Sylvester claims. And enormously powerful."

Perdita sat down on the uncomfortable little couch that did not encourage lingering. She bent over to wind and tie the dyed green laces of her sandals around her legs. "But what is it?"

"Leith wasn't certain. Something like a cup. Maybe a bowl. Anyway, Sylvester is very excited." Perdita tried to imagine the frail, scholarly Lord Sylvester Skelton inflamed by a piece of crockery. "Yes," her mother agreed. "It's hard to picture. But he is impassioned enough to persuade the king to send his knights out to look for it."

Perdita leaned back on the slippery couch and stared at her mother, astonished.

There was a tap at the door. "Come," Genevra said, and

Mystes Holly Halliwell entered, followed by Perdita's great-aunt, the previous King Arden's sister, Lady Morrig Seabrook.

Lady Seabrook, an absentminded relic from an earlier era, had vague gray eyes and a face contained within a labyrinth of wrinkles. She had worn black since the death of her young husband seventy years earlier. She served, for a couple of decades, as Mistress of Acolytes in the sanctum. As she aged, her duties had lightened; now she accompanied Mystes Halliwell to rituals and ceremonies, and she checked to see that the acolytes were at their designated daily posts within the sanctum whenever she happened to remember.

Holly Halliwell, a plump, pretty woman, was colorfully dressed in a blue and green silk robe overlaid with a web of jade and turquoise beads. She wore a crown of willow branches. Metal, which belonged to Severen, was never permitted in Calluna's sanctum. She carried the staff of her office: myrtle wood topped with the goddess's haunting face carved in pale green jade, inset against a full moon of ivory.

The mystes looked, Perdita thought, as though she'd swallowed a wasp. She gave the queen a formal bow before she raised the staff in her hand and let it thump sharply on the floorboards. Genevra, whose many subtleties of expression Perdita knew well, eyed her guardedly, as though she might peer under the couch or fling open the wardrobe door in search of the queen's hidden lover.

But it wasn't that.

"Queen Genevra," Holly said indignantly, "have you heard what Sylvester Skelton is up to?"

"I heard," the queen said, choosing words carefully, "he

has asked the king to send the knights out looking for something of Severen's."

"Ha!" Holly lifted the staff again, then caught herself. "I do beg your pardon, Your Majesty. It's just that I'm extremely upset. He has no right—I mean Sylvester, of all people, should know better. He's a scholar, for Calluna's sake! How can he have made such an idiotic mistake?"

The queen glanced down at her hands, looking perplexed. She wriggled off a ring of gold and sapphire she had left inadvertently on one finger, dropped it among her other jewels. "I'm sorry, Holly. I'm just not following—"

Morrig interrupted. Her voice, for one so aged, was unexpectedly clear and sweet. "Lord Skelton and I are also having a difference of opinion. He's not listening very well. Hard of hearing, I suspect, from viewing a thing one way for so long. Hardening of the earways."

"What Sylvester wants the knights to find never belonged to Severen!" Holly insisted, overriding her. "It belongs to Calluna."

"I still don't—"

"Oh, I know that story," Morrig said with delight. "Calluna found the dying god when they were young—back when the world itself was young. I was, too, then, I remember. She revived him with water from her fountainhead."

Holly eyed her askance, surprised, then found her voice again. "Yes. That's what the king will send his knights searching for: the cup or vessel of power that returned life to the dying god." Her mouth tightened; she refrained from whacking the floor again. "All its power is Calluna's. I've been arguing for days with Lord Ruxley, ever since he came to tell me about the mistranslation Sylvester had discovered in a very early text, and what Lord Ruxley, as Severen's Mystes, advised the king. But he won't hear a word I say."

"Neither will Sylvester," Morrig said. "He complains that I have no textual proof. Textual proof. As though written words alone contain the truth about anything." She smiled at Perdita. "He lets me borrow his books, you know. He trusts me with them."

"Stubborn old men," Holly fumed. "Both of them. You know the god Severen. Everything his name inspires turns to wealth or war. If the king's knights find that vessel, no good will ever come out of it."

Perdita, intrigued by the matter, said slowly, "Maybe it doesn't exist to be found. Maybe the artifact is just a detail of a very ancient story."

Morrig's misty gaze held her a moment, speculating, Perdita sensed, about some completely different matter—new shoes or a bottle of aged brandy—for which her great-niece might come in handy.

Holly's busy mind had already shifted toward possibilities. "Well," she said, some of the annoyance melting from her face, "we have to assume it exists, as long as Lord Skelton and Mystes Ruxley are going to shake up the realm looking for it. There are at least a half dozen of Calluna's former acolytes among the knights. We'll convince one of them—or bribe her if nothing else works—to find the vessel and give it to us. And then we'll hide it here in Calluna's sanctum, where not even Severen himself would bother looking for it."

Morrig opened her mouth; so did Perdita and the queen.

A bell rang, soft, sweet, from within the sanctum.

They closed their mouths, for the language of the sanctum was water, not words, and even Mystes Halliwell would not speak again until the ritual began.

Perdita checked the bone buttons on her tunic. The queen set a circlet of ivory and bone on her head. Perdita stepped to the door, opened it, and followed the mystes, the queen, and Morrig toward the slowly opening doors of the sanctum, where a young acolyte, surrounded by attendants and other acolytes, waited in the warm, steaming, gently swirling waters, to give birth.

# 9

While knights from all over Wyvernhold gathered in Severluna, Daimon found himself spending pearly dawn hours, blue, windy afternoons, flame-streaked dusks on the Severluna streets. As though his heart had turned to thread and Vivien held the end of it, he would lose interest, leave whatever he was in the middle of doing or saying, and find the quickest way through the twists and turns of byways and alleys to the inelegant, backwater neighborhood where she waited. Somehow she knew; she was always there, opening her door before he knocked. He didn't ask. Her stray powers, like her smile, seemed at once very old and all her own.

The city changed in his eyes when she tugged at him. It lost its past, its history; it existed only as the place he traveled through to reach her.

Even the streets transformed themselves when he was with her. The cracked sidewalks, stunted trees along them

guarded by broken iron railings, the hot, blustering whirlwinds of litter, food-cart smells and old leaves, the groan
and belch of trucks, the constantly clamoring traffic inter-
woven with stray snatches of music, sirens, ringtones, shifted
focus in his perception. He glimpsed wonder in the dusty
whirlwind, a fierce and ancient energy within the raucous
voices of the road; he overheard, within the passing drift of
song from an open car window, an otherworldly language.

"What is it you do to me?" he asked Vivien, incoherently,
he thought, but she seemed unsurprised.

"Nothing," she answered. "You're remembering."

"Remembering what?" She didn't answer. He took her
arm, held her fast in the jostling foot traffic streaming along
the bumpy sidewalk, the worn shopfronts. In the scrap of
shadow from a sapling whose wind-whipped leaves flecked
her eyes with gold, then shadow, then again gold, he asked,
"Remembering what?"

She gazed at him. He heard the distant voices within the
wind, the song beneath the squeal of tires, the quickening
water that flowed, in truth or memory, down hidden paths
beneath his feet to find the sea. The leaves that played with
light above her copper hair seemed suddenly ageless, lovely
in their flick and glitter, both new and older than all he knew.

His fingers opened, slid down her arm; she caught his
hand. They walked again down some path that he had never
taken but that he was beginning to remember.

The next afternoon, she took him so far he lost his way.

"There's a special place we want you to see," she told him
as they walked. Sun dazzled on the hot streets, angled ach-
ingly bright off chrome and spinning hubcaps. It melted

stucco, wood, stone, blurring lines and corners until buildings shimmered like light-struck water. Had she said *we*? he
wondered. What happened to *I*? And how could he see
anything at all in this light-drenched world? A building in
front of him, small shops topped by weary apartments,
melted completely under the sun; he glimpsed the green
meadow where it had stood, the long grass freckled with
wildflowers. The building returned raggedly, missing corners, windows. He shook his head to clear it.

"Who is 'we'?"

"Oh, people I know. I hope you like it. Look!" she
exclaimed with delight, and he turned his head into a splash
of gold. He blinked, saw the water flowing from beneath
the meadow, pooling in the grass, carving its bed as it grew
stronger, more defined, feeling its way into the world. "Calluna," he heard Vivien say, then the city came back, rising
rigidly around him; the rill of water faded into hot streets
smelling of asphalt and exhaust. He stopped, then realized
he had stopped. He was taking quick, sharp breaths, trying
to catch the scent of the spring again, the wet earth. He felt
water on his face, sweat, or maybe tears from the searing
glance of the sun.

"Where are we?" His voice shook. "Where were we?"

"Don't worry." She kissed away the tear under his eye.
"It's not far now."

They turned at a street corner, and the city vanished.

A cobbled street ran silently between a huddle of cottages
built of stone and thatch. At the end of the street, a small
bridge arched gracefully across a reedy, lily-filled brook.
Beyond the bridge, a castle rose, its towers tall and slender,

its walls pale as the open lilies massed around it as the brook turned to embrace the castle. It was a beautiful, colorful affair, its turrets and corner towers painted blue and green, rose vines climbing its inner walls, long pennants streaming everywhere. A pair of wild swans flew down, settled into the moat, glided serenely among the lilies. Like a fairy tale castle, he thought. And then the words took on power and life, and he closed his eyes, feeling as though he had stepped off the edge of the world and had no idea how far he would fall.

"We're in your photograph," he heard himself say.

"Well, not exactly," Vivien answered, and he remembered the ruins of that lovely castle, its towers broken, its bridge drawn up tight, closed. "That is now," she explained, or thought she did. "This is then."

He dragged his eyes open, found some comfort, even in free fall, at the sight of her smile.

"Where are we?"

"In Ravensley. Inside its memories. In Ravenhold."

"Ravenhold."

"One of the earliest realms in this land. Far older than Wyvernhold." She regarded him steadily, willing him to see out of her eyes, know what she was not saying.

"And not on any map," he breathed.

"How do you map a memory? A dream? We have never had much use for maps. It was the Wyvernbourne who drew lines around things, who declared boundaries. Air has no borders, nor does light. Nor should water though it does."

"How did you—how did you bring me here?"

"I didn't. You found your way. Those memories are your heritage."

He felt himself grow cold, seeing too much, seeing himself. "I am Wyvernbourne."

"You are the raven's child."

"I am—"

"You are both." She took his hand, even though his bones had turned to ice. "Come with me. I want to show you one more memory."

He heard traffic again, groaning and thundering as they moved. Thunder thinned to wind, roiling noisily, busily around them. She drew him down the road, over the bridge, into the meadowlands around the castle. In the midst of the green, a single tree branched high and full against the sky. Half-hidden in green, ravens or the shadows of ravens watched them among the leaves.

Vivien stopped just beyond the tree's shadow, as though it formed some kind of windblown, constantly shifting boundary. On the ground within the shadow, an enormous, lovely vessel shed light from within itself, as well as from its bronze-and-gold surface, every inch of it etched with patterns. The cauldron bubbled and steamed, though it rested on grass, not fire; its fires were invisible. A woman stirred it. She spoke to it; she sang; small birds flitted around her head, commenting cheerfully in liquid splashes of sound.

The woman raised her head, saw the pair at the boundary between light and shadow. She was barefoot under her long skirt; her sleeveless vest revealed the muscles in her arms, strong from wielding the great paddle. Her face was plain, friendly; her eyes, like Vivien's, were extraordinary. She said something and laughed. She gave the great pot one more swirl, then raised the wood out of the mix. She held it out to them, sliding it beyond the boundary just a little, just enough, so that the bowl at the end of the long handle was filled with dark and light, sun and shadow, day and night.

Her face changed, grew beautiful. Her hair turned from tree-bark brown to palest gold; the fantastic colors in her eyes misted into smoky, opaque gray. She looked at Daimon out of those eyes, and he saw himself in her.

He felt his heart fly into birds, all trying to burst out of him at once. He heard his own voice, an incoherent warble. Then he stood on the noisy street corner again, cold with shock, while, at his side, Vivien took his hand, blew on his chilled fingers.

He stayed with her that night, not trusting himself to find his way back to anything he knew.

Finally, the world caught up with him, in the form of his oldest half sibling, Roarke, who waylaid him the next morning when he returned to the palace to change his clothes.

"Where have you been?" he asked, then surveyed Daimon's clothes. "You're attending the formal lunch to welcome the knights in less than an hour; you should be in uniform. Where have you been?" he repeated, more slowly, his eyes, like the queen's, as green as a mermaid's scales, taking in more than what they saw.

"Around," Daimon answered briefly; his brother looked skeptical.

"Not around here, you haven't. Whoever it is, she'll have to wait, or there will be an empty chair with your name on it around the dais table at lunch and hundreds of knights all asking the same question—"

"All right," Daimon said, backing as he spoke. "All right."

"Not to mention our father."

"I'll get changed."

"You look—" Roarke hesitated, groping; the intense gaze under black, level brows reminded Daimon forcibly of their father. "Like you've been seeing visions. Like you've been in some other world."

Wyvern's eyes, Daimon thought, but without wonder: Roarke was the king's heir. "Well, I'm here now," he said with regret. "I suppose I should thank you."

"Don't bother," Roarke answered cheerfully. "Just be there."

Daimon slid into the empty chair between his other half siblings, Prince Ingram and Princess Isolde. As he sat, his father rose to give his welcoming address. Round tables, clustered thick as lily pads in the Great Hall, were ringed with men and women in black; only the beasts, real and mythical, embroidered above their hearts, and the great, long-necked, amber-eyed wyverns flying across their backs, were permitted color.

"Welcome, Knights of Wyvernhold," King Arden began, and Daimon's attention promptly wandered to the far regions of Severluna, where a woman with marble skin and eyes colored like a peacock's tail was no longer expecting him.

He quelled an urge to push his chair back, throw his jacket with the wyverns clinging to it onto the empty plates, and lose himself in the city. ". . . Mystes Ruxley will now bless this Assembly in Severen's name."

Across the table, the dour, ivory-haired mystes rose, his robe of office glittering with threads of gold and silver, the

symbols of the river god, along with the jewels the mystes wore
in his belt, on the collar around his neck, and on both hands.

"In Severen's name," he intoned sonorously, the last thing
Daimon heard until a salad plate glided under his nose, and
he realized that Isolde was talking to him.

"Where have you been, Daimon? No one's seen you for
days."

He had the entire table's attention, then, even the king's.
Mystes Ruxley, on one side of the king, opened his mouth
to expand the question. The slight, wiry magus Lord Skelton, who was straightening his spectacles to observe Daimon
more clearly, somehow dropped them into his water glass.

"Clumsy," he commented, and held his open hand over
the water. The spectacles rose, neatly folded and drip-free,
into his palm. He blinked at everyone watching him now
instead of Daimon. "I beg your pardon."

He slid the glasses back on his nose and looked again at
Daimon. What he saw through the circular lenses seemed
to surprise him; his pale blue eyes, enlarged by the lenses,
widened to fill them with the peering, questioning gaze.

"Where have you been?" Daimon heard him wonder.
Attention had drifted away from the question; it got lost in
the sudden ring of fork against porcelain. Servers in their
bright uniforms circled the table, proffering buns; others
stood attentively behind the king, holding pitchers of water,
bottles of wine, ready to replace the slightest sip. Daimon,
absently pulling a bun into bits, helplessly pondered the
magus's question.

Where, indeed?

Finally, there seemed some end in sight to the endless

occasion. The king rose, spoke again; a few words drifted into Daimon's head: a supper, a tournament, the formal opening of the Assembly, the purpose of which Lord Skelton and Mystes Ruxley would explain. And then everyone was rising, including Daimon, who left only his empty chair to answer some question that had begun with his name. In a blink, he was one of hundreds of black uniforms; after a blur of time, he was finally out, away, on his bike and leaving the tediously familiar behind him as rapidly as he could.

This time, Vivien met him in the past.

He tailed a roaring truck as it turned down the street where she lived, and there she was, waiting. There they both were, he realized suddenly, standing in the miserly shadow of a sidewalk tree. He stopped his bike, staring, oblivious to the screech and bellowing horns and curses behind him. Vivien gestured; he moved again, finally brought the bike to a halt under a NO PARKING sign.

The gray eyes, he saw, held the familiar, magical parings of gold in them that would catch fire under any passing light. She wore a flowing skirt, a tunic; her long, white-gold hair was pinned carelessly; blowing strands framed her lovely face. The expression in those eyes, fierce and watchful as she studied him, was not something, he guessed, she would have let his father see in the brief hours they had been together.

He swallowed dryly, tried to speak, suddenly as confused as the small whirlwind in a nearby alley, gathering up scraps, torn paper, dust, then letting them all go without knowing why.

"All these years," he said finally, raggedly, "you've been dead."

She smiled a little, fierceness melting into unexpected tenderness. "I never went that far away from you. Lady Seabrook found me various masks to wear so that I could sometimes see you, watch you grow."

"Lady Seabrook," he repeated, astonished. "My dotty great-aunt Morrig?"

"Your dotty great-aunt made me a field squire so that I could watch you train. I sold ice cream in Calluna's Cave when the queen first took you there to see it. I taught you how to drive."

"No. That was—"

"Me. I've worn a hundred faces so that I could see your face."

He was staring again, stunned. The little whirlwind spun down the walk behind her, plucked at her hair. She raised a hand, pushed the whirl gently aside, and it went around them, then dwindled into nothing, dropping grit and a feather black as a raven's eye. Vivien picked it up, tucked it into her own hair, and smiled at Daimon encouragingly. As though his mother's hand had reached out to him as well, into his whirlwind heart, he felt the turmoil lose force, let go of some of its bewildering flurry of questions.

He asked the simplest, the most entangled: "Why?"

"I am Ana, your mother. And I am the descendant of the scattered realm of Ravenhold, which lived at peace within the human world for thousands of years until the wyvern king destroyed it. To him, the Ravenhold that he could see was simply one of many small kingdoms he wanted to put into his collection. This one was ruled by Berenicia, a woman, an aberration in the nature of things, so Arden thought, and all the easier to conquer. But he would have failed completely and for all time, except for the loss of our most precious possession.

"The fact that the Wyvernbourne kings have never used it, nor even their most powerful magi, indicates to us that they have never known where it is either, or even that it exists. Until now."

"What is it?" he asked, even as he heard the echoes, the suggestions, of such power reverberating through the past days.

"You saw it. Child of the Wyvern and the Raven, you were born to see. That great cauldron beneath the tree, stirred by the raven-magus, has such powers that no Wyvernbourne king can begin to imagine. It was stolen from Ravenhold the day Arden Wyvernbourne overran our realm. The one who stole it tore the fabric of our realm, like waking tears apart a dream. He was the first and last king we ever had, and we had banished him from Ravenhold long before that for misusing our great cauldron and causing such distress across the realm that even the ravens helped us chase him out. At least we all thought he had gone; he had hidden himself among us so well. But when he finally fled with the cauldron, he opened the path into time, into the human world, that permitted Arden Wyvernbourne into our land. Left powerless, we could not fight back. Our warriors died like humans; we could not resurrect them.

"We want our realm back. We want our power back. Our cauldron. Whatever shape it has taken, you have the eyes, the heart to recognize it. Find it for Ravenhold. Find it for us."

He felt his heart crumple a little, bruised, at her words. "That's why you chose my father? That's why you had me?"

She took a step toward him, her stern, beautiful face changing again, becoming human. "It's not the first time, during our long defeat, that we have tried this. But none of the children we brought into the world were less loved for that."

He was silent, imagining her hundred different faces as she had wandered in and out of his life. Then he looked at Vivien, watching him beside his mother.

"And you?" he asked, the whirlwind in his heart beginning to stir again, catching at any straw of understanding. "What do you want me for?"

"I am the direct, living descendant of Queen Berenicia, whom Arden Wyvernbourne killed," she answered. "I hope you will be my consort when I am crowned Queen of Ravenhold."

# 10

S ome kind of pot," Gareth told Princess Perdita. "Or a vessel. A lost thing belonging to Severen. That's the rumor going around."

"The king will ask you to go out looking for a flowerpot?"

"Surely not."

"A fishing boat?"

He looked perplexed. "I can't imagine."

"There is an astounding array of pots in life," she reminded him. "Including crock-pots. And vessels from sailboats to gravy boats."

He caught her hand to make her stop, pressed it against his lips. "I won't know until the Assembly opens, in three more days. And then, I promise I will tell you everything."

She had joined the audience in the amphitheater seats on the first day of the tournament, to watch Gareth win a kick-boxing match, then blow more flying objects than anybody else into a fine mist with the Wyvern's Eye, then hit the center of a round, painted target more often than anyone else with an antique crossbow. He had clambered up into the seats to find her after that, relaxing after his victories. She wondered, as he sat beside her, if he had ever lost a contest in his life.

"Of course I have," he said. "I'm sure of it." He looked uncertain. "Everybody does."

She smiled, then asked him what Mystes Halliwell had sent her there to find out: how much he knew about what the knights had been assembled for.

She repeated what little that was to her great-aunt Morrig, Mystes Halliwell, and the queen, who seemed to appear as three as often as Perdita saw them. Holly Halliwell knew best what she was upset about, but not even she could shed much light on the obscurity.

"How," Perdita asked, "can anyone recognize something that has no name?"

"Go and ask Sylvester," Mystes Halliwell told her. "See what you can find out from him. Be subtle."

"Sometimes he has licorice," Morrig said, and three faces turned to her, all mystified. "Slip a handful in your pocket for me?"


The king's magus was most likely to be found in the ancient keep that had been part of the first Wyvernbourne king's castle. It stood on a lovely swath of green overlooking the sea, walled by worn stones salvaged from the original ruins. The tower was massive, and so high it had attracted the attention of a pair of wyverns, among the last before they went extinct. They took up residence on the top of the keep, with an eye to nesting there. The first Arden's magus was able to charm them away, then decided to live there himself. Magi, gifted as they were, had no need for stairs. But Perdita, who had been in and out of Sylvester Skelton's library since she was small, was grateful when he thoughtfully installed an elevator.

She was surprised to find a knight sitting on Sylvester's floor with an open tome on her knees.

Sylvester, who was at his desk, stroking his long mustaches with both hands as he read, glanced at Perdita vaguely, and then, after blinking her into place, with great interest. Knight and magus got to their feet.

"Princess Perdita," Lord Skelton said, "you might remember Dame Scotia Malory? She has traveled from the mountainous northeastern parts of Wyvernhold, where the last of the wyverns were seen five centuries ago in King Hodder's time."

The young knight, a foot taller than either of them, with a knot of long, honey-colored hair, bowed her head to the princess, and said ruefully, "The time also of my appalling ancestor, Tavis Malory, Princess. Lord Skelton kindly let me come to borrow some books about him."

"Tavis," Perdita exclaimed with delight. "He wrote *The Life and Death of Arden Wyvernbourne* while he was in jail for— What was it? Stealing sheep? Hiding in a hayrick during a battle?"

"I believe that time he was accused of assaulting Calluna's acolytes, Princess. I'm trying to find out if he was malignant or maligned. If I could borrow this, Lord Skelton?"

"Of course, Dame Scotia."

She wedged the huge book easily under her elbow and bowed her head again.

"Then I'll leave you—"

"Wait," Perdita said impulsively. "I don't suppose you ever trained as an acolyte yourself in Calluna's sanctum?"

Dame Scotia smiled apologetically. "I never had the chance, living that far north. I came to court so seldom that I only became a knight by accident."

"That doesn't sound easy," Perdita commented.

"Growing up so big and gawky, I felt most comfortable among people whose feet and elbows might be lethal to others. So I lived on the practice field at home, and here, whenever my father brought me to the king's assemblies. I caught the king's attention by knocking Bayley Reeve off his horse in the antique-tournament style of fighting."

Sylvester chuckled. "I remember that. The king knighted you, he said, before you had a chance to think about it."

"And I've never had a second thought." She paused, her calm, violet eyes on Perdita. "Why did you ask, Princess Perdita? Is there something I can do for the sanctum?"

"Perhaps," Perdita answered lightly, aware of the magus's swift attention. "I'll let you know."

She came to another abrupt decision as Dame Scotia closed the study door behind her. The slight, bespectacled, spindle-shanked magus disguised startling powers behind his mild manner. Perdita had seen him untangle the technology of her stalled Greenwing by absently patting its hood while he expounded on the migratory habits of the bird singing on the tree branch above them. His predictions were eerily accurate; he could boil water by whispering to it; he could change the shape of his shadow to anything he wanted, which he had done many times to the delight of the royal toddlers. He could find any lost object he was asked about. Even those lost, apparently, in lines of poetry for thousands of years.

"Be subtle," Mystes Halliwell had warned. But at that moment, under the magus's clear, interested gaze, she sensed that his dedication to scholarship would outweigh the preferences of Mystes Ruxley, and the king, and even the god Severen himself.

She said baldly, "Mystes Halliwell sent me here to find out what you're searching for, and if you have any idea where it is. I understand that revealing all this is the point of the Assembly of Knights. But since we are not knights, we are not invited. Mystes Halliwell is convinced that the lost vessel belongs to Calluna, not to Severen. Where should we—acolytes of the goddess—look for it? If, on the off chance, we do?"

"Intriguing, yes," the magus admitted, "that argument. Lady Seabrook brought it up to me as well. Oh, while I'm thinking about it, would you mind?" He pulled a bag out of a drawer and shook pieces of candy-coated licorice into an envelope. "She is the king's aunt, his own father's sister; she could ask for a tower full of sweets and get it. For some reason she prefers mine. If you would be so kind as to pretend you pilfered them?" Wordlessly, Perdita took the packet he made and slid it into a pocket. "Thank you, Princess. Now. As to your questions: What is it, where is it, and to whom does it belong?"

There followed a bewildering weave of scholarly references, lines of poetry, each older than the last, a briar patch of arguments about a badly translated word, a foray into the book Tavis Malory had written five centuries before, then into other older works the writer had used as reference points. By the time Lord Skelton came to a barely comprehensible conclusion, open books were strewn all over the desk and the couch, and decades of disturbed dust motes floated in the shafts of light from the lowering sun.

"So there you have it," the magus finished. "I would never call Mystes Halliwell wrong about her conclusions. I can only say that what fragments I have seen for that argument tend to be either fairly modern, or, if very old, imprecise and speculative, with only the weakest of scholarly underpinnings." He paused, reached again for the licorice. "As far as where it is, that's a completely different thicket of argument, and every bit as dense." He proffered the bag, then took a piece himself. Chewing, they looked at one another, startled, suddenly, at the angle of light through the tower windows.

Perdita glanced quickly at her watch. "I'm due at the sanctum in five minutes. Luckily, it's just the guardian's watch, keeping the peace and discouraging men and other such strangers from entering. Thank you, Lord Skelton. I'm not sure exactly what you said, but I'm fascinated by it anyway."

"Thank you, Princess," Sylvester said, looking pleased. "It's high time I put my ideas in order; I'll have to explain all this at the Assembly. Mystes Ruxley can deal with the practicalities of sending the knights across the realm searching for an ancient mystery. He's best at mundane details, despite his calling. But then, Severen himself was never a subtle god. Just rich."

Crossing the yard from the keep to the sanctum tower,

Perdita was surprised to see her half brother wheeling his electric bike along the sward.

"Daimon?" she called, and he started, then glanced back at her and reluctantly waited. "What are you doing? You look as though you're sneaking out of here."

"I am," he said. "Or I was."

"You look strange," she said, frowning at him. "All awry, somehow. I've hardly seen you for days. Not that I would anyway since you're busy doing knightly things. Like creeping through the sanctum gardens to the back roads beyond the practice field. Are you all right?"

He started to speak, shook his head a little, and started again. "Yes. I think so. And, yes, I am trying to slip away."

"Affairs of the heart?"

"Oh, yes. Very much so."

"Is she married?" He stared at her. "Well, you don't seem entirely happy. Whatever it is—"

"She's not married," he said shortly. "You're prying."

"Of course I'm prying. I'm your sister."

"Half. Half sister."

Something in the emphasis tossed her a clue; her eyes widened. "You know something," she breathed. "You found out something. About the other half. Daimon—"

He shifted edgily, began to walk his bike again, quickly. "Don't be ridiculous. There's nothing—" He seemed to feel her eyes boring into his head as she kept up with him; he stopped, said without looking at her, "I'm thinking something through. Just let it go. It's mine to figure out."

"Are you—"

"No," he said, with an odd, sharp urgency. "No more."

She took a step away, swallowing; he moved again, doggedly, his eyes on the route he would use to escape to or from whatever troubled him.

"Let me know," she said, too softly for him to hear except with his heart, "if you want to talk."

She hurried up the sanctum-tower steps to the royal chamber; she had pulled the long guardian's robe over her head and was putting on her sandals, when the door opened abruptly. Both the queen and Mystes Halliwell stood in the doorway, the mystes emitting incandescence like a burning stove. The queen's face wore a familiar, guarded expression. Perdita assumed that the fuel that stoked the mystes' ire was either Leith or Lord Skelton.

"Sorry I'm late," Perdita said; she saw the book in Holly's hand, then, and guessed Lord Skelton.

"Princess Perdita," Holly said stiffly, formally, as she tended to when she was beyond furious. "Please come with us."

Perdita did so, hopping on one foot as she finished tying her sandal.

The mystes led them into the sanctum, past its birthing and healing pools, its meditation streams, its fountains for worship and for drinking. The place was empty, soundless but for the faint rill of the goddess's waters flowing in from the antechamber. Holly did not stop there but headed for a closed door made of unadorned black wood in the back of the sanctum. A wooden sconce beside the door held an unlit candle. Lit, it requested privacy for those within. Holly barely waited for Perdita to light the candle before she flung open the door. The room was not empty. It was, however, occupied by the one woman who would not have fled from the look on Mystes Halliwell's face.

"Aunt Morrig," Perdita exclaimed as she recognized the darkly clad figure beside the pool, her aged face a pale blur in the dimness.

"My fault," Morrig said. "I didn't light the candle. I come in here sometimes to remember my dead. They become more numerous when you're as old as I am. And they seem to have much more to say."

The heart of the sanctum held only one broad bowl of a pool, lined with river stones. Water flowed silently out of a blue-green marble globe in the center of the pool. Above the water, the ancient face of the goddess, carved in moon-white marble, gazed from the domed ceiling down at its own reflection. The pool was ringed with candles. Marble benches alternating the colors of the goddess were scattered around the water. It was a place for stillness and solitude, built for those who mourned.

It was also, when the door was closed and the candle lit, the most private place in the palace.

"I'm sorry to disturb you, Lady Seabrook," Holly said tightly. "We came here to talk."

"Then you might as well join us," Morrig said, waving a hand at the shadows. "They won't mind. They like company. And they're incredibly discreet. They won't say a word outside this room."

The mystes shook her head, unable to speak. Abruptly, she walked out of her shoes, pulled up her robe, and stepped into the water. She shifted candles, sat down on the edge of the pool, the flickering reflections of light around her ankles rippling across the gentle fall of water from the endlessly weeping globe. She held the book out to Perdita.

"Will you read this, Princess? Where I have marked it. I'm too upset."

Wondering, Perdita opened the pages. The queen settled herself on a bench beside the mystes; the princess sat under a tall branch of candles and began to read.

"'The god Severen lay dying. His mighty rush from mountain to sea slowed. His shores became barren as waters ebbed. Fish died in great numbers, all down the long path he made to the sea. The great herds that drank from him fought and thinned and dwindled for the lack of him. No cloud hid the burning sun from dawn through night and again dawn. No rain fell. The god lay dying. Frogs and salamanders died; mosses grew dry and died; the great birds that fed on the creatures of the river died for the lack of them. Daily, the water grew shallow, grew inward, far from its shores; the river bottom grew hard and dry as stone. And the great mouth of the river dried as it opened to the sea; no water came down to give life to those that spawned in sweet and followed the salt to the sea.

"'In his weakness, in his dire distress, the river god took his human aspect and prayed for water as it left his veins.

"'She came then, in answer to his call. Though he had overwhelmed her, carried her to the sea over and over without thought or shame, she came to him. She raised his head up from the dead mosses and reeds and held her healing vessel to his lips. He drank. He drank.

"'His veins filled. His waters quickened. He drank. He

opened his eyes and saw her face between his face and the sun, shading him like a cloud.

"'The sky remembered how to fashion cloud; cloud covered the sun everywhere across the land, and everywhere from dawn to night and again to dawn the hard, sweet rains began to fall.'"

"You see?" Mystes Halliwell said in bitter triumph to the princess and the queen. "Calluna and her cup. Her power. Not Severen's. She saved his life."

"Surely Lord Skelton knows the tale," the queen said.

"He does, my lady. He says that since the only written version of that tale is less than four centuries old, and he has never seen an older reference to the tale, it is too recent to be of interest."

"Is that where you got the book? From Sylvester?" Morrig asked.

"No, of course not. He wouldn't lend me the time of day. The book belongs to us. I found it in the sanctum library. I've been searching the archives for anything that pertains to this tale. Anything that Lord Skelton didn't find first, that is. I wouldn't put it past him to have a few things hidden on his shelves that could point toward the truth of the matter."

"Oh, I doubt that," the queen said quickly. "He is too much a scholar."

"And another thing," Holly said, with great indignation. "Dame Cecily Thorpe, who was one of my acolytes before she decided to train for knighthood, told me that some of the knights, who are speculating wildly over nothing but rumor at this point, are planning to search Calluna's cave for the mysterious object of power. They can't just go barging through the sacred shrine, wading down the water, and shining headlamps on everything. The idea is outrageous. First they bury the cave and forget it completely; now they want to excavate it." She kicked at the water angrily, sent it splashing, dowsing candles in its wake. She blinked as the queen wiped her face. "I beg your pardon, Your Majesty. I'm frothing, and it's all Sylvester Skelton's fault."

Perdita got up to relight the candles, tipping flames to smoking wicks along the pool. "We have to find an earlier version of Calluna's tale," she said. "Lord Skelton may be obsessed by his version, but he's not at all devious. If we could prove the cup belongs to Calluna, he could be persuaded out of his certainty."

"Or we could just find the cup," the queen said.

Perdita, lighting a final wick, found the queen's eyes on her above the flame. She was looking, her daughter realized, for a reason.

"We," she echoed. "You mean me."

"Why not? Nothing in the stars says that only knights should go on this quest. People are used to seeing you in Calluna's cave. Nobody would question your presence there. You could look for the artifact anytime you want. Tomorrow morning. Before the cave opens to the public."

Mystes Halliwell lifted her feet, splashed again with excitement. "Yes. That's the perfect idea, Your Majesty."

"I've been trained to give tours of the cave," Perdita reminded them. "I've seen all the images, and I know what the scholars say about them."

"Scholars," Morrig said, stirring the water with her fingertips. "Always getting us into trouble, putting up walls, naming things. You must look beyond those walls, Perdita. Beyond the designated path. Trespass into the past."

Perdita sat down again. She contemplated the reflection of the goddess in the water, and the wild, wide-eyed face in the pool seemed to come alive, her expressions changing at every flare of candle fire, every riffle of water.

"If the artifact is Calluna's, it wouldn't be metal," she mused. "There would not be a jewel on it. A river stone, maybe, hollowed to hold water. A wooden bowl. A clay cup. She might have carried the water in a leaf." She paused, thinking again, while the walls of the cave formed in her mind, images covering them, symbols, the silent language of tales telling and retelling themselves. "I've never looked at the images in the context of that story. That gesture of the goddess. What would she have used to carry water to a dying god?" She looked up, aware of but hardly seeing the watching faces of women, flickering with light and shadow, like the goddess's reflection. "If anyone asks, I'll say that I'm studying the cave as a form of worship. If I don't find any-thing, I'll try Sylvester's library again."

"Be careful around Sylvester," the mystes warned. "He reads minds."

"He won't pay any attention," the queen said dryly, "if it's only about Calluna."

Perdita drove to Calluna's cave early the next morning. She brought a set of keys to the outer and inner doors, and a pair of bodyguards, who stationed themselves at the cave entrance, one watching the stairs, the other the steamy, murmuring pool. Nobody else was there at that hour. The constant darkness edging the frail lights around the pool made true time vanish; it might have been any hour of any lost century Perdita stepped into as she followed the water flowing away from the pool. She had turned on every light; most illumined the visitors' path along the narrow river and the images carved and painted on the walls. Those— handprints, trees, and flowers dedicated to the goddess, toads, dragonflies, deer, strange, huge-eyed faces—she knew well; they were in every souvenir guidebook.

What she did not know so well lay in the dark beyond the path, beyond the reach of light.

The bodyguards had given her an assortment of lights, tools, flares, even a weapon. She carried them to the little bridge across the river that marked the boundary of famil- iar tourist territory. She left everything on the bridge but the candles and matches she carried in her pockets. The oldest images had been made under the earliest form of light; they would speak, she guessed, more clearly in the flickering uncertainty of fire than in the glare of a flashlight.

She carried several tapers together, enough to illumine the shallow water, to draw an image on the stone walls out of the dark, then let it melt back into black. Most repeated the patterns of the early ones in the sacred cave. But as she wandered farther from the pool, now and then something would surprise her: the goddess's face, with its stark, pow- erful gaze, its wreath of hair, attached to a human body, or that same face with light, or water, or power streaming from its eyes. The Calluna itself quickened under that gaze; the water's voice changed, became stronger, cleaner, as its waters gained depth on its journey to the sea.

The paintings came to an end where all the books Perdita had seen on the subject ended: the goddess's face on one side of the river's wall, on the other a pair of hands, cupped, angled down, spilling drops of water shaped like tadpoles or tears. Beyond them, two massive wedges of stone leaned against one another across the river. The water pushed through the narrow opening between them, carving more deeply into its bed, its voice grown assured, imperative, echoing against the walls as it ran on, clamoring for the world and light.

The dark beyond the huge stones, Perdita knew, was caused by the human hands that had shaped the tunnel above the Calluna River to support the busy street named for the goddess. In an earlier century, the river had unearthed itself, glittered with sunlight, expanded in the luxury of meadows and fields for a brief, innocent moment of freedom before it met the Severen and was swept into the embrace of the god.

There, at that point of collision, a god dying of thirst, a mighty river drying up, might well have drunk gratefully and ceaselessly from the stream of water whose birthplace was buried underground, its source untouched by the light that had burned with such ruthless destruction across the whole of the land from the wyvern-riddled mountains to the sea.

Here, where the princess stood, was the goddess's face on one wall. There, on the opposite side, were her hands, water flowing out of them. In this form of the early tale, the

sacred, powerful, life-carrying vessel took the simplest shape
of all: the open hand.

Perdita, gazing perplexedly at the goddess's face, at her
hands, wondered if they had ever truly taken any other shape.

Then she thought: The story isn't finished. Where is the
god in distress?

On impulse she stooped, held her bouquet of flames
above the dark water rushing between the slabs of stone.
She tried to see beneath the surface to the river stones and
what they might reveal if, perhaps, they had once been part
of the ceiling or the walls. They might have spoken, continued the story long before the monstrous machines of a later
era had shaken them down into the water.

A face formed in her light.

Her own reflection, she thought at first, seeing only the
suggestion of a human in the coiling, rippling flow. Slowly
it took on color, dimension. Her lips parted. She sucked air,
felt the quickening, terrifying touch of the goddess on the
nape of her neck. She knew that face like she knew her own.
She stretched her hand toward it, her mouth opening soundlessly; her fingertips touched the water, and the face, the
reflection in the goddess's eye, misted away.

Daimon.

# 11

Pierce drove through a cleft in a dry, golden hill and found himself on a six-lane span across the astonishing breadth of Severluna Bay. The city sprawled at the end of the bridge, a tidal wave of civilization spilling so completely over land bordered on three sides by water that the land itself had vanished under it.

Pierce's hands grew damp, locked on the steering wheel. He was surrounded by more vehicles than he had seen in a lifetime; it took every nerve he possessed not to stop the Metro in the middle of the bridge so that he could get out and slink back into the hills. The Metro kept moving; the city grew. Streets appeared, going everywhere at once. Signs gave him choices, all unfamiliar. Since he would probably die, chewed up by the monsters snorting on all sides of him before he got safely off the bridge, choices seemed moot. He was slowed, at the end of the bridge where waves roiled and broke far under him, by traffic bottlenecking toward a toll-booth. The bill he proffered in trembling fingers was snatched away by the wind. The toll-taker eyed him implacably as he rummaged through his wallet. Finally, he did something right; a light turned green; the man waved him on, nodding, even smiling a little, while sounds of Severluna—horns, wind, engine growls, gulls, tide—poured through the open window like some kind of maniacal welcome.

He drove. Signs queried him constantly. Me? they asked him. Do you want me? He was frozen again, unable to say yes or no, right or left; he could only stop when everyone stopped and move forward when everyone else did.

He had no idea where to go.

Finally, catching sight of a quiet street, he reeled onto it, scarcely seeing the great stone houses along it as he drove, just relieved to be able to slow a little. He had a city map somewhere in the car but not a clue anywhere why he should go one direction instead of another. He drove aimlessly a bit, peering at street signs, smelling an oddly pungent scent of leaves from a park running along one side of the street. A broad road, lined with trees and very quiet, veered un-expectedly into the park. Pierce followed it eagerly, wanting only to find a place to park the car in the sudden peace and sit until he stopped trembling. Then he would look for his map and pretend he knew what he was doing.

He had followed the road's long curves deeper into the park, looking for a place to pull over, when he passed a little hut with heraldic devices painted on all four sides of it. Someone without a face popped instantly into his rear-view mirror. A line of metal teeth rose out of the tarmac, pointed, with lethal intent, at the Metro's tires. He shouted wildly, shaking again, and braked hard; the car slewed to a stop inches from the teeth.

A loud metallic voice said, "Step out of the vehicle." He managed to find the latch, tried to get out; his seat belt pulled him back. He cursed, heard the eerie voice again, and finally fumbled himself loose. He pushed himself upright, wondering wearily what he had done wrong, what ruthless laws he had broken just trying to find a place to sit among the huge old trees.

Two humanoids in black leather and full-facial visors that made them resemble giant, eyeless ants walked briskly to either side of the Metro. They each held something that lit up a strand of air between them and hummed. They passed the line of light fore and aft over the car, let it hover for a moment across the pack in the backseat. They reached the front bumper; the light vanished. Dark head consulted head, soundlessly to Pierce's ears. Then one walked back toward the little hut, and the other raised his visor, revealing a young, tanned, expressionless face.

"You have a knife in your baggage."

"I do?" Pierce said, and then remembered. "Oh. I do. The kitchen knife."

The guard murmured something into his chin, listened a moment. Behind him, the malevolent teeth slowly sank into the tarmac. The young man looked at Pierce again.

"You need to continue on, take the next right, then the immediate left. You took the wrong entrance."

"Oh."

"After you go left, the entrance will be on your right."

"Ah—"

The guard held up a hand, listened. "They're expecting you."

"Could I—like—just turn around?" Pierce pleaded.

"No. This really is the shortest way from here. You can drive on now."

Wordless, Pierce slid into the driver's seat, started the engine. "Right, then left, then right again," the guard reminded him as he crawled over the hidden teeth. Pierce saw him watching, visor down again, from the middle of the road. He swallowed, his mouth dust dry, and gave up any thought of peace in that demented city.

He followed directions carefully to avoid another yawning gape of vicious road teeth. An entrance of some sort into something loomed beyond another tiny guardhouse. As he took the second right turn, he saw the guard watching him, commenting to someone invisible about Pierce's passing. The end of that brief drive was a parking lot filled with vehicles of every kind. Pierce pulled in among them, not knowing what else to do. He wondered what would happen if he just took his pack and snuck into the trees surrounding the parking lot. Then he saw the vast stone wall running endlessly behind the trees.

There was a thump on the Metro roof; he started, expecting the insect-men to reappear. A girl in a black tunic and trousers, her hair bundled into a net, peered at him. She gave him a crooked, cheerful smile as he rolled down the window.

"At least I'm not the only one who's late. Walk in with me?" She added, as he stepped mutely out of the car, "Don't forget your stuff."

"Ah," he said tentatively. "I'm not sure— Is this the right—?"

"The royal kitchens, back entrance. They needed so many extras for the king's Assembly that you'll probably meet everyone you know here. Come on."

Dumbfounded, he grabbed his pack and hurried after her.

He caught up with her as she pulled open a door into what looked like an enormous cave filled with dimly moving figures. A cloud of steam smelling of bread, chocolate, onions, roasting meat blew around them and out.

"You're late," a voice grumbled amid the cloud. A lean, black-haired man carrying a clipboard took shape, scanned their faces and his list. "Marcia Holmes. You know your station."

"Yes," she said, vanishing into what looked like rows of counters half a mile long, cooks lined at them, vigorously chopping, clanging pot lids, whirring machinery, shouting for this or that.

"And you—" the man said. "I'm not seeing you. Who are you?"

"Pierce Oliver."

"You're not—" He flung up his hands, his list taking flight, settling again. "Never mind. What have you got in there?" Pierce pulled the knife out of his pack. The broad blade picked up light from somewhere, flashed silver. The man stared at it, his harried face suddenly slack with wonder, as though he recognized it though he could not remember why or from where. He pulled his thoughts back together abruptly. "All right. We have seven hundred and forty-nine knights to feed in seven hours, including the king and his knighted children. And, of course, everyone else in the palace not invited to the formal dinner must be fed as well. There are extra uniforms and aprons on that rack, and an empty station at the third counter. Get dressed, get over there, and start chopping."

Pierce threw on black trousers and a tunic, found his place, and began to feed the knife whatever anyone put within his reach. He had no time to think, except to marvel that he had somehow muddled his way under the king's roof. The knife melted through anything it was given. It minced garlic, chopped onions, sliced tomatoes, diced potatoes. The wicked edge, neatly balanced, rocked its way across walnuts or celery as easily as it cleaved slabs of raw beef into fine ribbons, and fresh chives and parsley into airy flakes. He had no idea what he was making, only that the thinnest rounds of unpeeled lemon were involved, endless narrow strips of red pepper, vast quantities of apple wedges and butterflied prawns.

After an hour or three, Pierce felt he had merged, melted into the kitchen. Its relentless heat, its endless alphabet of smells, its clatters, whirs, bangs, whacks, and sizzles had become his skin. His hand had grown a knife at the end of it; his feet existed in some other universe. He could toss a lime and part it six different ways before the wedges landed on his board. He could pare an avocado and catch the falling pieces. He could notch the green end of an onion in three strokes as it flew. He could julienne a carrot in midair.

He wondered if his father would be among those he would help feed.

He hardly noticed the chaos he was creating around him. Odd strands of light caught and swirled around the blade, then flashed across the counters, snagging themselves in metal and steel, in bowls and whisks, in other blades. Things groaned, smoked, clattered to the floor. Equipment froze or overheated; squalls of black smoke, hot, oily steam, collided with shouts and curses from the cooks. Pierce, oblivious, tossed yet another of a seemingly endless supply of oranges to peel it in one spiraling stroke when he realized abruptly that the knife was no longer in his hand.

The orange thumped down on his cutting board and bounced off. A woman wearing the king's crest on her hat and apron caught it with one hand. With the other, she laid the knife across the board, where, for the first time in hours, it was still.

She said succinctly, holding Pierce's eyes in her dark, furious gaze, "This is not working. I don't know you, I don't know what that knife is, but you are creating havoc every time you move. Whatever purpose that knife has, it does not belong in my kitchen. And neither do you. Remove it and yourself so we can at least try to function again." Pierce opened his mouth; she pointed her finger. "Out!"

"I'm sorry—"

"Just go away before something else breaks."

Pierce tucked the knife into his pack and, following the rigid finger that seemed to him to point the wrong direction, he slunk out of the kitchen.

He got lost before he could find his way.

He roamed through empty classrooms, dorms, a staff room, and a dining hall before he found a door around a corner beyond the hangar-sized bathrooms. He pushed it open and heard the world cheer, as though he had done something of magnificent import. The cheering died away. A voice spoke loudly, incoherently. He walked outside, found himself in a small, walled garden with a couple of benches, shadowed by huge trees with narrow, silvery leaves. A statue stood among the shadows, its face broken and blurred, its eyes blind with mold. Its head was angled toward the invisible crowd cheering again somewhere beyond the old stone wall.

Pierce walked across the yard, slung his pack straps over one shoulder, and hoisted himself into a tree beside the statue.

The wall dropped dizzyingly on the other side into a vast bowl shored up by brickwork and concrete and ringed with tier upon tier of seats. Groups of dark figures lounged here and there watching what was going on across the field below. From that high place, he could see, across the bowl, what seemed a miniature city of graceful buildings and towers, the past and present of Wyvernhold history, the lacework of stone ruins among high, colorful, modern designs, all surrounded by enormous, sprawling walls. Beyond them, he saw the busy span of the bridge he had driven across, so long ago it seemed impossible to him that it had been only that morning.

He took his eyes off the restless, mesmerizing roil and glitter of sea, and looked down at the movement below.

There seemed a number of things going on at once, some of which he recognized from programs that the antiquated television in the only sports bar in Desolation Point pulled out of the turbulent air around the cape. He had seen the ancient jousting games: riders and horses arrayed in colorful swaths of cloth galloping headlong toward a wooden figure that spun if it were struck by the long pole in the rider's hand. It hit the rider with its own straw-stuffed cudgel if

the rider missed. The scattered watchers seemed to be root-
ing for the wooden knight: they clapped and whistled vigorously whenever a rider got walloped by the cudgel.

They were knights, Pierce realized: the darkly clad among
the audience in the seats, and the contenders on the field.
They jousted; they raced; they shot arrows that spanned the
millennium between longbows and tech bows. They fought
with broadswords, with rapiers; they fought without weapons in a dozen different styles, none of which Pierce could
name. On a far end of the field, behind which the seats were
empty, they shot weapons that spat blood-red streaks of
lightning; the most accurate of them caused their small,
flying targets to mist into oblivion.

Pierce couldn't see faces; language from the microphone
came to him garbled with echoes. He moved impulsively,
drawn by the knights, wanting to be among them. He slid
off the tree branch onto the top of the wall, then rolled to
hang by his hands before he dropped to the platform behind
the last row of seats. He rose cautiously, not wanting to
attract the attention of any of the wicked weapons on the
field. He still wore the black kitchen uniform; at a distance,
he might be unremarkable. He found an aisle between the
tiers of seats, walked down the steep slope, and finally
understood the announcer's voice.

"Sir Val Duresse has won the Dragon Claw match. Dame
Maggie Leighton's team has scored highest in the jousting so
far. Second place in jousting is still held by Sir Block of Wood
and Straw. Team Sir Jeffry Holmes places third. Next team
of challengers led by Dame Rachel Thistledon please get your
mounts to the lists. Good luck to you against Sir Cudgel. Sir

Alexander Beamus has won Section Three of the longbow tournament. Whoever it was that just dropped over the wall from the kitchen yard, please proceed down the aisle and onto the field, where you will be allowed to prove your right to be among us. Good luck, Sir Kitchen Knight."

Pierce, one foot suspended, nearly lost his balance and bounced down the aisle onto the field. He righted himself, arms flailing, pack bouncing, and heard laughter, applause. If he turned then and there, he could make it back without anyone likely to recognize him later. But scrambling back over the wall using the backs of seats and dangling tree limbs would become an event in itself, to be won or lost by the red-haired chopper whose long black apron was luffing like a sail in the wind. It made no difference, he realized, whether he humiliated himself up a tree or on the field; one or the other was inevitable.

He untied the apron; it whirled off like a runaway shadow. He continued down, his face burning at the cheers and whistles from the crowd.

He saw the announcer gesturing to him as he reached the field. He dodged around a whirling pair of kickboxers and nearly found himself one of a row of targets in a sports bow contest.

"Careful, Sir Kitchen Knight."

Sir Kitchen Clown, more like, Pierce thought grimly.

"Watch out for— Oops."

Pierce dove across the grass, out of range of a pair of knights in full antique armor flailing broadswords half-blindly at one another. He got to his feet, looked around wildly for the next attack.

"This is not a country fair, Sir Kitchen Knight," the

announcer said reproachfully. "You can't just wander around among the exhibits. Sir Guy Morton is now the top contender in the Ribbon Dance style of street fighting. Challengers welcome. Dame Cynthia Barkley has so far scored highest in the Wyvern's Eye competition, obliterating eight out of ten targets."

Pierce reached him finally, after coming unnervingly close to getting scrambled under the hooves of a charger finishing a gallop down the tilting list. The announcer was a burly blond knight with an easy, confident smile that Pierce guessed he had worn sliding out of the womb. He stood on a platform overlooking the field, with a microphone in one hand and an earpiece in one ear, receiving information from the enclosure high in the seats above him.

"Welcome, Sir Kitchen Knight," he said cheerfully, then held the mike under Pierce's nose. "Do we have a name?" Pierce opened his mouth; the mike was suddenly no longer there. "No? Then Sir No Name it will be, since a knight without a name is a knight without a history, kitchen or otherwise, and who can say what feats and marvels you might perform on the field? Who can say, that is, but you?"

The mike was in front of Pierce again; the announcer cocked a brow, said briefly into it, "Anything?"

"What?"

"What," the announcer asked more precisely "is your weapon of choice? Hands, feet, longbow, lance, pistol, Wyvern's Eye—"

"Kitchen knife?" Pierce said uncertainly, all he could think of. The mike swooped back to him; he said into it, "Knife?"

A cheer went up. "Knife it is. What style?"

"What?"

"Longshore Style, Double-Handed, Chained Blades, Eastern, Old Style—"

"Ah," Pierce said, and got the mike's attention. "Deli Style?"

The announcer grunted with amusement. "Not familiar with that one. Do you have your weapon with you?"

"Yes," Pierce sighed.

"A field squire will escort you to the Field of Knives. Wait there for your challengers. Let's hear it for Sir No Name, who will introduce us to the art of knife-fighting Deli Style." He held up the mike to catch the raucous reaction. Pierce closed his eyes, wishing he had taken his chances with the tree.

He followed his escort to a square patch of grass with mysterious colored lines painted on it. He unpacked his knife and stood bleakly in the center where the lines converged, waiting. Around him, in other painted squares, men and women fought with unbelievable dexterity and grace, with and without weapons, their patterns of movement as varied as dance and likely as old. Surely, he thought, none of those skilled in such subtle and deadly moves would be interested in the knife-weavings of Slicing the Onion or Cubing the Tenderloin.

He was wrong.

A tall, lithe knight with long red hair in a knot on his head walked up the front of his opponent, did a backflip off his chin, and knocked the feet from under him on the way back up. The explosion from the nearby crowd obscured the announcement of the knight's victory. He held out his hand, helped his dazed opponent up, then he bounded into

Pierce's square and bowed gravely. Pierce, stunned, could only stare at him and hope one of them would disappear.

"Since you have no name to give," the young man said briskly, "I won't bother you with mine. Anyway, I expect to lose to you since I've never heard of Deli Style fighting. Can you show me a few basic moves before we start?"

Pierce found his voice finally. "You just walked up that knight."

"Yes, but that was a totally different style."

"You don't even have a knife."

"I'll get one," the nameless knight said patiently. "If you could give me an example of the style, I'll know which knife to choose." He waited, while Pierce's mind went blank at the idea. "Please? Just one simple move?"

Pierce stirred finally, an underwater slowness in his bones. Feeling ridiculous, he tossed an invisible fruit in the air with one hand; with the other he sent the knife flashing after it, describing a little circle in the air, before he caught the falling fruit. "Coring the Apple," he said, and tossed it again, cutting the air with five vertical, precisely parallel turns of the blade. "Wedging the Apple." He caught the wedges, which usually fell on the cutting board, and stood awkwardly, his empty hand cupped, wondering what to do with the nonexistent pieces.

The knight's eyes had narrowed. He gazed at Pierce out of eyes the pale blue of a winter sky; his lean, comely face, with its red brows and lashes, was without expression. "Can you do another," he suggested finally. "I'm not quite getting this."

Pierce drew breath, held it. It seemed easier to acquiesce than to try to explain, which would probably result in his getting walked up and knocked down, then jumped on a few times. The explanation was inevitable.

"Look—"

"Just show me."

Pierce closed his eyes briefly, then, in rapid succession, showed him Scalloping the Potato, Fine-shaving the Ham, and Butterflying the Flying Prawn. The knife had warmed to his grip by the time he finished; he was vaguely aware of the flashes that came from it as metal caught the sun. When he stopped, the knight was regarding him with a peculiar, skewed stare, blinking rapidly as though light from the sun's reflection had streaked across his eyes.

He said finally, very softly, "Who are you?"

"My name is Pierce Oliver," Pierce answered, relieved that the knight had asked before he attacked. "And I'm not a knight. I was just in the kitchen accidentally—"

"Yes. You made me remember something. My mother used to chop like that. That same magical blinding tangle of knife moves. I loved to watch that when I was little. She was—is still, I think—a sorceress."

Pierce swallowed. His heart seemed to shift and glide in his chest like a fish easing from shadow into underwater light. His eyes stung, blurred. "On Cape Mistbegotten?"

There was silence. When he could see again, the knight had crossed the battle lines to stand in front of him. His pale, intent eyes were very wide.

"Heloise Duresse. She is my mother."

"Heloise Oliver." Pierce heard his voice shake. "She took her maiden name when—after she left you here in Severluna. She is my mother."

The knight, still holding his eyes, gave a short nod, as though in recognition. "You look like her. I remember that, now, too. And your father?"

"My father—" He paused to swallow again. "She didn't tell my father about me when he returned to Severluna after he saw her for the last time at Cape Mistbegotten."

"So." The knight's hands rose, clamped above Pierce's elbows. "So you are my brother." He smiled then, the astonishment and pleasure in his face making Pierce's eyes burn again. "This is amazing. I always felt I lacked a brother and finally here you are. My name is Val Duresse. Our father is—" He stopped. His eyes flicked away from Pierce, then back again, an odd, wry expression in them. "Well, he's not on the field. I'm not sure where he is now. He's not good at keeping his cell turned on. We'll find him later, at the Assembly."

Pierce's heart pounded suddenly at the thought, which had been, until that second, only a marvelous possibility. "Will he—I mean, he doesn't even know I exist. And I'm not a knight; I can't just—"

"Yes, you can. You walked onto this field in a kitchen uniform and challenged every knight here. I accepted your challenge, and you won before we even began to fight."

"I haven't got a clue—"

"There is that," Val agreed, with his quick, charming smile. "We live in enlightened times. Not every knight chooses to fight or carries a weapon. There are other ways to serve. Come and choose a knife for me. I want to learn more of your Deli Style. And if that's all you know about fighting, so should you."

# 12

On another part of the field, Daimon faced an unknown knight.

Like a shadow, the knight matched Daimon's height and reach. He wore black from head to foot; his head was rendered invisible by an acorn-shaped helm with a finger's breadth of a slit across it for sight. Nothing on the mantle flowing from his shoulders indicated, by ancient beast or heraldic device, who he might be. Daimon was similarly hidden in red, his body sheathed in metal, his helm densely padded against the mighty heave and thrust of the black knight's broadsword. The helm smelled of oil, copper, and old sweat; the air he breathed was thick and hot and merciless.

He was battling, it seemed, something maddeningly unnameable, as old as time and as elusive as mist. This dark, faceless knight was a manifestation of the idea he had been struggling with since the moment his mother had appeared out of nowhere and offered him a realm of enchantment and a consort's place beside the young woman who already ruled him. That offer was weighted with implications heavier than the shield he raised against the dark knight's sword hammering away at it. He could not decide which was more incredible: the intriguing, compelling, and even justifiable offer itself, or the faceless, nameless stranger Daimon saw in himself who might accept it.

He got tired of the endlessly battering blade and shifted his bulky, ponderous weight out from under his shield. He let the shield drop. The knight's sword met air instead of metal and kept going, dragging the dark knight after it. He drove his blade into earth and clung to it, maintaining a perilous balance.

Sun leaped off Daimon's blade and into his eyes as he lifted it. Somehow, the black knight pulled his own sword out of the ground and angled it upward to block the fall of Daimon's. Metal sheared against metal. The two knights pushed against one another's weight, lumbering around the crossed blades. The muscles in Daimon's arms and back, wrung to the utmost, could only maintain their thrust against the dark knight's strength; the knight seemed equally unable to change the equilibrium of their power.

Then the black knight let his own blade shift, yield, just enough, as he twisted to one side, that the weight of Daimon's body armor pulled him off-balance. The step he tried to take to catch himself was blocked by the knight's blade, run into ground against Daimon's foot.

He fell facedown with a grunt of breath. The black knight rolled him onto his back, not without some difficulty. The tip of his blade found a delicate, defenseless line of skin between helm and breastplate. Daimon gazed at the hard, expressionless, inhuman head looming over him. The knight's shadow fell into his eyes; he heard the harsh, weary rasp of his breath within his helm. Who are you? he demanded silently, urgently of the shadow-knight, of himself. Who are you?

"I yield," he said to the exasperating uncertainty, and the cold metal left his throat. He heard the thud of the massive hilt hitting the ground. The black knight raised both hands, wrestled off the helm, and Daimon saw the elegant, broad-boned, smiling face beneath it.

His breath stopped. Field squires swarmed around them both. Hands hoisted him upright, drew off his helm. The distant whistling and cheers from the onlookers grew suddenly loud; he sucked in fresh, sweet air, and heard Jeremy Barleycorn's amused voice from the announcer's stand.

"Dame Scotia Malory has defeated Prince Daimon Wyvernbourne in knightly combat with armor and broadsword. Beware, House Wyvernbourne, the powers of the north."

He looked for her as the squires helped him rise. But he only saw the back of her head, the severe braid of honey-colored hair suddenly fall out of its coil and down the black mantle, as she was escorted off the field.

Later, Daimon sat among the wyverns in the huge, ancient hall named after them. The great, winged, long-necked, barb-tailed beasts swarmed across the stone walls and the ceiling, shadowy with age, memories of themselves. The throne built for the first Wyvernbourne king stood on a simple dais against a backdrop of the great stone caves and peaks where the wyverns lived. When the king arrived, he would sit there, as his ancestors had done, surrounded by wyverns' faces rearing out of the black wood of the back and the armrests, their wild, staring eyes golden lumps of amber forged long before Wyvernhold existed. A podium with a microphone, looking bizarre among the wyverns, had been placed on each side of the dais.

Knights who had spent the earlier hours on the practice field crowded into the rows of black-and-gilt chairs. Their faces were sunburned; they smelled of soap and shampoo. Daimon, adrift in his thoughts, barely heard their greetings. A lovely scent of lavender beguiled him out of himself as someone took a seat near him. He straightened, glancing around for the source of the lavender, and saw his half siblings, the two princes Roarke and Ingram, and the sister born between them, Princess Isolde. They scattered themselves around Daimon; as knights shifted to let them pass, he caught again the faint, elusive fragrance.

"Too bad you bothered to fight in full armor," Ingram said, taking a seat behind Daimon and prodding his shoulder. "You missed the sight of Isolde smacking the head off the joust dummy with her lance. It went flying. Nearly took out Jeremy Barleycorn in the announcer's stand. He ducked just in time, or it would have been his head flying after it. What's this all about? Anybody know?"

"Not a clue," Daimon answered shortly.

"Something Lord Skelton found," Isolde said, settling her ivory braid over one broad shoulder as she sat. She and Ingram had their mother's hair, and the only blue eyes in the family for several generations. "Something in a book, I think."

"A book," Ingram marveled. "Our father gathers an assembly of knights from all over the realm because of a book? A real one, do you think? Or one of those floating around in the cloud?"

"Parchment, I would guess," Roarke said. He added, at his younger brother's silence, "That's paper made of goatskin."

"You're joking."

"No, but I am stunned that you actually know what a book is." Roarke leaned over the empty chair beside Daimon. "I could have used you this morning on my street-fighting team. We were overwhelmed by Graham Beamish's team, who had both Leith and Val Duresse on his. Machines, both of them. Even at Leith's age." He paused, glanced around cautiously, as though the elder of the fighting machines might be listening. "You had lunch alone with our father earlier this week. Did he say anything to explain this?"

Daimon shook his head mutely, then made an effort. "Some artifact of the god Severen's, I think he said Sylvester found."

"Our father invited you to lunch with him alone?" Ingram exclaimed. "What for? What?" he demanded, as Isolde smacked him upside the head.

"Thank you," Daimon said gravely.

"You're welcome."

"I don't see—" Ingram said indignantly, then saw. "Oh, that. Well, nobody cares about that. Do they?" he asked, as Daimon, shifting abruptly in his chair, felt the blood rise in his face. He sensed Roarke's intense, speculative gaze on the back of his head and quelled his own impatience, turning to meet his siblings' eyes, as well of those of others around them listening without compunction for royal gossip.

"The king told me, for the first time in my life, about the woman who was my mother," he said carefully, and his siblings were suddenly motionless, entranced.

"Who was she?" Ingram demanded. "Did he love her? Were you an accident?" He dodged his sister's hand that time. "Sorry. Stupid."

"And then he talked about this Assembly. Nothing that I understood." He paused; they waited expectantly, as did those in the island of silence around them. "He said she was the descendant of a very old realm that no longer exists. She vanished after a night, and"—he lifted a shoulder—"somehow he found me."

"How?" the listeners demanded at once.

"Ask him," Daimon answered pithily, and with great relief saw their father come in at last.

The Assembly rose. The king, followed by Lord Skelton and Lord Ruxley, stepped onto the dais and seated himself among the wyverns. The magus and the mystes moved toward the podiums. Lord Skelton wore a suit of scholarly black and carried an armload of books and papers, one of which he promptly dropped and pursued across the dais before he reached the podium. Mystes Ruxley, magnificently robed in gold embroidered with jewel-toned threads, had already set a single, thin screen upon his podium. He gripped the podium with both hands, summoning patience while the magus dithered with his books and papers, sorting through them, changing their order, mislaying one or the other, and searching through them again. The king watched him expressionlessly, while the gathering settled again into their chairs.

Finally, the hall and the magus grew quiet, and the king rose.

"Knights of Wyvernhold, I have summoned you here from all over this realm at the request of the court magus Lord Skelton and of Lord Ruxley in his aspect of Mystes of Severen's sanctum. This concerns a matter of Wyvernhold history. It is a matter of enormous power, lost for millennia and brought to light through the painstaking scholarship of Lord Skelton. He will present the matter to you within the framework of his studies. Mystes Ruxley will explain the matter within the context of the sacred powers of the god Severen. What I will ask is that you consider this matter within the context of knightly endeavor along the lines of the court history of the first king of Wyvernhold. I will ask those of you who are willing to undertake a modern version of the old-style quest."

There was an insect-chirp of chairs creaking all over the room at the unexpected notion.

"Lord Skelton and Mystes Ruxley will explain what that means," the king said, and returned to the wyvern throne.

Both nobles silently queried one another, then the impassive king. Dourly, Mystes Ruxley flipped a palm at the magus.

"Since you brought it to light, Lord Skelton," he said grudgingly, and the entire pile on the magus's podium slid onto the floor. "Well, then," the mystes said with more complacency, as Lord Skelton disappeared abruptly after it, "since you're busy, I will begin."

He touched the screen in front of him and began to read.

"'The young god felt the year dying within him. Frost whitened his bones, his brows, his lashes. The dying leaves in their journey floated through his veins, blocking light, blocking warmth from his heart's blood. The voices of the birds cried of the coming end. They sang cold; they warned cold; they flew away and left the god to die. The old moon, the withering crone, showed no mercy, only cold. Animals fled from her, buried themselves in the earth. The pale webs of spiders, their tales, turned to ice and shattered.

"'The god began to turn to ice, began to die.

"'In his despair, he called to the vanished sun. He summoned its warmth, its fires into himself. With his power, a great mountain burst into flame in the snow. Ice melted from the cliffs carved by the footsteps of the river god. Stone itself melted. Stars of fire blazed like jewels and fell into the icy waters, warming them. The river ran gold with molten light. The wild, swirling waters, freeing themselves from the prison of ice, spun and spun. They shaped and fashioned. They made a vessel of pure gold, brought it into light. The pale moon, now the full and barren queen, reached down with her fingers of icy light to snatch the vessel, to steal its warmth and beauty as it whirled in the flow of the god to the sea.

"'The moon caught it, held it in her fingers of mist. But the river god pulled it down into its rapid, foaming waters, pushed it down deep, hiding the brilliance from her. Weighed with the god's great power, the vessel sank, warming the waters as it drifted down, turning over and over in the flow, filling and emptying, gold warming god, gold burning water as the great river flowed to meet the sea.

"'The new moon, maiden now, made one last attempt to steal the god's treasure. Her face looked down; she saw herself reflected in the river god's face. She snatched the vessel his power had made, hid it there in her secret place, her pool buried under the earth. But the god found it and took it back. And he took her, for she was rightfully his, part of his great and powerful godhead.

"'He bore her with him to the sea.

"'There in the fountain of the world, the great cauldron of life, the vessel floats and falls, filling and emptying. The moon still searches, walking the path she weaves in the dark across the sea. The sacred vessel is now lost, now found, full and empty, carrying sun and moon, the power of water, of gold and god. It waits to be found. It is never lost. It waits.'"

"Little of that," the magus said, his gray head with its furry brows and long mustaches rising unexpectedly like a wayward moon from behind his podium, "makes any sense whatsoever."

"I am aware of that," Mystes Ruxley answered acidly, looking a trifle unsettled by the apparition. "But, confused as it may be, it is the first written reference to the sacred vessel holding the god's power. It is the tale most learn first."

"For most, the only version they know." Lord Skelton brought up his collection from the floor and dropped it onto the podium with a thud that made the microphone ring. "The dying and reviving god is certainly the central symbol of the tale. But it would be ridiculous for the king to send his knights out in boats searching for a floating bowl of gold. For one thing, that much gold would sink like a stone."

"It is also light," Mystes Ruxley reminded him, restored

to equanimity by his pun. "Granted the tale is already muddled by antiquity, but it is a place to begin the discussion.
The vessel has been, from very early times, an astonishing
source of power. And you have come to the conclusion that
it exists. Today. In this world. It can be found. We could
argue that it must be, before the evil represented by the
moon finds it first. If it is not in water, then where should
the knights look?"

The magus's brows peaked; lines fretted his forehead.
"That is the mystery. My search into the early myths, the
tale of the vessel at once empty and full, lost and found, the
great cauldron of life, brought me to unexpected conclu-
sions. The vessel can only be seen through the clarity of
understanding. It must be named in order to be truly seen.
It can only be truly seen by those who, in the most profound
way, already possess it."

"There must be something wrong with your translations,"
the mystes said with asperity. "It is sacred, yes, but it's also a
physical object. You have been pursuing it for years, and now
you are convinced that it exists to be found. Yet you say that
it only exists for those who can see it? That makes no sense."

Lord Skelton gripped his mustaches with both hands, a
sign of mounting exasperation. "And you call yourself a
mystes."

"My lords, please," the king said. Both men started as
though one of the painted wyverns had spoken. "I understand that if it were a simple matter, the vessel would have
been found long ago. It might help us if you present your
ideas about the vessel without interruption. You can argue
later. Lord Skelton?"

The magus presented his views with many rustlings of paper, much riffling through pages of books. Odd bits of arcane philosophy, ancient names and poetry, folklore and allusions to the writings of the early mystica formed a roiling sea in Daimon's thoughts, upon which the golden vessel floated aimlessly. "You must see with your heart. The vessel will find you. It will recognize itself in you. The vessel belongs to anyone who desires it, but no one can possess it. Its powers are as ancient as the world; it holds all the mysteries of the world."

One of which, Daimon noted, lay hidden in his father's expression; the king listened to Lord Skelton without a thought revealing itself in his face, while all those amorphous ideas of power stirred to life under his roof.

The magus stopped, seemingly at random in the middle of a thought, and asked if anyone had a question. Half the hall rose. He looked nonplussed at the response. Even the wyverns flying across the ceiling seemed to peer bewilderedly down at him.

"I have as well," the king said, quieting the hall again. "But perhaps Mystes Ruxley's thoughts on the matter will answer some of our questions."

"Thank you, Your Majesty," the mystes said with what sounded like equal portions of indignation and relief. "And thank you, Lord Skelton, for a presentation that was scholarly to the point of nebulousness."

"You're very welcome," the magus said imperturbably.

"I'm sure the question uppermost in your thoughts is: Where should I look for this vessel? In the sea? In the streets of Severluna? On a mountaintop? Lord Skelton seems to think that it can be found only by not looking for it, or only by those who have already found it. Some such. The vessel is formed in the Severen; it might be somewhere along the river. Or at the estuary, where the Severen meets the sea. There are, as well, references to the moon in her aspects of child, queen, crone. The phases of the moon might suggest clues. There is also a reference to Calluna's cave. Perhaps there are ancient clues on the walls of the cave, even an image of the vessel itself." Lord Skelton opened his mouth; the mystes lifted his hand. "Yes, yes, I know that every scratch on the cave walls has been studied. But maybe that's why the vessel has not been found: Nobody would recognize it if they saw it. A cooking pot, they might see. A simple drinking cup." He paused, hearing his own words. "I suppose," he added reluctantly, "in that idea, Lord Skelton may be right. Perhaps only the heart, not the eye, would recognize the power in it."

Daimon, motionless in his chair, heard his mother's voice again, on a noisy street corner in Severluna, not far from where he had been born: *Whatever shape it has taken, you have the eyes, the heart to recognize it. Find it for Ravenhold. Find it for us.*

# 13

On the far side of the Hall of Wyverns, Pierce, sitting
with a wyvern glaring from the stones on one side of
him, and Val in his formal black leather and silk on the
other, tried to render himself invisible. He was still in his
black server's uniform; he would, Val assured him, be all
but inconspicuous wearing that among the knights. Two old
men had been droning on the dais for an hour, with the king
between them. Pierce hadn't heard a word they said. He
had taken one look at the king's sharp, golden eyes, his
strong, inscrutable face, and his own head had tried to
recede, turtle-wise, into his untidy collar. He stared at his
feet, waves of anticipation and dread rolling through him,
sweat running down his hair, down his back like brine.

Val turned to him once, his ice-blue eyes wide. *Calm*,
they said. *Calm*. Pierce swallowed dryly, kept sweating.

There was a sudden stir throughout the hall. Something

had happened; knights turned to speak to one another; others rose. Pierce jumped at the touch of Val's hand.

"We're taking a break," Val explained, and stood up. "Come on, let's find my father. Our father," he amended, as Pierce stared at him incredulously.

"I can't go out there among the knights. Not like this. If I even stand up, I'll melt into a puddle of kitchen-server black on the floor."

His brother's brows crooked. "You've come this far," Val reminded him. "Just a little farther—" Something in Pierce's expression, his inextricable huddle, made him relent. "Stay here, then. I'll find him. Don't go anywhere."

He shifted his way through knights down the aisle, then disappeared among them. Pierce slid down in his chair a few more inches and closed his eyes.

They flew open again as a hand clamped onto his shoulder.

"What are you doing in here?" a voice barked indignantly into his ear. The hand pulled him to his feet; by some miracle, he stayed on them. "You're that kitchen knight. You were on the field. You had no business there; you have even less business here. Wearing black doesn't make you a knight any more than climbing over a wall to wave a knife around on the practice field."

Pierce, tongue stuck to the roof of his mouth, gazed speechlessly at the knight who had dragged him out of his chair. He wore his sandy hair in a tightly shaped bristle that peaked down his forehead and along his ears like spearpoints. Even under his quilted jacket, Pierce could see muscle. His long, lean face was pinched with extreme irritation.

"Why are you still in my eyesight?" he demanded. "Go. Get back to the kitchen where you belong."

Pierce, his brain dissolving into a nebulous cloud under the furious, hazelnut stare, found a salient point. "For one," he heard his tongue say, "you're still holding on to me."

The knight scowled. Pierce felt his fingers open, the weight finally lift. The knight jerked his head at the nearest doors.

"For another," Pierce said without moving, "I've been told to stay here."

The knight's face flamed. He pushed it so closely into Pierce's that the wrong word, Pierce felt, could spark and ignite them both. "If you were anyone at all in this palace, you would know me. I am Sir Kyle Steward, first cousin of the king and seneschal of this house. Whoever brought you in here will answer to me. Go. Now."

Pierce's knees gave way; he sank back into his chair. In the gathering their squabble had begun to attract, someone loosed a faint gasp. Someone else chuckled.

"Sorry," Pierce gabbled with genuine regret to the fury looming over him. "I am so much more willing than you could imagine to get as far away from you as possible. But if I do that, I will never find my way back to this chair where I was told to stay so that for the first time in my life I can meet my father. I have come all the way from Cape Mist-begotten and through all the years of my life to get to this chair."

All expression flowed out of Sir Kyle's face; his eyes emptied even of contempt. He pulled something out of his jacket, said into it, "House guards to the Hall of Wyverns. South doors. Now."

"Wait, Sir Kyle," an unexpected voice said. A woman, half a head taller than most of the knights, broad-boned and graceful, eased toward them through the growing crowd. Her hair, shades of honeycomb and gold, was swirled into a severe knot; her eyes, a lovely, pale violet, seemed recklessly fearless in the face of the fuming seneschal. She said simply, "Sir Kyle, we are here for reasons most of us barely understand yet. As Lord Skelton pointed out, we can't make assumptions. Nothing on this path the king has asked us to take may be as it seems. Not even a kitchen knight."

The seneschal seemed to struggle between various responses as he looked at her. "Dame Scotia," he said lamely, "we haven't started the quest yet."

"How do you know? We don't even know what we're looking at now. He has a name. You could ask him."

With reluctance, the seneschal looked away from her to Pierce. His face tightened again; he said brusquely, "Who are you?"

Pierce pulled together some tatters of dignity under the young woman's calm gaze; he stood up before he answered. "My name is Pierce Oliver."

He heard the whispering begin, ripple through the crowd, which had grown by then to fill a quarter of the hall and was still growing. His eyes followed the whispering and found, with vast relief, the wicked grin on his brother's face.

Then he saw the broad-shouldered, black-haired man beside his brother, staring at Pierce with complete astonishment.

He jostled his way through the crowd, his eyes, a warmer blue than Val's, never leaving Pierce's face. He would have walked through the seneschal if Sir Kyle had not gotten out of his way. In front of Pierce, he finally stopped.

"I had no idea," he said. He put his hands on Pierce's shoulders. "You look so much like her."

Pierce was struck mute again, this time with wonder. He took in the strands of gray in his father's hair, his deep voice, the expression in his eyes of tenderness and rue. His own hands rose, fingers closing on his father's arms; he felt the muscle like stone. He dwindled, somehow, knee high to the knight, staring out of a child's eyes at someone he should have known but never had, and wishing for a sixth sense that might have shown him all the missing years.

He took a breath finally, sharply. "I'm sorry," he said. "I didn't— I'm sorry to surprise you like this. I didn't know— any other way."

"Well," his father said. "There it is. How many other ways are there to tell a man you are his son?" He paused, while some sort of chaos disturbed the back of the crowd, and it began to separate around a single moving figure. "How is your mother?" Leith asked.

"She's—she's fine. She's—at least she was before I left. She—" His voice stuck again, as he recognized the force approaching. His father glanced around, finally remembering their transfixed audience, and saw the magus.

"I suppose," he said reluctantly, "this must wait."

Pierce let go of his father. The slight, cob-haired Lord Skelton eased through the brawny crush of knights as if they were not there. Behind his circular lenses, his unblinking eyes seemed enormous. They caught at Pierce, held him; he could not look away. Leith said something; he scarcely heard it, so compelling was the magus's focus on him.

The magus reached them finally, stood silently, his gaze like a mist enfolding Pierce, separating him from time, past and present, giving him nothing to see except himself and the confusion of unknowns surrounding his next step.

Lord Skelton blinked, set them both free in the world again, and smiled.

"You," he said, "have already begun."

The wyvern was not far behind the magus.

The king had, it seemed, finally found a use for an expression. "Sir Leith," he said, "is this yours?"

"Yes, my lord. My son Pierce Oliver. His mother neglected to tell me. I'm sure she had her reasons."

The king studied Pierce, who bowed his head belatedly, not having a clue what else he should do.

"That's a kitchen uniform," the king noted with interest. "What were you doing there?"

"My mother taught me how to cook. Sir. My lord." He gave up, flushing deeply, but his father was nodding. "I found my way to the kitchen by accident. I think."

"Which doesn't begin to explain—" The king left it there, shaking his head. "We have an assembly to finish, a quest to consider. Welcome to my court, Pierce Oliver. From what I understand Lord Skelton to say, you have already begun the search for this ancient object of power, which may or may not, depending on magus or mystes, be seen or possessed, and which may resemble the sun or a stewpot. Join us at supper;

you can explain then how you found your way into my kitchen."

He turned away. The knights began to drift toward their chairs. The seneschal lingered, regarding Pierce with mystification.

"You can't wear that at the king's table," he stated, then queried Leith silently.

"He'll stay with us," Leith said, "of course."

"I have clothes in my pack," Pierce said.

"I doubt you brought much that would be suitable here." He crooked a finger with distaste, slid the pack strap from the back of Pierce's chair. "You'll find this in Sir Leith's rooms. Along with clothing more appropriate to your status."

He ended that with a curl of a question in his voice. Pierce considered the matter blankly, having no idea either.

Mystes Ruxley called the Assembly to order again, and Pierce sat with his father on one side of him, his brother on the other, and himself so full of astonishment at his sudden wealth of breathing, shifting family surrounding him that not a word from magus or mystes, knight or king penetrated.

Later, he sat clothed in finer and more formal textures of black, again between his father and his brother, his eyes and throat powder-dry, his fork making ineffectual movements over his plate, never quite touching what the silent servers had placed upon it. The wyvern, the magus, and most of the wyvern's children filled the rest of the circular dais table. All of them, even the king, assumed that Pierce's path led back out of the palace door in quest of some mythical whatnot made by the sun or the moon, he couldn't remember which or find a single reason under either why he should care.

The magus, Lord Skelton, was not helping any by picking things at random out of Pierce's head.

"'All-You-Can-Eat Friday Nite Fish Fry'?" he said abruptly, staring at Pierce, and putting conversation on hold around the table. "That's where you got your kitchen knife?"

Pierce felt Val's silent tremble of laughter.

"What's a fish fry?" the king asked Pierce with interest. "And why do you, Lord Skelton, think that a knife has anything to do with finding Severen's sacred artifact?"

The magus, his foggy eyes enlarged and luminous behind his lenses, answered, "It is part of an ancient ritual. He recognized that. Wherever it was."

The wyvern's eye caught at him then, transfixed him. "Where did you see the ritual?"

"I didn't—I—" he stammered, and felt his father's light, reassuring touch above his elbow. "My lord, it was at a bar and grill. In Chimera Bay. A sort of diner. They served fish. All kinds of seafood."

"Deep-fried in Severen's pot, I'll bet," the king's second son, Prince Ingram, said irrepressibly. He shifted under the weight of the wyvern's regard. "Sorry, sir."

"I take it," the king said to him mildly, "you are not drawn to this quest?"

"No. I mean, yes, I am. I wasn't so much at first, until Niles Camden inspired me. He's gathering a group of us he calls Knights of the Rising God. He used to be an acolyte in Severen's sanctum, when he was young, and was very torn, he explained, between the two callings when he decided to become a knight. That's why he takes this quest so seriously. His idea is to find the holy artifact and use it to proclaim Severen's ultimate power over Wyvernhold." He paused to cut a bite of meat, oblivious to his father's sudden stillness. "He wants to separate us into various groups, some to search the headwaters of the Severen, others to the more important sanctums across the realm, maybe another to stay here and search Calluna's cave. Anyway, after we find the artifact, the worship of Severen will be the dominant sacred force over this kingdom." He raised the bite to his lips, then became aware of the silence around him. His eyes flickered from face to face; he put down his fork. "What? What did I say?"

"Beyond threatening to offend every other ancient god and goddess in this land?" the king said dryly. "None of you seem to have listened at all to Lord Skelton."

"I tried," Ingram said earnestly. "I really did." He looked at Lord Skelton, who was tugging one mustache and gazing incredulously at him. "I didn't really understand much of what you said. Niles put things much more simply."

"He won't find it," Lord Skelton predicted abruptly. "None of you will, with your hearts blinded with power."

Prince Ingram flushed, but said doggedly, "I'm sure you're right, Lord Skelton. But there's no reason we can't look anyway."

The king's eyes moved to Leith. "You'll go, of course." It sounded to Pierce like both a command and a plea. "And your sons?"

"Yes, my lord," Val answered eagerly, for them all. "We can travel together to this mysterious Friday Nite Fish Fry."

I just got here, Pierce protested silently.

Leith opened his mouth, then closed it, and gave Val a quick, warm smile. "I yield to my son's fervor and to your bidding, my lord. I doubt that I'd recognize such a complex object, but at least we can promise not to disturb even the slightest of the old powers in this land."

"Don't make promises you can't keep," Lord Skelton warned. "Wandering around in the realm in search of its oldest power is liable to cause all kinds of disturbances and consequences. There were always unexpected dangers on those early quests." He sipped wine and added more cheerfully, "Very colorful, sometimes deadly, often mysterious, random, occasionally verging on the ridiculous. No quest was ever safe. They exist to reveal."

"Reveal what, exactly?" Leith asked in his deep, sinewy voice that Pierce was coming to love. "Lord Skelton?"

"The landscape of the heart."

There was a little silence that sounded, Pierce thought, bewilderingly like a comment. Then the king murmured, "Indeed an unpredictable place." His eyes went to his daughter. "And you, Isolde? Are you joining Niles Camden's expedition?"

She shook her fair head, her face, unlike her father's, expressing exactly what she thought. "I am so underwhelmed by Niles's ambitions. I've made plans to travel with Maggie Leighton. We haven't yet decided where to start looking."

"Good."

"I want to go," Prince Roarke said, taking his knife to the small bird on his plate. "There's something compelling about this quest, even if, as Lord Skelton says, you may not know what you're looking for until you see it, and if you look for its power, you may miss it entirely. It's like taking the wyvern in the north. Maybe you glimpse the ancient memory of it, maybe not. But you bring home its shadow in your heart and the feeling that you have been seen."

The king's face loosened toward a smile. "I do remember that. It's something you never forget. But no. You've been away from court long enough. I want you here with me."

Prince Roarke looked at him silently, surprised. The king regarded his youngest son, who had scarcely said a word after greeting Pierce. Prince Daimon, busily deboning his bird with a culinary precision and eating very little of it, laid down his fork and met his father's eyes.

"Yes," he said. "I will go. I'm not yet sure where. Or with whom."

Expression flowed through the king's eyes, surfaced on his face, complex and fleeting; he studied Daimon with a stranger's scrutiny, as though, in that moment, he did not recognize his son.

Daimon's eyes dropped, hid from the wyvern's gaze, and from the magus, who, frowning vaguely, seemed to be trying to remember something else lost in the mists of time and history, and whether or not it might in any way be important.

"Well," he breathed finally, "what will come will come. We shall see in the end what shape, what face it takes." His tangled brows knotted suddenly; he shifted the glasses on his nose, looking pained. "You need," he said to Pierce, "to call your mother."

———

The next afternoon, Pierce stood between his father and his brother among hundreds of knights in the sanctum of the god Severen. Like Val, he wore the dark uniform and the quilted jacket embroidered with the sign of Leith's family: a black swan floating on a silver-blue lake, silhouetted against a full moon edged with a circle of stars. The sanctum was a huge, diamond-shaped structure whose great colored windows were so rich with coiling seams of silver and gold that light reflecting off them burned Pierce's eyes and inspired the tears that were his first gift to the god. Through centuries, its lofty walls had acquired a crust of wealth that astonished the eye in every possible shape and from every possible cranny. In the center a great fountain shot sacred water upward through a lavishly decorated pipe, imitating the perpetual, vigorous power of the Severen River.

Mystes Ruxley, high above the gathering on an ornate, gilded pulpit, also endlessly imitated that flow.

"You will at all times uphold the laws of Wyvernhold. You will use all weapons in the name of the god Severen, and lead your quest in a manner that reflects the ancient traditions of this land and its king. You will . . ."

Pierce's thoughts strayed to the small town on Chimera Bay that, no matter how far he traveled, would not let him go. Random memories surfaced: the strange ritual in the ghost of the old hotel; the past that clung there, a collection of fractured relics and small mysteries; the young woman with her smiling green eyes, her flowing golden hair and generous smile, those eyes reddened, heavy with unshed tears. Trapped in a fairy tale, she seemed to him, by the chef who refused to show his face. Again Pierce felt the pull of her, even across the distance, and his impulse to step once more onto that convoluted, obsessive path to her door.

"Go in peace, return safely with what you find, for every one of you, searching for such a prize will, according to the magus Lord Skelton, bring back what you need most. In the name of the god Severen, and with King Arden's sufferance, go into the world with courage, humility, and the worthiest of intentions. As Lord Skelton might say, and probably did: Follow your heart, and you will always know where you are. This Assembly is ended. Praise Severen."

The knights did so with such enthusiasm that the phrase bounced from wall to wall and even overwhelmed, for an instance, the incessant voice of the river god. Pierce felt a hand grip his shoulder; he turned his head, met Leith's smiling eyes. He followed his father and his brother out of the sanctum into the long shadows and bright, sun-streaked late afternoon of Severluna, and he wondered what he could possibly find of value on this quest that he did not already, amazingly, possess.

Late that night, he finally called his mother.

# 14

News about the Assembly reached Calluna's sanctum in piecemeal fashion. Short of listening through a keyhole, Perdita had to wait for Gareth to reappear, which he finally did late in the evening after the Assembly ended. They slipped out of the palace, away from knights and acolytes, to a quiet, discreet pub to talk. From Gareth, the princess heard the incredible tale of the secret son of Leith Duresse, whose wife Heloise had kept from him all those years.

"We actually met him," Gareth told her, looking amazed. "Prince Roarke and Bayley and I, when we got lost on Cape Mistbegotten, coming home from the north. The sorceress who cooked our lunch was Pierce's mother. Now he is going off questing with his newfound father and brother."

"And you?" Perdita asked grimly, fascinated as well but refusing to be distracted. "Are you going off, too?"

He gave her a rueful look that was overshadowed by a

vision. She recognized that distancing between them, the feeling that part of him had already left her. "Yes," he said. "I'm sorry."

"You just got back from the north!"

"I know."

"That time it was for a falcon—"

"The winter merlin."

"This time—for what? Exactly?"

"Nobody seems to know, exactly. It's hard to explain."

She took a cold swallow of beer and eyed him dourly. "Try."

He did, earnestly but not very coherently, through another beer, and most of what was left of the night. They parted company in the morning, he to pack, she to Calluna's sanctum, where she had the first shift of the day keeping watch, among the pools and fountains and flickering candles, over the ancient peace of the goddess. She opened the chamber door to change into her robe and found herself face-to-face with Leith Duresse.

She froze on the threshold; he blushed; the queen said quickly, "Close the door."

Perdita did so, a bit crossly, guessing that he had been telling the queen much the same thing she had listened to for half the night. "Good morning, Sir Leith. In a few minutes, it will be my duty as Calluna's guardian to tell you to leave this holy place, where no one dedicated to the god Severen is permitted to cast a shadow or loose a breath in the goddess's sanctum. I hear you are going off on this quest as well?"

"Only reluctantly, Princess," he said, and added with wry

honesty, "I'm too old to go looking for such mystical powers. I would have to relive my life."

She nodded, hearing as well what he didn't say. "The king wants you to go."

She looked beyond him at the queen, who was adrift beside the window, her hair disheveled, her expression unsettled.

Genevra said, "I asked Leith to come here before he left, to give us details about the Assembly. It seems to have been confusing, well-intentioned, and entirely mystifying."

"Father didn't tell you?"

"It probably didn't cross Arden's mind that we might want to know." She looked quickly at Leith, as though, far away, she had heard a footstep turn their way. "You should go."

"I will see you before we leave."

"Yes."

"Take the tower stairs," Perdita advised. "Aunt Morrig hovers near the inner stairway to check on the acolytes. Just don't breathe," she reminded him dryly, as he slipped out across the goddess's tranquil antechamber. Perdita closed the door behind him, met the queen's eyes long enough to recognize her own expression in them, mingling love, exasperation, and the aftermath of a very short night.

The queen opened the wardrobe, handed Perdita the long turquoise guardian's robe, with its collar and cuffs of mossy green. "So Gareth is going as well," she said.

"Yes," the princess sighed, drawing the robe over her clothes. She kicked off her shoes; the queen handed her sandals. Perdita sat down to put them on, and added tightly, "From his description of whatever it is he's searching for, he's very likely to find it, perfect, gentle knight stuffed full of rectitude as he is. There will be no room left for me."

"Don't worry," the queen said, a rare, cold glint in her eyes. "Nothing involving Severen ever had much to do with perfection."

Perdita finished tying her sandals, sat for a moment gazing at them. Memory pursued memory; she retraced them, shod in Calluna's sandals, and remembered what had gotten misplaced in the past chaotic days.

She looked up, found the queen watching her. "What is it?" Genevra asked. "What do you see?"

She had long ago stopped being surprised at her mother's unexpected leaps of perception. "I had a vision," she answered thinly. "In Calluna's cave when I searched it. Under the last images in the stones at the very end of the passage: the goddess's face on one side, and her hands, across the river, letting water spill out of them. I saw Daimon's face, reflected in the river, looking up at her."

The queen drew breath sharply, loosed an imprecation in the general direction of the river god. "My fault," she said harshly. "I told Arden it was long past time to explain to Daimon who his mother was. Apparently—"

"Do you—"

"I don't. I never wanted to know. She died; I never had to live my life wondering who, among those I might meet every day, was Arden's lover and Daimon's mother. Now I want to know."

"That's not all," Perdita said slowly. "Daimon seems to be in love. And very short-tempered about it, as well as secretive."

"Is she married?"

"He said no. He also said—" She hesitated, frowning. "Something that made me realize he knows more about his mother's family—and cares more—than seems likely. We used to tell each other everything. Now he barely talks to me. As if there are things he doesn't want me to know. Or anyone. He leaves the palace through back ways. He seems troubled."

"Enough to draw the attention of the goddess," Genevra said tightly. She stood silently a moment, arms folded, staring at the floor. "Who," she said finally, drawing a solution out of a rumpled turquoise rug, "do we trust to follow him?"

"Me," Perdita said promptly.

"No. I'm not sending another of my children into the wilds of Severluna. We have no idea where he goes. One of the knights, who can fight for him if need be."

"They're going off questing."

"Well, somebody must be questing around Severluna. Is Daimon?"

"I don't know. I'd guess, by the mood he's in, he wouldn't want to tear his heart away from what it wants. What about Sylvester Skelton? He finds lost things. He could watch Daimon in water."

The queen mulled that over a moment, then shook her head. "The goddess has her eye on him; now so do we. Sylvester would tell the king; word would get out. I don't want to intrude so far into Daimon's life that I drive him away. Maybe he can work whatever this is out for himself. For now, I just want to know what it is. And I want him protected."

A figure formed in the princess's memory, clad in antique

shining armor, wheeling a huge broadsword in the air at
Daimon, pinning him down, then smiling genially at him
afterward.

"Dame Scotia Malory."

"Who?"

"I saw her fight, and I met her in Sylvester's tower, reading a book. She's very strong, competent, and she offered her
services to the sanctum if we needed her."

"Really? What made her do that?"

"Something I said. Something she heard that I didn't say."

"Indeed," the queen murmured, her tense face regaining
some of its calm. There was a faint tap at the door then,
followed by a cat scratch; Perdita stood abruptly.

"That would be Aunt Morrig, wondering why I'm not at
my post."

"Go, then," the queen said softly. "I'll send for Dame
Scotia." She opened the door, smiling at the aged, inquisitive
face behind it, peering into the chamber for the missing
sanctum guardian.

Perdita took the customary station in the antechamber,
seated upon a great stone among the smaller, candle-bearing
river rocks taken from Calluna's cave. There, she could
watch both the tower and the inner stairwells for intruders,
the stones for guttering candles, and keep an eye out for
glitches in the movement of waters gliding soundlessly down
the walls. She could, as well, meditate upon the ancient,
powerful face of the goddess on the sanctum wall. She could
also, if so inclined, pay attention to the comings and goings
in and out of the changing chambers along the far wall near
the stairs. She did not see her mother leave. She did see the

tall, graceful young woman in knightly black who came up the inner stairs to knock on the queen's door.

Perdita was waiting for her beyond a curve in the stairwell when Dame Scotia came down.

She put a finger to her lips; Scotia closed her mouth, bowed her head silently, and waited.

"I'm coming with you," the princess whispered.

"The queen warned me you would say that," Dame Scotia said softly.

"Then I'll go alone."

"Prince Daimon hardly knows me, Princess Perdita," the knight answered, her brows crooked doubtfully. "If he sees you, he may take us in circles."

"And you hardly know Daimon. How will you recognize what's important to him? Calluna showed his face to me, in her waters." The princess added, at the knight's silence, "Maybe she knows I can help."

"I may be dedicated to Severen by my status," Scotia said finally, "but I'm not about to argue with the goddess. If Prince Daimon sees us, we can tell him we are questing together: both looking for the same thing for very different reasons."

Perdita heard the sanctum door open and close softly above them. "Lady Seabrook," she breathed. "She's on the prowl this morning. I'll see if Daimon is still in the palace. Meet me at the road nearest the sanctum tower in half an hour."

Dame Scotia went down; the princess went up, rounding the curve just as Morrig appeared at the top.

"I'm here," she said to the elderly, darkly clad figure staring confusedly down at her. "I thought I heard forbidden voices on the stairs."

"That's odd," her great-aunt commented. "So did I."

Instead of her well-known Greenwing, Perdita took one of the fast black sedans out of the garage that the knights donned like a second uniform when they drove. She picked up Dame Scotia and parked on the quiet, tree-lined side roads behind the palace. There they sat, arguing amicably about who should drive, and almost ignoring the sudden streak of black that curved around them, and away. Perdita started the engine hastily.

"He's in uniform," Dame Scotia commented. "I wonder if he's questing."

"He's after something," Perdita agreed. "And he's liable to get stopped for speeding before he finds it. I wonder if he knows we're behind him . . ."

He led them on a long, winding chase through the city, once they left the palace grounds, by way of the truck routes, alleyways, and side streets of Severluna, thoroughly snarling the pathways that Perdita thought she knew so well, and revealing, after she thought she had seen everything at least twice, portions of the city she did not know existed. Some had been frozen in time, streets still cobbled, buildings low, thick-walled, and unfashionably ornate; the cars and buses on them seemed to have wandered in from the future and were involved in a rambling, futile search for the way back. Perdita stubbornly tracked the helmeted figure on the electric bike ahead of her, no matter how frequently he made his turns or how abruptly he sped up and left behind only the memory of where they had seen him last.

She always found him again.

"He's playing us," Scotia said finally, calmly. "I've done that to fish."

"Then why doesn't he just disappear? We must have driven through most of Severluna. If we are still in Severluna. I have no idea where we are. I wonder if even he knows. Now where did he go?"

Finally, the streets grew broader, less congested; the knight on the bike stopped his sudden veering, held a steadier path, as though finally he could see in the distance the object of his search. Intent on him, Perdita scarcely noticed the wealthier neighborhood she drove through, the parklike setting of stately trees, the gently curving streets that held no traffic now, only the strange little hut that appeared in the middle of the road as though it had dropped there from some tale.

"Ah—" Dame Scotia said; Perdita heard the astonishment in her voice.

She braked abruptly. They watched the figure in black speed past the guardhouse without generating any interest whatsoever from the guards chatting outside it.

"Either he's that familiar to them," Perdita said incredulously, "or he's invisible."

The sedan was not; the guards gestured it forward, looking into the tinted windows as the princess neared. They straightened quickly, waved her past. She drove on, her mouth tight, looking for the black-clad cyclist down footpaths, hiding in bushes, though without a thread of hope.

She yielded finally with a sigh, and said to the tactfully silent knight beside her, "All right. He may not know you, but he knows me far too well."

"It seemed a very good idea," Dame Scotia said fairly.

"But how did he know? And why, of all things, did he bother leading us on a wild-goose chase all over the city?" She slowed at another checkpoint, guards standing rigidly as she passed, and wound her way toward the palace garage. "He could have stopped and asked us not to follow. And he could have lost us easily enough a dozen times. What possessed him?" She watched another bike pass them, this one traveling at a more sedate speed. The rider, wearing jeans and boots, and a helmet with a familiar crest on it, did not glance at them as he passed, so intent was he on his own pursuits.

She braked again, sharply. They both turned to stare at his back as he followed a curve out of sight.

"That was Daimon," Perdita said. Her voice shook. "That was the Wyvernbourne crest on his helmet and bike. That was his pale hair."

"Then who—" Dame Scotia exclaimed. The princess turned to meet her amazed eyes. "Who else knew we were going to follow him?"

"No one. No one but you, and I, and the queen."

"Then who did we follow through that tangle of streets? Someone must have known—"

"No one," Perdita whispered. And then she was silent, looking back at the face of her aged, charmingly scattered great-aunt as she watched the princess from the top of the sanctum stairs.

Morrig.

# PART THREE

# KINGFISHER

# 15

Pierce floated out of Severluna with his father and his brother in a black limo the size of a small yacht. It bore them effortlessly northward, surrounding them in a cocoon of soft leather, perfect air, small luxuries of every kind to while away the hours. Beyond its tinted windows, Pierce watched the highway he had driven down in the Metro scant days before. It looked completely different now, as though he saw it through the eyes of someone he barely knew. This strange Pierce unreeled a past to his new family that seemed, compared to theirs, scant of detail, monotonous, inexplicable.

"It took courage," Leith said, "to leave the only place you ever lived. Even more to brave the complexities of Severluna and the court, where you knew no one and neither of us knew you existed."

"It's magical," Val said, sprawled easily along most of a seat and picking out the almonds from a can of roasted nuts.

"If you hadn't done this thing or that, if you had been two fighting squares away from me instead of next to me, if you hadn't announced a style of fighting I'd never heard of—"

Pierce's face burned. "Deli Style fighting. I can't believe I invented that. Lucky for me it was you. Anyone else would have just smeared me into the grass and left me there to be dumped back into the kitchen."

His brother's pale blue eyes flicked at him. "It was perfect. The way you used that knife—"

"You asked me to show you. You spoke to me."

"You used it the way our mother did. You unburied memories."

"You asked my name."

"It was your mother in you," Leith said. "Both of you. You recognized her magic in each other." He reached out, took the can from Val. He shook his head, gazing at his sons as he chewed. "I can't believe the pair of you. I thought I had done only one good thing in my life. Now I find I have done two." He passed the can to Pierce. "Did you talk to Heloise?"

Pierce nodded. Leith waited while he stirred the mix, located a cashew, and ate it. He said finally, "She isn't very happy with me. I think she didn't really expect me to find you. She thought Severluna would terrify me, and I'd run back home. And it did. But I didn't." He paused, added wryly, "I didn't have time to run."

"Does she know that you're with us? Heading north toward the coast highway? Does she expect to see you?"

Pierce shook the can, peered into it, looking for words. "I told her we were traveling north together. I couldn't explain the quest—I wasn't listening very well at the Assembly. She didn't say much. She didn't ask if we would be going as far as Cape Mistbegotten."

Leith shifted. "She wouldn't want to see me, but I'm sure she'd want to see you and Val. Maybe you could—"

"She's a sorceress," Val reminded his father. "We're here with you. We're on a quest, not a vacation. If she wants to, I think she could find us. Though she hasn't exactly made the effort so far." He took the can from Pierce, rattled it, his eyes wide as he gazed into it. "She left me with you and never looked back."

"Maybe that's why she let me go," Pierce said abruptly. "So that I would find you both. She couldn't come looking for you. She is too proud. And too—and too hurt. But now she knows that we are all together. Val is right, I think. She has her ways. If she wants to, she'll use them."

The driver's voice came over the intercom from behind the closed glass partition between them. "Sirs, this is the last largish town before we start climbing. Do you want me to stop somewhere for lunch? Once we get into the mountains, no telling what we'll find."

They stopped.

In the midafternoon, surrounded by mile after mile of huge trees marching up and down peaks and valleys holding only hints of civilization, a glimpse of a door, a sign, an abandoned fuel station, the steadfast vehicle ran aground. One by one screens flicked off, lights failed, the car slowed, drifted. The driver, his cursing becoming audible, got the partition between them half-opened before it, too, stopped moving. A pickup careened around them, honking wildly. They were in the fast lane of a steep, curving, four-lane highway, rapidly losing power and fortunately on a downslope. The driver eased the limo across the road, avoiding the swift cars dodging to the left and right of them. It settled finally onto an unpaved pullout as a semi peeled around them, making a noise like an indignant whale.

The driver spoke to the dashboard. No one answered. He pushed this, flicked that. Val leaned through the partition, making suggestions, while Pierce tried a door, and Leith pulled out his cell.

The door opened, to Pierce's relief, but the phone screen remained black.

The driver pulled off his crested uniform cap, threw it on the floor, then picked it up, put it back on, and turned.

"Sorry, sirs. I don't have a clue what to make of this."

Val looked at his own phone. "It's a dead zone," he said curiously. "Nothing tech works."

"Everyone else is still moving," Leith said tersely. He got out, roamed around the car with his phone.

"Sorcery, then."

"Might as well be," the driver said, exasperated. "This vehicle was thoroughly tested before the wyvern on its hood got a look out the garage door."

He tried his own phone, then got out and waved at passing traffic until a Greenwing small enough to fit in the pullout behind the limo stopped. The driver bent down to talk to the young women in it. Val joined him promptly. Pierce got out, stood looking around, half expecting to see Heloise sitting on a branch above them.

Gigantic pillars of trees stood tranquilly on the steep mountain, maybe napping in the warm, golden light, maybe commenting in slow tree-thoughts on the grand vehicle that had hobbled to a halt in their shadows. In the distance between two high peaks, he glimpsed the sea.

A car door slammed; he glanced around to see Val settling in the midst of the young women in the little car. The car pulled back onto the road, sped away. Leith watched it, startled.

"They said they'd take him to the nearest garage," the driver explained. "Their phones work fine," he added bitterly, as Leith walked to the edge of the road, stood frowning at the Greenwing disappearing around a bend.

"I don't like this."

"They seemed very nice," the driver assured him. "Students on their way back to the local college. I offered to go, but—"

"I know. An otherwise appealing young knight except for his brains. Or lack of them. He was the one who reminded me that we are on a quest. Sylvester Skelton said we must assume nothing."

"I'm sorry, sir," the driver said uneasily. "I thought—"

"Well," Leith said, leaning against the limo beside the tiny bronze wyvern rearing on the hood. "You may be right. We'll wait."

The driver got back inside, tried rousing the engine again. Leith, his arms folded, brooded at the highway. Pierce went looking for a bush.

He walked farther than he intended, lulled by the soft breeze, the smells of needles, pitch, sun-burnished bark, the shadows and gentle whisperings of the immense trees. For the first time since he had left home, he feared nothing, anticipated nothing, just rambled without thinking through the quiet afternoon. A squirrel chided him; a bird sang briefly, then fluttered away, a streak of yellow against the green. He rounded a tree trunk that might have taken a couple dozen arms to span its girth. At the other side of it, he saw the sea again, the brilliant light across it that, in a tale, might have been the blazing wake of a vessel made of gold.

From somewhere in the trees above him there came a sudden, high-pitched scream.

His head snapped around; he took a step uphill and heard a gunshot. He froze. Someone shouted from below: Leith, he thought, but had no time to answer before he began a scrabbling run among the stones and swollen tree roots. The girl cried out again; this time it sounded like a curse. Another shout came, this one from uphill as well. Pierce crashed through a thicket; the ground leveled on the other side of it, trees opening up in a crescent around a strange stone ruin.

Water flowed out from under the ruin, a quick little rill that vanished back underground beneath a brake of ferns. The ruin, three broken walls and an archway, had been built around what looked like a cave in a steep, sudden rise of earth, slabs of stone, more trees.

The voices sounded very close, a tangle of men, the girl crying at them fiercely, rhythmically. Pierce saw the mountain bikes lined along both sides of the dark opening.

All of them carried the familial devices of the Wyvernhold knights.

The girl's voice rose sharply. Pierce looked around wildly for a weapon, saw a lovely glass pitcher lightly chained around its neck to a tree branch above the froth of water.

During the moment it took him to reach it, break it against a stone and turn, armed with a shard of jagged glass attached to the pitcher's handle, some of the confused knot of voices began to break into words.

"Put that down! I'll shoot, I swear—"

"All weapons belong to Severen—you can't shoot us. Just put it down—"

"You put that down!"

"This is holy ground. We are Knights of the Rising God on a quest in King Arden's name, and this gold mine is dedicated to Severen—"

"This old shaft is as empty as your heads, you assholes; it went dead a hundred years ago!"

"If you'll just listen—"

"Put that down, too! This is Tanne's holy ground, not Severen's, and I swear—"

There was an odd snick of metal that Pierce associated with weapons in very old movies. He plunged into the ruins, wielding his broken glass in the air, and found an elderly man with white hair down his back swaying on his knees and trying to pull himself upright. His eyes widened at the sight of Pierce and his weapon. He threw himself sideways to grasp at some kind of long-handled implement. Pierce moved quickly through the ruins and into the open earth beyond them, the mouth of an old shaft crisscrossed with miners' lights, young men's faces flaring and disappearing as they roamed, and rummaged, and the girl cursed them in the constantly shifting shadows.

One turned headlamp illumined her face finally: a young, freckled oval, narrowed gray eyes beneath flaming red brows, lips pared thin as thread with fury.

Then she vanished as light drenched Pierce's face, then flashed across the broken pitcher.

Pierce heard her gasp. A thundering boom sent dirt scattering down from the ceiling. There was a tortured groan from very old timber. All of the headlamps pointed up.

The world went black.

When Pierce's eyes flickered open, he saw the spare, freckled face again. He felt water misting over him instead of the dry dust of centuries. He made a sound, and Leith shifted into view, crouched beside him, Pierce realized, under sky and trees, not earth and rotting boards. The empty chain that had held the pitcher swung aimlessly above his head.

"I'll give you a drink, but you'll have to take it from my hands," the girl said dourly. "You broke my pitcher."

That, Pierce thought, would explain her disgruntled expression. He tried to speak, then nodded. Leith held up his head; the girl cupped her hands in the bright rill, and he opened his mouth.

He drank the pure, cold water falling from her fingertips three times before he could finally speak.

"Sorry," he croaked. "I needed a weapon." He paused a moment, remembering. "Did you shoot everyone?"

"No. But they didn't wait around for the ceiling to make up its mind." The frown on her face was easing; she added, "I thought you were one of them when I saw the broken pitcher. They were taking things—small, sacred things we keep in there—looking at them with their unholy lights, then just tossing them on the ground. Searching for gold, I think, though they kept yammering about something sacred belonging to Severen."

"Can you sit up?" Leith asked, and helped him. The world whirled, then slowed and steadied. He felt at the back of his aching head, wondering if one of the mineshaft timbers had swung down and smacked him. Sitting, he saw the old man finally, with his white hair and his beard down to his belt. There was not much room for expression on his hairy face, but his eyes were rueful.

"Sorry," he said. "I thought you were one of them, too. You're all dressed alike but for the emblems. Sir Leith here explained who you are."

"What hit me?" Pierce asked bewilderedly.

"My garden shovel."

"Oh." He sighed, his eyes going to Leith. "So much for knightly prowess. Armed with a pitcher and felled with a garden tool."

"You should have— You should never have—" Leith began, then gave up, shaking his head.

"It was very brave of you to try," the girl said staunchly. "My grandfather tried to stop them. They just threw his crutch over the wall and let him fall. He has a bad knee."

"Where— What is this place?"

"It's Tanne's shrine."

"Tanne."

She gestured at the crescent of enormous, hoary trees around the ruins, so tall their lofty tips seemed to lean together as their great boughs stretched toward the sky. A rosy wave swept up her face, making her red hair, glowing in the sunlight, even more fiery. "This is his forest. My grandfather has been the shrine guardian here all of his life since he was twelve. This old shrine was built thousands of years before anybody discovered the gold behind it. The miners ran that guardian out and let the shrine fall down while they took out all the gold. Now travelers come to see the ruins and fill their bottles with water fresh out of the earth. But nobody remembers the forest god. People born here pass the tales along. When my grandfather can't climb up here any longer, then one of our family will take his place."

"You?"

She shrugged, almost smiling at the thought. "Maybe. Tanne chooses. Sometimes with a dream. Sometimes, if the wind is just right, the one who is chosen hears him call."

"He called me," the old man said. "I heard him clear as an owl's cry, and I came. Up every morning, down the hill at sunset by myself for decades until my knee gave out and Sara here came along to help me." He looked at her fondly, added, "I had no idea you could shoot that thing."

"Neither did I. We found it in the cave," she explained. "I think some miner left it there a hundred years ago." Her smile deepened with satisfaction. "Now we know it works."

"Forgive the knights if you can," Leith said grimly. "Nothing they did here was sanctioned by King Arden, who has deep respect for all the gods and goddesses of Wyvernhold. Those young men are arrogant louts on an idiotic quest; their behavior here was despicable and cowardly, and I'm sorry not to have come in time to make that clear to them." He paused, gazing at Pierce, his expression still dark. "I am enormously grateful you did not shoot my impulsive son. My other impulsive son."

"Oh," she sighed, "me, too."

"You have another?" the old man said, surprised. "He didn't come running to help?"

"He went off in a car full of young women to look for a garage. No telling when we'll see him again."

"A garage."

"Our car is stalled on the road below. It shut itself down for its own reasons; our driver can't get it started again, and none of our phones work either."

The old man raised a shaggy brow, musing a bit. "Everything just went dead?"

"Everything."

"For no reason."

"None."

"Well." He scratched his head and smiled a little; above him tree boughs swayed and spoke in a wind from the sea. "That happens, sometimes, around the shrine. On the odd occasion—rare, mind you—that the forest senses it might need some help. Go down and try your car again," he added, as Pierce and Leith stared wordlessly at him. "It may have cured itself by now."

When they reached the bottom of the hill, the limo engine was gently idling, and the tow truck from which Val had emerged was on its way back down the mountain.

# 16

Carrie sat with Zed in his narrow bed, sharing a bottle of wine and the events of their long days. It was past midnight. Zed had come home from the Pharaoh Theater; Carrie had stayed late with Ella, scrubbing the hoary kitchen floors. Around them, the small cabin was a shadowy mix of candlelight and camp lantern. Thrown together as a duck blind, remodeled into a rental with the world's tiniest kitchen, it still smelled of damp logs, and occasionally sprouted a mushroom. A potbellied stove, one broken leg on a brick, exuded the scent of damp ash. There was an actual braided rug on the splintery floor. Outside, the night itself was soundless, no weather and a sky so clear the lace of streams through the long grasses ran with moonlight instead of water. The slough made its own noises: hooting, rustling, grunting, and peeping. Distant car engines mingled with the constant musings of the sea. Carrie's ears sorted through every noise, pricked for the sound of Merle's voice.

"What is he, anyway?" she wondered. "Magic?"

"Merle?"

"I always thought he was just demented. My mother always said so. But no matter how crazy you want to be, you can't turn yourself into a wolf without knowing something more than most. Where did he learn it?"

"There's magic around."

"Not in Chimera Bay."

"There's Merle," Zed said. "There's the Friday Nite ritual. There's mystery in that old hotel."

She poured herself more wine, took a hefty swallow. "There's Stillwater."

Zed looked at her silently, quizzically; in that moment, she made up her mind about what she had been pondering since the afternoon she had walked into Stillwater's restaurant to talk to him and got a glimpse of something in his face too old to be still alive and human at the same time. *Eat*, he had said.

"And I did," she said hollowly.

"What?"

She stirred, getting her thoughts in order, what to tell, what not to so that he wouldn't worry. "I told you that Stillwater wants me to work for him."

"Yeah."

"So when I went to talk to him about it—just to talk—he offered me samples of his cooking. Little, complicated layers of color and texture, so wonderful to look at, you don't want to eat it, and at the same time, you imagine how much more wonderful all those colors could taste, all at once in your mouth. Like a sweet explosion of fireworks, like edible music. So I ate." She reached for her glass, took a sip to reassure herself that she still had taste buds. "That beautiful little piece of art, food jewelry—it tasted like nothing. Mist. Not even sea mist. That has a bite of salt in it. Just cloud. Just. Nothing." She drank again. "So of course I ate another. And another, since whatever was wrong must have been in me, not in those perfect Stillwater bites. He must have known. I kept eating, trying to taste, and he just kept smiling. He has the most wonderful—"

"You keep saying."

"Anyway, I think I ate everything in sight. Or I would have, except that his wife came in with her arms full of groceries, and we got up to help her. She seemed nice. Friendly. Really beautiful, of course; you'd expect that, since she's married to a Greek myth—"

"Yeah, yeah."

"When I left them, I still wanted more. More little beautiful bites of nothing."

"So are you going to work for him?"

"Yes. I have to. He's the only piece of the mystery around the Kingfisher Inn that will talk to me."

Zed shifted closer to her, put his arm around her. "Be careful," he pleaded.

She nodded, whittling another half inch off the scant distance left between them, then another, after she put her glass on the floor and let the hollow in the old mattress cant them together.

"I intend to," she said somberly. "I don't know what he is, I don't know what my father's afraid of, I don't know what Ella hates, and I have no idea if I'm capable of figuring out all the whys of everything. I can't imagine why Stillwater cooks like that. Or why my father can turn into a wolf. I need to stop thinking like me and start thinking like them."

"How?"

She looked at him silently, studying the sweet, caramel brown of his eyes, while she contemplated mysteries going back farther than she did, back under the magnificent chandelier in the days when every prism flamed with light. "Stillwater lies even with his cooking; my father refuses to tell the truth. Where? Where does that story begin?" She turned her head, held Zed's eyes. "I will fry fish for Ella," she told him fiercely. "I will eat Stillwater's not-cooking, I will learn wolf and howl back at my father if that's the only way I can talk to him. I want to understand this story if that's the last thing I do. If nobody's talking, I'll find a new way of listening. If nobody's talking, then nobody can say no."

She went to work for Todd Stillwater during her hours off at the Kingfisher: lunches on Tuesdays and Thursdays, and dinner on Wednesdays. She did not so much as whisper to a soup pot or tell a fork in Ella's kitchen that she was cooking for Stillwater. She kept the word "water" out of her head when she took Hal's daily note up to Lilith. She avoided even looking out the window at the bay. Chowder, she thought. Butter, cream, clams. Onion cheddar biscuits. Endless sizzling fries. The sudden flick of storm-green glances Lilith sent her way hinted that she suspected something. But for once in her life, Carrie was doing the not-talking, as though her life depended on it. She babbled randomly instead, about Zed, about the aging pickup truck, about the old fruit trees and vines the early farmers had left behind still alive and blossoming again. When Lilith pressed her about Merle, she drew upon old memories: he had left her a seashell, laundry, a wild lily in a beer bottle; she had heard him singing deep in the woods at midnight.

Except when she glimpsed him brooding at her in the Kingfisher bar, she had no idea what he was doing, or thinking, or where, or in what shape, he slept. He knew what she had done. She knew he knew. Neither one of them was talking.

The first of the questing knights came at the beginning of a Friday Nite Fish Fry. Carrie walked out of the kitchen holding the huge cauldron full of steaming oyster stew with tiny crackers buttered and broiled to a crisp floating like gold coins on top of it. She heard their voices break the traditional silence, the worship of smells, before she saw them. She glanced across the room toward the sound, found a cluster of noisy, muscular, handsome men, all of them dressed in black. They were laughing, she realized incredulously; they were joking about the peculiar backwater ceremony going on in the dilapidated old inn.

Hal did not waste a glance at them. He simply stopped, leaning on his staff, gazing ahead. The line behind him, Father Kirk with the bloodstained gaff, Merle carrying the salmon on the gold platter, Carrie, all stopped. The diners gathered for supper stood silently in their places, waiting. Through the swinging doors that Curt Sloan and his son Gabe held open, Carrie heard not a whisper, a step, a clatter from inside the kitchen.

The laughter thinned, died away. Carrie recognized the uniforms then, the little heraldic shields embroidered on their jackets. One of the young men looked at Tye, behind the bar.

Tye said before the knight could speak, "Bar's closed."

"Private party," another man murmured, and asked Tye, "Could you tell us—"

"Try Stillwater's," Tye said without compunction, and stood unblinking, hands flat on the bar, until the young men finally drifted toward the door and out.

Hal spoke then, smiling, welcoming the gathering to supper.

My father knows what all this means, Carrie thought coldly, as she carried the cauldron back into the kitchen to ladle out its contents. He won't tell me.

Maybe, she thought later, bringing the cleaned and polished cauldron back to the bar to be locked away, Stillwater knows. Maybe he'll tell me.

"It's nothing," Stillwater said, when she asked him about the ritual a few days later. "A family thing. You know how families are. Always looking back, doing things the way they were always done, acquiring habits, ceremonies over the years. Actually, if I were making that choice, I wouldn't put that in there."

Actually, Carrie didn't say, I have no idea how families are, and neither do you. "That" was a lemon, and "there" was one of Stillwater's many odd kitchen tools, machines of various sizes with no obvious ways of behaving.

"Sorry," she said. "I thought it was the slicer."

He opened a drawer, took out a paring knife. "This works."

He had an extremely eccentric kitchen; the small stove and a blender were among the few things she recognized. He did nearly everything in his collection of machines. He showed her how to fry an egg in one, to roast a parsnip in another, to fashion a seven-layer cupcake, complete with a lovely ribbon of frosting tied in a bow on top, in something that looked like a martini shaker.

"Forget everything you know here," he advised. "Experiment. Invent. Create. That's why I built these."

She spent the first working hours doing just that: tossing food at random into his inventions just to see what would happen. She turned a red onion into ice cream, a potato into sea foam, bread into what looked like curly shoe leather; she made sequins and stars out of radishes, frothed an egg yolk, then deep-fried the froth into a golden lace. She found herself eating constantly, licking a finger or a spoon handle, desperate for a taste of anything besides air. Sage wandered in occasionally to nibble Carrie's experiments, give critical comments about how something looked, make suggestions about what to pair. Now and then, she said simply, warmly, "Yes. That's good. Todd was right about you."

"It's nothing," Carrie said helplessly.

"No, no. It's wonderful."

Maybe, she thought, lying beside Zed and listening to him breathe in rhythm with the sea, that's what magic is. Believing that nothing is something.

"You haven't been cooking the way you used to," Ella commented wistfully as they prepped for the next day's lunch. "I miss your tidbits. Your little bites."

Carrie looked at her, surprised. She seemed to be inventing all the time, coming up with this and that, plate jewelry, edible ornaments. But that was for Todd Stillwater, she remembered; she had neglected them in this kitchen, where every tool and recipe was predictable.

"I forgot," she said lamely. "I've been distracted, I guess."

"Something worrying you?"

Carrie shook her head, speechless. Working two jobs, skulking to Stillwater's three times a week, trying to find her father, deceiving Ella, hiding her thoughts from the scarily perceptive Lilith, had put her beyond worry. Maybe that was why she was hungry all the time, at least at Stillwater's. Here, she barely remembered to eat.

"Not more than usual." She whacked at celery for the soup of the day, the old workhorse chicken-veg. She never chopped vegetables in Stillwater's kitchen, she realized. If he served soup at all, it would be in the form of a custard, maybe, or a cone of little frozen pearls. She made an effort, shoved his kitchen out of her mind. "I'll come up with something today," she promised, and later, she combined several things lying around in such a fashion that there were visible signs, on many plates, of bites that had been spat back out.

"You've got some serious weirdness going on here," Jayne declared, eating Carrie's creation. "I like anchovies. I just never knew I liked them with sweet pickles before." She swallowed and added, "There are knights at one of my tables. Three of them, from Severluna. I had to explain what a shrimp basket is. What's with these knights coming through Chimera Bay? Are they all lost?"

"Maybe someone's making a movie," Bek suggested, hefting a tray of plates to his shoulder.

"You're probably right," Jayne said, absently munching more anchovy bites. "Real knights can't all be that gorgeous."

They were that gorgeous in Carrie's dream that night: they all had Stillwater's face. The knights had gathered in the Kingfisher Inn to watch the solemn ritual Fish Fry. Women from an era of crimped hair, red lipstick, heart-shaped bodices, full skirts made of satin and chiffon accompanied the knights. The high-hatted chef led the ritual, holding a great platter of beautiful little bites. He carried it around the room, offering it to the richly dressed, smiling women, to the knights who all looked alike, to Hal and Merle, who wore their tuxedos, to Ella, even to Lilith, who had come down from her tower to join the merry gathering.

Everyone ate. The platter never emptied; more and more bites appeared and disappeared. Colors in the dream began to flicker, vanish, return. The rich hues of women's gowns paled, melted into grays and whites and blacks of old photos. People kept talking, laughing, even as one by one lights in the chandelier went dark. Airy skirts began to tear, part into shreds; high-heeled sandals vanished, left the women barefoot. Their glittering diamonds winked out like the prisms above them. The knights' beautiful faces became hollow, haggard, even as they kept eating. The walls of the prosperous inn grew thin; moonlight came through them, and the sound of the gulls. Here and there a rafter fell. Still the party, the celebration, continued, as if nothing were wrong, nothing at all, everyone talking, laughing, eating from the chef's inexhaustible platter, even though shadows crept over the walls, and Lilith had vanished, and so had Hal, leaving a crippled old man in his place, leaning painfully on a staff, and beside him, Merle turned into a wolf.

The wolf opened its jaws, howled.

Carrie sat up in bed, knowing even before she opened her eyes that the wolf was at the door. She stumbled through the farmhouse, flung the door open, and saw the lovely, silvery lines of streams growing dark, lifeless, as the stars blanked out, one by one, and the darkness swirling over them reached out toward the moon.

She opened her mouth, heard herself howl with the wolf as the moon began to disappear.

She woke and heard the wolf at the door.

This time she rolled out of Zed's bed and tripped over the brick under the broken stove leg, so she knew that she was finally awake. She heard Zed moving behind her, muttering drowsily until he tripped over the same brick and cursed.

Carrie threw open the door and saw moonlight drenching everything in a misty glow, burning the tidal strands running through the grasses, the dark and bright mystery of living water flowing out of the hidden source within the trees, the silent, glowing hills.

The moon's ancient, beautiful face, her spangled fingers of light, the streams milky with her reflection, the glittering air all but transparent over the distant, luminous source stunned Carrie. As she stood on the threshold of the night, she heard the song of the wolf within the eerie light transform itself in her ears.

It was not the language of fear, she realized, but the language of love.

And then she saw her father, in the meadow under the soft touch of moonlight, changing into shape after shape in an intricate dance of power, or the constant folding and refolding of life in all its variations. Man became wolf became deer became hare became bear became cougar became porcupine became salmon leaping out of the water, became white heron became owl, soundless in the transfixed eye of the moon. Then owl became man, hair and long beard of moonlight, tall, hale, and older than time. Then man became Merle, her father, the shape she knew.

She swallowed fire; she was shaking; she tasted tears catching in her smile. Zed put an arm around her, held her tightly.

The man became raven, followed the path of the moon into night.

# 17

On the narrow coast road beyond the ancient forest, a mountain face covered with trees on one side, and a long craggy drop to the sea on the other, the limo rounded a curve and drove straight into a blinding wall of fog.

It was so thick, the world vanished. Pierce could not see so much as a weed in a ditch beside the road. He could not, he realized, see the road. Even the little wyvern ornamenting the long hood of the limo wavered in and out of the sluggishly drifting fog. The driver slowed to a sudden caterpillar crawl, causing Val to pull out his earbuds, and Leith to blink the abrupt nothingness out of his eyes and channel the intercom.

"This is not good."

Pierce stared incredulously at the nothing and waited for the strike from behind, the beginning of the pileup along the steep, two-lane highway.

"Shall I try to back up, sir?"

"Mist," Val observed with seemingly pointless interest, as though it were a hitherto mythical sea creature.

"No," Leith said tersely. "Don't back up."

"I think you should get out, sirs. I'll keep inching along. I think now, sirs, would be a good time for you to get out."

"So do I," Val said, and promptly opened a door. It scraped against something invisible, but left room for him to slither out. Leith motioned for Pierce to follow; Pierce hesitated.

"You're coming, too," he said.

"Yes. In a moment. Go," he added, and Pierce moved finally, reluctantly, out of the car and into the cloud. It was annoyingly damp and chilly, oddly silent as well, he noticed, then realized why.

"I can't hear the waves," he said to the fraying figure of his brother, whose red hair was the most visible thing left of him.

"No," Val agreed. "Fascinating, isn't it?"

"It's fog," Pierce protested. "It's blinding, it's dangerous, it is not fascinating. And where's our father? Did he get out of the limo? Where is the limo?"

"Mist," Val said again, a point of argument so pointless that Pierce ignored it.

He turned restively, trying to spot Leith, trying to see the car, listening for the inevitable collision of traffic, tires screaming, metal accordion-pleating against the rear end of the limo. He heard nothing, not even the cry of a gull. He took a few steps, one hand out to feel the trees he could not see: a steep slope full of them, tall, thick pillars of red whose green boughs stretched out endlessly, greedily, to gather up the cloying, obscuring wet.

They were all apparently receding from him as he moved. The ground that should have been running sharply uphill was simply lying there, no matter which way he turned, flat and vaguely rocky underfoot. He heard something finally: his own heartbeat, uncomfortably loud, as if the fog had pushed powerful, invisible hands against his ears.

"Val?" he said, suddenly without much hope of an answer. He had wandered out of the world he recognized, leaving even Val and their father behind, along with his sight, his hearing, and, once again, any kind of a weapon.

He heard an inhuman snort, an answer to his call, as though he had awakened something within the fog. He froze, hoping it would go back to sleep. A stone skittered across the ground. Something enormous yawned, sucking in mist; it swirled, ebbed toward the indrawn breath for a long time, it seemed, before fog blew back out again, accompanied by an odd smell of charred, damp wood.

Pierce stopped breathing. His skin grew colder than the fog. The fire-breathing cousin of the wyvern was, unlike the extinct wyvern, a myth. It had inspired a rich hoard of tales in early Wyvernhold history, especially those illuminating the prowess of legendary questing knights. It was a fantasy, a symbol, no more than that. At least it should have been.

He heard the dragon's voice.

*Pierce.*

He caught a breath, coughed on cold, ash-soured air. The deep voice seemed to resonate from the stones buried beneath the earth; Pierce felt it underfoot, heard it with his bones. The constantly shifting mist frayed just enough to give him a glimpse of an outline paler than the mist: an enormous, crested neck, a lizard's maw trickling smoky mist out of nostrils the size of platters and ringed with a red, pulsing glow.

*Go no farther. You are not welcome in the north.*

"I'm— We're just on our way to Chimera Bay," Pierce stammered. "Only that far. At least for now."

*No.*

He cudgeled his brain a moment, trying to remember any scrap of story that gave him a clue about how to talk to dragons. Mostly, he guessed, there was not a lot of talking, just fire and gore. He gave up, asked baldly, "Why not?"

The mist flamed in front of him; he felt the warmth, smelled the harsh, dry dragon's breath.

*You have chosen. Come no closer. This is my world.*

He blinked and recognized the cold encircling him, the soundless, invisible landscape, the baleful dragon: the heart of the matter. Val had seen it, felt it, immediately.

Mistbegotten.

"Mom?" he whispered, and the dragon roared.

That cleared the air, though Pierce, dropped and clinging to earth under the weight of the vast, endless, reverberating thunder, didn't notice until the sound growled and echoed away into the distance. He raised his head cautiously, opened his eyes, and heard the plaintive cry of gulls, the surge and break of the waves.

"Pierce!" his father called, and he got up, brushing away the needles that clung to him, dropped from the finally visible trees.

He stumbled downhill, saw the limo across the road, waiting in a viewing area overlooking the sea. Val and Leith stood with their backs to the water, trying to find Pierce among the thick, silent ranks of giants climbing up the mountainside.

"I'm here," he said, reaching the road, still feeling the smoldering glare of invisible dragon between his shoulder blades. Its thunder echoed in his heartbeat, his blood. The mist clung to his skin like the touch of the sorceress's hand. He wondered if even his shadow had turned pale.

As he crossed the road to the overlook, he saw Leith's face grow tight, his brows knot. Val's normally unruffled expression mutated into an odd wariness.

"Mist," he said for the third time, and Pierce nodded wearily. Leith's eyes flicked between them.

"What?" he demanded. "What was up there? What happened to you? You look white as a ghost. You're shivering."

"Ah—" Pierce said, and stuck. One angry parent seemed more than enough. But this was between the two of them, he remembered; the seeds of the dragon's wrath had been sown before he was born. "She—ah—she doesn't want to see us. Any of us. She thinks that's why we're travelling north. I must not have explained things very well when we talked."

Leith took a step closer, his hands tightening. "What did she do to you?"

"She roared at me."

"She what?"

"Well, it probably wasn't her. It was her making. Her illusion. I couldn't see it too well in that mist. But it was huge, and it smelled like burning embers, and it made a noise like a mountain blowing its top."

"Dragon." Val's face had gone pale, but it had lost its

tension; his eyes, vivid with sudden comprehension, nar-rowed at his father. "She still loves you," he said incredu-lously, and Leith's face flamed as though the dragon's fire had scorched it.

"I doubt that her passion has anything to do with love at this point," he said brusquely.

Val gazed quizzically at him, looking unconvinced. Pierce, remembering his last evening with his mother, the fierce anger in her that had shaped flames, that had shaped tears, wondered at his brother, who could draw such conclu-sions out of a seemingly impenetrable mist.

He said uncertainly, "Maybe you should talk?"

Leith spread his arms wordlessly, dropped them. "She doesn't want to see me. You just said." He turned abruptly, walked back to the limo, then paused before he opened the door. He spoke again, his back to them. "She told me as much the last time I saw her, before you were born. From what I understand of quests, we go where they lead." Val opened his mouth, promptly closed it again. Leith added, as though he had taken the unspoken point, "It led us here. Yes. But was that the quest, or was that your mother interrupting it? Let's get back on the road, see where it takes us next."

Not far, Pierce saw with disbelief. They might as well be walking, considering how difficult it had become to move just a few scant miles along the road. They had passed through an elegant little resort town with wide beaches and monolithic rocks crusted with sea life wandering in and out of the tide, when the town's four lanes dwindled again into two, then into none. The limo came to a halt at the end of a long line of traffic curving along the water and disappearing around the next bend.

"Sorry, sirs," the driver announced upon consultation with his dash. "Both lanes are blocked up ahead for nearly a mile. They don't know how long before the road is cleared." He paused, listening again. "They're—ah—they're advising people to turn around, catch another road back in town that runs through the hills around the—ah, the—ah—problem."

He sounded oddly shaken. Leith asked, "What exactly is the problem?"

"Seems to be a mythological beast in the middle of the road, sir."

Val ducked instantly over his cell phone, working rapidly. Leith closed his eyes briefly, opened them, and said grimly, "Which beast?"

"Ah—they're not sure, sir. The fire department managed to get some trucks through from the next town before traffic got too tangled. They tried to chase it away with hoses and sirens. The beast is sitting on top of one of the trucks. They've sent a photo to the Royal Herald in Severluna."

"I've got it," Val said briefly, and held it up.

Pierce broke their mystified silence. "It looks like a snake with a rooster's head."

"Basilisk," Val murmured, entranced by the vision, the enormous, upright coils balanced between the fire-truck ladders; the fiery cockscomb fanning the fowl's head above its huge, open beak; the visible eye, round, golden, with a mad red flame in its center. "Isn't there something weird about the basilisk's eye? Oh, here it is, in the Royal Herald's description. Its look can kill." He paused; his brows went up. "So can its breath."

"I doubt that your mother is planning to kill anyone," Leith protested. "Except maybe me."

"I've been eyeballing the situation, sir," the driver said over the intercom. "I'm fairly certain I can get the limo turned around soon. There's a wide bit in the road ahead, and we're creeping closer to it as more cars ahead are turning for the detour."

"It's probably just another illusion," Pierce guessed. "It won't hurt anyone, and it can't get hurt."

"No," Leith said abruptly. Val looked at him, his eyes narrowed.

"No, which, sir?" the driver asked.

"No, don't turn. Stay in line." He reached across Pierce, opened the door, and stepped out. "And you stay here," he told his sons.

"But—" Val began.

"You told me to talk to her."

"But what if it's not her? I mean, not her making?" Pierce argued. "I might be wrong about that."

"It hasn't done anything more dangerous than commandeer a fire truck. Besides, what are the odds that two mythological beasts appear along the same road within half an hour of each other, and they're not from the same source?"

"What if it's not sorcery?" Val asked simply, balancing halfway out the door behind Leith. "Do you know how to kill a basilisk?"

"Look it up," Leith said shortly. "Call me and let me know how if I get into trouble."

"I think you should—"

"I think this is my fight and not yours." He pushed against the limo door until Val yielded, shifted back, and Leith closed it. "My fault, my affair, and my basilisk. Find your own mythological beast."

They waited until he had glanced back once, several cars ahead of them, before they followed him.

Val slipped an assortment of chains, sticks, and metal balls into various hidden pockets, along with the small, deadly Wyvern's Eye. Pierce, blankly considering his own arsenal, pulled the kitchen knife out of his pack. Val showed him one of the sheaths sewn into his jacket lining. The driver stuck his fist out the window as they passed, and raised his thumb.

"Good luck, sirs. Be careful."

They did not have to walk far before they saw the beast.

Its body, uncoiled, would have been longer than two or three fire trucks. Its head, with its blazing frill of cockscomb and the great wheels of its eyes, was raised, alert, over the front end of the truck, peering out of one eye, then the other, at the people milling around it with weapons, news cameras, cell phones. Leith, walking toward it on the opposite side of the road, was half-hidden by the idling vehicles. The fire truck the beast had landed on was angled across the road, stopping traffic in both directions. Its former occupants had abandoned it hastily, judging from the wide-open doors. A man spoke into a bullhorn, trying to persuade people back into their cars. They ignored him; so did the beast.

"I wonder if it knows—" Val started, then answered himself. "Of course it knows we're here if it's our mother's making. That's why it appeared."

"It's another message for us," Pierce said tightly. "She knows we didn't listen to the dragon. Maybe I should call her."

"A basilisk with a phone?"

"She's probably at home in Desolation Point, watching us in water, or in the mist, or in a pot of chicken soup or something. I had no idea she could make anything like this. I had no idea—" He paused, added heavily, "I'm glad I didn't know. It wouldn't have been so easy to think of leaving her."

"Maybe she didn't know either," Val suggested. "Maybe she was never this angry before." He sounded unusually somber. Pierce glanced at him, and he added, "I haven't seen her since I was a child. I've been with my father most of my life. She doesn't have a reason to think that I care about her. That I even remember her. You, at least, she knows she loves."

"She's mad at me, too."

"Only by default. You're with us."

Pierce started to reply, didn't. He had no idea any longer what their mother might do or not do. He watched Leith, who was hidden from the basilisk's eye by a long moving van. He reached the end of it, and the strange, upright coils of the snake's body rippled suddenly. Its head turned almost completely sideways, staring down at the man walking toward it, visible now beside a small convertible with its top down. The driver, in the shadow of the beast's oddly tilted head, dropped his cell and tried to crawl under the dash.

"That is the weirdest combination of creatures imaginable," Val said, wonderstruck anew. "A variation of the feathered serpent, maybe? I wonder if it crows."

"I think," Pierce said uneasily, "we're about to find out."

The huge beak was opening wide above Leith. Weapons

appeared in open windows: Wyvern's Eyes, hunting rifles, bows. Leith shouted something; so did the man with the bullhorn. Leith moved to the middle of the empty lane, walked down it in full view of the basilisk. Behind him, cars stopped in the middle of their turns, transfixed by the knight on foot challenging the monster on top of the fire engine. One of the trucks let out an ear-piercing wail, an effort to distract it, Pierce guessed. Val moved impulsively from behind the line of vehicles to walk behind his father. The snake's coils shuddered again all down the long body. The rooster beak answered the fire truck with a fierce, shrill cross between a rooster crow and a snake's hiss that must have shaken windows all along the highway. Then it caught sight of Pierce emerging behind his brother.

The basilisk's beak opened again. It made no sound this time. It enveloped Leith in a cloud of breath that was black, completely opaque, and stank of such acrid bitterness that a flock of starlings flying overhead rained down suddenly among the fire trucks.

The whiff Pierce caught made him gag, forced tears into his eyes. He heard children screaming and crying, people coughing and cursing all around him. He moved blindly, bumped into Val, who was bent over and throwing up his lunch. Pierce wiped his burning eyes with his sleeve, blinked vision desperately back into them, taking in dry, shallow breaths through his mouth.

When he could finally see again, the basilisk had vanished, leaving its cloud of appalling breath for the sea winds to shred. The body of his father, his blurred eyes told him, lay motionless on the road.

Pierce staggered toward him, still hearing sobs, moans, convulsive noises all around him. Those nearest the basilisk were dazed, hunched over and stumbling into the trucks, or tripping over one another. No one had yet come to the aid of the fallen knight. Pierce reached Leith finally, dropped to his knees. He put a hand on Leith's chest, felt his heartbeat, then the breath move through him. Val staggered next to him, sagged down. He couldn't speak; he queried Pierce with a bloodshot stare.

"He's breathing," Pierce told him. "I don't see anything broken or bleeding. I think he just fainted."

"Felled by the basilisk's breath," Val muttered hoarsely. "He'll never live that down." He held Leith's shoulder, shook him gently. "Father? Are you in there? It's safe. The beast is gone. Come back. Sir Leith Duresse. We need you. Please come back."

Leith showed no signs of doing so. Val gave Pierce another haggard glance, then looked around helplessly at the still-afflicted fire crew.

A shadow fell over Leith. Pierce raised his head and found the most beautiful woman he had ever seen in his life standing over them.

She was speaking, he realized belatedly, still half-stunned, as flowers, pearls, jewels, fell from her full, rose-petal lips.

"My house is just up that drive." She motioned toward a palatial estate on the cliff above them. "We've been watching the excitement from our deck. My driver can help you carry him to my car. The drive is clear of traffic, and he can wait for the paramedics in my guest room. I think it would be much quicker than waiting for an ambulance trying to get through this. Will you let us help you?"

Val was trying to tell him something, Pierce sensed. His wide-eyed, insistent gaze, his two-handed grip on their father, his alert, motionless warrior's stance, all spoke, all said the last thing Pierce wanted to hear.

Pierce said, "Yes."

# 18

Daimon rode through the streets of Severluna, paying no attention to where he was going. Where didn't matter anymore: every street would take him there.

"Our world," his great-aunt told him, "is always just a step away from anywhere. Don't bother looking for it. You are already there in your heart."

That much was true: he felt the moon-tug of that realm, the tidal pull of it overwhelming the kingdom of the wyvern, until very little of that world seemed important any longer. He lost the need of it, except in necessary ways: the place he went for clothes and food; the place where he was occasionally expected to appear, talk to faces that he remembered vaguely, in a dreamlike fashion. As in dreams, they were losing predictability; he was losing hold of their past. He saw them as from a distance: the queen who had never been his mother, the king who looked at him through wyvern's eyes and knew nothing of the raven, the princess who fretted over him but no longer knew him, anything about him at all.

He had thought that the fay realm of Ravenhold was a dream; he learned that Wyvernhold was the unreal world. Its magic had fragmented; few possessed it. Every moment of its days was time-bound, counted, measured; the end of time was not forever, but death, and death waited every-where, in every shadow.

"Silly way to live," Morrig said. "What's the point of being so tidy you can't see beyond the rules you've made for every-thing? Look at this world instead." He could see it now, as she and Vivien and his mother had taught him: the lovely, timeless place hidden within the noisy, jangling, quarrelsome, troubled world where even the wyverns were nothing now except a word. "Once our true realm ran from one horizon to the other, from day to night; you could move from one end to the other with a wish. A step. What Sylvester Skelton calls his magic flamed in every blade of grass, every flowering tree. Now, time gets in the way. It scattered us; we withered in it, even those of us closest to being human. The world of the wyvern king trampled us without even knowing we exist. We need our cauldron to remake our world. Find it."

"Find it," his mother pleaded.

"Find it," Vivien said, always with a kiss, "for us."

"Where are you these days?" his father asked, startling Daimon on his way out. No one really knew him anymore, so why would anyone pay attention to what he did? "You drift in and out like a ghost; your body is here, but your eyes never are. And then you vanish entirely, and I think you've followed the path of the questing knight. Then you're back; you've gone nowhere at all, except that you've never left the place you think you come home from." Daimon, his mind in the wyvern's world at that moment, saw the wariness in his father's eyes. "Who is she?"

"No one," Daimon told him, feeling the long, powerful flow and drag on his heart, the summons of the invisible on the verge of becoming visible if he took that step, that leap. "I'll get over it," he added, absently, words his father wanted to hear. "Just give me time."

As he learned how to see into that timeless place, he learned more of its past.

It was a piecemeal process: he never knew what he would see, or when it might have happened; as in dreams, there was no past, only now.

He parked his bike at a crossroad, took a step, and Severluna vanished. The broad meadow where the Calluna River found its way into light surrounded him. What he thought was the sun flashed on the horizon. But his shadow lay in front of him; a twin sun above him illumined the vast flow of green around him. The second star on the horizon was rich bronze-gold; it pulsed with a clamor of hammering that echoed across the plain. Great black flocks of ravens swirled up and out of the glow, as though somehow they had been forged within its fires. Everything—the genial sky, the flowering grass, the earth itself—seemed to emit a low, sweet hum he could feel reverberating through the ground, up into his veins and sinews. He stood rapt, a note the earth sang.

At the corner of another street, he stepped into night, and saw the source of the second sun. It was the cauldron he had seen before, under the familiar tree. The woman he remembered stirred the shining liquid within it with her great wooden spoon; this time she sang that pure, constant hum. So bright the cauldron was that it blotted out the stars. The moon, awash with its light, was a faint, thin pair of bronze horns tilted above the tree.

A procession made its way from night into light: four women carrying a long bronze shield with a dead man lying upon it. He had no eyes; there was a bloody hole where his heart should have been. Following him, a man carried a spear that wept blood; another held a knife, its blade curved like the moon in the tree.

The woman stirring the pot raised the bowl of her spoon, poured the molten liquid over the blind face. Then she gestured.

The women raised the shield, tilted it, and the body of the fallen warrior slid, disappeared into the cauldron.

"That's what you want me to find?" Daimon asked Vivien, who was suddenly on the sidewalk beside him, surrounded by endlessly moving bodies dodging around them.

"Yes," she said. "But after being in time all these—well, however long—we don't know exactly what it will look like. You'll recognize it as we would." She smiled; her palm rested briefly on his heart. "Here."

"Did the warrior come back to life? Or did he get eaten?"

Her mouth crooked; she answered patiently, "He was drinking beer and toasting the moon an hour later."

"Are you certain my heart is big enough for this?"

"I'm certain that your heart will grow large enough to take that great power when it reveals itself to you. As it will. You are the raven's son."

He rode in a daze, found himself back on the palace grounds. He got off his bike, walked it behind the sanctum tower to the royal garages, where he found a woman crouched on the floor beside her bike and wielding a wrench.

She rose swiftly when she recognized him.

"Prince Daimon."

She looked familiar: those long bones, the honey-colored hair, that height. Standing, they were eye to eye, and suddenly he remembered.

"Dame Scotia. You were the black knight who forced me to yield to you."

She smiled; that, too, he remembered.

"It is strange," she commented, "not knowing who you're fighting. In tales, it seems romantic: the nameless, invisible knights, the shining armor, the great swords. That's why I took to it. In truth, it's stifling and awkward, lumbering around wearing all that weight and trying to see out of a slit in your helm."

"You made yourself good at it."

She shrugged lightly. "I had several older cousins to practice on. You made yourself good at it, as well."

He was silent, trying to recall exactly why. His own past blurred into another; he could scarcely envision a time before he had known Vivien. Who had he been, he wondered with a strange, quick tremor of panic, before he was the raven's child?

He heard a clink, blinked, and saw Dame Scotia bending to pick up the wrench she had dropped. He saw her, he realized, as he saw no one else those days. Perhaps only because she was a stranger, and therefore not tediously predictable.

He shook his head a little, settling a bewildering stir of thought.

"Anything I can help with?" he asked.

"Just tightening this and that, Prince Daimon. Making sure things don't fall apart. Thank you." She smiled again, left an imprint on his mind of calm, violet eyes, an expression absurdly free of complications. "That's another thing I accidentally became good at."

In the middle of the night he woke himself up thinking: Chimera Bay.

The words haunted him when he woke again at dawn. He didn't recall where he had heard them, or why they might be in any way important. He threw on some clothes, fended off the usual meaningless questions and conversations, and rode back in time to the one place left that made any sense to him.

This time, he found himself at Vivien's door. As always, she opened it before he knocked. He entered wordlessly. She put her arms around him and took him nowhere and everywhere at once. Memories his own and not his own drifted like richly colored dying leaves through his head; he did not know, any longer, who he was except in her enchanting eyes.

He asked his mother about his vanishing past. She had put on a hundred masks to watch him grow; she would remember.

But she did not seem interested in it, either. "That was the wyvern king's world. The place I couldn't enter unless I was disguised. I juggled colored cloth balls at your fourth birthday party; I measured you for your first formal suit. I watched you in your first tournament from a concession stand. Glimpses of you were all my life, then." She gave him a lovely, bittersweet smile that touched his heart. "Now I can stand here looking at your face." She cupped it lightly with her hands. "And showing you mine. Why should I want to remember that past?"

They were in the tiny village called Ravensley, sitting at a sturdy wooden table in the cottage that Vivien's apartment sometimes mysteriously became. She was out in one world or the other. Ana had poured tea in the pot on the table; neither of them drank it. The village was a place of shallow dimensions, Daimon sensed, like its photograph. He had never seen another cottage door open or anyone walking on the street. In a place beyond eyesight, it held villagers, tourists, traffic of every kind. In this moment, this memory, it held only an open door, a table, a teapot, no voices but their own.

Morrig entered then, glanced around for another chair, and there it was, along with another teacup. Daimon watched her guardedly, aware now of the power she hid behind her dithering ways.

"Tea," she remarked, gazing into the cup. "Why never brandy? What is Chimera Bay?"

She looked questioningly at Daimon; he tried to grasp a slippery recollection, not easy in a place that seemed to be somebody else's fraying memory. For some reason the queen's lover, Leith Duresse, surfaced.

"I woke last night," he explained, "and the words were in my head."

"I know," Morrig said. "I heard them, and I wondered." She linked her fingers, clad in lacy, fingerless gloves, beneath her chin and regarded him out of mist-colored eyes older than Wyvernhold. "Try," she suggested gently, and it came: supper on the day of the Assembly, Leith sitting beside his newfound son, Pierce Oliver, who was explaining something to the king, and to Sylvester Skelton.

"A fish fry?" Daimon said. "Can that be right?"

"Chimera Bay is a fish fry?"

"The fish fry is in Chimera Bay." She nodded encouragingly, looking baffled, while his thoughts blundered about in the mists of her gaze, trying to see. "Friday fish fry," he amended, then glimpsed another piece. "A ritual. Lord Skelton called it a ritual. Yes. Pierce Oliver had taken something from a ritual in Chimera Bay, involving fish. A knife, I think it was." He hesitated, hearing fragments he had been paying little attention to, until now. "Lord Skelton seemed to make a connection between the knife, the fish fry, and Severen's sacred artifact."

He felt wind stir through the door of the cottage, smelling of asphalt and brine. Somewhere, in the past or future, brakes screeched, then an owl. Morrig's attention had withdrawn so far from him or anyone, she might have been one of the cottage's memories: the old woman sitting over her tea, motionless, shrouded in shadow.

Then she raised her cup, took a sip of tea, and made a face.

"Where is Chimera Bay?"

Ana shook her head. "Somewhere north?"

"I have no idea," Vivien said. Daimon started, and she smiled, sitting among them unexpectedly, holding her own flowered cup. "Daimon, my love, do you?"

"Not a clue."

"What might be there," she persisted, "to make it at all important? To us, that is? A shrine? A well?"

"A place," Ana said more clearly, "that might hold our past? Anything of Calluna's?"

"I don't know," he said helplessly, and added, "I could ask Lord Skelton."

"You could," Morrig said, "just go there and see what you see. Be a questing knight. Take a look. You know yourself well enough by now to recognize what might be important to us." He looked mutely at Vivien, appalled at the idea, wondering how she could expect him to leave her and go off searching for a fish fry in the nether regions of Wyvernhold.

"Come with me?" he pleaded. She reached across the table for his hand, gripped it tightly.

"I can't travel with you," she said gently. "Not openly. None of us can. It would attract attention, especially from the king and his magus, who have their eyes on you already. Lord Skelton might begin to think too much and discover us. We must have that cauldron back first." She raised his fingers to her cheek, her brows crooked. "But don't worry. We will never be far from you. No farther than it takes for you to find me now. Do this for me?"

Reluctantly, later, he nerved himself to enter the vast, dusty, overwhelmingly packed rooms of the Royal Library to look for maps. The older the better, he decided, since no modern map would have anything to do with Ravenhold. He needed one map to pinpoint Chimera Bay, which he was not entirely sure how to spell, and another, the oldest he could find, to look for words, place names, that, like fossil footprints, might indicate the values of a forgotten realm.

He got vague directions from a librarian and wandered

through collisions of architectural styles, as rooms expanded through the centuries to admit new collections. A map framed on a far wall beckoned; he followed its summons and found himself in a room so cluttered with moldering tomes that it made him sneeze.

Near him, an elbow slid off the page of a tome and hit the table hard. A head, haloed with sunlight from stained glass, turned toward him as the elbow's owner rubbed it. They gazed at one another with surprise.

Then the knight hastily pushed back her heavy, ornate chair, and Daimon said as quickly, "Dame Scotia. I didn't mean to startle you. Don't tell me you read as well?"

She subsided, showing him the enormous, gaudily illustrated work. "I'm researching my ancestor, Tavis Malory, to find out if he was truly as dreadful as his contemporaries said. I do intend to go questing. I keep intending to go. But I can't seem to find my way past all the books, these and Lord Skelton's."

"Tavis—" Past surfaced unexpectedly; a title came to mind. "*The Life and Death*—of course."

"Have you read it?"

"Hasn't everybody? That's what made me want to run around in armor swinging a broadsword at people. I remember now." He glanced at her curiously, wondering what it was about her that seemed to clear his head, convince him, for just a moment, that he belonged back in the mundane world. "Where will you quest, when you do?"

"I haven't decided yet, Prince Daimon. It seems such a complex notion: finding a vessel belonging to a god, lost for who knows how long except in tales. I'm at a loss trying to find a beginning point. If you don't mind my asking, how did you make the decision?"

"I didn't."

"Oh."

"Like you, I'm still here. But I have decided to look at a map. A very old map. Like this one."

He crossed the room to study the map on the wall that had lured him in. It was large, studded with wyverns' nests, a realm with borders puffed and vague as clouds, mountains like inverted V's, forests of what looked like brown chimneys billowing green smoke, abounding with animals extinct, and imaginary, and occasionally, like the spouting whales frolicking off the coast, still existent. Wyvernhold, in huge gold-leaf letters, spanned the landmass. "Later than I thought," he commented, studying it closely, and came nose to nose with a peculiar creature. It appeared so suddenly that it took his breath away. "And there it is. So that's what a chimera looks like . . ."

He heard the chair scrape stone again. "May I?"

"Of course."

She came to stand beside him, silent for a moment, until she gave a sudden chuckle. "There." She tapped the glass over the northeastern, mountainous portion of Wyvernhold. "The Triple-Horned Mountain Sheep. My family crest. Not lovely, but fearless and quite strong. They would even attack wyverns who were after their young."

"Everyone fought the wyvern, once, it seems."

"Where is the chimera?"

He pointed to the fire-breathing lion with the body of

a goat, and a writhing serpent for a tail, hovering over a bay in the northern coast of Wyvernhold. "Chimera Bay. That's where I would look. If I were questing."

"Why there?" she murmured, studying the strange beast. "Is a chimera particularly dedicated to Severen?"

"I don't know."

"The goat part looks female."

"So it does," he said, recognizing the very full udder. "I need an older map. A map older than Wyvernhold, to know."

"To know what, Prince Daimon?"

"If the bay had other names. Older names. What early beings might still be living, forgotten, in the chimera's shadow." He glanced at her; she still studied the map, fascinated, it seemed, by the variety of beasts.

"So you are?" she asked. "Questing? That's why you need the map?"

"Yes." He turned away restively, full of sudden impatience, to go so that he could come back. "As soon as I can. Tomorrow. At dawn."

She looked at him, gave him her quick, generous smile. "I hope you find your chimera, Prince Daimon. Wish me luck with mine."

# 19

I told you so," Val said.

"You did not," Pierce said. "You didn't say a word."

"I told you with everything but words. You read my mind."

"I heard your 'no,'" Pierce conceded reluctantly. "But you didn't say why."

"How could I? She was the basilisk."

They were sitting in what looked like an old library in the basilisk's house. At least it was full of bookcases. A dusty volume lay here and there on the shelves, which mostly held an impressive collection of cobwebs. The books seemed discarded leftovers: *A Beginner's Guide to Butterflies*, *Do It Yourself Plumbing*, *A History of Irrigation Methods in South Wyvernhold*.

There was also their supper, which they had chanced upon by roaming around the countless rooms in the house above the sea. How long they had been there, Pierce had no idea. After adroitly separating them from Leith, sending him off under the care of her attendants, the sorceress had stripped them of everything but their underwear and left them a pile of old shirts and assorted bottoms to pick from. Somehow, they could not move while she did this. They could not speak, not even when she pulled Val's Wyvern's Eye out of his jacket and examined it curiously.

"What is this?" she asked, waving it at them; they could not blink, let alone duck. "Oh, well." She tossed it on the small pile of arms that included the kitchen knife. "You won't need it."

Pierce wondered how he had ever imagined her beautiful. Her lips were too rosy, her teeth too white, her curly hair too golden, her eyes an unpleasant shade of cornflower blue. Her smile deepened slightly, offering him an absurdly placed dimple.

"It's called glamour," she told him. "Works like a charm. Now. Here are the rules. You can go wherever you like. I'll feed you when you're hungry. After Sir Leith recovers from his unfortunate affliction—which he will do, I promise—I'm sure we will all become the best of friends. Any questions?" They stared at her. "Good. Then I will see you—when I see you." She laughed lightly and disappeared, along with their weapons and uniforms, without bothering with the door.

Still wordless, too worried and disgusted to speak, they pulled on some faded, fraying clothes and went looking for Leith.

The house, which had seemed from the road a large, light-filled coastal mansion, full of windows and decks to watch the sea, bore no resemblance to itself inside. It rambled interminably like an underground cave. Its hallways were shadowy, its ceilings low, its rooms moldy and overflowing with shabby furniture, or else, like the library, looking as though they had been hastily abandoned. There were no windows anywhere. There were no visible doors leading out-side. There was no sign of Leith.

"Why did she do that to him?" Val demanded explosively, when, weary and strewn with cobwebs, they stumbled into the library and found their supper. "She turned into a bas-ilisk, knocked him out with her breath, brought him here to cure him—for what? It makes no sense."

"Did he break her heart, too?" Pierce asked.

Val blinked, made a visible effort to think.

"He never mentioned anyone but our mother. And the queen. He had to tell me about that before gossip did." He paced, an incongruous knight in a torn pink T-shirt and fire-engine-red pajama bottoms. Then he paused over one of the supper trays, complete with a wineglass full of water and a plastic rose in a bud vase. "Do you think this is safe to eat?"

Pierce shrugged and speared a forkful of some kind of fish covered in green. His brows went up; he swallowed. "Olive sauce. Someone here can cook. I don't know if it's safe, but it's good."

They ate, then continued the search. When they began to stumble over their feet, they came upon a room with two frightful iron beds, thin mattresses unrolled over bare springs, covered with rumpled, yellowing sheets and thread-bare blankets. They fell into the lumpy, sagging embraces and slept.

The house looked exactly the same when they woke.

"There is no time," Val breathed. "There is no day or night."

"There are no toothbrushes," Pierce said glumly from the stained, rusty bathroom.

"I think we're inside a spell."

"No kidding."

"Our father isn't in the house we're in," Val said more coherently.

"Well, there's one. I think it was last used by something with mold on its fangs."

"No matter how long we look, we won't find him. We're in some kind of magic bubble. A sort of alternate universe inside the real house. We could be in the same room our father is in, right at this moment, and never know it."

Pierce, splashing water over his face, leaned back and peered out the door at Val. "Then how do we get to where he is?"

"I have no idea."

They continued searching, and found their breakfast in a drab little room with an unplugged dishwasher in it, a box of laundry detergent on the bottom of a set of shelves, and an empty birdcage.

"Our mother," Pierce said as they leaned over the dish-washer and ate scrambled eggs, peppered bacon, and cran-berry muffins, "is a sorceress. One of us must have inherited something of her magic. We should be able to think our way around this." He paused, looking expectantly at Val, who shook his head. "You recognized the basilisk when all I saw was what she wanted me to see. You recognized the Mist-begotten mist. You recognized me. You piece things together far better than I do."

"That's not sorcery. That's perception. What you do with that knife—that's magical."

"It's in the knife, not in me."

"Is it?" Val waggled his fork at his brother. "What could you do with this, for instance?"

"Eat," Pierce said flatly. He did, then added, "I still think we may have some of her powers. We've just never had to use them before. If you wanted to make all of this—"

"It's illusion," Val pointed out.

"You mean it's all in our heads? We're imagining this house?"

"No. The sorceress is. It's in her head."

"Well—" Pierce grappled a moment. "Can we—can we change it with our minds? Put a door in it that leads out?"

Val considered the question, then answered simply, "I'm a knight. I'm better at bashing things apart than imagining doors through them."

They tried that for a while, swinging at scarred plaster and torn wallpaper with whatever they could find: removable shelving, a rolling pin with a missing handle, a mop. The sorceress appeared as they were battering at the walls around a chimney, raising clouds of soot but doing no discernible damage to her spell.

She sat down on a couch with a few springs sticking out of it, and said, "I need some help with your father."

They gazed at her, still holding makeshift battering tools, which she ignored.

Val said, "Of course we'll help. Just take us to him. What's wrong with him?"

She brushed his words away. "Not that kind of help. He's fine. He just— Is he always so stubborn?"

Val took a step toward her, still wielding the mop handle. He asked tightly, "About what?"

She waved her hand again; the mop disappeared. "About— Well. His feelings? I've been doing everything for him. I put him in the loveliest room in my house. I removed the basilisk's spell. He has only a bit of a headache. My attendants bathed him, dressed him in clean clothes; I cooked for him myself. I would have fed him with my own hands. He refuses to be grateful. All he does is ask for you."

"Why wouldn't he? He's our father. We were traveling together."

"I explained that to him," the sorceress said a trifle querulously. "More than once. That everyone around him was incapacitated by the monster, that I saw the incident from a distance and went to help, that he was alone when I found him, and in such distress that of course I did all that was possible to get him out of there, and quickly. The roads were blocked, so I brought him here. I saw nothing of a limo, a driver, or two young, red-haired men wearing uniforms. They must have driven on to search for him when the road cleared."

"He doesn't know we're here?" Pierce said, appalled.

"No. He has no idea where you've gone." She brooded a moment. "I suspect that—in some tiny way—he doesn't entirely believe me. I don't know why." She stood up restively, paced a moment across a rumpled, faded hearthrug. They watched her in complete bewilderment.

"What is it you want from him?" Pierce pleaded. "Maybe we can help? Is it something he did to you? Are you that angry with him?"

"Of course not. He has never met me before in his life.

But I've known about him all of mine." She paused, studying them, nibbling on a fingernail. "It may be that you'll both—no, maybe just one of you, to be on the safe side—will have to appear at my door asking if I've seen him. He will be so grateful to me when he sees at least one of his sons. But we'll need some convincing story of where the other one has gone."

"How about this?" Val said sharply. "That one of us was kidnapped by the incredibly stupid and selfish sorceress who turned herself into a basilisk and attacked our father."

The sorceress took her finger from between her teeth and pointed it at him. "You," she said coldly, "can stay here. I'll take your brother with me to see your father."

"I'm not going to lie to him for you," Pierce said adamantly.

"Fine. Decide for yourselves who stays and who goes free to see Sir Leith. But if I glimpse the faintest falseness in your eyes, in your face, hear it in your words when you speak to him, the brother you left behind will share stale bread and moldy cheese rinds with the rats."

Val gazed at her, his eyes narrowed and so intent on her that Pierce wondered uneasily what, by word or action, he might trigger in her. He only asked, with unexpected gentleness, "What is it? If you want our help, tell us what you need."

Her face crumpled suddenly; she dabbed at the corner of one eye with her forefinger. "I need him to understand how deeply I am in love with him. That he holds my heart in his. I need to move him as he moves me. Can you help me with that? He finds it so difficult to be grateful despite all I've done for him. Can you persuade him? I want to rule his heart, to make it tack and turn toward me, always toward

me, until all the world understands the poetry that he feels
for me. I want him to forget the queen. I want to be known,
from this time on, as his legendary love. Can you help me?"
She flicked a finger at her other eye, then gave them both a
dark, tearless stare. "If you can't, then stay out of my way.
Now. Choose. Which of you remains here, which of you
sees your father. Be ready to tell me when I return."

Val said quickly, after she vanished, "I am older than you,
far more experienced with fighting whatever she might conjure
up, and I've been with him my entire life. Please. Let me go."

"I can lie better than you," Pierce said.

"How do you know?"

Pierce gazed at him helplessly. "Because there's so much
I don't know about either of you. I could invent all kinds of
things and believe them at the same time. And I've been
around a sorceress all my life. Look at your face. Have you
ever told a single lie?"

"Of course I have."

"That must be the first. You can't even lie convincingly
about lying. Your eyes don't know how."

Val said nothing, just looked at him with such burning,
pleading urgency that Pierce yielded and stayed behind to
await the cheese rinds and the rats that, he expected, would
be inevitable.

It did not take Val long to get into trouble. After some
roaming and futile banging at walls, during which time stood
around and watched, judging from the lack of even a hair-
breadth of movement from light or shadow, Pierce found a
plate on a cracked and blistered wooden chest. As promised,
it held some furry cheese whittled to the rind, and a couple

of rock-hard heels of bread. He looked at it glumly, wondering how his father and brother were faring. Also as promised, a rat popped up from behind the chest, eyed Pierce warily.

"Help yourself," Pierce told it, and turned away to find another wall, another weapon.

He dumped the dead plant out of a cast-iron pot, and was trying to put a dent in a windowless wall inset with an incongruous window seat, when the rat leaped up onto the seat and stood staring at him.

"Sorry," Pierce sighed. "You'll have to wait for the next meal after whatever that one was." He whacked at the wall with force, determined to fight his way back into the world by whatever worked. The rat did not move. Pierce glanced at it again. Something in its dark, fixed gaze, its complete lack of instinct or common rat sense, made Pierce's skin prickle.

He lowered the pot, whispered, "Mom?"

The wall around the window seat blew into fragments. The rat, squealing, leaped one way, Pierce another. When the shards of lath and plaster finished falling, and the dust settled, he felt light and heard the distant roar of the sea.

A series of muffled explosions thundered methodically around him, followed by some furious shouting just before the floor collapsed under his feet. He thudded down an inch or two, and walls around him collapsed, dissolved, like the long spiral of chambers within a shell fraying apart, opening up to reveal its outer structure. He stood in the lovely mansion he had seen from the road, with its airy rooms overlooking the highway and the sea, its windows stained the mist and pearl of what he finally realized was dawn.

Across the road, down a long, empty beach, a crow chased

a seagull. Their cries were audible even above the waves. Pierce, watching the crow gain air and peck at the gull's feathers, shivered suddenly, amazed at the power that his mother possessed to have torn apart the sorceress's spell like a squall hitting a haystack. He watched for a time, wondering if she would turn and fly back to him. Both birds vanished behind a jut of headland. He waited, as the sun revealed its waking eye between two layers of cloud, then closed it again and carried on unseen. Pierce opened a sliding deck door, stepped outside, taking deep breaths of the briny, chilly air. He heard voices, and went to look over the side of the deck.

Val and Leith stood below. Val was pulling on his jacket and sliding weapons into its hidden pockets. Leith, holding Pierce's clothes and boots and the kitchen knife, was scanning the lower windows and shouting his name.

Pierce called back, then found his way down swiftly and joined them. Leith, looking pale and harried, reached out, hugged him tightly with one arm, then handed him his pants.

"Hurry," he begged, "before she comes back. I'd rather face the kraken at the bottom of the sea than that again."

Val was looking askew at Pierce, astonished. "How on earth did you break that spell?"

"I didn't. Our mother found us."

Leith stared at him. "That was Heloise?"

Pierce nodded, pulling on his shirt. "The sorceress made a mistake and let a living animal into her spell. I told you," he added to Val, "that you couldn't lie."

"You were right."

"What animal?" Leith asked.

"A rat. My mother has a habit of watching out for me.

She uses just about anything with eyes." He paused, added with wonder, "I can't believe she came all the way down from Cape Mistbegotten for this."

"She was the dragon," Val reminded him.

"No. That was only her making. She probably borrowed some other local creature for that illusion."

"But she wasn't the basilisk."

"No. I was wrong about that."

"We were all wrong," Leith murmured. He gave Pierce his jacket and the knife. "Where is she? Where did they both go?"

"Last I saw, they went flying down the beach. And I think you're right," Pierce added uneasily. "We should get out of here before the sorceress comes back."

Val produced his cell. "I'll call our driver."

Leith, still looking unsettled, incredulous, said, "I can't believe . . . I had no idea she could— Did you have any idea she was that— Do you think she knew that Val and I were in trouble? Or did she only do this for you?"

Pierce sighed. "Honestly? I don't know. You should ask her that. You should find her. You should talk."

Leith, his gaze shifting toward the sea, said nothing; after a moment, he gave a short nod.

They had walked halfway down the long drive from the sorceress's house when they saw the limo pull up at the end of it.

# 20

There were knights everywhere, suddenly, in Chimera Bay. Carrie, shopping for Stillwater's, saw them strolling down streets, eating lunch in the brew-pub, getting their bikes and cars looked at in the local garages, roaming through antique stores and the flea market, even appearing at weekend garage sales. They were hunting, Carrie learned from Jayne and Bek, who paid attention to lunchtime gossip. The knights were in pursuit of something inexplicable, indescribable, that might resemble a mixing bowl, or a wine goblet, or a flowerpot made of gold. They would know it when they saw it.

They didn't stay long, overnight at the most, though it was hard to tell when they all dressed alike. Chimera Bay, a serviceable wayside along the highway between greater, more complex cities, presented a friendly and ingenuous face to strangers passing through. No one would stay long to look for wonders there. A few found Stillwater's restaurant, though, busy as she was in the kitchen, Carrie rarely knew until after who had eaten her cooking.

Some workdays were longer than others: when she cooked for lunch at Stillwater's, then dinner at the Kingfisher. She scarcely saw Zed on those days, much less her father, who, after his amazing shape-changing dance in the moonlight, had vanished again. She thought, after that vision, nothing else could surprise her. But, on one of the long days, which started early when she bought groceries for Stillwater's before lunch, she walked in hauling bags and found Sage Stillwater on a stool at the bar eating a sandwich.

Carrie nearly dropped the groceries.

"Is that tuna?" she asked incredulously, catching a whiff of it.

Sage nodded, making a little face. "Out of a can, even. Todd's funny that way. He gives me such ordinary food now and then. I have no idea why. Maybe he just gets tired and runs out of ideas. And he is so hurt if I don't eat it." She lifted the thick, graceless slabs of bread with the grayish ooze of tuna salad between them, gazed at the concoction reluctantly, and forced herself to take another bite. "Pickles," she said, grimacing again after she swallowed. "Mayonnaise from a jar. Celery. Onions."

"Sounds like something on the Kingfisher menu," Carrie said with disbelief.

"Capers."

"Well, maybe not." She noted the salad beside the sandwich plate: tomatoes that looked exactly like themselves, undisguised red onion and pepper, a mass of greens for all the world to see. "Does he eat that, too?"

"No," Sage said, laughing. "Never. He wouldn't be caught dead eating anything less than beautiful." She had another face-off with the unlovely sandwich. "It hasn't killed me yet, and it makes him happy." She sighed, and bit into it again.

Carrie, mystified, took the groceries into the kitchen and began to prep for lunch.

When Stillwater came in later, she was turning truffle oil into a mist to give a delicate, subtle flavor to thin diamonds of raw beef for the bottom layer of a lunch bite. He tasted one, grunted something approving, and passed on before she remembered the tuna sandwich. She went on to the Kingfisher Grill with the scent of truffles in her hair. By the time she helped Ella replenish the dessert tray and started cooking suppers, the homey smells of banana cream pie and frying fish overpowered any lingering mementos from Stillwater's kitchen.

But Ella kept giving her little fretful glances whenever she was between whirlwinds of this or that.

"You're getting too thin," she commented as she finished making up half a dozen salads and put them on a tray for Marjorie.

"Am I?" Carrie said, surprised.

"Have you been eating?"

"Of course. All the time."

Ella gave her one of those narrow-eyed looks of pure perception, the last thing Carrie wanted to inspire. "Are you working another job?"

"No," Carrie said, shoveling halibut over to sizzle on its other side. She felt cold, hollow with the lie; she peppered the fish, not meeting Ella's eyes. "I have been looking," she temporized. "Just for a part-time, something mindless and easy, to make a little more money. But I don't want to change my hours here. I'm fine with here." She paused to test the silence, the weight of Ella's regard. "I'm worried about my father. We seem to be at odds, these days. We can't agree on things, and most of the time I never know where he is. When I do see him, he doesn't talk to me."

"Ah." Ella went back to bustling, spooning green beans, garlic mash on a plate for Carrie's halibut, then filling bowls, two chowders and a split pea ham for one of Bek's tables. "You want to leave him. Like your mother did. No wonder he's balking."

Carrie laughed a little, inhaled a pepper flake, and turned away quickly to cough. "Can you blame us? He doesn't exactly make things easy."

Bek backed into the door, arms lined with salad plates; he slid them into the sink, picked up the two chowders, and vanished again.

"Busy tonight," Ella commented. "Strangers all over town, I hear." She grated some carrot curls on top of the split pea bowl, and handed it to Bek as he reappeared. Then she stopped moving again, standing in the middle of the floor, staring down at the ancient linoleum as though it were expressing something profound, or just revealing old memories.

"Nobody, living or dead, makes things easy even when you love them. Especially then."

Jayne whirled through the double doors like a dancer,

her purple hair swirling, her tray full of dirty dishes. "There's a pair of black-haired, blue-eyed twin knights out there I think we need to keep. I'll take one and you take the other, Carrie. They need a blue cheese dressing and a chowder."

Ella reached for dishes; Jayne popped some corn muffins and butter into a basket and danced out again.

Carrie checked the bar when she finished work but found no Merle there. She went home and crept gratefully into bed. Sometime in the night, she woke up feeling odd, somehow amiss, then realized it was nothing, only hunger. Zed came in then from working the late shows at the theater, and she took in a long breath of the smell of hot buttered popcorn on his skin as he rolled in beside her. She went back to sleep and dreamed of Merle, or maybe she heard him in her dreams, singing his song of love or loss or dire warning to the night.

"You're working too hard," Zed told her sleepily the next morning, as they drank coffee together in the farmhouse kitchen.

"I'm not the one who has to get up at the crack of dawn and walk Harlan Jameson's puppy."

"That's only for a week, while he's out of town. I think you should quit working for Stillwater. He hasn't told you anything. All he's done is make you feel guilty about working for him. Your tightest pair of jeans is starting to sag on you. You're getting some killer cheekbones, but I don't think all this is good for you."

"I'm fine," Carrie said without really listening. "You should eat something. I could scramble some eggs."

"There are no eggs. I looked. There's no bread for toast."

"Milk and cereal?"

"There's a wilted stalk of celery and a jar of mustard."

"Seriously?" Carrie put her cup down, went to stick her head in the fridge. "Well, where did— Who's been eating—" She opened the freezer. "There's ice cream. No. Frozen yogurt." She stared at it, and felt something dark, constricting, ease around her thoughts, her heart. "He hates frozen yogurt. He says it's unnatural."

"Who?"

She looked at him, smiling. "My father. He's been here laying waste to the kitchen."

Zed didn't smile back. "And this took you how long to notice? How many sandwiches ago did he finish your bread? How many bowls of cereal?"

"I don't know. What does it matter? I miss him, Zed. I want so much to be able to talk to him again. I'm just happy he's been here at all."

"It matters because you've stopped bothering to feed yourself." He got up abruptly, pulled the yogurt out of the freezer, and handed her a spoon. "Yogurt. It's good for you. People eat it for breakfast. Eat some human food for once instead of those airy nothings you eat at Stillwater's. I'm not moving until—"

"Oh, all right," Carrie said. She prodded a spoonful out of the box, sucked on it until it melted. "Here. Your turn."

"Finish it."

"I will, I will, I promise. You'd better go before the puppy chews its way out of the house."

He lingered, his forehead creased, his eyes dark, watching her excavate another bite, until the thought of the ravaging, whimpering beast tugged him away. "I'm bringing groceries tonight." It sounded like a threat. "Somebody around here needs to exercise some common sense."

She tossed the carton and the spoon into the freezer when she heard his engine start, and went outside to see if she could spot the errant wolf.

She found him by his singing.

Crooning, more like, she thought. If a wolf could. It was a gentle sort of whine, hitting notes of love, lullaby, and play, the sound a creature might make that had spent an entirely satisfying night, and looked forward to another just like it. She could not see the wolf though it sounded close, just behind a tree, or around the great fallen snag of a root-ball lying partly in the grasses, partly in mud the ebbing tide had uncovered. She followed the wolf song through the trees behind the house, the hemlock and cedar, the occasional apple tree orphaned by a long-forgotten farm, scattering the last of its blossoms among its roots. She saw the deer the wolf ignored, nibbling on a shrub. The song, a tangible thing now, like a beckoning finger, or the wolf's shadow sliding out of eyesight every time she saw it, led her deeper into the forest, but never far from the tranquil shallows reflecting the flush of light in the wake of the rising sun.

The wolf sang. The song flowed into her ears, into her head and heart, then, like sunrise, it illuminated her eyes. She heard herself humming with it, now, seeing what the wolf saw, what it sang to, what it sang about. The daily ebb of water, the blue heron in the tree, the sleeping owl, the patient, peaceful trees, season after season of leaves falling, petals falling, needles flying, cones budding, petals forming again, opening again. The rich, tangled wealth of smells

from the water, the living treasure buried in the mud, clinging to the long grasses, waiting for the tide to turn, return.

At last she saw the wolf, sitting on its haunches, waiting
for her.

She walked up to it. It had stopped singing, just sat there,
silent, motionless, its eyes the color of the drifts of morning
mist above the waters.

Its eyes closed. When they opened again, her father stood
there, gazing at her out of weary human eyes. He was mud-
stained, disheveled; there was dried eelgrass in his hair. He
didn't speak; neither did she. She just put her arms around
him tightly, clinging to him thoughtlessly as she had when
she was a child and believed he could protect her from
anything.

Then she dropped her arms, stepped back to see his face.
He lifted his hands, gripped her arms, staring into her eyes.
She saw crow wings in his, the full moon, lightning flashing
in the dark, turning every hidden thread of slough water
into molten silver. The sudden light ignited, turned to amber
and fire; she stood reflected in the wyvern's eye.

She drew a deep breath, seeing herself finally, answering
the one question that she hadn't even known to ask.

Daughter of the wolf. Daughter of the magus.

"Yes," she said tightly. "I want this. I need this. Whatever
you can give me."

"You need to see this world before you can recognize the
other."

She nodded, not entirely understanding but trusting him
to arm her.

"I have been calling for help," he added. "I think I have

finally been heard. I had to find someone who would remember me. Not many left who remember back that far."

Her eyes stung suddenly because he was finally talking to her, telling her, and because she could finally hear him. She did not have to ask how far back. He had seen the living wyvern, that was how far. He stood with his old, gawping boots rooted so far into the deep they probably reached bottom, down where the new things had started to crawl out of the sea onto the first of the drying mud.

She saw the glimmer of a smile: *Not quite that far.* He went back as far as that, at least: to the beginning of laughter.

She said, "Tell me what to do."

"I'm going to give you something. Give it to Lilith when you take her Hal's note this morning."

"All right."

He leaned forward; she felt his lips brush her cheek, before they paused over her ear.

He left a word there.

Then he said, "Sorry about the empty cupboards. I didn't have time—"

"That's okay. Zed is going grocery shopping."

"Good. He's a good man. I hope he stays around."

He lingered, filling his eyes with her, even while a pointed ear nudged through his hair, one hand wavered into claw and back. "Be careful," he said, his voice sliding between human and howl, between now and then, so ancient and unwieldy it might have been a slab of granite trying out a human word.

Her eyes burned again. "Okay."

Then she was watching the wolf slip shadowlike through

the trees, giving away nothing of itself, not even a scent to
startle the grazing deer.

L ilith barely gave her a chance to speak when Carrie
brought Hal's note to the tower suite and knocked on
her door later that morning. She opened the door and
whirled away, phone to her ear, papers taking flight off her
desk as she passed.

"No," she was saying. "We haven't caught sight of them
yet. I've never heard of a sorceress on that part of the coast.
I'll keep some eyes on her down there. I'm glad to hear you
trimmed a few feathers out of her wings. It was astonishing
to see their faces on the news—" She came to the edge of
the carpet and turned again, a tide in full flood, until she
saw Carrie and stopped so abruptly the breeze in her wake
seemed to flow past her and out the door.

The blood ran completely out of her face. It crumpled,
shadows and lines appearing, underscoring the terror in her
eyes, the sudden, overwhelming grief over something invisible between them, roused from memory by whatever she
saw in Carrie's face. She dropped the phone from her ear
to her shoulder, held it there like a lifeline.

As abruptly, the tide of color washed back into her face;
the terror vanished under an upwelling of rage.

"No," she said to Carrie, chopping words like vegetables.
"Tell me. You are not. Working for Todd Stillwater."

The voice on the phone rose in volume and jumped an
octave, repeating the same word over and over, like an angry

songbird. Lilith didn't seem to hear; Carrie held all her attention.

Carrie said, "My father told me to give you something. A word. I don't know what it means. Miranda."

For a moment, Lilith only stared at her as though she had no idea either. Her face seemed frozen, unable to shape a thought. Slowly, her eyes changed, grew large, flushed, glittering with what Carrie realized were unshed tears. She dropped the phone on the floor, beginning to tremble. Carrie, suddenly terrified, took a step toward her. But Lilith caught her balance and finally found her voice.

"Miranda," she said, and again, "Miranda." The name seemed to comfort her. The frozen, stricken face eased a little, expression melting through it. She seemed to look through Carrie, past her into an immeasurable distance.

Then her eyes quickened, saw Carrie again.

"He said her name."

"Yes," Carrie whispered.

"I haven't. Said her name. None of us has, not even Merle. Said her name. In all these years."

"Who—who is she?"

"Was. She was our daughter. Hal's and mine. She fell in love with Todd Stillwater, when he cooked for the Kingfisher Inn, so long ago. His cooking—it made the inn famous. It was wonderful. Spellbinding. His spell bound my daughter. His spell bound us all. Me. He fed us all so well that we were always hungry, always happy, always wanting more. People came from all over Wyvernhold to tie up at our dock, stay at the inn, eat Stillwater's magic in that magnificent old dining room that has never been used since—" She stopped, absolutely still again, looking inward, lost to the world.

"Since?"

"Miranda." Her eyes filled again; she turned her head, looked out over the water. Like Carrie's voice, her own dwindled, burrowed. "Only Merle saw. Only Merle saw clearly. What we had all become. What Stillwater was. Is.

"He destroyed this place. Merle and Hal fought him, finally drove him out. But the terrible battle left Hal crippled, Merle lost in his own mind half the time. Stillwater sucked the magic out of this place, left it shattered, and us still spellbound. We couldn't—we couldn't speak. That's why he's still here in Chimera Bay. We could not speak. He's safe here."

"From what?"

"From those who drove him out of his world into this one." She raised her hand, brushed her eyes with her wrist. "They couldn't stand him, either."

"You're speaking now."

"You said her name. We could never—we could never say her name. After she died. She died wanting more, always wanting more of Stillwater. He left her here, went his way. He took her name away with him. I could never forgive myself." She looked at Carrie again, her eyes dry now, the unnatural green of sky and sea mirroring dangerous weather. "I encouraged her. Even I was a little in love. I thought our love, our fortune, our beautiful, enchanted life would last forever."

"That's why you always stay up here. Why you never come down."

"There was no point. I couldn't forgive myself for not—
for not seeing my own daughter in such horrible danger, not
helping her— How could I expect Hal to forgive me?"

"What's changed? Now?"

"Merle said her name. He sent you up here, looking like
you do, feeding on emptiness, wasting away without even
noticing, even your hair thin and hungry for what's real,
what's true. But somehow you learned to see like Merle sees.
You are his daughter, and what he sees in you is hope."

When she left the Kingfisher Grill after lunch and
went to Stillwater's to prep for dinner, she was not
entirely surprised by the cracked and rain-darkened oak in
the old bank door. She walked inside, saw the splintered,
warped floorboards, the tattered tablecloths, the long-dead
flowers in the vases. Sage Stillwater sat at the bar, taking
notes. She turned her head, smiled at Carrie. Her hair was
limp, her face wan, hollowed, fretted with tiny, worried
lines, and so pale it might have been the color of her bones
seeping too near the surface of her face. Her eyes seemed
huge, hungry for something she no longer remembered.
Stillwater, his back to Carrie, read labels of nearly empty
bottles, some of them so dusty the writing was hardly visible.
Sage jotted down what he needed: limes, olives, brandy, new
glasses to replace the cracked. He glanced toward Carrie and
smiled absently as she greeted him. He looked, she thought,
like a sort of shriveled, pallid mushroom, his skin damp, grayish white, not enough hair on his head to bother leaving it
there. One eyebrow had vanished completely. His eyes had

sunk so deeply into his furrowed face that he looked like something furtive peering out of a fallen tree trunk.

After seeing Merle shaping everything under the moon, she wasn't afraid of the magic, just suddenly, profoundly curious about this ancient, nameless power who, in trapping those Carrie loved within all their memories, seemed to have trapped himself as well.

She passed them, headed into the kitchen, and saw something she hadn't noticed before. Or maybe her attention had just skittered over it before, since it was nothing much to look at, just a dented old pot gathering cobwebs on the floor in a corner. As she wondered idly what it was doing there, a lovely bronze light glided over it, barely visible beneath the dust and old grease clinging to it.

Something of Stillwater's, she guessed. Maybe one of his early, experimental machines. Being Stillwater's, it would most likely still contain a surprise or two.

She lifted it out of the shadows to see what it could do.

# 21

Perdita and the queen received the news of Daimon's quest from the king himself, who summoned them out of a ritual midseason salute to the goddess by appearing at the top of the sanctum stairs and startling the guardian on duty to the point of incoherence.

"Your Majesty," she whispered to the queen within the sanctum, as Mystes Halliwell led the acolytes in their chant. "His Majesty—he's—just outside. Inside the antechamber. He wants you and Princess Perdita."

Perdita, watching the queen grow pale, thought instantly: *Daimon.* She turned, followed the queen easing through the crowd around the central pool with its feathery wisp of a fountain murmuring a musical counterpoint to the chant. For no reason, Perdita glanced back as they left the sanctum. She saw her aunt Morrig's face turned to watch them, her gray eyes looking oddly dark and birdlike.

Observing the sanctum's rules, the king waited courteously on the top of the antechamber stairs. The rare uncertainty on his face made Perdita swallow dryly. The queen quickened her pace.

"Please," he said softly, as they reached him. "Can we talk?"

The queen's mouth tightened. As she had done many times through the years for her lover, she opened the chamber door for her husband.

"Arden, what is it?" She closed the door behind him, leaned against it. The king glanced around the small, cluttered room strewn with clothes, shoes, jewels, the open wardrobe door whose mirror reflected his presence. He picked up a sweater Perdita had tossed on the little couch, then stood holding it, hesitating. "Sit down," Genevra said, and he did.

Perdita took the sweater from him and sat on the arm of the couch, gripping the soft wool tightly. "It's Daimon," she said with that strange certainty, and the king nodded.

"What is it?" the queen said again, sharply. "What happened? Where is he?"

"He has gone questing, like half my other knights." He paused, his eyes on his wife, narrowed slightly as against a dark and imminent tempest. "You asked me to tell him about his mother. I did. And now I think I should tell you."

The queen stared at him. "She's dead. That's all I have ever wanted to know."

"That's almost all I know of her," Arden said heavily. "We were together one very short night. Nine months later, she was dead."

"And now?"

"Now I'm not so sure of anything, even that."

The queen pulled herself from the door, sank into a chair. The blood rose swiftly, brightly, into her face. "You think she might be still alive? Does Daimon know her?"

"He's been behaving very strangely. He comes and goes without a word; he is distant, preoccupied, and—most of the time—simply not there."

"Not there where?"

"Behind his eyes. It's as though he sees us as strangers. He can't seem to remember who he is, why he's here in this family. He has spent entire days, and even nights, away. He won't say where. Sylvester thinks he's enchanted."

"So it sounds," the queen said, her frown easing a little. "So he's in love? Is that what you're worried about? That she's in some way inappropriate? So is he, for that matter. We all are, at one time or another—"

"Spellbound," the king interrupted, and she was silent again, her eyes wide on his face. "As I might have been," he added slowly, "so long ago."

The queen gripped the hardwood arms of her chair. Perdita had never seen her eyes so cold. "Arden. What is the point of all this? He is in love the way you were in love?"

"No. It's not my word. It's Sylvester's," the king said, with odd emphasis, and Perdita's lips parted.

"Yes," she exclaimed. "Of course that's it. That's why Morrig— But who? Who is doing the enchanting?"

Her parents stared at her now.

"Morrig?" the queen echoed faintly.

"What do you know about this, Perdita?" the king asked with bewilderment.

"He as much as told me he had glimpsed his other heritage—his other half."

The queen's voice ratcheted up a notch. "So who was his mother?" she demanded of Arden. "And what," she asked Perdita, "does Lady Seabrook have to do with any of this?"

"I think," Perdita said, keeping her voice low in case Morrig was hovering around the keyhole, "that Great-aunt Morrig is anything but dotty. I believe she—or someone who does her bidding—led Scotia Malory and me on a wild-goose chase over most of Severluna when we tried to follow Daimon to see where he goes."

The king held up his hand, patted the air between them. "Please. Let me say what I came to say. Sylvester put the pieces together, taught me the words for it. There was a realm once named Ravenhold. It existed along with many other small kingdoms before Arden Wyvernbourne conquered it. At least the human realm of Ravenhold disappeared within Wyvernbourne. The hidden realm, the invisible realm, whose boundaries once stretched across the whole of Wyvernbourne and beyond, never entirely disappeared. Neither did its powerful, magical people, who, Sylvester guesses, still live among us. He also guesses that, after all this time, they want their realm back.

"And that realm is Daimon's other heritage. Where his mother came from. Where she still might be, for all I know. He is half-Wyvernbourne. His other—"

"You didn't know?" the queen interrupted incredulously. "You did not know her well enough to know that?"

"I was enchanted," the king said simply. "All that the word means. All."

"And Daimon—"

"Spellbound as well, by the powers we have all forgotten, until they transform our hearts. My ancestor overran their realm, called himself their king. My son, half-wyvern, has been enchanted by the raven. I can't guess what will come of it."

"Why should anything come of a broken realm? How powerful can it be?"

"Lord Skelton has found evidence, in old myths and poetry," the king answered steadily, "that they were powerful enough to make a great cauldron that brought their dead warriors back to life."

"A cauldron," Perdita said blankly. Then her eyes widened, riveted on her father. "A bowl. A pot. A vessel of enormous power—"

"Yes." The wyvern's eyes, holding hers, seemed dimmed, diminished by the idea of it. "And I have sent the knights of Wyvernhold out looking for it. Including my youngest son, who is under the raven's spell."

The queen rose abruptly, pacing the small room in six long strides. "It's a tale," she said harshly. "A scrap of myth." She whirled, paced back. "Anyway, if it's real, and your knights find it, they will bring it to you. Not that such a thing could possibly exist. Could it?" She came to a halt in front of Arden. "What does Sylvester think?"

"Sylvester himself sent the knights out questing for it. He is convinced it is real. But he isn't certain, any longer, that it ever had anything to do with Severen."

Perdita saw the look in her mother's eye of a woman on the verge of kindling lightning with her hair. "And this has exactly what to do with Daimon?"

A dark flame wavering in the air near her made her whirl. A figure seemed to push its way into being, shaping and pulling itself free from the mist and vagueness clinging to it. Perdita, fascinated, expected Lord Skelton to emerge from the nebulousness. The thin, sharp angles suggested his spare figure, his pointed elbows. But the face coming clear was not his.

"Lady Seabrook," the queen exclaimed.

"Morrig," the king echoed, rising, and responding, in Perdita's view, to the least significant aspect of her great-aunt's appearance out of thin air. "In ordinary circumstances, I would come nowhere near this sanctum. I know your rules. But—"

"Don't worry," Morrig said sweetly. The gray eyes still carried the suggestion of shadow, like aged silver. "That's why I came: to tell you not to worry."

"About—" the queen said faintly.

"About Daimon, of course. Everything will go as planned. We will keep him safe."

"We."

"The three of us."

"Three," Perdita whispered. The word came alive in her head, busily making connection after connection through time, across poetry, familiar images turning unfamiliar faces toward her, linking themselves across the whole of Wyvern-hold history and farther back, so far back that they became themselves, words so old they were new, and they meant only what they were: Moon. Raven. Death. Night. Life. Morrig's eyes flicked at her, and Perdita saw in them every ancient word.

"Three," the king echoed, sounding mystified.

"Daimon's mother, his sweet friend Vivien Ravensley, and his great-auntie Morrig. I know you must be fretting. You have always been so kind to him."

The king's face flamed; the wyvern glowered back at her. "He is my son," Arden said explosively. "What have you done to him? Are you setting him against me?"

"Of course we don't want it to come to that. And I can't—"

"Daimon's mother is alive?" The queen's voice hit a note so high that her voice cracked.

"Very much so, yes. And I can't stay to explain. Just be patient." Her head cocked suddenly, as at an undercurrent of sound. "I think I'll take the stairs. The airways are congested."

She went out the door without bothering to open it. The queen, white as spun sugar, glared incredulously at the wood, asked without sound, "Who is she? And who," she demanded, her voice swooping up several notches again, "is Vivien?"

The king, his face still fiery, drew a breath as though to bellow himself. The air, taking on density in front of them again, checked his impulse. They watched breathlessly. This time the face sculpting itself out of airy streaks and disturbances wore two long mustaches and circular spectacles.

"Your Majesty," he said without a mouth, then achieved himself and settled his glasses. "I heard you call."

"Did you find Daimon?"

"I did. He is on the coast road, heading north, as are any number of questing knights."

"How?" the queen demanded. "Did he call you and tell you that?"

"I found him in water, Queen Genevra," Sylvester said. "It's really the simplest way, especially since he left his cell phone in the royal garage's garbage bin. At a projection of thought or memory onto the reflection of water, the surface will mirror the—"

"Where is he going? Will it mirror that?"

"Not yet, my lord. But as I watch his path unfold, I can see where he is, where he stops, and eventually, I hope, why." He was silent, his eyes moving from face to fraught face. His hands rose, gripped his mustaches. "Now what?"

Later that day, as she sat in the soothing calm of the goddess's antechamber, guarding its peace a bit belatedly, she felt, and trying to imagine the state of her half sibling's mind, Perdita saw yet another vision emerge from the cross-hatch of candlelight and shadow.

This one was no longer young but beautiful despite her years, like the queen. Gazing at her, surprised, Perdita felt her heartbeat suddenly. This apparition she recognized. This apparition had given Daimon her pale hair, her light eyes, the shape of her face. Perdita found herself on her feet, wondering if she were seeing a ghost, or a vision, or what she actually thought she might be seeing.

"Yes," the woman said, reading her mind. "Daimon is my son."

"Has he— Does he know—"

"Oh, yes. He and I have met." Perdita saw another thing the woman had given Daimon: that friendly but closely guarded smile. "My name is Ana. Daimon and I have met many times through the years. So, a time or two, have you and I."

Perdita glanced around her, wanting her father, Lord Skelton, even the queen to prove she was not dreaming. "No. I don't remember."

"You wouldn't. I had to wear many faces, many disguises, to watch my son grow up. Morrig helped me on every occasion, with every changing face. It was the only way I could see him."

Perdita backed up a little, felt the stone on which she had been sitting reassuringly solid against her. "What is it you want? My father? My mother? Daimon isn't here."

"You are, Princess Perdita. Morrig sent me to answer questions; she said she left you in a mist—"

"Totally blank," Perdita agreed with feeling. "Who are you?"

"We are remnants of an ancient realm. We have all our hope in Daimon to help us recover our lost land. And we are all very grateful for the queen's care for him, for your love—"

"You—you sound as though you're taking him away from us. You, and Aunt Morrig, and that Vivien—"

"Vivien Ravensley. She is heir, by a very long bloodline, to both the human and the not-so-human thrones of Ravenhold. The realm had a king once, in its early days. He grew so terrible we had to drive him out. Since then, only daughters rule. When they marry, the child of both the wyvern and the raven will unite the wyvern's power as well to Ravenhold, in the daughter who will be their heir."

Perdita felt her knees give way; she sat down abruptly on the hard granite. "Marry? Exactly how far away from us are you taking him? Does he know? Or is he too spellbound—"

"He knows, of course. How far he goes is up to him."

"Is it? Are they in love? Or is it an enchantment of convenience?"

Ana paused before she answered. "I think," she said with surprising honesty, "that, beyond the enchantment, they are in love enough. Certainly attracted. And not, so far as I know, in love with anyone else. Vivien is extremely ambitious. And Daimon is—"

"Like his father," Perdita finished tightly. "Susceptible."

Ana was silent again, gazing at the princess. "We have made our decision. How simple or difficult the matter will be will depend on the king. If he chooses the wyvern over the raven, then Daimon will make his own choices. One of which may well be the Wyvernhold throne."

Perdita felt the blood leave her face. "You have that power over him?"

"If that's what Daimon wants, we will get it for him. My own preference for the return of our realm would be under far happier and easier circumstances. The king could simply offer it to the new queen and her consort as a wedding gift."

"Who are you?" Her voice shook. "You three?"

"We are different faces of the raven. We have survived in many bodies, behind many faces, for time beyond measure." She smiled again, a cold moon's smile; Perdita glimpsed the raven's eye within hers. "We hope for all the best. But we will spread our wings and bring on the night if we are challenged." She paused again, looking at once inward and into the distance. "I must go. I am attracting Lord Skelton's attention."

"Wait," Perdita pleaded, and the blurring lines stilled. "Does my father know all this?"

"In his heart he knows. It is what he fears most."

She was gone, drained out of the air like the candle flame on a river stone, dwindling into the memory of fire.

Perdita, her wyvern's eyes narrowed, gold reflecting fire, left the goddess to her own devices and went to call the questing Scotia Malory.

# 22

At the waning end of the endless day on the road that had begun at dawn in the sorceress's driveway, Pierce recognized the snapped sapling, the gashed tree trunk, and the mangled milepost he had damaged in passing during his previous existence. He realized that they were nearly at Chimera Bay.

He opened his mouth to say so, groggy with travel and full of wonder that here he was again, in such unpredictable circumstances, and for far different reasons. He was with family; his life had purpose, destiny, if only, at the moment, to return what he had stolen from the kindly owners of the Kingfisher Inn. It had, he thought dazedly, fulfilled its own unlikely purpose. Val, listening to music and lightly snoozing across from him, opened one eye blearily, as though he had sensed the languid tremor of mental activity. Leith, texting someone as his sons sprawled in weary stupor around him, glanced at them, thumbed a brief end to his message.

Pierce said, "We're here."

A dark tide roared up behind the limo on the quiet stretch of highway, washed around it in a fragmented whirl of faces, emblems painted on helmets, black leather gloves trailing colorful windswept leather ties raised in greeting, or maybe just signaling, bulky baggage tied to every possible space on the noisy bikes, all of which bore familiar crests. They forced the limo to slow, then abruptly turned in one long dark stream around it and onto a side road whose modest sign proclaimed it: Proffit Slough Lane.

"Follow them," Leith told the driver abruptly as the fellowship swarmed around a curve and out of sight. The limo veered like a bus, rattling the last shreds of lethargy from Pierce's brain. Val pulled his lax limbs together; straightening, he twisted to get the driver's view of the winding road ahead.

"What's a slough?" he wondered. "Slow? Slog? Did you recognize them?" he asked his father.

"Several of the crests. Niles Camden's among them. Their leader. They seemed to know exactly where they wanted to go."

Pierce pulled a memory, a pointed sliver, out of the past days. "Knights of the Rising God?"

"And up to no good," Leith answered grimly, "in Severen's name."

Val pulled out his cell. "Let's just find out what's got their attention . . ."

He regaled them for a while with an intermittent lecture involving tides, grasses, worms, mud, microscopic crabs, and salmon finding their way back home. "The great nursery of the sea," he intoned, then was silent, causing his brother and his father to pull their eyes off the road ahead to look at him.

"What is it?" Leith asked.

"There is an island in the middle of the sluff. The slog."

"Slough," Pierce said.

"Slew. According to this article, which of course is suspect since Severen only knows who wrote it, it was once, to ancient indigenous peoples, a holy place. They believed, because of the positions of the moonrise around it, that the island was the birthplace of the moon. It had attributes, this island. It had powers of healing. Women came there to give birth. Small things left as gifts have been found by archaeologists and picnickers. Painted clay beads, bone flutes, shell belts. Fieldstones carved with pictures of objects used in daily life, or birds and animals, were transported to the island and laid down in shapes corresponding to the phases of the moon." He glanced up at Leith's sudden shift. "Yes. That's probably where the knights are going. They seem fond of disturbing holy places. The site was most recently used, a century or two ago, by prospectors who built an alehouse on the island to carouse without complaints from the gentlefolk of Chimera Bay. There were rumors of a brothel as well. When the prospectors moved on, and the structures fell down, the island reverted to its former wild state."

"Is it accessible?" Leith asked.

Val studied his screen. "It is . . . yes. By means of a footbridge, too narrow for cars."

"But not for bikes."

"If they want to risk it. I wouldn't. It looks pretty rickety to me."

"They are risking it," Pierce said, looking over the driver's shoulder at a distant span above silent waters surrounded by the gentle rise and fall of thick, sprawling forests.

The driver echoed him. "There they are, sirs. And losing no time about it. Sorry to be so slow around these curves. The limo doesn't like to bend."

A dark smudge moved across the span, which seemed cobbled erratically to begin with, and gently dilapidated, swinging a slat here and there. One dropped off, shaken loose by the powerful vibrations of well-kept machines. It seemed to Pierce to fall a long way before it hit the water, causing a raptor to change its mind and veer sharply out of its dive.

As he watched, a piece of high ground detached itself from solid ground and shifted, as the road slewed, to reveal the water around all sides of it. The bridge disappeared into the tangle of green near the top of the island.

The first of the knights vanished into it.

"What do they think they'll find there?" Val wondered. "Gold the prospectors missed? The brothel?"

"What do you think, sirs?" the driver asked. "There are a couple dozen of them and, from the look of it, not much trouble they can get into."

As he spoke, a streak of blood-red lightning shot up from the trees, made a smoking blur of the uppermost branches. The driver braked hard, nearly tossing his passengers onto the floor.

"Sorry, sirs," he panted. "What was that?"

"Wyvern's Eye," Leith said tersely. "Step on it."

The driver pulled up finally at the end of the narrow bridge. As he tumbled out, Pierce heard faint cries across the water that might or might not have been gulls.

"Are you armed?" Leith asked him. He had to think.

"Yes." He touched his shoulder, where the knife lay in its hidden sheath. "Since this morning." He added, as another bolt of fuming red lit up the crown of the island, "For what it's worth."

Val, standing still, his eyes narrowed at the island, said, "There's a woman's voice among the birds."

"Not again," Leith breathed, and began to run.

By the time they reached the island and stumbled, panting, into the trees, the shouting had stopped. Even the birds had quieted. There was a faint, calm rill of water, which, as they moved toward it, transformed itself in surprising fashion to Pierce's ears. The water spoke a human language. The water was not water. The rill, low, sweet, calm, was human.

They followed the trail the bikes had left along a hiking path that was littered with torn branches and tire-scarred ground. The tangle around them opened to a wide clearing. Surrounded by brush and trees, it edged the top of the island, overlooking the waters of the slough as they were pushed inland by the tide toward the distant conjunction of water and earth, silver flowing and disappearing into the endless rise of green.

The woman, her back to them, was addressing the entire company of knights. They stood among the sunken patterns of fieldstone, small, dark standing stones, the drifts of shell and little piles of sea-polished stones left by more recent visitors. Their faces, half-hidden by visors and sunglasses, seemed both baffled and incredulous. The woman in black with the Wyvern's Eye in her hand aimed it not at them but at the line of bikes that had fallen one over the next as though they had been ruthlessly shoved.

"It's a long walk back to Severluna," she said.

Then she was facing Leith, Val, and Pierce, her pale violet eyes unblinking, her face composed, ready for whatever came. In her other hand, the weapon's red fuming eye still stared at the bikes.

There were stray movements among the knights, but Leith had his weapon out, aiming at the young men rather than their transportation. The woman smiled suddenly, and Pierce recognized the very tall, broad-boned, amber-haired knight who had rescued him, in the Hall of Wyverns, from the wrath of the king's seneschal.

"Sir Leith. Where on earth did you come from?"

Leith nodded, his taut face loosening almost enough to smile back. "Dame Scotia. I'm very happy to see you here."

"Sir Leith," one of the young men called across the clearing. "Can you get her to stop pointing that at our bikes? She has us at a disadvantage. We are Knights of the Rising God. We don't fight women."

"Oh, yes, you do," Pierce exclaimed indignantly. "Last I saw of you, you were harassing a girl at the mountain shrine."

"I'm sure that wasn't us."

"I'm counting," Val said, "what? Twenty-three of you? And you need my father to rescue you? I have an idea. Why don't you just do whatever Dame Scotia wants you to do?"

"We haven't done anything yet! We just came to look around, and she started shooting."

"I've been on the road long enough to see what happens when you just stop to look around," Dame Scotia said tartly. "Things get stolen and broken. Sacred shrines to gods other than Severen get totally trashed."

"We seek only what belongs to Severen—"

"You seek to destroy any hint of power other than Severen's. You're a rude, wicked lot, and I should just make you walk back across that bridge without your bikes."

"How about we slash their tires?" Pierce suggested.

"Let's toss their boots into the slough," Val said with enthusiasm. "After they tell us exactly what they hoped to find here."

There was a brief silence, during which the knights, without moving, seemed to shift closer together, and the partially hidden faces calculated the changed odds.

"You wouldn't understand," another indistinguishable face said slowly. "We are searching for something holy, precious, powerful. We move in Severen's name; his name moves our hearts. You, Sir Leith, might think yourself worthy of this quest. But Lord Skelton and Mystes Ruxley both spoke of the need to see with your heart, and how can you, blinded by the king's unfaithful wife wherever you look, and by your two sons at your side whose mother you abandoned for the queen? How can you possibly understand what we seek?"

Pierce, standing very still beside Val, could not hear him breathe. When he breathed again, Pierce knew, in that split second, the tiny, peaceful island would no longer be the same. Birds would die, maybe trees; stones would go flying; bikes would roar into flame. New ghosts would inhabit the place in Severen's name; they would roam without peace among the ghosts who still worshipped the moon.

Val drew breath. He turned his head to look at his father, and said mildly, "He's got a point. What do you think? Are they holier than thou?"

"Damned if I know," Leith said. "I do know that I don't want to litter the mudflats with their boots."

"If we slash their tires, we could find someone to haul the bikes off the island," Val suggested. "That way, we wouldn't offend the moon."

"Just try," another of the company dared them. "There are twenty-three of us and three—"

"Four," Dame Scotia said dryly.

"Actually, I wasn't counting the kitchen knight, Dame Scotia. That's five to one. At least."

"Ah," Val said. "That would be seven to one. Three times seven—"

"I knew that."

"Actually almost eight to one, Prince Ingram."

There was another brief silence. "How did you—"

"Don't," someone hissed between teeth. "He's just baiting you."

"Well, I can't go home and tell my father we attacked Sir Leith—"

"Why not? Would he care?"

"I have the strangest feeling that yes, he would care. More than I have the feeling that there's anything in this place we need to dig up. It's only a bit of tangled wood that everyone has already forgotten."

"That's not the point!"

"The point of this quest is to find something sacred and powerful," the prince said doggedly. "Not go around killing people. Especially people you just had dinner with a few nights ago."

"Oh, for—"

"He might be right about one thing," someone else said reasonably. "I don't see anything here worth fighting for."

"Prospectors came here. There might be gold that belongs by right to Severen, not the moon."

"This place has been well picked over for decades. A few fieldstones aren't worth the argument. Anyway, the sun is about to set. I'd not like to ride across that bridge in the dark. Nothing but bed slats and toothpicks."

"Well," their leader said disgustedly, "we can always come back. And we will, Sir Leith, Dame Scotia, if this is the direction the compass of Severen draws our hearts." He turned his back on them, strode to the toppled pile of bikes. "Let's untangle these and get out of this pathetic backwater."

"Can I reach for my cell without starting a war?" Val asked. "I need to tell our driver at the other end of the bridge to move out of your way."

Nobody bothered to answer him.

They followed the company of knights to the trail's end, stood watching them ride carelessly, noisily across the trembling bridge. It held, by some miracle, possibly Severen's, Pierce thought. But he doubted that the god would be at all interested in the mud, the trees, the moon just cresting the distant forest where the channel, pared to its narrowest, caught the first of the pale, ancient glow.

"What are you doing here?" Leith asked Dame Scotia when the knights had gotten safely across the bridge and back onto the road.

"I was looking for a place to camp for the night," she answered. "I saw the bridge and wondered where it led."

"It drew you."

She looked at him thoughtfully. "I suppose you could say."

"That happened to us," Val said, "in the mountains. Knights of the Rising God attacked a shrine. The forest god there summoned us by making our limo go dead for no reason at all until we finished his business."

"And here?"

"The knights passed us on the road, and we recognized them. We followed them to the bridge."

"They are troublesome," she murmured, frowning. "Brave and silly fanatics in love with Severen's power and wealth. I wasn't crazed enough to ride across the bridge. I walked my bike and found the trail to the ancient site. It seemed the perfect spot to build a fire, watch the night fall. And then they all came roaring out here. I hid myself and my bike until they started unpacking shovels. I'm so glad you showed up. I wasn't at all certain, once I got their attention, what to do with them."

"Neither was I," Leith admitted. He dropped his hand on Val's shoulder. "You had me worried there for that split second. But I should have trusted you. You rescued us. You have a gift for recognizing what matters. That what he said was true."

Val slewed a quick, perceptive glance at his father. But he only said wistfully, "I could worship the moon for a bit. Smell the tide, feel the wind, after all those hours in the limo. Do you want some company around your fire, Dame Scotia?"

Her smile appeared again, like something unexpected and lovely breaking the surface of an unruffled pool.

"Yes. Very much."

They gathered up twigs and fallen branches for a fire and sat around it among the stones and memories of the island. The night enclosed them quickly; the moon, a luminous eye, watched their fire with them, turning the complicated channels, the coils and threads of water, a silver that the god Severen had never thought to claim. Dame Scotia shared her wine with them, passing a camp cup around, as well as nuts and olives, smoked fish and chocolate. Pierce, leaning against one of the little standing stones, watched the stars form and hang among the tree branches like strange, fairy tale fruit. His thoughts reeled backward through the past amazing days, the scant weeks since he had left Cape Mistbegotten. A face appeared among the stars, long rippling hair, eyes the gray-green of her name.

"Tavis Malory," he heard Scotia say from the shadows. "Yes. The depraved knight who could not stay out of trouble and was in jail when he wrote the history of the first Wyvernhold king. Part of the land my father holds along the northern marches was once his. At least it was until Tavis had to sell it to pay compensation for one of his despicable crimes. His grandsons managed to buy back the land. They tried to restore his reputation, too, saying that his enemies betrayed and maligned him. But it was a tough sell. Everyone liked the other version of his life better. He did write a fine book, though." She leaned forward to prod the fire, and Pierce saw her profile, strong and graceful, the shining braid down her back now, loosed from its coils.

"We don't often see you at court," Leith commented.

"I'm with my father most of the year, helping him care for the land, especially when he's in Severluna himself, supporting parliamentary issues affecting the north. Water usage, fish habitats, that sort of thing. This time, when the king called the Assembly, my father had to send me alone. He sprained his back swinging a broadsword with too much enthusiasm for his age, and he can't travel easily yet."

"So you're questing," Val said. "Like the rest of us. Do you know where you're going?"

"Not entirely."

Val nodded, reaching out to stir the flames. "Following your heart."

In the sudden flare of firelight, Pierce saw her eyes widen with surprise, then swiftly fall. She turned, reaching into the shadows for more wood. Pierce's thoughts drifted again, this time back to the Kingfisher Inn, with its odd ceremony that seemed, at the time, as old as the stone at his back. What strange urge had that been, to steal the ritual knife, take it all the way to Severluna to end up coring a nonexistent apple on a field full of trained knights? Had the fish fry suffered because of him? he wondered. The wolf man, Merle, had known Pierce had it. *Take it to Severluna,* he had said in that hovel of a bar on the waterfront. *See what you can do with it.*

He had gone; he had seen. He had found his brother with it, then his father. Now he was ready to give it back. Was that the end of it?

His brother and his father were stirring, rising. He stood

up as well, feeling as pleasantly drunk with moonlight as with wine. Dame Scotia rifled through one of her packs and produced a flashlight, which they promised to leave for her at the other end of the bridge.

"What if the knights come back here?" Pierce asked uneasily.

"They won't cross that bridge in the dark. And I'll be gone at dawn."

They left her beside the fire under a watchful moon. Pierce glanced back at her before he turned onto the trail. She had risen also, and was standing at the edge of the cliff, looking out at the dark that defined itself best, to the human eye, by what it was not.

Light flared from a different night in the corner of Pierce's eye. He turned his head and froze at the reflection of fire in a pair of unexpected eyes. Something big, he sensed, just beyond the light. Something wild, powerful, undefined.

He opened his mouth to warn, then saw those eyes again, their human shape and expression, in his head, in memory. He breathed again, relieved by the thought of a closer, more dangerous guardian for the solitary knight than the wandering moon.

"Pierce," his father called from the dark ahead.

He nodded a greeting to the wolf and turned again to the path.

# 23

Carrie, veering around knights at any hour and on every corner of Chimera Bay, was hardly surprised, on one of her Stillwater lunch days, to see a darkly clad figure walk into the restaurant door ahead of her. It was too early for lunch, but Todd Stillwater rarely bothered with CLOSED signs. People would know, he told Carrie, and mostly that worked, though he didn't explain how. Carrie, causing the knight to turn as she followed him in, saw the expression on his face of someone amazed that he had actually found his way through a door.

Then she recognized the face.

That red hair, those vivid, blue-green eyes—there was a name attached to the face in some cluttered drawer or file holder in her head. He was frowning at her, recognizing her as well, but in the wrong context. She should, she remembered, have been carrying sheets instead of fresh basil and oregano from the Farmer's Market.

"Carrie?" she offered helpfully, and he nodded quickly.

"Yes. The Kingfisher Inn. I'm Pierce Oliver."

He looked older, she thought, than just a week or three. He had seen things, learned things, done something, at least, to be wearing that uniform.

"Did you get yourself knighted?" she asked with astonishment.

"No." The thought made him smile ruefully. "The only weapon I'm good with is the knife I stole. I plan to give it back," he added quickly.

"That's what my dad said. That it would bring you back."

"Really? Merle said that?"

"He did."

"How did—"

"He just knows things. If you want lunch, it'll be an hour or so before we start serving."

He shook his head. "I didn't come for lunch. I came to see if—" He paused; a little color streaked his face. "Is Sage here?"

"No," she said, amazed again, wondering how they had ever met. "She shops on Tuesdays."

"Of course. On Tuesdays." He sighed. "If I walked in here on a Wednesday or a Saturday, that would be the day she's out shopping."

She stared at him, recognizing that dazed look in his eyes. When on earth had he had time to fall in love with Todd Stillwater's wife? Then he was seeing Carrie again; he glanced puzzledly at the world around her.

"What are you doing here?" he asked. "Are you working for Stillwater now?"

She swallowed, stepped closer to him. "Listen," she said softly. "Please. Don't tell anyone I'm working here. Please. Nobody at the Kingfisher Inn knows. Nobody. I don't want them to know. Except my father. I mean, he already knows. But he's not talking about it. Maybe he'll talk to you."

"About what?"

"Just—please. Promise me? If you promise, I'll tell Sage you came here. But I won't tell Todd Stillwater."

He flushed again. But his eyes, on her face, were wide, curious. "I'll try to remember," he promised. "Might be easier if I knew why it's such a secret."

"It's too complicated to explain, and I can't, right now. You should go. I need to work. That way I'll have something to think about, and Todd won't pick you out of my head."

He frowned at that, still studying her. "Are you all right? I've never even met him, and he has that effect. Of making people not all right."

"I'm fine. I need to be fine. We'll talk later. Over a beer at the Kingfisher bar. All right?"

"Promise?"

"Yes."

In the quiet vault, she took the odd pot out of the corner where she always found it, no matter where else she had left it. Stillwater moved it out of his way, maybe. It had other quirks that she was beginning to expect. No matter how thoroughly she washed it, no matter how it brightened and glowed under her scrubbing, it would be, when next she saw it, in the same dull, cobwebby, grimy state as she had first found it. Stillwater, again, she guessed, though it was hard to imagine him not cleaning a pot, when she never saw as much as a speck on his gleaming machines. Another weirdness was the way it changed size according to what she put into it. It seemed to know what she wanted to cook: It grew huge at the proximity of live crabs from the docks; it dwindled down to the size of a soup bowl when she melted butter.

It could read her mind.

The first time she used it, she had no idea what to expect. None of Stillwater's machines ever did anything predictable. Would it, she wondered, transform a homely potato into a perfect nest of twigs, deep-fry them golden, and lay tiny eggs of potato ice cream in them? It did. Would it stack paper-thin slices of raw beef, black licorice, sweet cherries, white onion, and bittersweet chocolate into colorful layered bites, and add a rosette of red onion on top of it? It would indeed. Might it shred the boiled crabmeat, swirl cracked peppercorns, roasted garlic, and the tender green shoots of onions in such a magical fashion that the concoction could be inserted into hollow straws of deep-fried butter and breadcrumbs, to be sucked through them before the straws themselves were eaten? It might, it would, and it did. Carrie, so enchanted by the results, picked one without a thought out of the pot and bit into it.

Tastes filled her mouth: crab, onion, garlic, pepper, salt and spices from the breadcrumbs. She stood in shock, her mouth full, not daring to chew, just letting the wonderful wave of flavors flow and break across her tongue until, reflexively, she swallowed. The flavors did not vanish; they lingered, reminding her what charms and delights a simple, single bite of anything at all could hold.

She reached into the pot for another, then another.

Then she heard Todd's voice, Sage answering, Todd's voice again, coming closer as he walked into the vault. He wore his sweet Stillwater face since the restaurant would soon be open. At other times, he did not know, or perhaps he didn't care, what face Carrie saw. She turned to present him with her experimental crab bite, and found the pot had disappeared, along with everything she had made.

She stared at where it had been, then at the corner where it usually sat: it was nowhere to behold.

She still had a bite, she realized, in her hand. He looked surprised by the bare table, the silent machines.

"You haven't started cooking yet? It's nearly time to open. Business is doing well with all the knights coming in. They inspire me," he said, with a faint, thin smile.

"I was experimenting," she told him, glancing around again for the hidden pot. "I came up with this."

She gave him the crab straw; he ate it the way she had envisioned: sucking the crab out like a mouthful of milk shake, then eating the savory little straw.

He nodded. "Good," he said. "Very good. As always," which was what he always said, without a flicker of expression, as though he had just tossed back a vitamin pill. "Make more," he suggested. "And make it fast."

She gazed at his back as he went out to the dining room. He had tasted nothing, she realized suddenly. He had never tasted anything. He had no idea what she could feed his customers if only she could find what she had made it in.

"Come back, pot," she whispered, glancing under the table. "Where are you, pot?"

And there it was on the table again. She studied it a moment, wondering at this extraordinary vessel, able to change its size, wear protective coloring, see what she saw, imagine what she imagined, making it, then hiding itself at will from the cook whose machines transformed everything into illusion.

She made more, she made it fast, and she made it all in that peculiar pot.

Stillwater came in again to cook with her, later. She expected the pot to vanish again. But it stayed visible, all the while he worked with his machines and barely noticed what Carrie did. He looked straight at it a time or two, Carrie thought, but he did not comment. So why, she wondered, did it bother to hide?

She answered her own question finally, making tiny, braided loaves of bread out of white root vegetables and baked egg whites.

I can see you, she told it. Todd Stillwater, whatever he is, can't. All he sees when he looks at you is another of his machines. Point taken.

Sage came in, for a taste, as she usually did. Carrie handed her a bite from the rows lined on parchment paper. Sage wondered aloud about the time; Stillwater, whose attention was focused down the gullet of a machine, did not seem to hear. Waiting, Sage popped the bite into her mouth.

She chewed once, then stood transfixed, as though she were listening to music she had not heard in years or remembering a life she had misplaced.

She closed her eyes, chewed again. "Chocolate," she whispered. "Cherries. Licorice. Raw beef, raw onion. And one last— Oh. Yes."

Stillwater raised his head. The utensil in his hand dropped into the working machine and it made a noise like metal wrapping itself into knots.

Then his hands were on Carrie's shoulders, his face flowing in and out of other faces, other expressions, mostly furious and even more frantic.

"Where is it?" he shouted. "Where is it? It's mine! I rescued it—it belongs to me!" Shocked, she couldn't find her voice. His hands tightened; he focused an enormous, leaf-green eye on her that held a predator's senseless, malignant glare. "Where?" He shook her, then let go of one shoulder and raised his hand, shrieking, "Where? Is? It?"

"Where is what?" Carrie gabbled back, terrified. "I don't even know what it is! I just—I gave—I had it in my pocket— One of my bites from the Kingfisher Grill."

"No. You come here first—"

"I went in early to help Ella make cherry tarts for supper. Things were lying around. I just— So I just made something. Ella liked it, so I brought a piece here. I don't know why you're shouting at me. I don't have anything of yours. Everything in here is yours."

The eye, luminous and huge, seemed to stare into the bottom of her mind. But all it would have seen, she realized shakily, was a battered, stained old pot, worn beyond use, and most likely found under a sink in the Kingfisher Grill, catching a leak in the pipes.

He let her go abruptly. Sage had vanished somewhere

inside herself, standing motionless, unblinking, trying to make herself into air, nothing more noticeable or important.

Stillwater picked the utensil out of the machine, and shook it, listening to its inner rattlings. He put it under the table. When he spoke again, he sounded as calm and reasonable as ever.

"You should make more of those bites for us, since Sage likes it so much. Yes, Sage. Go ahead and let them in."

Carrie kept the small bites coming for a couple of hours, sometimes using Stillwater's machines, sometimes the ugly, magnificent pot.

Finally, the last diner left; Sage closed the door, and Carrie came out to help clear the tables, while Stillwater tidied his machines. Finished, he left the rest of the cleanup to Carrie and went out, as usual, to walk and think about tomorrow's lunch, since the restaurant was closed for supper that night. Carrie put plates in the dishwashers, handwashed the bar glasses, and scrubbed and polished the pot until she saw the gentle glow of its fires.

She put it in its favorite corner and stood for a moment, listening. Stillwater hadn't returned yet. The washing machines were running, full of napkins and tablecloths, which meant that Sage was back in the old bank office, adding up receipts.

Carrie turned, contemplated Stillwater's small, gleaming army of machines.

She went to work.

She took the pot with her when she finished.

# 24

Pierce was sitting at the Kingfisher bar late in the evening, alone and waiting for Friday or Carrie, whichever came first, when he became aware of a stirring in the air beside him, a shift of the empty barstool. Fingers gripped his arm. He turned, looked into a white, thin face with the wolf's pale, luminous eyes. Carrie, he realized with a start; still he did not entirely recognize her.

"You're a knight," she said, getting to the point without bothering to say hello. "At least you look like one. And you know something about magic. You knew which knife to steal."

He flushed. "I'm giving it back, I swear—"

"I meant that you saw the magic in it. The mystery. I need help. Isn't that what questing knights are for?"

"I suppose. I didn't really listen to the instructions. Of course I'll help, whatever it is. Can I buy you that beer?"

She nodded, raising a finger at Tye, who lifted an empty

glass in greeting and slid it under a tap. Pierce, studying her hollow, resolute face, wondered at the changes in it.

He said abruptly, "It's Stillwater. Isn't it?"

"Don't say that name," she breathed. "Not in here. He's got a history, here."

"Carrie," Tye said, setting her beer down. "Haven't seen much of you these days. Working too hard?"

"Thanks, Tye," she said, giving him a smile that he didn't return. His eyes, behind his glasses, seemed opaque, his thoughts withdrawn to some distant place. He didn't look at Pierce until Pierce spoke.

"Tye. About the knife—"

"Don't worry about it. We'll settle up later. You okay for now?"

"For now, thanks," Pierce answered, and Tye moved away, swatting at a cruising fly with his bar towel. Above him, the mobile of hanging Fools' heads swayed and turned as someone else came in. Pierce was silent until a couple settled at the other end of the bar, and Tye went to greet them. Then he said softly, "They know. Don't they? That you're working for him?"

Carrie gave a brief nod, huddling over her beer, dropping words into it as though they would dissolve with the beer bubbles. "He destroyed this place," she whispered, "and left them all spellbound. Not even my father could drive him out of Chimera Bay. He couldn't enchant my father, though. My father saw clearly enough what was going on. Like you do, even though you've never even met—never—" She paused, asked bewilderedly, "How on earth did you find your way to that restaurant? I thought you'd left town."

"I blew a tire and hit a tree. I stayed downtown while my

car was being fixed. Skulked, more like it, so that I wouldn't run into anyone here. I don't know why I wanted that knife. I just did. So I took it. Then I wandered by that restaurant and saw something else I wanted."

Her eyes widened. "Are you just naturally drawn to trouble, or do you go looking for it?"

"How would I know? I've never left home before."

"Well." Her voice went thin again, almost inaudible. "She could use your help. We both could. Very much. You saw what he wanted you to see. The way he wanted you to see her. He did that to me, too. To everyone in this place. He shows you a face to fall in love with, then he starves you. You can never have it, and you can't live without it."

"Sage," he breathed, suddenly cold. "Is she—"

"Not like him. No. She could use some rescuing." She linked her fingers around her glass but didn't lift it; she hadn't taken a single sip. "She's trapped. So am I. But at least I know now what I'm looking at."

"What can I do?"

She drew a breath. "Come for lunch tomorrow. Anytime after one—he should be open by then. I might need someone to fight for me."

"What are you planning?" he asked, startled.

"I made some changes. I'm not sure about anything I did, or can do. But maybe, while you're there, you'll think of something. If nothing I did works."

His eyes narrowed. "Does Merle know you're doing this?"

Her taut face warmed unexpectedly at the name; she almost smiled. Again, Pierce glimpsed the wolf in her eyes. "I haven't told him. But he'll know."

Pierce was silent a moment, absently running his finger around the lip of his glass and remembering Sage, her easy smile, her fairy tale face, the long, rich fall of her hair, so heavy, so full it could belong only in the realm of the imagination. The beer glass refused to sing; he dropped his hand, said hollowly, "I spent those two or three days in Chimera Bay trying to get back in to see her. Trying to outsmart the restaurant. But always when I went there, no matter what time of day, no matter what day, it would be closed. If he sees me coming, I might not be much help to you. He might just lock the place up."

"Maybe you can melt in with the lunch crowd. And if not—we'll have to think of something else. But try. Please? Just remember: If he actually lets you in the door, don't eat anything."

"Of course I'll try." He reached toward his back pocket, caught Tye's eye, and gave up on that thought. "He won't let me pay for anything," he murmured ruefully. "Not even my mistakes."

"You're family," Carrie said. "Your mother has been calling Lilith ever since you left home. She knows you're here." He stared at her, aghast. "You could invite her to lunch. I'm just saying," she added as he stood up. "We need all the help we can get."

"Believe me," he said grimly, "joining me for lunch is the last thing she'll do if she finds out who else I'm inviting."

He was amazed any number of times before he actually saw Sage's face. The small, elegant restaurant stayed on its corner as he approached it and did not shroud itself in mist. The door opened when he thumbed the latch. There were actually diners inside, filling most of the tables, as though there were nothing at all extraordinary about the place. He saw Sage standing with her back to him, speaking to a table of four, most likely telling them what they were going to have for lunch. Then she turned, and above all, he was astonished at the sudden, pleased smile on her face.

"You came back!" she exclaimed. "We hoped you would. Todd asked me to tell him if I ever saw you again, so that he could make something very special for you. Now let me see. Where can I put you?"

Pierce glanced around, found his father and brother at a table in a corner near the bank vault. "With them," he said. "They're waiting for me."

"Oh, that's perfect. As you can see, we have so many guests today." She paused briefly, her attention snagged by his clothes, or by the scrutiny he gave her face. A line, the faintest thread of thought, formed and vanished on her brow. "I don't remember that you were a knight," she said slowly. "I remember—someone younger."

"I'm a kitchen knight," he answered wryly, and realized, as he heard himself, how it was true.

She said nothing, bowed her head, showing him her perfect profile against her shining hair, and led him to the table.

Val glanced up from his phone as Pierce sat; his pale blue, burning gaze homed in on his brother, and then on the tall, lovely server. "Are you all here now?" she asked, then paused, as though distracted from a script. "You look so much alike."

"They're my sons," Leith said with satisfaction, and her

eyes widened, as though even she, the sorcerer's enchanted wife, recognized the man behind the gossip.

"We might have other friends coming," Val told her cheerfully. "They're very rowdy. You probably shouldn't let them in."

"As long as Todd cooks, he will feed whoever comes in. We'll find room. Have you had a chance to read the menu? It's unusual, but everything he cooks is wonderful; you won't be sorry about letting him choose. And we have an amazing new cook working with him. Our well-kept secret. We hide her in the shadows so no one can steal her away. What would you like to drink?"

"Water.

"Water."

"Water."

"Perfect. I'll let the kitchen know you're ready."

"Who else did you invite?" Pierce asked Val softly when she was out of earshot.

Val picked up his cell again, and fingered through it. "I'll show you."

There was, oddly enough, what looked like real bread on the table. Both Val and Leith had broken a piece on their plates, scattering a deceptive path of crumbs onto the cloth. Pierce, eyeing the board with the tiny loaf on it, felt a sudden urge to taste it, find out if it was real. Val raised his eyes from the phone, narrowed them warningly at his brother.

"She's very beautiful," he murmured. "I can see why you came back here."

Pierce opened his mouth, found no coherent response in his head. I came back to return a knife, he thought. I came

back to show you what a fish fry is. I came to rescue a cook
who asked to be helped. I came because I couldn't not. "She's
not what you see," he said shortly. "That's why we're here.
What are you looking at?"

Val turned his phone around, showed him an image. It
was of a huge cauldron, polished so that it seemed to shine
from within by its own brilliant, mystical source. Every inch
of it held pictograms, ancient writings, birds, fish, animals
both legendary and extinct. Light filled the cauldron, spilled
out and around it in a swirling pattern that curled through
the air as it flowed upward. It was fashioned, Pierce guessed,
out of solid gold, and looked big enough to steam the three
of them together.

"That should do it," Val said with satisfaction.

"Should," Leith agreed, smiling.

"What's the name of this place again?"

Pierce pushed the Stillwater's menu under his nose. "But
what is it?"

"In life? About as big as my fist. It lives in a Severluna
museum. I added a few things to it." He worked silently a
moment, then put the phone down and leaned over the
table, his head very close to his brother's. "I'm certain that's
what our lunch is made in. Don't you think so? I just sent
the image to Niles Camden and Prince Ingram. They're still
in town. I saw them last night in a brew-pub. We got into a
philosophical argument. Or was it metaphysical? I can't
remember who won."

Pierce, gazing at the golden, shining pot, swallowed dryly,
his eyes prickling with wonder. "You're diabolical."

"Thank you. We can only hope they take the bait."

Sage came over to them, carrying a tray. She set down three glasses of water, three small plates, and a slightly larger plate holding three layered ovals of jewel-like colors, and three little cones made of what looked like frozen gold foam, out of which black pearls or fish eggs spilled over frozen waves of white. "Something special to waken your appetites," she said. "Enjoy."

She left them staring warily, bemusedly, at their lunch. "Now what?" Val breathed. "We forgot to think about this part."

"Use your uniforms," Leith murmured. "Surely you don't have an arsenal in every opening." He guided a cone toward his mouth, dropped it adroitly down the sheath in his sleeve.

"Magic," Val said wryly, and disappeared a cone somewhere under the table.

Pierce picked up one of the oval bites. It teased him with its half-recognizable layers. Fresh raw tuna, it suggested. Candied lemon peel. The thinnest slice of rose-golden peach. Roasted purple beet. A mouthful of mysteries. A chord for the palate. Carrie made it, he thought. How could it harm?

"Don't," Leith said very softly, "even think about it. You warned us, last night. Remember why."

There was a shriek from the kitchen; it sounded like a machine being tortured. A human shout followed it, then a muffled thump. Something shot out from between the bank vault's closed curtains, skimmed a tabletop or two, then flattened itself against a far wall above the heads of two transfixed diners. A formless clot of translucent purple slid very slowly, inch by inch, down the wall, leaving an oddly glistening trail of green.

The two diners leaped up, overturning their chairs. The vault curtains whipped open, and Pierce finally saw Todd Stillwater's face.

It seemed, for a blink, oddly layered, like his bites. The self-deprecating face of an inhumanly comely god fallen to earth was stretched, at the temples and eyelids, over a bulky, twisted, sunken-eyed tree burl, which had been hastily pulled over something else entirely, with pallid skin glistening like decaying mushroom and clinging tautly to a white frame of bone, through which yet another face drifted like a dream or a memory of a wild, ancient, darkly haunting beauty.

In the next blink, the layers collapsed under the perfect, disingenuous human face, reassuring in its concern for the dismayed crowd of common mortals.

"I am so, so sorry." Even his voice was perfect: resonant, sweet, expressive. "We're having a little trouble with the kitchen equipment. Please. Don't feel you have to leave. We've gotten the trouble under control. And I'm more than happy, in apology for your inconvenience and distress, to cook lunch for all of you for free today. If you—"

There was another explosion. Stillwater whirled; the frozen diners waited. But nothing flew out this time. The thing creeping down the far wall detached itself with an audible squelch and fell on the floor.

Someone laughed. Then everyone was laughing, bent over their plates, wiping their eyes, sliding out of their chairs. Stillwater, mingling apology and relief in his smile, took his apron off and tossed it over the mass. Sage appeared between the curtains. Her own face had lost its cool serenity. Pierce saw the anxiety, the wariness in it, as she hurried across the room toward her husband.

Pierce rose, turning against her wake, and stepped quickly through the curtains.

The vault, a wine cellar now, opened at the back to the expanse of kitchen beyond. It looked peculiar at first glance. It lacked essentials, Pierce realized. Like pots and pans. Grills. An oven. Mostly it held a large table covered with machines, one of which Carrie seemed to be trying grimly to stab to death with a pair of tongs.

She jumped when she saw Pierce. "What are you doing back here?" she hissed.

"Can I help with that? I've seen machines like these in Severluna."

"No, you haven't. There are none, anywhere, like these. They turn perfect food into air. Air into art. You didn't eat anything, did you?"

"No. What are you doing?"

"Trying to make it eat tongs."

"I can—"

"No. Don't let Stillwater see you back here." He hesitated; she glared at him fiercely. "Go and watch over Sage. She doesn't have a single weapon."

She has you, Pierce thought, and stepped back out of the vault into a battlefield.

So it seemed, with all the darkly uniformed knights pouring through the doors. Pierce heard Stillwater's voice trying for reason, humor; the young men ignored him, milling among the indignant diners, picking up this and that, invading the tiny space behind the bar, rattling through bottles and glassware. Then one stepped through the vault curtains, and Stillwater's voice cracked a martini glass with his shout.

"No!"

The knights stared at him, motionless. Then, like a wave, they broke, tumbled across the room, and flowed through the steel walls of the vault toward the kitchen.

Pierce heard Carrie scream.

He spun, dove into the flow.

By the time he had shouldered his way back into the kitchen, he found Carrie standing on top of the table among Stillwater's machines. She held the tongs like a weapon, vigorously smacking hands probing the strange machines that could turn their fingers into froth.

"What are you looking for?" she demanded. "This is just a kitchen! I'm cooking here! If you'll tell me what you're looking for—" She paused to whack the head of a knight who had turned a machine upside down and was shaking it. "Be careful with that! You have no idea how dangerous it is."

He glanced up at her with sudden interest. "Seriously? It's a weapon?"

"You would not believe."

"Then it belongs by right to the god Severen."

She stared at him, her tongs suspended. She said slowly, "I never thought of it that way. You're right. Take them. Take them all."

Across a noisy, chaotic distance, Pierce heard a hoarse, deep reverberation, as though the air had growled. Then Stillwater was in the kitchen, melting through the crush of knights, leaping lightly onto the table beside Carrie like some graceful, powerful creature made of air and muscle, for whom bones were optional.

"What are you doing?" he demanded; his voice still held the snarling edge to it. His eyes were on Carrie, but it was a knight who answered.

"We are here in Severen's name. We are Knights of the Rising God, come to proclaim the god's ascendancy above all others—"

"This is a restaurant, not a church! We cook in here."

"You cook in a vessel that belongs to Severen." Pierce recognized the knights' obstinate, humorless, boneheaded leader, Sir Niles Camden. "A great cauldron made of pure gold, that feeds everyone who comes here whatever they crave, and it constantly replenishes itself, it is never empty. We want it. Such a vessel is dedicated, by its nature, by its never-ending power enclosed in gold, to the god Severen. Praise him. In the name of King Arden, we have come to return the sacred vessel to the god."

"You disgrace the name of King Arden." Somehow Leith and Val had pushed their way into the tightly crowded kitchen. "You disrupt people's lives and steal from them," Leith continued sharply. "You are not true knights, and no true god would accept your worship. You're nothing but marauding thieves."

"We are questing knights, Sir Leith," Prince Ingram protested. "You can't change facts by calling people names."

"You're trashing a restaurant kitchen. How proud would your father be of that?"

"Enough!" Stillwater roared. The sound filled the kitchen and seemed to vibrate through his face, shake it free to reveal the bole and burls beneath the mask. This time, Pierce was not the only one to see it. Carrie stared at him, her eyes huge. Stillwater reached out, gripping her with fingers that coiled like bindweed around and around her arm. "There is nothing in this kitchen but what you see. I don't cook in gold. It is soft, malleable; it changes shape too easily under pressure. I make my own machines; they work their wonders by such power that you would never understand. A god who values gold possesses no more than human powers. I feed the hungry. You knights won't find what you're looking for under this roof. But if you stay, I will cook for you, with my machines, a meal that you will never forget. If you stay, my wife Sage will seat you and bring you whatever you want to drink. Carrie will help me cook for you. Stay. Sit at our tables. Enjoy what we bring you; that's all you need to do here."

"That's all you'll ever do," Carrie cried. "Don't listen—"

Stillwater, his open, genial face restored, tapped her lips lightly with a forefinger. "She worries about me working too hard. But I feel like cooking. Cooking for you. All day and through the night, as long as you want to stay."

In his grasp, Carrie, her lips tightly closed, turned her head frantically, trying to push out words. Pierce, swayed hither and yon by the murmuring, surging crowd, felt something sharp threaten to dig into his elbow. He straightened his arm slowly, jostling for space, and pulled the kitchen knife out of his sleeve. His fingers closed tightly around the familiar handle, something to hold on to when there seemed nothing else. Val had a weapon out, too, he saw: The Wyvern's Eye was cupped in his hands, though, surrounded by the eerie magic of Stillwater's machines, the eye remained oddly dark.

The knights were looking at Niles Camden, who finally proffered judgment. "If you let one or two of us watch you cook—"

"Certainly."

"To see that nothing handled is of metals dedicated to Severen."

"Yes."

"And that these machines truly cook, and are not weapons, and therefore dedicated to the god—"

"Of course."

"Then maybe we can—"

The knife slid out of Pierce's hand as someone passed him. His fingers tightened on air. He glanced around, startled, but saw only the listening knights, and Sage, who had slipped in somehow, likely at the sound of her name. Her back to Pierce, she eased herself around, between, toward her husband on the table, whose hold on Carrie had taken on a less fantastic shape.

"Ah," Stillwater said, smiling at the ripple through the crowd. "And here Sage is to help you all find places at our tables. If you would follow her—"

*Out*, he meant to say, when a seam of silver parted the air above Sage, caught light as it spun itself down. Somehow, Stillwater's word got stuck. His mouth opened wider and wider around it; still he could not push it out. His fingers uncurled; Carrie stumbled away from him as he bent down over himself. Knights near the table backed abruptly into one another, away from Sage and the strangely afflicted Stillwater, who was losing masks like leaves dropping away from him, until only one was left.

The word came out finally, a stunned shriek, and Pierce saw the kitchen knife again, nailing the chef among his machines to the table by one bloody foot.

"Take the machines," Sage cried, turning away from him to face the knights. "Take them all to Severluna and throw them into the river. They are weapons. They are as powerful and destructive as any you carry. Go away and take them with you and never, ever eat anything they might tempt you with, because you will never again want anything but air until you die."

The bones were sharp in her wan, wasted face; her long hair hung limply; her eyes were hollowed with a human hunger. Behind her, Stillwater was tugging at the knife in his foot; it refused to give him up. Pierce would not have recognized him. His hair was a cloud of tangled dark, his eyes an astonishing peacock blue flecked with gold, his lean, high-boned face wild in its beauty, a face that had been once worn very close to earth.

A wolf howled from the street outside. Then it howled at the door, and again, within the walls. Stillwater stopped moving, gazed incredulously toward the sound. Carrie, who stood holding one of his machines, a soda siphon by the look of it, above his head in case he escaped, smiled suddenly at what bounded through the knights, knocking half of them off their feet.

"Hey, Dad."

The wolf leaped up onto the table; machines wobbled and crashed. The wolf snarled, showing teeth inches from Stillwater's face.

"You can't be here," Stillwater panted raggedly. "You can't get past my wards. You never could. You—"

He stopped speaking. His face turned reluctantly, angle by angle, toward what his eyes did not want to see.

Three women stood across the threshold of his escape.

At first glance, Pierce guessed, they were family, stopping in for a bite: daughter, mother, grandmother. Their eyes held a similar expression of recognition, satisfaction, the successful completion of some task, maybe something as simple as finally finding the time to meet together. Then he felt his skin prickle. What they recognized was Stillwater, or whatever went by that name, now that he had shed every disguise. They knew his oldest face.

An odd cast of light behind them caused their shadows to meet in front of them, form one long, straight line of dark that rolled through the old vault, into the kitchen to the table. Knights, oddly silent, swallowing their words, shifted away from that dark, pushing against one another to avoid its stark edges.

"There you are," the oldest said. Her eyes were smudged silver, her hair white as moonlight.

"And about time," the younger said. Her face looked backward and forward, lingering in the mellow season of beauty between young and old. "You've lived so quietly up here, you must have thought we had forgotten you entirely. But we have never for a moment forgotten. The wolf recognized you. He called us until we finally heard him."

The youngest of them, slight and ethereally slender, gazed at him curiously out of his own rich, fay eyes. "You stole our cauldron, that feeds anyone, everyone, and is never empty. Yet you made these machines. You make hate with them, and you feed it to humans. You hated your own world; you hate this one as much. What a strange existence. You never used what you had stolen. What did you do with it?"

Behind the creature that was Stillwater, Carrie lowered the machine she held over him. She set it very quietly on the table and backed away from the impending storm. Leith, his eyes never leaving the three, held out his hand to her, helped her down. The wolf, turning restively on the table, shoved against the trapped cook once or twice, knocking his body out of its precarious huddle over the knife, its compromise with pain. His mouth opened again; the anguished word that came out was incomprehensible. Then the wolf flowed carelessly down onto the tangle of shadows and turned human.

He turned his back to Stillwater, asked the three tersely, "You? Or me?"

"He might prefer you," the oldest said, her silvery eyes as cold as the metallic machines around the cook. "You are powerful, Merle, and you might find a way to give him oblivion. We can take him back to the place he fled so long ago, the place where he was born. He has something that belongs to us; he will not die before he tells us where it is."

Another word came out of the cook, a wild bird cry, echoing itself again and again. He pulled frantically at the knife, his hands growing slick; the kitchen blade seemed rooted in the table, oblivious to any power but its own. He spoke again to the women, words entwined with the sounds of birds and insects, frogs and snakes, creatures that ran on four legs and named themselves with other than language.

"Promises," the youngest said, the one who had his eyes.

"Promises. I am only part fay, the tiniest breath left from those days when human and fay crossed paths, and yet I feel I know you. What have you done to yourself?"

"Time to go," the third said, her pale eyes pitiless. "Time to go home."

"I don't know!" he shouted, finding one final way to say what he needed. "I don't know where it is! It vanished from my sight years ago. Maybe decades, maybe centuries—I don't remember! It was useless to me—I stopped seeing it, and it was gone."

They had no faces suddenly; they had no substance; three shadows stood together, hollows of air and space. On the floor, the path of their true shadows deepened, took on dimension. The thing that had been Stillwater was losing its shape, blurring into a slurry not unlike one of his strange culinary inventions. So were the walls and ceiling of the kitchen; the machines, the table, everything that was not human dissolved. Colors ran, whirled, shed light, as though, Pierce thought, the world itself had gotten snagged in one of the machines and was turning into something only almost familiar. Then, for the briefest, most exquisite moment, he saw the world that engulfed the fay: such a wealth, a treasure of beauty, of scents and sounds, air as fine as silk, heavy gold light falling extravagantly everywhere, free for the taking, loveliness wherever he looked, as though he had never fully opened his eyes before, and now he could see what he had missed, what had always been there, all along, if only he had looked.

Then all he saw was that long stretch of shadow, opening like a door. The cry of loss that came out of it as it closed sounded completely human.

# 25

Daimon, stopped at a light on the highway running along the water in Chimera Bay, saw a sign ahead of him, swaying from the scaffolding covering much of a dilapidated old hotel. ALL YOU CAN EAT, it said, FRIDAY NITE FISH FRY.

The light changed; he started forward. He angled across the next lane and pulled into the parking lot, sat idling, gazing at the extremely unlikely sign, and the even more improbable Kingfisher Bar and Grill, whose customers all seemed to own one version or another of the same dented, rackety pickup.

He heard another bike turn in behind him. In that same moment, the world began to ripple around him. His inarticulate protest was echoed by a sudden shift of gears behind him. The stranger's bike roared; the town vanished into mist and trees, and he heard another voice raised in a cry of complete astonishment.

He turned, found Dame Scotia Malory, pale and breath-less, searching the air for whatever was left of Chimera Bay.

"What— Where— What just happened?"

"Dame Scotia," he said, astounded. "What are you doing here?"

"Following you."

"Here?"

"Here is where you went. So I—" Her voice wobbled; so did her bike. She got off it, kicked its stand in place, and turned a slow circle, blinking rapidly at the tall, silent trees, pennants of mist hanging from their boughs. "Princess Perdita asked me to follow you. So I—" Her voice trickled to a whisper. "So I did.

"Here?" he repeated sharply, and she shrugged helplessly.

"It's where you went."

Daimon parked his own bike, frowning, watching her turn another bewildered circle, searching for anything famil-iar. Memories appeared in his mind like stepping-stones; he tracked her backward to the royal library, to the palace garage.

"Why on earth," he asked with some annoyance, "would Perdita ask you to follow me all the way up the north coast?"

"Well." Her face, still colorless, seemed to shield itself then behind a warrior's mask, calm, watchful, focused on that fraught question. "It seems she met your mother. Who explained what she, and Lady Seabrook, and your friend Vivien Ravensley have in mind for you. At the least, a wedding. At most, war between Wyvernhold and Ravenhold. Between you and your father. The end of the rule of the Wyvernbourne kings."

Daimon, staring at her, felt the fog that had taken up residence in his head fray a little, breeze-blown, hinting at the precipice on which he stood. "That sounds," he said, his eyes narrowed against the mist, "that sounds like some old story."

"Doesn't it?"

"How did it end?"

"Badly. Very, very badly."

He was silent again, his eyes on her face now, using its calm to look as clearly as he could into the swirling, unsettled mists of the past weeks. He had met a young woman with astonishing eyes. She had taken him into another world, showed him marvels, the most marvelous of which was how she had made him see so clearly the drab, pointless, unfeeling world he had been born in, devoid of vision, trivial to the extreme, and completely unworthy of his curiosity and his love. In return, she had asked him only the simplest of favors: to find a cauldron, to help her regain her lost realm, to become her consort when she was crowned queen.

He closed his eyes and glimpsed the edge of the precipice at his feet, the long, long fall into the unknown.

Where had he been? he wondered, seeking Dame Scotia's face again to steady himself as he balanced precariously between worlds.

He remembered then the knight in black he had battled with a broadsword, whose impervious, implacable strength within the armor, behind the expressionless helm, had seemed to him the shape and invincible face of his own confusion, his conflicted impulses. The lovely, smiling, unexpected face that appeared beneath the helm as he lay vanquished on the ground had transformed the dark.

"How did you do that?" he demanded, incredulous again. "Is there some Ravensley in your past? Is that how you could follow me even here?"

"Ravensley? Not that I know," she answered, looking baffled. "The family crests tend toward beasts that get along very well with this world. Is that where we are? In that fay realm?"

He glanced at the silent trees, the bay streaked with long sluices of mudflat as the tide slowly, gently, pulled back into the sea. "I'm not sure. In someone's past, I think."

"Is that why you stopped here? Because you sensed something? It drew you here?"

"I stopped because I heard a rumor that within a shabby diner advertising all you can eat there might be the vessel of ancient and enormous power I was requested to find and return to Ravenhold."

"Ravenhold. Not Wyvernhold."

"I have the raven's eyes. So I'm told. And the raven's heart. I would recognize what belongs to the raven." He wandered restively a few steps to where the Kingfisher Inn should have cast its shadow, should have hidden the water from view. "Apparently, the inn vanished when it saw me coming."

"The entire town vanished," she breathed. "It's like a dream. A spell cast over us."

"Yes."

"Has this happened to you before?"

"Oh, yes," he said, memories flooding into his head, a colorful wave of scraps, moments, brief and timeless.

"Well, how— What do you do to find your way out of it?"

He looked at her from within the tide, no longer seeing

her. "What makes you think I have ever wanted to find my way out? Have you ever been spellbound?"

"Not until now."

"This is where I found everything I thought I wanted. I left the world behind to come to this place. I left my heart here, always, so that I could find my way back. Now I can't even find that."

"What?"

"The face I loved. My heart." He paused, searching for one face in memory, and finding someone else entirely. "You should not be here."

"No," she said softly, somberly. "But I am. Lord Skelton warned us about quests. How they reveal even when they seem to conceal, or confuse, or make no sense whatsoever. Maybe this is not the spell that binds your heart; maybe it is part of the quest you are on."

"This has nothing to do with Lord Skelton's quest—"

"You are searching for the same thing," she said inarguably. "What would you have done with that extraordinary vessel if you had walked into the Kingfisher Bar and Grill and found it there? You recognize this marvel, you take it—and you do what with it? Use it to threaten your own father with war if he doesn't return a long-forgotten land to its rightful ruler? Would you really do that?"

He was seeing her clearly, then, and wondering at the question, which took on dimensions he hadn't noticed before, or had so completely forgotten why he should care about them. "Yes," he said finally. "Yes. I would have. If I had walked into the Kingfisher Inn instead of into this mystifying, exasperating no-place. This mist would still have been in my head instead of all around us. Now, my head is appallingly clear. And when we are finally allowed to leave this place, I will be of no use any longer to the one who enchanted me. Or to myself," he added with wry sorrow. "I will be disenchanted."

He was astonished at the sudden sheen in her eyes, the well of tears from some source hidden within her prowess, her composure.

"I am so sorry," she whispered. "I should never have followed you so far."

"I didn't think anyone could." He was silent again, thinking clearly for once, and finding it disconcerting. "If this isn't within the definition of Lord Skelton's idea of a quest, and it isn't the enchanting place I had begun to know so well— if some power is guarding that vessel from both the wyvern and the raven, then where are we? Who brought us here?"

"Good question," his mother said, and he saw the three familiar faces behind Dame Scotia.

She whirled, as though she felt the intent gazes homing in between her shoulder blades.

"Who is this," Vivien wondered, "standing between you and me, my love?"

Scotia moved again, quickly, stepping to one side of Daimon. "Lady Seabrook," she exclaimed, and Morrig smiled suddenly with delight.

"Dame Scotia Malory. I met your ancestor Tavis once, you know. Well, of course you don't, but I did. You'd think, writing all those tales of valor and romance, he would have led a more respectable life. But then, how would he have recognized me?"

"You knew Tavis?" Scotia said faintly.

"Of course. I have been at the Wyvernhold Court since the first King Arden overran Ravenhold. I thought it would be the best place to hide."

"But how," Vivien asked, her wide, lovely eyes never moving from Daimon's, "did this knight find her way here?"

"Well," Morrig mused, considering the question, "that might be Tavis's fault, too. We might as well blame him. Everyone else did. He was always finding himself where he didn't belong, and with those who might have given him a glimpse into overlapping realms. Dame Scotia could have inherited some of his sight. Fore and hind, over and in, as well as second—who knows exactly which sight drew her here?"

"She serves the wyvern," Daimon's mother said abruptly. She was veiled in black from hair to shoe, as they all were, shadow black, raven black, and she held what looked like a chain made of raven feathers that linked her to an odd, blurred bundle containing broken branches or bones, all of them constantly shifting, testing the strength of what held them imprisoned.

"Yet she sees us," Vivien said, her voice curling to a question, a caress, in Daimon's ear.

"He brought her here," Ana said simply, and Daimon, startled, shook his head.

"Of course she serves my father," he said, glimpsing undercurrents, and choosing words very carefully around them. "So do I, for that matter, though it hardly matters to you. She was following me only because she was asked to. She has no idea how she got here, and I'm sure, if you show her a way out, she'll take it with great relief."

"She has a voice," Vivien commented, and gave Scotia a glimpse of her charming smile. "She could ask."

"I could," Dame Scotia agreed. "Ask."

But she did not, just waited silently, while they gazed at her, waiting as well, then consulted one another.

"Generally speaking," Morrig said to her, "you must be wanted."

"Wanted?"

"Invited. To come here. As we asked Daimon. We permitted him to see our realm. Sometimes we allure, beguile, bewitch—we do whatever catches the attention of the one we wish to bring into our world. All that is a form of invitation. We did not invite you."

"Yet here you are." Under the changeless gray of water and sky, Vivien's eyes found nothing to kindle the fire in them. "Who invited you?"

The controlled expression that had settled over Scotia's face melted suddenly. She stared at the three, looking wide-eyed and tense, and answered incredulously, "Nobody invited me! I exceeded the speed limit on my bike and rode out of the world, maybe that's how I got here. What can one knight pledged to serve the wyvern king matter to you? You're already battling King Arden for his son, so that you can fight him for his realm. There's nothing I can do except stay and bear witness, to do what I was asked to do: to stand with the king's son until he casts me out. What else can I tell you?"

"You took something I want," Vivien said simply.

"I didn't—I have nothing—"

"You took Daimon's attention. He brought you here."

Daimon, astonished, gazed at the fay, enthralling face

that had again and again drawn him across the threshold between worlds. Vivien smiled ruefully at him; he remembered the touch of her long, graceful fingers, the eerie, magical fires in her eyes. He had a sudden vision of her being crowned queen of her realm, while he stood beside her yet alone, watching without a word to say and with no one he knew at all standing with him in that strange land where he had lost himself.

He drew breath slowly, deeply, wondering what peculiar dream they had inhabited together, until they woke and neither knew where they were now.

"It's called glamour," Vivien said softly. "What you saw in me. I enchanted you. Now the glamour, the magic, is gone. You are disenchanted."

"I didn't intend to be," he whispered. "I'm sorry. I don't— I can't seem to find my way back to where we were. That place seems terrifying. If not impossible."

"It's not the first time we have tried this," his mother said reluctantly. "I was hoping— I wanted this so much. For us. And for you."

He gazed at her, the woman who had given him her face, and half his heart. "Maybe you could change the story? Talk to my father. Without the threats."

"Oh, piffle," his great-aunt declared to that. "Without the cauldron, what do we have to—"

"You have no cauldron. But still you have such power."

"What power?"

He felt it again, the lingering touch of pain and desire, the dream of what had ensorcelled him. "All that power," he said huskily, "you had over me. That still exists. Ravenhold exists. You showed it to me in so many ways. Open your boundaries. Invite others in. Show them what you showed me. The magic. The poetry. Invite my father."

"I did, once," his mother reminded him.

"And he never forgot you. Ever. You could show the human world what Wyvernhold is lacking. You don't have to fight my father's realm to get back your own. They can exist together. I know that. You revealed that in so many ways. Open your doors; let the magic flow into Wyvernhold. The more humans know of the lost Ravenhold, the more they will want it back. It is beautiful, dangerous, magical, frightening, ancient, and forever. I know that. You took me there."

"Piffle," Morrig murmured again, dourly. But he saw in her eyes the faint, unexpected gleam of possibilities. "I still want that cauldron," she added. "If only because it's ours, and I don't see why Wyvernhold should have it."

"No," Daimon said fairly. "I don't, either."

"This led us here." Ana raised a darkly shod foot, nudged the odd, shifting cloudy bundle of bracken with it. "To Chimera Bay. We heard pleas for help that his evil caused, and finally understood them."

"What is it?" Daimon asked uneasily.

"Our first and only king," Morrig said, her voice so cold and thin that Daimon felt it chill his heart. "He and the cauldron vanished at the same time, during that battle with the wyvern king. He keeps telling us he has no idea where it is. But he is here in Chimera Bay, and so are you with your raven's eyes. If it's here, you'll recognize it."

Daimon gazed with horror and fascination at the bundle. "What will you do with him?"

"We'll ask him one last time," Morrig answered. "If he refuses to tell us, we'll trap him somewhere, I suppose. I don't know if such power truly can die, but he's too dangerous to let loose." Out of the corner of his eye, Daimon saw the wordless Scotia shift half a step closer to him. "Where in your world are we?"

"We're in the parking lot of the all-you-can-eat diner."

"Ah. Good. That's what you came here to find. There are ways we can see without being seen. Can you take us where the inside of it might be?"

Daimon, remembering vaguely, led them through the trees to where, if another world had shifted into view, the old hotel would have stood. Trees thinned into a clearing; forgotten ruins rose around them as they entered it. Within the slumping, crumbled stones, a little circular pool ringed with shells serenely reflected the sky above it.

"Something of Calluna's?" Vivien guessed. "They put their inn on top of this sacred shrine?"

"Or they built the inn there because they felt the power in this place," Ana suggested. "Perhaps a place worthy of some great vessel that fell into their possession."

"It certainly didn't look worthy," Daimon commented. "The roof is half–blown away, and most of the walls are held up by scaffolding. The inn itself looked closed."

"Sounds like the perfect place to keep a secret," Morrig said with interest. "Water knows everything; it goes everywhere, and it never forgets. There's an eye; let's see what it sees."

She moved toward the little pool. Daimon heard an odd whimpering from the bundle as Ana tugged the raven chain.

The whimpering subsided to whispering as it bumped along the ground. Daimon, following behind the three veiled figures, risked a glance at Scotia. Her face was as chalky pale as the shells scattered around the pool; she met his eyes clearly but without expression, recognizing, in that dark company, the dangers of coherent thinking.

They stopped at the edge of the pool. It gazed limpidly back at the cloud, mirroring its grays. The odd clutter at Ana's side was gabbling breathily in some demented language. She pulled on the feathery links, and it fell abruptly silent.

Morrig bent over the pool, touched the water with one finger as though to wake it. It stirred faintly, forming a ripple, like a thought. Another followed it, and another, ripples growing stronger, faster, spreading in overlapping rings across the pool until its surface ruffled as under a private wind.

It stilled. Colors streaked across it, formed shapes. Figures moved, spoke soundlessly, though Daimon suspected Morrig heard them. A burly bartender wearing glasses poured beer for an invisible customer. A cascade of painted Fools' heads above his head turned, watching this way and that, all smiling the same knowing smile. The scene shifted: a glass cupboard holding such incongruous items as a fishing gaffe and an elaborate silver bowl appeared. Morrig studied it a moment, then waved it away, as well as the unlit chandelier, the old photos on a wall, the motley clutter of worn furniture. A door swung open; a girl with purple hair came out carrying a hamburger. The eye peered through the door, found a diner engulfed by the looming, shadowy bones of the old hotel. Plastic flowers, vinyl chairs, half-filled jars of condiments, and the diners themselves, working through plates and baskets of food, passed swiftly across the water.

Another door opened to sinks full of dirty dishes, people busily cooking, filling plates, deep-frying, ladling soup from pots, boiling crabs in other pots. Pots of every shape flowed past, hanging on racks, stacked on shelves, one in the hands of an elfin old woman as she lifted it onto a burner, another, oddly battered and grimy, sitting on a chopping block while a dark-haired young woman chopped chives beside it. The lines of that pot paled, grew vague as though it sensed itself being looked at. It was not there, it told Daimon's eye. It was nothing, not a worth a glance, let alone scrutiny.

He blinked. Or maybe it was the pool blinking, as Morrig loosed it from its visions and her attention.

"Odd," she murmured. "I would have thought . . ." But she did not say. She stood silently, gazing puzzledly at the waters that had grown still again, reflecting only mist. She stirred at an eerily human noise from the cloudy collection of underbrush. "Well," she said, distastefully, "let's get this to the place where it can do no more harm. Say your farewells, Daimon and Vivien. Somewhere, in some world, you might meet again. There's nothing for us here now."

She took the raven chain from Ana's hand; the howl of despair that came out of the churning pile swept through the tree boughs like a breeze and sent a black cloud of birds swirling into the sky.

Mist filled the pool, as though it had drawn cloud down into it. It flowed upward, a column as high as the trees, then higher, and higher than that, sculpting itself out of blur and drift, a ghostly shape that formed and firmed, became enormous, forcing the eye to constantly reenvision it, until, piece by piece, it became impossibly familiar.

A woman made of mist, clothed in cloud, her hair a pale, drifting wreath around her face, looked down at them from such distance she might have been the moon, regarding them. Daimon, recognizing her, felt his own skin turn cold, colorless. One bare foot, longer than he was tall, stepped from the water to earth; the other followed. She stooped then, her body folding with enormous grace, her face, constantly flowing, shaping itself at every movement, even managed a discernible expression. She reached down with one immense hand, snapped the raven chain.

A man appeared, lying where the earthy pile had been. He was dirty, half-naked, clothed here and there in bracken; one foot, bloody and badly chewed by something, was turning black. His eyes, swollen and raw with tears, opened painfully to the mist. Daimon caught his breath, glimpsing the treasure in them, the fay, familiar colors. Three dark figures, motionless as standing stones, watched the woman cup one hand, dip it into the pool, and raise it, dripping, over the soiled, damaged, pain-ravaged face.

Slowly, gently, she let the water flow over his eyes, into his open mouth.

He drank eagerly for a long time; her hand never emptied. He drank until he began to fray, to dissolve back into the earth, and even then the water flowed, and he drank.

He grew across the ground, bones and sinews sliding into vines, lashes and fingernails into grass. The earth turned green; the vines wrapped themselves around and up the stones of the broken ruins, winding everywhere, and opening, one by one along the way, lovely trumpets of gold, ivory, blue, red. The arching tendrils flowed to encircle the pool with a wall of leaves and bright flowers, until nothing was left of the dying man but life.

The goddess let the last drop fall from her fingers. She rose to her full height, gazed silently down at the three, whose faces, turned upward, were as white as her own.

"This is what you are looking for," she said on a sigh of wind.

And then she was gone.

The still, gray pool watched them like an eye.

# 26

Pierce returned the knife to the Kingfisher Inn not long after what came to be known as the communal hallucination due to food poisoning at Stillwater's restaurant.

In the chaotic aftermath of the chef's disappearance, his fall into shadow, Sage had also vanished into one world or another, leaving Pierce with only the memory of her driving the kitchen knife through Stillwater's foot and into the table. She left it there. For some reason, so did the Knights of the Rising God. They collected Stillwater's crazed, dangerous machines eagerly enough but ignored the one thing actually used as a weapon. They wanted nothing to do with the knife. Maybe, Pierce thought as he wrestled, coaxed, pleaded it loose, the color of Stillwater's blood had deterred them. It had turned from human red to the amber brown of sap, glittering on the blade like slow, viscous tears. It even smelled like trees.

When the kitchen knife finally let go of the table, the strange tears melted down the blade into the wood. Pierce stared at it, musing over its unexpected destiny, the powers it possessed along with what seemed to be a will of its own.

What else could it do? he wondered.

The blade glinted at him, a metallic glance, as though reminding Pierce where it belonged, where he needed to take it next.

"Oh, all right," he breathed. He slid it back into the sheath in his jacket and realized then how quiet the restaurant was.

He was alone in the kitchen. He wandered through the vault; its bottles were mostly intact though those precipitously fleeing through it had left some shard-laced puddles on the floor. The restaurant itself was a bigger disaster: tables knocked askew, chairs overturned, tablecloths and broken plates and little edible jewels scattered across the floor. The diners had long gone; Pierce had heard the knights' bikes begin to roar, along with some sirens, during his struggle with the knife. Sage was nowhere Pierce could see, which, he realized, was pretty much the place she inhabited whenever he looked for her. The screen door sagged on its hinges, swaying back and forth in the breeze. The entire place looked as though it had dropped its own mask, exposed its warped floors, chipped paint, the bare, flickering bulbs, all its warts and wrinkles, for everyone to see.

It was completely empty. Not even his father or his brother had waited for him. He stood aimlessly in the wreck, perplexed, and felt the phone in his jacket vibrate.

He pulled it out, found a message from his brother: *At police station. Starving. Will call when they let us out. Cheers!*

He walked along the bay to the Kingfisher Inn and was greatly relieved to find one familiar face at the bar.

He slid onto the stool next to Merle, pulled the knife out of his sleeve, and laid it in front of them. "I don't think it needs me anymore," he said to Merle, and to Tye, who reached for a glass and began filling it.

Merle smiled. "You did well with it. The knife fit the hand that wielded it. In this case, both the hands."

"Where is Carrie?" Pierce asked. "The restaurant was completely empty when I finally got the knife out of the table. Did everyone but me get arrested?"

Tye was smiling, too, as he set the frosty glass down in front of Pierce. "Maybe that's why they didn't find you. The knife was guarding you." He picked it up with both hands, reverently. "I'll just put this back where it belongs. We'll need it tomorrow."

Merle took a sip of his own beer. He looked different, Pierce thought: a weight off his shoulders, a few centuries out of his eyes. "Carrie and I slipped out through the fuss in the street," he said. "Nobody noticed our shadows. There were reports called in of weird events at Stillwater's: people screaming, running out the doors, somebody stabbed, people disguised as knights looting the place. Lots of disorderly conduct. It didn't look very orderly at the police station, either, so we walked on by. Everyone recognized your father. He and your brother were taken along as witnesses. It will be a while before all that gets sorted out. I found Carrie's friend Zed Cluny and sent Carrie with him to get a decent meal."

"Good." Pierce took a sip, felt the cold seep through him, and shivered suddenly, shaking memories loose in his head.

"What was all that? Stillwater? Those three women? What did they do to him? And what does it all have to do with this place?"

"It's a long story."

"That's all right. Sounds like I'll be here for a while."

He caught up with Leith and Val several hours later, eating pub food at a brewery around the corner from their motel. Val, whittling down a mountain of deep-fried seafood and talking on his cell, flashed a grin at him. Leith, looking weary and relieved, pulled him into a hug, then dragged the nearest stool closer to his. "Sit down. Have you eaten?"

Pierce nodded. "I've been with Merle at the Kingfisher."

"How did he miss being pulled in with the rest of us? He was running around in wolf shape one moment, and talking to those three women in the next as if he had grown up with them."

"Maybe he did."

"I could swear—actually, I might have at the station—that the oldest of them was Lady Morrig Seabrook, the king's aunt. What she was doing in Chimera Bay tracking down that malevolent chef absconded from some depraved fairy tale I cannot begin—" He didn't try, just rendered himself speechless for a moment with a slab of steak.

"What happened to the Knights of the Rising God?"

"They got charged with theft, destruction of property, violation of an ordinance against loud noises within city limits, and a few more things. Then someone recognized Prince Ingram, and the whole business started all over again. Neither Merle, nor Merle's daughter, nor Stillwater's wife were on hand to testify that the knights were not stealing those machines, nor did they wreck the place, and the diners who actually saw what happened to Stillwater kept contradicting one another." He chewed another bite, gazing incredulously back at the endless afternoon. "Where was Merle when we needed him? And where were you?"

"It took me some time to get that knife out of the table. I wasn't going to leave it there. When it finally decided to let me free it, everyone had vanished." He caught sight of the expression on Val's face, one he didn't recognize, even after days of close company, dealing together with mysteries, enchantments, and other assorted crises. "Who is Val talking to?"

"Your mother."

They waited for her in the Kingfisher Inn the next afternoon. Leith, as tense as Pierce had ever seen him, kept trying to leave.

"She won't want to see me."

"She does," Val insisted. "She said so."

"She said that to please you. She didn't mean it."

"Well, I want you here," Val said patiently. "I haven't seen her since I was a child. Stay to please me."

They were sitting on one of the sagging velveteen couches in the bar. Luckily, Pierce thought, most of the old springs were shot, considering the edgy, restive fidgeting on either side of him. He wondered, studying Leith, if bravery in the face of impending angry spouses counted in the code of knighthood, especially when the knight was in the wrong. He wouldn't have blamed Leith for justifying his absence as a kindness, to

give Val and Heloise more time to talk. But Val wanted his
company and would recognize any excuse for the abject cow-
ardice that it was. Their father, who could have faced a living
wyvern without flinching, had to force himself to stay put.

A woman walked alone into the bar; their three faces
turned at once. But it was not Heloise. It was no one, Pierce
thought at first, no one he knew, just a young woman with
drifting hair, and a thin, tired face. She went to the bar;
Leith and Val went back to fidgeting. Pierce watched her.
Something in her movement, her tall grace, the tilt of her
head within her lank, untidy hair, made him rise abruptly.

He crossed the quiet room. It was nearly empty in the
midafternoon, too early yet for the Friday Nite gathering.
She was talking softly to Tye, who said, as Pierce joined her,
"You should talk to Ella. I know she's been needing more
help, but I don't know if she'll admit it yet."

Pierce said, "Sage?"

She turned quickly, startled. He smiled; she didn't,
couldn't yet, he guessed. She was very thin; her gray-green
eyes were haunted by what she had seen. The lovely, heavy,
champagne-gold hair he remembered looked dry and
unkempt. The beauty of her face existed only in his memory as yet: it was hollow, pained, shadowy with sadness.

"Pierce," she breathed. Something in his eyes brought
the faintest color to her face, the barest hint of a smile.

"You were amazing," he said. "Yesterday. What you did
with that knife."

"You took it out, showed it to me."

"I stole it. From this place, actually. I never knew why
before."

"It's a powerful magic," Tye said. He was cutting fruit into a blender, pulling peaches, strawberries, oranges out of his enchanted garden behind the bar. "It goes where it wants, finds who it needs, does what it must." He scooped ice into the blender and splashed liquid from some bottle over it, adding a scent of melon. "Pierce is right. You were brave to recognize what you had to do."

"I don't feel brave," she said ruefully. "I'm just a woman who lost her husband, out looking for a job."

Tye ran the blender, poured the thick, colorful concoction into a glass, and passed it to her. "Good riddance to the husband."

She nodded at that, raised her glass. "Good riddance. Thank you, Tye."

"So you're looking for work here?" Pierce said.

"I thought—it wouldn't hurt to ask. I used to be able to cook. At least I think so. Before I met Todd." She swallowed a sip of fruit and ice, then another. "I had forgotten what tasting is like," she sighed. "This is so good. It's like learning to walk again, remembering my life before. Todd fed me enough real food to keep me alive, but he made it taste so dreadful, I never wanted more."

"Do you have a place to stay?"

"He owned the old bank building; we lived upstairs. It's mine, now. For what that's worth. I hate being in it. But I'm not afraid of it. I might clean it up, open it again. But first I need to find out what I can do in a kitchen."

I can cook, Pierce thought, and saw, with wonder, his life take yet another turn. He had left this magical backwater once; life had brought him back. He had found the family he needed, but he did not need to become a knight. He could sand a floor, paint a wall, put a restaurant back together, help create new memories in the face of the woman beside him.

"Ella's in the kitchen, probably prepping for tonight," Tye said. "She's between meals. Why don't you go and talk to her? She'll be happy to see you, anyway, after what you did to help get rid of Stillwater. She was getting pretty worried about Carrie. Take that with you," he added, as Sage put the glass down. "It's good for you."

She smiled then, a thin, tremulous thing, but genuine. Pierce watched her cross the dim room, push open the kitchen doors to a sudden stream of light. He lingered, riffling through his own memories of her, letting thoughts roam idly between past and future.

"Do for you?" he heard Tye murmur; he shook his head. Then he heard Tye's voice again, still soft but oddly shaken. "Holy shit."

His mother walked into the bar.

He heard the couch lurch as the two knights rocketed to their feet. She nearly walked past Pierce without seeing him, so riveted she was by her tall, flaming-haired son with his ice-blue eyes, and by the darker shadow behind him. Then she seemed to feel the tug from the bar, the pull of heartstrings, and her attention veered. So did her step. Pierce felt his throat close as she came to him, threw her arms around him.

"I have missed you so much," she exclaimed, kissing his eye, his jawbone. "I had no idea you would get into so much trouble in such a short time. I chased that demented sorceress clear up into the northlands." She lowered her voice, pitched it to his ear. "Is that your father?"

"Yes."

"So strange. I almost didn't . . . I suppose we've both gotten older." She loosed Pierce, took his arm, walked to Leith through the twenty-odd years of distance between them both. She stood silently, gazing with wonder at Val. She turned to Leith; Pierce saw the glitter of tears in her eyes. "When I was so busy not forgiving you, I forgot that one day I would need to ask our sons to forgive me. One because he never knew you. The other because, for all those years, I hardly knew him. Forgive me?" she said to Val.

"What's the alternative?" he asked, and she stared at him, tears sliding down her face. Then she laughed, and he put his arms around her.

"I could tell you," she told him. "I know it well." She stretched out one hand to Leith, still holding her son. "Thank you," she said. "Thank you for this."

Gradually, as they sat and talked, the bar began to fill. Smells wafted from the kitchen, rich, briny, pungent with herbs and spices. Carrie came in, waved at Pierce, smiling for once before she vanished through the swinging doors. Pierce recognized faces from his first Friday Nite ritual: the father and son who held the doors open, the young priest who carried the gaff. A few knights wandered in, including, he saw, a couple of marauders from Stillwater's. They looked subdued; they spoke quietly, very politely to Tye, who relented and gave them what they wanted. A party of elderly couples entered, and behind them, another knight, whom Pierce remembered immediately as the first he had ever seen.

The knight with the hair like lamb's wool and the eyes

of balmy, tropical blue, carried his wine over to the family gathering on the couch, and toasted them with it.

"Sir Gareth May," Leith said. "This is Heloise Oliver. The mother of my sons."

"Strange how I knew that the moment I saw you," Gareth said to her, smiling. "That hair, those eyes—such generous gifts to your children. I see this is the place to be for supper tonight."

"You weren't in town earlier, Sir Gareth, were you?" Val asked.

"No. I just got here and saw a few familiar crests in the parking lot. I stopped on impulse. I'm on my way back to Severluna."

"So soon?" Leith said. "Is there trouble?"

Gareth shook his head. "No. Suddenly, it didn't seem very important, going off looking for something so vague and mysterious when what I really want is where I left her." He heard himself and flushed a little, but Heloise nodded.

"That seems by far the most sensible thing I've heard yet about this odd quest."

"Thank you. I keep smelling the most wonderful things . . . Where do we find them?"

"Just wait, Sir Gareth," Pierce suggested, watching Carrie come out and hand the key to Merle, and the priest turn away from friends to follow him. The sentinels, the golden-haired father and son, moved to their places beside the door. "The magic will come to you."

Two other knights wandered in before the ritual began. Pierce pulled their faces out of memory: Prince Daimon and the formidable Dame Scotia Malory. They both looked unsettled, wary, Pierce saw with surprise. They moved cautiously across the room as though the unexpected might take shape at any moment out of the worn floorboards. They returned greetings absently; their smiles faded quickly. Beside the bar, they stood very close together, finding comfort in one another's presence. He wondered, amazed, what power, what magic had crossed their paths to leave those shared memories of uncertainty and awe in their eyes.

The crowd, recognizing familiar signals, began to quiet. Faces turned, bright with anticipation; people rose from chairs and couches and barstools, their eyes on the closed doors. Pierce stood up; Leith, behind him, rested a hand on his shoulder.

The doors opened. The gasps and murmurs of astonishment and pleasure that rolled through the gathering welcomed the tall, white-haired, green-eyed woman beside Hal Fisher, who held his arm, accepting the weight of his halting steps, as the ritual began.

Pierce, moved by the smiles on the aged, tranquil faces, watched them until Val gripped his arm suddenly. Startled, his eyes shifted, were caught by the odd pot Carrie was carrying, not the seriously decorated silver soup tureen he expected, but something plain, a trifle battered, looking as though it had been around and well used for any number of centuries. As he wondered at it, a bronze glow illuminated it, gliding over its surface like a secret smile of its own making.

He had no idea why, a few moments later when the solemn gathering grew vociferous and merry, his brother could not stop laughing, or find any known language to explain.